# Halstad House

# Halstad House

CHRISTY MARTENSON

Text © 2019 by Christine K. Martenson

Cover Illustration by Marjorie Somerville, Life lines Creations
Cover Design and Interior Layout by Roseanna M. White

Edited by Rachelle Rea Cobb

This is a work of historical fiction. The town of Emmett is fictitious but other locations in Northeast Washington are real. References to World War I are all based on facts. The characters in the book sprang out of the author's imagination. Any resemblance to actual persons, living or dead, is a happy—or in some cases, unhappy—coincidence.

My heartfelt thanks to proofreaders Karen, Kristen, Abigail, Sara, and Sarah—and the rest of the launch team—for their invaluable input!

Scripture is taken from the American Standard Version.

ISBN 9781690886075 (paperback)

*Lovingly dedicated to my mother*
*Karen Ann Wang Shute*
*1933-2018*

# *Prologue*

No two ways about it, she was beautiful. The most beautiful baby in the world. Grace Halstad knelt beside the quilt-lined cradle where Allie slept in peaceful innocence. One pudgy arm supported her head; bent knees sent her pink-and-white checked backside poking into the air. Grace smoothed a tuft of honey-gold hair from her daughter's face. "Your daddy's missing all this," she whispered. Sitting back on her heels, Grace looked across the kitchen at her sister. "I can't believe she's almost a year old. How can time fly on one hand yet drag on the other?"

"Makes perfect sense to me." At the butcher-block table, Esther paused in her work. "Allie's changing so fast it's hard to keep up with her, but your husband being gone for months, well, that's a different story." She turned her attention back to peeling carrots.

"I suppose you're right." Grace stooped to kiss Allie's cheek before she rose. "I could watch her all day, but I'd better take advantage of naptime to get things done." At the counter, she rinsed her hands in a basin of warm water, picked up a cutting knife, and grabbed a carrot. "Thanks again for staying last night. Wash day goes much faster with an extra pair of hands."

The sweet fragrance of locust trees in bloom wafted through an open window while a bee buzzed against the screen in frantic determination to get inside. Grace hummed a tune as she chopped, then broke out in a soft soprano. *"He's the Lily of the Valley, the Bright and Morning Star…"*

Esther's smooth alto joined in. *"He's the fairest of ten thousand..."*

Their voices blended in sweet harmony as they had since childhood, above the steady beat of knife blades against wood.

All three verses done, Esther grinned. "We haven't sung that one for a long time. How about we sing it at church Sunday after next?"

"Sounds good to me."

"All right." Esther scooped a handful of diced onions into the pot. "I'll run it by Pastor Grant, but since he pretty much leaves the music up to me, I don't think there'll be a problem."

A comfortable silence filled the kitchen, along with the mouth-watering aroma of beef stew simmering on the cookstove. Esther glanced at Grace. "What did that good-looking Norwegian husband of yours say about you having a boarder while he's gone?"

"He's fine with it—for now." Grace added her pile of carrot slices to the pot. She smiled when she thought of Søren's remarks about Mary Talbot living here. "What he sees as timid and mousy—and don't you dare repeat that, Esther Rose Browne—I call quiet, reserved, and very easy to have as a house guest." She counted off on her fingers. "She doesn't complain about my cooking. She pays her rent on time. She says Allie is the cutest baby she's ever seen."

"Oho. That's how she wound you around her little finger. Well, I'm afraid I agree with him. Mary's always been afraid of her own shadow. I don't know how she manages the school kids, especially the older boys. A couple of them could chew her up and spit her out. And don't *you* dare repeat that, Lillian Grace Browne Halstad."

"Poor Mary." Grace reached for a potato. "She jumps at the slightest sound. But she's sweet. You have to admit that. She's no trouble, and the extra money comes in handy. When this awful war is over and Søren is home, there'll be a tidy little nest egg laid by. In fact..." She raised the knife and pointed it at Esther. "I told him I might add two or three more boarders. Imagine the nest egg then."

"What? You can't be serious." Esther pinched her lips together and leaned against the worktable. "You're going to call me a bossy big sister again, but I'll say it anyway. You're out of your mind. What about Allie? You won't have time for her and everything else." She hesitated, then touched Grace's arm. "Dad and I talked before I came into town yesterday. We still think you should both move back to the farm with us until this is over."

Grace stiffened. *Here we go again.* "That's not going to happen, Esther. I'm a big girl. You don't have to take care of me anymore. This is our home and we're staying."

Esther didn't look convinced. "I'm not trying to take care of you."

"Really?"

"Well, maybe I am. I've been taking care of you since I was eleven. It's what I do. But that doesn't mean I'm wrong." She seemed to take a different tack. "And just what was Søren's reaction when you told him about more boarders?"

Grace's cheeks warmed. She'd written a glowing account of her plan, afraid he would flat-out say no. But she could be just as stubborn as he could. Almost. "In his last letter, he told me he wasn't crazy about the idea, but to go ahead if I could handle it, just to be careful not to overdo. Although he did say the minute he sets foot through the door he's booting them all out, lock, stock, and barrel. He wants to fill Halstad House with Halstad kids, not a gaggle of simpering women."

"I can see it now." Esther chuckled, but a moment later her face sobered. "Just don't take on too much. Remember, *you* can always boot them out if they get to causing you trouble." She placed a lid on the pot. "Grace, I really think—" She shut her mouth with a snap and shrugged. Grabbing a damp rag, she swiped it across the work area, avoiding her sister's eyes.

Grace rubbed a gentle hand over Esther's arm. "I promise not to do anything foolish." She gave her shoulder a squeeze. "Look on the bright side. If I do, you can always say, 'I told you so.'"

Esther snorted. "All right, Smarty." She gave Grace a swift swat with the rag. "I may take you up on that."

Grace relaxed and wiped her hands on the sides of her skirt. "You know, a letter from Søren is overdue. I have a feeling there'll be one today. I can feel it in my bones, as Dad says."

Esther glanced at the clock on the wall and swatted her again. "The mail should be sorted at the post office by now. What are you doing just standing here?" She shooed Grace away. "Skedaddle. I'll keep an eye on Allie."

With a quick hug, Grace headed out the door.

On the porch, she took a deep breath and leaned against the rail, lingering to survey the town. To her left, scattered houses and businesses came to life as people prepared for the day ahead. She loved living here. When Søren brought her home to his rambling white house on Main Street two years ago, she was a new bride, not quite eighteen years old. He teased her about filling the second-floor bedrooms with kids and having them spread into the attic even. He was over the moon when Allie was born eleven months later. So was Grace. The dimples in that little girl's cheeks melted her heart every time she saw her smile. When her fine-looking man returned, they'd pick up where they left off, chasing their dreams together.

She set off down the porch stairs and onto the dirt road. A perfect summer morning greeted her. Blue sky, no clouds, the air fresh from last night's gentle rain. Grace's spirits rose as she crossed the street and stepped onto the boardwalk. Maybe a letter from Søren really would be waiting. She glanced at the sign above the door of a false-fronted building sporting a fresh veneer of white paint. *United States Post Office, Emmett, Washington. Ben Guff, Postmaster.* She peeked through the window at the empty room. The bell over the door jangled when she entered, but no one came through the connecting door from the house beyond. Grasping the knob on mailbox seven, she rotated it left - right - left. She opened the little door and—Yes! At the sight of Søren's handwriting, she clasped the letter to her chest and almost skipped out of the office.

Back on the street, Grace touched the letter to her lips. "Thank You, Lord."

The sun glinted off the Kettle River at the far end of town. Beyond the river, pine trees stirred in the breeze. When she reached Halstad House, she lifted her eyes to watch a fat-bellied robin fly from the massive maple tree to the porch eaves.

At the gate, Grace hunkered down to pet the beagle sniffing her flowerbeds, his brown, black, and white coat hidden behind a mask of dust. "Uffda, you are filthy. Have you been digging again?" He nuzzled her palm, licking her fingers with his rough tongue. She ruffled the top of his head, sending a cloud of dust airborne. "There may be no holes in sight, but I'm keeping an eye on you."

In the back of her mind, she'd heard the putt-putt of a motor, but it didn't register until the crunch of tires on her gravel walk caused her to look up. She stood slowly, sucking in her breath.

A man wearing a cap emblazoned with the words *Western Union* pulled his Model T to a stop in front of her. His gaze shifted in her direction. He swallowed hard. "Mrs. Halstad, ma'am. I..." He swallowed again, reaching into the dreaded canvas bag on the seat next to him.

Grace stared, afraid to move. *No, please no.* Uffda whined, nudging her knee with his nose. She fumbled for the envelope with one hand. Søren's letter lay in the other.

After hesitating a moment, the man shifted his car into gear and drove away without a backward glance.

She squinted at the envelope addressed from the war department, trembling as she ripped it open. Hateful words sneered at her. *No.* She struggled for air. *It can't be.* Søren? Her faithful, levelheaded Søren? Her best friend, love, champion? Grace looked back and forth at the letters in her hands, then pushed open the gate. Her legs faltered at the first step. Lead weights seemed to be chained to her ankles.

In the kitchen, Esther rolled out pie dough. She glanced up with a grin. "So was it there?"

Grace's eyes roamed the room like she'd never seen it before.

Esther straightened. "Grace?" She brushed a wisp of hair from her forehead with the back of her hand.

Grace brought her eyes back to her sister. She dropped the telegram on the dough.

Esther grabbed it. She clapped a hand over her mouth, the color draining from her face as she read. She rounded the end of the worktable, but before she could reach her, Grace staggered to the stairs.

Hot, stuffy air met her when she opened her bedroom door. She'd forgotten to raise the window to ward off the morning sun. It didn't matter. Nothing mattered. Lowering herself to the edge of the bed, she twisted to gaze at Søren's picture on the bedside table. He gazed back, his eyes holding a look she'd seen a hundred times, a look that said *I love you*. His rumpled blonde hair in need of a cut, his jawline covered by the beard he was so proud of. She touched the glass, her thumb caressing the handsome young face she'd never see again. A shuddering breath escaped her lips. She squeezed her eyes shut against the stranglehold that threatened to crush her, forcing it deep within. A moment more she sat, then, as if in slow motion, she stood and walked to the bureau, removing the lid of the precious wooden box he'd carved for her. Inside lay a stack of letters tied with a blue ribbon. She laid the unopened letter atop the others, along with her hopes, her dreams, her very life. Maybe even her God. With unsteady fingers, she replaced the lid.

## One

*June 1922*

"Mommy! Geoffrey Chaucer has a bum leg!"

The orange-and-white tabby hung in long-suffering silence from Allie's hands, stomach bulging with her every step, tail threatening to fall victim to the four-year-old's brown oxfords. His whiskers twitched as he caught sight of Grace; otherwise, he remained a dangling, motionless blob in the arms of his small human.

"Oh my." Grace took one look at them and scooted into the nearest kitchen chair. "Set him in my lap, sweetie."

Allie waddled over and tried to lift Chaucer. Only his head and front paws made it. Grace reached around his middle. "Heave ho," she said. Chaucer plopped across her knees.

"He was holding that one up." Allie pointed to his right foreleg.

Grace fingered his leg, then searched the underside of his paw. "Sis?" She glanced at Esther who stood at the worktable, mixing batter for apple dumplings. "Do you know where the magnifying glass is?"

"I do!" Allie darted to a cabinet near the back door. She jerked the top drawer open and, with a triumphant grin, held up the magnifying glass. She scampered to the table.

"Okay, let's see what we can find." Chaucer tensed but stayed put under Grace's poking and prodding.

Allie peered over her shoulder, stroking the long chestnut-colored braid hanging down her mother's back. "When Chaucer's all better, can you come out 'n play with me?"

Grace rested her head against Allie's for a moment. "I'd like that." After a few minutes of exploring, Grace straightened. "I see a sliver in there. It'd be best to put some black salve on and let it draw out the splinter."

"I can help. I know where it is." Allie bolted across the room to another cabinet.

Just as she returned with the jar, Grace heard a fretful voice behind her. "Excuse me, Mrs. Halstad."

*Oh, for Pete's sake.* Swallowing her frustration, Grace turned to the parlor door. "Yes, Mrs. Gibbons?"

The face of one of her boarders, lined with wrinkles and re-morse, eyeballed her. "I'm afraid the slat has fallen off the bed frame again, and the mattress is not secure on one side."

Grace let out a sigh. Those wrinkles may be genuine, but Grace knew from experience that Mrs. Gibbons' contrite expression was simply a ploy to wangle her into doing what she wanted. Unfortunately, she couldn't afford to offend and perhaps lose a boarder. Grace would have to grin and bear it. "Can it wait?"

Mrs. Gibbons' wrinkles and faux-remorse deepened. "Oh dear. It's not that I want to be a bother, but I'm going out for the day, you see. I want to have my room in order because I'm afraid I'll be too tired to deal with it when I return. You understand, don't you?"

Grace looked at Esther, who frowned and shook her head. Okay, she was an adult. And the landlady. This was her respon-sibility. Besides, if her sister spent two minutes alone with this particular boarder, she'd either flatten Mrs. Gibbons or run screaming from the room. Maybe both.

Grace swung her eyes to Allie's anxious face. She was going to have to disappoint her. Again. "I need to take care of this, sweetie." She gave Allie's earlobe a playful tug. "I'll be back as soon as I can."

Allie's lower lip quivered.

This happened far too often. Maybe if she hurried, she could still spend time with her daughter before the rush of meal prepa-ration. She glanced at Esther. "Would you mind finishing this?

Wind some gauze around the paw once the salve is on. We'll keep an eye on it."

She kissed Allie's forehead. "I'm sorry."

Esther pulled up a chair. "Come here, you." She hauled Chaucer onto her lap.

Grace followed Mrs. Gibbons to her room. The smell of the boarder's *eau de cologne* permeated the room, almost knocking her over. It's a good thing she cleaned the rooms once a week or the smell would be terrible. Attempting to take shallow breaths, she marched to the bed. "Which side?"

Mrs. Gibbons pointed to the side pushed against the wall.

The mattress rested at an odd angle, but honestly, was this woman helpless? Grace grabbed the post of the footboard with both hands and yanked.

Her boarder hovered like a mother hen, albeit an idle one. She hovered. Grace did the work. It took all of ten minutes to remedy the situation.

Mrs. Gibbons' tale of woe lasted much longer. "I suppose I could have done that myself, but you are so much younger than I am. Although I am not old and infirm by any means, perhaps I would have wrenched my spine moving the bed." She wrung her hands. "My late husband always told me to be careful. I think there may have been a weakness there even when I was a child, so I am cautious. One must be prudent concerning one's health. And a childhood weakness is no laughing matter. Don't you agree?"

"Um-hmm..." Grace straightened the bedspread.

"That thought occurred to me before I went in search of you. Odd that I should think of my childhood just then, though it was no doubt a good thing. And good that I should remember what my late husband said."

"Um-hmm..." Grace took a step backward. The floorboard squeaked.

"My mind strays in that direction often. To my late husband, that is, not to my childhood. He had such wise and practical advice. Many times I have reflected on his words and am grateful indeed for his guidance every day."

"Um-hmm..." Another step, another squeak.

"Even he commented on childhood weaknesses, though he never had one. He was at all times of the strongest constitution, except when he passed away of course, although it must be said that it was not the result of a childhood weakness. Nor a long-draw-out illness."

Grace suspected that one day the lady's longsuffering husband had reached his tiresome chatter limit and turned up his toes then and there. She inched her way back toward the door. "Excuse me. I really must get downstairs."

"Yes, of course, and I would not keep you another minute. However, I wanted to explain why I didn't undertake the task on my own. On account of my spine. And of what my late husband said. You being a widow yourself can understand. Although I have been a widow much longer than you have—"

"Yes, yes." Grace thrust her hand behind her and grasped the doorknob. "Have a nice day." Without giving Mrs. Gibbons a chance to comment further on weak spines, widowhood, or dead husbands' wise words, Grace closed the door and dashed for the back stairs.

Her heart sank when she found Esther alone in the kitchen. Allie must have given up and gone outside to play. She peeked at the clock on the wall, clucked her tongue, and rejoined her sister at the worktable.

Mrs. Gibbons' monologue left no room for the other boarder to get a word in edgewise. Grace and Esther carried two steaming platters into the dining room, one laden with pot roast, potatoes, carrots, and onions, the other covered with a bulging white tea towel. Allie trailed behind holding a small bowl of bread and butter pickles, her robin's-egg blue eyes fixed on the table, lips pressed together. Grace placed the pot roast on the table as her daughter laid down her own bowl.

Esther set her platter next to the roast. "Allie and I will get the butter and the water pitcher."

Allie bolted through the kitchen door, returning a minute later with a porcelain butter dish.

"Oh dear. Do be careful." Mrs. Gibbons waved her hand as if to ward off impending disaster. "Don't you think she's too young to be trusted with china, Mrs. Halstad? I hope she doesn't drop it."

Allie shot her a scornful look through narrowed eyes.

"It's all right." Grace stroked Allie's head. "I trust her." She'd like to tell the old coot to mind her own business, but she pasted a smile on her face instead.

Allie beamed. When she turned that angelic face to Mrs. Gibbons, she scrunched her nose and stuck out the tip of her tongue.

Since Grace was tempted to do the same, she decided to let it slide.

"Hmmph." Mrs. Gibbons turned her eyes to the young woman seated across from her. "You know, Izzy, my dear husband and I never had children. But if we had, I'm sure they would have behaved as models of decorum."

Grace stiffened and wrapped an arm around Allie's shoulders.

"Yes?" Izzy glanced at Allie and gave her a wink, then turned back to Mrs. Gibbons. "I'm afraid I was anything but a model of decorum. My father would frequently frown and call me impudent." Nineteen-year-old Isobel Sommers ran her hands over her unruly hair, which only served to make it spike every which way. "I was a bit flighty and always said the first thing that came to my mind. I didn't mean to be sassy; it just came out that way, I guess." She laughed and laid her napkin over her lap.

"Hmmph." Mrs. Gibbons grimaced and laid her own napkin across her lap.

Esther reentered the room and poured water into their glasses, while Grace removed the tea towel, revealing fluffy golden biscuits. "You ladies enjoy your meal," Esther said.

Grace brushed a spot of lint from the tablecloth. "We'll be

in to clear up later." She steered Allie toward the kitchen, with Esther close behind.

As they walked through the door, Mrs. Gibbons sniffed. "I do so hate to complain, but I prefer bread with my pot roast."

Esther stopped in her tracks.

Grace grabbed her arm and pulled her inside. "Ignore her. Let's eat."

Esther jerked a chair back from the kitchen table and dropped into it. "That woman. If I'd made fresh bread, she would've said she preferred biscuits. Why do you put up with her?"

Grace shrugged. "Simple. I need the money." She dished up meat and vegetables for Allie. "I might have taken a couple slices of bread out to her but there's only enough for breakfast tomorrow. I could have sworn I had more. Oh well." She clucked her tongue and buttered a piping hot biscuit for her daughter.

Allie took a bite. "Yum. Can you teach me to make these someday, Auntie Esther? Yours are the best."

Esther smirked at Grace over her own biscuit.

"Don't worry." Grace sighed. "I know yours are much better than mine. Try as I might, I can't get the hang of it."

Allie reached across the table to rub Grace's hand. "It's okay, Mommy. You make better cinnamon rolls."

Grace met Esther's eyes and chuckled.

After a few minutes with only the sounds of cutlery clinking against plates, Allie raised her head. "Know what Chaucer did this morning?"

Grace leaned forward. "Besides sleep for hours in the sunshine?"

"Uh-huh." Allie's eyes sparkled. "There was this bird—"

"Excuse me." Mrs. Gibbons stood in the doorway. "I know you are always meticulous about these things, but the salt shaker is almost empty. We may run out before the end of the meal."

Grace ran a hand over her face. "I'll get some right away." She glanced at Allie as she stood. "I want to hear the rest when I get back."

Moments later, seated at the table again, Grace flipped her braid over her shoulder. "Go ahead, sweetie."

Honey dripped over the side of Allie's biscuit. She caught it with her tongue. "Well, there was this bird. Maybe a robin. Chaucer slunk clean down on his tummy and started to crawl right toward it. He looked so funny." She took another bite of biscuit.

Grace wiped the corner of her mouth. "He must have been intrigued to exert that much energy."

Allie scrunched her eyebrows. "What's a zert?"

"Exert." Grace grinned. "It means to—"

"Pardon me."

*Good grief.* Mrs. Gibbons again. "You know how much I hate to disturb, but might I trouble you for another napkin? I don't know how I came to do it, but I spilled some food by my plate and used my napkin to wipe it up. So I will need another right away... If you would be so kind... "

"Of course. I'll be there in a moment." She looked at Allie. "Be right back."

At the table again, she spread her napkin across her lap. "Okay. One more time."

Allie's eyes had lost a little of their sparkle. "Well, he did the zert thing and snuck closer to that fat old bird. Closer and closer and closer. His tail swished back and forth. Just then—"

"Mrs. Halstad?"

*I can't believe it.* Grace turned to see Isobel's face through the slightly opened door. "Mrs. Gibbons wonders if you have any chutney for the roast."

"Chutney?" She plopped back against her chair.

Esther jumped up. "I saw a jar in the icebox the other day." She walked across the room and examined the contents of the cooler, then rose with a puzzled expression on her face. "That's odd. It's not there. Well, I know there are a couple of jars in the root cellar. Want me to get one?"

Grace hesitated. "No. It's my responsibility." She shifted her gaze to Allie. "Sweetie, I am so sorry. I'll be as fast as I can."

But by the time she hunted through the root cellar shelves,

finally locating the chutney behind several jars of canned peaches and a misplaced tin of buttons, delivered it to the dining room, and listened to a prolonged thanks from Mrs. Gibbons, both Allie and Esther had finished their supper.

Esther heated wash water on the stove. She looked over her shoulder at Grace. "I let Allie go out to play. She was chomping at the bit to find Chaucer and Uffda." Her expression softened. "She understands. It was just a crazy night."

Crazy or not, frustration pressed in on her. Tears filled her eyes. "I let Allie down again." She sat back at the table, but after stirring cold food around the plate a few times, she tossed her napkin aside and took her dishes to the counter.

Allie sat on Grace's lap, feet swinging back and forth under her pink-and-white nighty. Grace removed the band from her daughter's hair and loosened the thick braid with her fingers. She grabbed a brush. Grace loved this part of her day and knew Allie did, too.

Allie's fingertips tapped against Grace's leg. "Know what? I caught Uffda in the flower bed again. He dug two holes under the rose bushes."

"That stinker. I wish I knew how to break him of that."

"I told him he was naughty, but he just licked my hand." Allie groaned. "What's to become of him? Maybe we're doomed."

Grace bit her lip. Which one of the boarders did Allie pick that up from? "Let's not give up yet. There's always hope."

"'Kay." Allie gave a little bounce. "'Member. A hundred strokes just like you do."

"Yes, ma'am."

They counted together as Grace brushed. Allie lagged behind when they got past twenty, but persevered, repeating each number after her mother. That done, Grace worked another braid into her hair, nestled Allie into the crook of her shoulder, and grabbed a book from the nearby table. "All right, missy-moo, where were we?"

After turning several pages, Allie pointed to a picture of a bonnet-clad girl and a floppy-eared dog walking through a field. "Right here."

Grace set the rocking chair in motion and began to read. Allie rested her head against her mother's chest, patting Grace's arm in rhythm with the chair. Shadows from the oil lamp flickered across the wall, adding to the peace in the room.

Fifteen minutes later, Grace closed the book. "The end."

"I liked that book. I wanna be good and brave like that girl." Allie brushed a wisp of hair from her eyes.

"Oh, you are." Grace kissed the top of her head. "Brave and good as can be."

Allie reached around Grace's neck to take hold of her mother's braid. "Now my song." She swirled the curls at the braid's end along her chin and cheeks.

"Which song would you like?"

"The one you made up when I was a baby."

Grace paused. "Okay." She took a breath and began. *"Close your eyes and go to sleep for Jesus is watching you. He will guard you, He will keep you…"* Grace sang from memory, letting her mind drift. She knew it was Allie's favorite. She had believed the words once. But now? The corner of her heart reserved for God held only numbness, deadened because He had not returned Søren to her. It was just Allie and her now.

She rested her cheek on Allie's head when she finished the song. "To bed with you, young lady."

Allie scooted off Grace's lap, heading for the trundle bed beside her mother's. She knelt, folded her hands, and squeezed her eyes shut. "Please bless Mommy and Auntie Esther. Bless Grampa and *Farfar* and *Farmor* and Chaucer and Uffda." She started to rise, then fell back to her knees. "And bless the biddies even if I don't like 'em all."

"Biddies?"

"Oops. Boarders." Allie scrambled under the covers and flashed Grace a cherubic smile.

Grace sat on the edge of the bed. She tucked the covers under Allie's chin. "Goodnight."

"G'night."

"Sweet dreams."

"Sweet dreams."

"See you in the morning."

"See you in the mornin'."

Grace kissed Allie's forehead. "I love you."

"I love you, too, Mommy." Allie turned to her side.

Grace ran her fingers over her daughter's face with gentle tickles, softly singing a sweet Norwegian lullaby Søren's parents—Allie's *farfar* and *farmor*—had taught her. Bit by bit, the four-year-old's eyelids lowered until she sighed and her breathing slowed to a smooth rhythm.

With Allie asleep, Grace took care of her own routine—cleaning her teeth, washing her face, brushing and re-braiding her hair. Once in her nightgown, she glanced at Allie, then opened the closet door. The glow from the oil lamp on her bedside table cast a pale light inside, but she knew what was there. His shirts still hung on their hooks, trousers folded on a shelf, the wool fisherman's sweater knitted by his mother, his sweet *mor*, tucked beside them. Esther said it was time to clean everything out. Time to move on. Esther didn't understand.

She pulled his favorite shirt from its hook and slipped into the sleeves, wrapping it around her like a hug. She closed her eyes, picturing him in this very shirt, smiling as he looked up at her from the workbench in his backyard woodshop, or over a cup of coffee at the kitchen table, or—At a slight sound from the bedroom, she swiveled to peek through the door. Allie had kicked off the covers in her sleep. Grace turned to replace the shirt, letting her fingers linger a moment over the rough fabric before closing the door. She pulled the blankets over Allie, then slid under her own blue-and-white quilt, the one her mother had made before she was even born. She lay on her side, propping herself on one elbow, and brought two fingers to her lips. After kissing their tips, she moved her hand to his picture on the table and laid the kiss on Søren's mouth. "Goodnight, Sweetheart." Only then did she blow out the lamp and settle back on her pillow.

# Two

The veranda of Halstad House stretched around three sides of the white structure, all shaded by an overhanging roof. Serenaded by the morning's chorus of birds—a medley of robins, meadowlark, and quail—Grace swept scattered leaves over the edge of the porch to the flower beds below. At the melancholy whistle of a locomotive, she set the broom aside and leaned against the weathered corner post. Across the Kettle River, a train pulled out of Emmett Station, spewing billows of steam high into the July air.

Geoffrey Chaucer brushed against Grace's ankles, and she bent to stroke his tawny coat. "Well, good morning to you, too, sir. What do you think? Want to give me a hand with chores?"

The tabby leaped to the top rail of the balustrade and sat back on his haunches. His tail hung over the rail, swishing back and forth across the faded balusters. Lifting a paw to his mouth, he swiped it with his tongue and rubbed it over his face—repeating the action again and again.

Grace scratched his head. "Do you want to mend sheets or weed the garden?"

Chaucer only purred and continued his bath.

The banging of the kitchen door and thudding of feet interrupted their discussion.

"Mommy, 'member you promised to take me to the store today."

The grocer's store. The grocer's bill. Even though she needed a few items, Grace wished she could pay off her account at

Walters' Mercantile before she shopped again. Harv and Ada understood. They always did. They knew things were tight and replacing the broken parlor window had cut into her already-meager reserves. Maybe...maybe she could put this trip off until rent checks came in? She looked at her daughter.

Allie hopped from one foot to the other, eyes twinkling, the corners of her mouth nudging matching dimples into her cheeks. No. She'd have to deal with it. She wouldn't go back on her promise. "Let me finish up here and we can be on our way."

Allie spun around and took off.

"Grab your shoes and stockings!"

"'Kay!" Allie disappeared through the kitchen door.

Mother and daughter strolled hand in hand along the boardwalk, Allie chattering, Grace breathing in fresh pine-scented air and nodding at appropriate intervals. Uffda walked beside them one minute, scampered off the next, investigating what he must have deemed any suspicious object or smell. At Walters' Mercantile they turned in, leaving their canine companion to explore to his heart's content. Harv and Ada Walters may not have carried as wide a variety of articles as Temple's in the nearby town of Orient, but their stocked shelves contained most everything she needed, as well as what Allie dubbed *oodles of things*. In fact, Allie was in seventh heaven whenever they came.

As soon as the door closed behind them, Allie headed straight for the candy display. No surprise. Glass jars of colorful candy lined the countertop—peppermint sticks, horehound, taffy, lemon drops, and an assortment of other sweet treats.

When Ada saw Grace, she stepped to the yard goods and waved her over. "Look what came in yesterday." Her plump cheeks dimpled. She held up a cream-colored bolt of organza. "Isn't this beautiful? It would make a lovely shirtwaist. I thought of you as soon as I saw it."

Grace fingered the dainty fabric. She hadn't seen anything this lovely in ages. Temptation knocked at the door.

Ada pointed a finger at her. "I can tell you love it. Just a little extravagance this once?"

Temptation dispensed with the polite knock and took to pounding instead. Wouldn't it be fun to have something new? And she could work wonders with her treadle sewing machine. She'd been so good for so long, perhaps—Heavens to Betsy, what was she thinking? She shook her head. "It's lovely, but not today."

Ada's mouth dropped open. "Are you sure? We could put it on your account."

Grace shook her head again. "There's enough on the account as it is. Maybe someday." She touched the fabric, then squared her shoulders and handed Ada a list of needed staples. She pulled a coin purse from her pocketbook and extracted two bills. "Would you put this against my account?" She glanced at Allie ogling the candy jars and chewed her lower lip. Frugal was fine and necessary. On the other hand, her daughter was only young once. She pulled out a coin and set it on the counter. "And a penny candy."

Ada stepped to the cash register. "My Lydie Sue will be sorry she missed you, Allie. She's visiting her grandma and grandpa today." After taking care of the business at hand, she moved to the candies and opened the jar of peppermint sticks Allie pointed to. Removing one, she handed it to the grinning girl and looked back at Grace. "I'll have Harv Junior deliver your supplies as soon as he gets home from school."

"Thank you, Ada." Grace bumped her daughter with her hip and gestured toward the shopkeeper.

"Thank you, Mrs. Walters." Allie took a lick of her red-and-white striped sweet. "It's yummy."

"Let me know if you change your mind about that organza."

Grace smiled and took Allie's hand. "Thanks. Have a good day."

Once outside, Grace turned toward home. After two or three steps, Allie tugged her mother's hand. "Can we walk some more?"

The myriad of chores awaiting her at Halstad House called. But so did time with her daughter.

Allie tugged again. "Please?"

The breeze played with a wisp of hair on her forehead. Why not? Chores weren't going anywhere. Grace made an about-face.

With Grace's sudden stop, Allie collided with her. Grace caught Allie's shoulders and spun her around. "All right, missy-moo. Let's go for an adventure."

"I like 'ventures." Allie switched the candy to her other hand and grabbed Grace's with warm, sticky fingers.

They walked past three houses, the laundry, two more houses, the schoolhouse, the church. Allie popped the peppermint stick out of her mouth and aimed it at the white clapboard building. "Grampa says we got a awful good church 'cause Preacher talks about God there."

"Grandpa says we *have an awfully* good church," Grace corrected.

"Mm-hmm." Allie took another suck, then pulled the candy out again. "Grampa says you use'ta play piano at church. How come you stopped?"

Grace tensed. Church? She tried not to think about it. What kind of an explanation could she offer her four-year-old daughter, though? Uffda saved her. He bounded to them, running circles around their legs until catching sight of Allie's hand. He jumped up, front paws on Allie's stomach, pleading with his eyes.

"Hey." Allie held her peppermint stick out of the dog's reach.

Grace pushed Uffda off. "Behave yourself, you goofy dog."

The distraction proved enough. Allie giggled and they continued their walk. Grace would deal with the church question later.

When they reached the livery stable, they took time to admire the horses in the corral, each pointing out the one they'd choose if they could. The blacksmith looked up from his work and waved. They crossed to the north side of Main Street with the piercing ring of hammer against anvil echoing behind them.

As they strolled by the Bluebird Café, the door opened and Isobel Sommers—accompanied by enticing mealtime smells—burst onto the boardwalk. Grace thought her hair looked wilder than ever. Freckles stood out on flushed cheeks, and her hat sat at a tortuous angle as if she'd plopped it willy-nilly on her head in a mad rush. She skidded to a stop in front of them. "Mrs. Halstad, Allie, how are you?"

Allie held up her peppermint stick. "See what I got?"

"Say, that looks good enough to eat." Isobel gave a nervous laugh, glancing back toward the café. "My boss wants me to go to the mercantile for sugar. I don't want to be gone long." She leaned close to Grace and gushed. "There are three or four gentlemen eating lunch in there. One is handsome as can be, but another one is simply *gorgeous.*" She jumped off the boardwalk, calling a hasty goodbye over her shoulder, then raced across the road. Halfway to the mercantile, her hat flew off. She screeched and whirled around to retrieve it. With a quick wave, she darted to the store.

Allie watched, taking a slow lick of her candy. She glanced up. "Does Izzy have a bunch'a handsome beaus in there?" She bobbed her head toward the café.

"I don't think she has one beau, let alone a bunch of them." Grace steered her daughter down the boardwalk. "I'm afraid she figures if she chases after boys, she'll catch one, get married, and be magically happy."

Allie stopped to pull up a droopy stocking. "I'm not gonna chase after boys."

"Good. It's best not to worry about beaus. Just be yourself— kind and brave and good—the best Allie you can be."

They wheeled around at a shout from behind them.

Isobel sprinted across the street toward the cafe, one hand snugging a grocery bag to her side, the other pressing her hat to her head.

"Maybe Izzy's mommy never told her 'bout that," Allie said.

"Maybe not. Anyway, when the time comes, you don't need a bunch of beaus. One will do. Grandpa always said, 'Pick 'em right and treat 'em right and everything'll be all right.' Of course, the same goes for a young man. You want someone who treats you right as well."

"Yeah. He better treat me right, or I'll thump him on the head."

There was a thought. Grace chewed the inside of her cheek to keep the laugh at bay.

A cloud passed over the sun, draping them in a momentary shadow. Grace watched Isobel disappear into the Bluebird. Poor silly girl. She was as boy-crazy as they came. When Uffda barked and zipped ahead of them, Grace took Allie's hand. Oh well. Allie was her concern, not Isobel.

The steady ticking of the wall clock resonated in the kitchen as nightfall laid a blanket of quiet over the house. That fixed motion of the pendulum marking time usually calmed her. Not tonight. Grace set her elbows on the table and dropped her head into her hands. No matter how many times she reworked the figures, the numbers in her ledger didn't balance. Frustrating? Yes. But the fact that the expenses column grew faster than the received column alarmed her. She wasn't going under yet, but she wasn't quite making ends meet either.

She ran a hand over her face. Okay. She had to make this work. With eyes closed, she inhaled, lifted her shoulders, twisted from side to side, slowly exhaled. Pencil in hand, she looked at the columns and tried again. The clock continued its rhythmic beat.

A half hour later, blurry figures pooled across the page. She dropped the pencil, rubbed her eyes, and groaned. *Why can't I get this right?*

When the parlor door opened, she turned.

Esther walked in, brown leather slippers scuffing across the floor. Clad in a faded blue dressing gown, her hair curled tight to her scalp with bobby pins, she patted Grace's shoulder as she passed. "Why are you still up?" At the icebox, she pulled out a bottle of milk, poured a little into a pan, and glanced at Grace. "Want some?"

"Sure." Grace stretched her arms over her head and yawned.

With the pan set on the stove, Esther replaced the bottle on the icebox shelf. "Looks like you're doing the books. How's that going?"

Grace closed the ledger with a snap, causing her pencil to shoot across the table and drop to the floor. She ignored it. "I'm not making much headway. I'll work on it again tomorrow."

Esther stirred the milk. "I could take a look if you want."

Grace's stomach clenched. "No, thanks. I can handle it." Esther was *not* looking at the books. The last thing she needed was a lecture on how running Halstad House wasn't feasible.

Esther nodded. Once steam rose from the pot, she tipped warm milk into two mugs. She placed one in front of Grace and one across the table where she pulled out a chair and sat down. Leaning back, Esther sighed. She saluted Grace with her mug and raised it to her lips.

Grace took a good look at her. Owing to good genes and Esther's faithful daily and nightly rituals, her complexion was lovely. Nevertheless, new laugh lines gathered at the corners of her mouth and a few crow's feet appeared by her eyes. Even with her brown hair in pin curls, several strands of gray stood out. At thirty-five, Esther was eleven years older than Grace. Always taking care of somebody, she was the only mother Grace had known, even though Grandma Browne had come to live with them after Mama died. But Grandma had passed away years ago. Every weekend Esther spent helping Dad on the farm. The rest of the time she spent here and for that, Grace was grateful. She couldn't make it without her.

Esther lowered her mug to her lap. "I'm worried about you. You're wearing yourself to a frazzle trying to keep this place going. Laundry, cleaning a huge house—including the boarders' rooms—meals, baking, the garden, figuring out finances. I know I help with a lot of chores, but is it enough? And Allie. Don't think I haven't noticed how much she longs for your attention." She set the mug on the table. "I've said it before, but I'll say it again. For your sake and Allie's, please consider moving back to the farm. It would be so much easier—"

Grace held up her hand. "No."

When Esther dropped her gaze, letting one hand fall to her knee, Grace realized her voice had come across sharper than she'd intended. She reached across to touch her sister's arm. "I want so much for you to understand. This was the home Søren brought me to and I—I want to stay. I want to raise Allie here. I don't have everything figured out, but I'm trying. Please, sis, I need your help."

Esther sighed and patted the top of Grace's hand. "I do understand, or at least I think I do. Don't worry. I won't abandon you." She gave Grace a crooked grin. "Except where Mrs. Gibbons is concerned. You're on your own with her."

The knot in Grace's stomach relaxed. She took another sip of milk.

They enjoyed a few more minutes of peace, then Esther took a deep breath. "Can I ask you something?"

"Sure."

She rubbed her fingers against the tablecloth. "Will you come to church with us this week? Dad and I would love it, and I know Allie would."

The knot slithered back. Grace shook her head in slow motion, her voice coming out in a shaky whisper. "I can't."

A pleading look shone in Esther's eyes. "You haven't been since—since it happened. Don't shut God out. Please. He can heal your heart. He can bring you through this."

*How?* Grace feared if she opened her heart, all the pain she'd buried would rush out in an avalanche, engulfing her in grief so unbearable she'd never recover. No, better to keep that door closed. Better to just survive. She blew out a breath. "I can't."

It might've been the coward's way out, but she needed to escape Esther's words and the feelings they aroused. She scooted her chair away from the table and stood. "Time for bed." Her voice sounded over-bright, she knew. So be it.

Esther looked up. "Okay. I'm not going to give up praying for you, though."

When Grace reached for her mug, Esther waved her hand away. "I'll take care of these. You head on to bed."

She planted a kiss on the top of Esther's head. "Goodnight." Esther might drive her crazy sometimes, but Grace loved this big sister of hers.

# Three

Ethan Myers gripped the top of the gate. Halstad House. Grace lived here. Maybe she rushed around the kitchen even now. A slight breeze brushed his cheek as he removed his hat, raked his fingers through his hair, and shoved the hat back in place. It'd been six years since he'd seen her.

He inhaled the scent of the yellow roses Grace had always favored. They grew against the fence, its white, peeling paint as much in need of attention as the boards on the house. The sharp staccato of a woodpecker mimicked his racing heartbeat. He wiped sweaty palms on his trouser legs and pushed on the wooden pickets, hearing the click of the latch as the gate opened and the gentle *thwack* as it closed behind him. He walked up the stairs, maybe not two at a time like he used to, but at least without a limp.

At the door, he paused, listening to the muted clatter of dishes, a woman's soft voice, a child's giggle. He took a deep breath and knocked. After an abrupt silence, the door opened and there she stood, a dusting of flour powdering her nose. Dark tendrils had escaped her thick braid and curled around her face. Those chocolate-colored eyes that had caught his attention when he was ten years old peered at him. Her eyes didn't have the same sparkle he remembered. Something lurked in the background—a wounded, haunted expression. He understood, but his heart twisted just the same.

She gazed at him, one hand still on the door. "Yes?"

He took off his hat. "Hello, Grace."

Her eyebrows raised, and a glimmer of a smile appeared. "Ethan?"

Ethan grinned.

She burst into a laugh. "Ethan Michael Myers!" She threw open her arms and launched herself at him.

Tossing his hat onto a porch chair, he wrapped her in a hug.

"I can't believe you're here. When did you come? Are you staying in Emmett?"

He just smiled and held on.

Too soon, she stepped back, looking him over. "We heard you were injured in the war, but you look good. In fact, you look wonderful." At a tug on her dress, Grace swung her head to a blond, blue-eyed pixie peeking at him, then to Ethan again. "Heavens to Betsy, come in, come in." She took his hand and pulled him into the kitchen.

Ethan gave her hand a quick squeeze. "You look wonderful yourself." He squatted to smile at the little girl who stepped in front of him without a trace of shyness. "Now, who do we have here?"

"Ethan, this is my daughter Allie. Alice Ruth."

Allie scrunched her nose. "I like Allie best."

Grace stroked her daughter's hair. "And this is Mr. Myers, one of your daddy's and my dearest friends. We all went to school together right here in Emmett and were best buddies."

The pixie surprised him by flinging her arms around his neck.

She must have surprised her mother, too, because Grace clapped her hand to her cheek and shook her head. "Allie doesn't ever do that. I guess she knows who the good people are."

"Well, I know who the good people are, too." Ethan returned the girl's hug.

Allie pulled back and looked him in the eyes. "It's almost my birthday."

"It is?" Ethan gave her braid a playful tug. "Birthdays are special."

He glanced up when Grace interjected, "My baby's not a baby anymore, I'm afraid."

Allie tapped his shoulder. "I'm gonna be five, and I'm gonna have a party. A real party. Wanna come?"

"I can't think of anything I'd like better. How about if I talk to your mom about it?"

"'Kay." Allie grinned and scooted next to Grace again.

Ethan straightened, letting his eyes roam the room. Not much had changed. The black cookstove, shelves stacked with pots and pans, the ornate walnut sideboard that had belonged to Søren's grandfather, plain wooden cabinets on either side of the window on the far wall. And that big, round oak table in the center of the room. How many times had he sat there with Søren as they dipped gingersnaps, Søren in his thick black coffee, Ethan in his preferred tea? They'd taken breaks there on the days Ethan helped him prepare this house for his bride. Søren's bride.

After Søren and Grace married, they'd invited him over for evenings too numerous to count. He'd pull up a chair, talking, laughing, playing dominoes, reveling in the company of his two best friends. Increasingly, though, the torture of seeing them exchange loving glances, of bidding them goodnight as they stood arm-in-arm at the kitchen door, of walking alone to his horse, and plodding back to his bed at the sawmill's bunkhouse, slowly squeezed the life out of him. When he heard Grace was expecting, he hitched a ride twenty-five miles south to the town of Marcus and enlisted. U.S. involvement in the war in Europe appeared inevitable. He'd been fighting an internal war here, so he volunteered to engage in a different kind of battle on a different kind of battlefield.

"Ethan, come sit down." Grace steered him past a butcher-block table, the only thing he hadn't seen before. Once they were seated, she plied him with questions. Where had he been all this time? What were his plans?

Allie scooted her chair closer to his, gazing at him with wide eyes and a crooked little grin that melted his heart.

He rested his forearms on the table, looking between them. "Well, I fought in Europe for three years, then spent quite a bit of time back East in a hospital when I was sent home. After that,

I started traveling. I've been here and there, seeing places I'd only read about. New York City, Yellowstone National Park, the Grand Canyon. Lots of places, lots of people."

For twenty minutes he regaled them with stories of his travels. Allie scooted her chair even closer and placed her hand on his arm. When she gave him a broader grin, dimples surfaced. She seemed enthralled with his tales of magnificent mountain peaks, rushing rivers, interesting characters he'd met, and a few dangerous situations he'd faced.

Even Grace seemed spellbound. She placed her elbow on the table and propped her chin in her hand. Her eyes took on a far-away look as she listened with a half-smile on her face.

Finally, Ethan inhaled, then slowly let out his breath. "All very impressive, but a few weeks ago I woke up and thought, *It's time to go home.*" He looked at Grace. "I'm sure you know my mom passed away while I was overseas."

"Yes. And I'm so sorry." She touched his arm lightly. "And I was sad when your dad moved away from Emmett only a couple of months later."

Ethan nodded. "My sisters and their families live in southern California and they talked Dad into moving down. I traveled to San Diego and visited them two weeks ago. Beautiful country, lots of sunshine, but it's just not home to me. So I packed my bag, bought my train tickets, and..." He spread his arms wide. "... here I am."

"I'm glad," said Allie.

"Me, too," said Ethan. "And almost as soon as I arrived, I talked with Mr. Emmett at the sawmill. He hired me on as a bookkeeper, and I start first thing next week."

Grace gave him a puzzled look. "Not surveying? You loved that job." She grinned. "I always thought it was a good excuse for you to hike around the mountainside and get paid for it. I figured you'd do it forever."

Ethan's stomach clenched. Even now he felt a little raw when he remembered the ordeal that had forced him to change his plans. No more surveying. No more dreams of building his own company, contracting out to businesses in need of survey-ors. He cleared his throat. "Just as you heard, I was injured in the war." He took a look at Allie and tried to smile. "Seems like my leg got in the way of a bullet. Can you imagine that?"

She rubbed his arm, her bright eyes filled with concern. "Did it hurt?"

"To be honest, it hurt plenty. But Army doctors in France worked on me, then they shipped me to that hospital I men-tioned where more doctors worked on me." He patted his right thigh. "Now, my leg is as right as rain. Or almost. My days of spending hours roaming the mountains may be over, but I'm a swift hand with a pencil and a ledger."

Allie's eyes turned thoughtful. "My daddy got shot in the war. 'Cept they couldn't fix him."

"I know, kitten." Ethan placed his hand over hers, gently stroking the top with his thumb. He glanced at Grace and fol-lowed her solemn gaze to the mudroom that led to the back porch. He swallowed hard when he saw Søren's jacket hang-ing on a hook like it always had. *Oh, Lils.* Lils. His special name for his childhood chum, Lillian Grace—saved only for when his heart was moved.

He coughed and ran his fingers through his hair. "Man oh man, I smell something scrumptious. Is that what I think it is?"

Grace blinked. "Heavens to Betsy, the cinnamon rolls." She dashed to the stove and with two hot pads, pulled a pan from the oven and set it on the butcher-block worktable. "No harm done, thank goodness." A bowl of white frosting lay on the counter. Holding it above the pan, she drizzled glaze over the golden buns in loops and swirls. Half a dozen she transferred to a milk glass platter and laid on the table in front of Ethan. "Ta-da."

The dense, spicy aroma hit him. He remembered her cin-namon rolls. Snatching a napkin from the pile on the table, he tucked it into his collar. "All set."

"Let me grab some plates and forks," Grace said.

"What?" Ethan grimaced. "Half the fun is eating them with your fingers."

Grace clucked her tongue. "We'll need to at least let them cool a bit."

He kept eyeing them as they chatted.

After a few minutes, Grace relented. "All right, I think it's safe."

Ethan nabbed a roll from the platter, closing his eyes as he took a soft gooey bite. "Mmm-mmm." He took another bite and winked at Allie. "I've had these in a whole lot of places, but nothing compares to your mother's cinnamon rolls."

Grace waved a hand at him. "Flatterer."

"How 'bout me, Mommy?" Allie's eyes held a pleading look. "Can I use my fingers, too?"

Grace hesitated, looking between Allie and Ethan.

"Aw, come on, Mom," he said. He picked up another napkin and slipped it into the neck of Allie's dress.

Grace shook her head. "All right. Just this once." She handed a much smaller piece to her daughter. "And remember to use your napkin, not your dress, kiddo."

Allie beamed. She dove into her first bite, coming up with frosting and crumbs clinging to her upper lip and dimples.

Ethan found her adorable.

Grace picked up a tiny section of roll and bit into it. She pointed a finger at him. "You always could talk me into things."

"Oh, yeah?" He swiped the napkin across his mouth. "Who talked who into jumping into the river from the top of the Orient bridge? Who got who into trouble with his mother?"

Grace giggled and tucked a tendril of hair behind her ear. "At least I didn't leave you in the lurch. I apologized to her."

"Fat lot of good that did me. She never did believe sweet little Grace Browne would suggest a thing like that."

"Can I help it if I have an innocent face?"

Allie's hand paused mid-bite, eyes wide as she glanced at Ethan. "Did my mommy do that?"

"Yep. That and more."

"Like what?" Allie dropped her hands, crumbly cinnamon roll and all, into her lap.

Ethan cocked his head toward Grace. "Once she begged me to make snow angels in the schoolyard with her when no one else would. Never mind that it wasn't what a self-respecting high school boy did."

Grace leaned toward Allie. "He was a good sport about it and very brave. Especially since every student in school, plus the teacher, gathered around to watch. Some of the boys snickered and poked fun at him."

"Oh, they did all right. I risked my dignity that day, I'll have you know." He watched Allie's head ping-pong back and forth between him and Grace. "The next morning Bobby Bowers called me *angel-girly-Ethan*."

Allie's eyes opened wider. "What did you do?"

He glanced at Grace when she coughed, then turned to Allie. "I persuaded him not to call me that again."

She gave a quick nod. "Good. I would'a thumped him on the head." She took another sticky bite. "What else?"

He hid a grin behind a hunk of sweet roll. This little one was capturing his heart, no mistake about it. "I remember another time she got me in trouble. She brought a chicken to school and—"

"Oh, no." Grace covered her face with her hands.

"A chicken?" Allie creased her forehead.

"Yep. She'd been telling everybody how tame it was and how she'd taught it to do tricks. So she brought it to school to show off."

Grace sputtered. "Not to show off. I just wanted to display the hen's talent."

"Right." Ethan shook his head. "Well anyway, someone's bicycle was leaning against the schoolhouse. Your mom claimed she could ride around with the chicken on the handlebars and it would sit quietly, enjoying the ride."

Allie looked to Grace. "And did it?"

"As a matter of fact, it did." Grace got a smug look on her face and wiped the corner of her mouth with her napkin. "I circled the schoolyard three times with my hen Betty holding tight to the handlebars, looking as pleased as punch. She acted like she rode a bicycle every day of the week and twice on Sundays."

"But..." Allie's eyes quizzed Ethan. "How come you got in trouble?"

"Well, that isn't the end of the story." He scratched the side of his jaw.

"What happened?"

"One of the boys said it was no big deal because the chicken was her pet. Of course, she sat quietly. If she'd been trained well, anybody could give that old hen a bicycle ride. His next words were *neener-neener* if memory serves me right. Your mother wouldn't stand for that. She challenged the boy to try it. He made some lame excuse about his folks not wanting him to ride anybody else's bicycle." Ethan glanced at Grace and smiled, lost in the memory for a moment.

"Then what?" Allie wiggled in her chair.

Grace rested her cheek on her hand. "Brave as ever, Ethan volunteered to prove my point."

"And rescue a fair maiden's honor." He placed a hand over his heart, dipping his head.

Grace picked up the knife and cut another cinnamon roll. "He exchanged places with me. Hopped on the bicycle, pushed off, and Bob's your uncle, wheeled around the schoolyard like nobody's business. My sweet Betty sat on those handlebars as calm and contented as could be. I was proud of them both."

Ethan took the roll she held out to him, but before he bit into it, he shook his head at Allie. "Everything would've been fine if I hadn't gotten too big for my britches."

Allie didn't move a muscle, just stared with round cornflower-blue eyes.

"I got carried away, thinking myself a pretty clever chicken wrangler. I kicked my feet straight out and hollered *yahoo!* For some reason, that upset the chicken. She flapped her wings and let go of the handlebar with one foot, which caused the bike to wobble. Which caused me to lose my balance. Which caused an abrupt and embarrassing end to our ride."

Grace giggled.

"Did you fall on the ground with a splat?" Allie asked.

Ethan couldn't tell if she was amused or concerned. "Yep. Wounded my pride and backside at the same time."

Allie wrinkled her nose. "You got in trouble for that?"

"The worst was yet to come." This from Grace's corner of the world.

Ethan hung his head in mock shame, then raised it to Allie. "The hen kept flapping her wings, so when the bike went down, she went up. As luck would have it, special guests were coming to speak at school. They arrived at that unhappy instant, sauntering past our group, both dressed to the nines. The owner of the sawmill, Mr. Emmett, strode over with his wife on his arm."

Allie gasped. "Hoity-toity Mrs. Emmett?"

"Allie." Grace gave her daughter a slight frown, but a chuckle escaped her lips.

"That's what I called her, too," Ethan whispered. "Anyway, the hen squawked and sailed over Mrs. Emmett's head, hooking her talons in the poor lady's hat. Off it came. Mr. Emmett must have become addlepated in the flurry of all the activity. He batted wildly at the chicken when it flew at him, missed, and he clocked his wife instead. Well, that got her goat. She smacked him hard with a frilly white parasol she carried."

A laugh from Grace ended in an indelicate snort, which she covered by clapping a hand over her mouth.

Allie's lips formed a perfect O. "And that's when you got in trouble."

Ethan raised his hands as if in surrender. "And that's when I got in trouble."

Grace let out a whoop and collapsed against the back of her chair, laughing until tears rolled down her cheeks.

Ethan's heart warmed at the sight. *There you are.* Her eyes shone, and the slight furrows he'd noticed in her forehead disappeared. One corner of his mouth slid up. "I seem to remember an incident with a watermelon patch."

Grace slapped the tabletop. "Don't you dare."

Before he could say another word, the parlor door opened. In poked the head of a young woman with hair so messy he figured she'd either misplaced her comb or got caught in a heavy gale.

"Mrs. Halstad?" She glanced toward the table. When she saw him, her eyebrows shot straight up and she stepped into the room. "Gosh golly, aren't you handsome?" She clasped her hands under her chin and...shivered? "Oh, my." She smoothed her skirt, tittering as she took two more steps into the kitchen.

Heat climbed up Ethan's neck and into his face. He looked to Grace for help.

She smirked and scooted her chair back. "Miss Sommers, may I introduce my friend Ethan Myers?"

Miss Sommers inhaled, then let her breath out in a long sigh. "Hello, Mr. Myers. It's ever so delightful to meet you."

Good grief, she batted her eyes at him. He remembered his manners and stood with a jolt.

Grace laid two fingers over her lips and cleared her throat. "Ethan, this is one of my boarders, Miss Isobel Sommers."

He gave a slight bow. "My pleasure, Miss Sommers."

She did that tittering thing again and touched her hair with one hand. "Oh, please, call me Izzy. Everybody does. Dizzy Izzy. That's me. And may I call you Ethan?" She moved toward him, hand outstretched, ankles wobbling on her high-heeled shoes.

Ethan felt like a fat, juicy trout with a piranha honing in on him. He shot a look at Grace that he knew bordered on desperation.

She must have sensed his panic and took pity on him. "Is there something I can do for you, Miss Sommers?" She placed a hand on Izzy's shoulder, turned her around, and walked with her through the parlor door. Izzy swiveled her head to give him a toothy smile, wiggling her fingers before it swung shut behind them.

In their wake, silence descended on the room like the calm after a sudden storm.

"Whew." Ethan plopped into his chair and looked at Allie. "I'm trembling in my boots."

The cinnamon-crusted imp giggled. "Be brave. She's just one of the biddies."

He held back a chortle in case he hurt her feelings but knew a wide grin creased his face. "One of the biddies, huh?"

"Uh-huh." Allie leaned toward him, eyes shining, and spoke in a conspiratorial whisper. "Mommy's not sure if Izzy has all her cups in the cupboard."

It was hopeless. Ethan threw back his head and gave in to a fit of laughter. He'd be this little charmer's slave for life.

# *Four*

"I like that Mr. Ethan."

"Me, too." Mommy kissed Allie's forehead, carrying the warm scent of cinnamon and vanilla with her. Her smile was different. Gentle and sweet like most times, but even softer. "Have a good nap, sweetie."

Allie traced her mother's mouth, still drinking in all the happiness that had danced across Mommy's face this morning. Mr. Ethan had done that. She'd never seen Mommy laugh so much—not ever. For a while, Allie didn't see a smidge of sad in her eyes.

She grinned when her mother tweaked her nose and rose from the bed. When she heard the click of the door, Allie nestled into her pillow. Mr. Ethan made her laugh, too. She got a cozy feeling being around him, like a big ol' hug. She felt safe and glad at the same time. And something else. When she looked at him, her tummy clenched in a funny way, the same way like when she saw Lydie Sue's daddy pick her up and put her on his shoulders, then run around like he was a pony. Allie always wished she had a daddy who could do that. Hers was in Heaven, but now she wondered—can you ever get another one?

Mr. Ethan made her think about that. She bet he'd be good at it. And another good thing about Mr. Ethan was his hair. He had lots of it. Dark brown with curly ends that crept over his collar. If Allie sat on Mr. Ethan's shoulders, at least she'd have something to grab hold of if she started to slip. Lydie Sue's hands would slide right off her daddy's shiny bald head and then where would she be? Flat on the floor, that's where.

Should she ask Mommy about Mr. Ethan being her daddy? Allie chewed her bottom lip. No. If he was, he'd have to live here. Mommy had enough people to take care of. Better wait.

But she heard Preacher say you can talk to God about anything. She clasped her hands and closed her eyes tight. "Dear God, I don't want to hurt my own daddy's feelings, but I sure could use a real-live daddy right here. Mr. Ethan is the only one I ever met in my *whole life* who might work. I like him." Allie's eyes popped open. "He's smiley and funny and nice and looks straight in my eyes when he talks to me. Not like some stuck-up grown-ups who act like I'm not even there. *And* he makes Mommy laugh." She gnawed her lower lip again. "Know what? I think it's a awful good idea." Allie yawned and scratched her elbow. "Maybe You could mull it over and let me know what You think?" A little more lip-gnawing. "And maybe You could do somethin' 'bout it?"

She rolled to her side but flipped back again a second later. "When You see my daddy, tell him not to feel bad. I still love him and he can give me shoulder rides when I get up there." She scratched the other elbow. "'Kay. Amen."

Back on her side, she smiled, happy to think about Mr. Ethan as she drifted off to sleep. All of a sudden, a memory hit her and she bolted upright. *Uh-oh.* She better talk to God about this too, seeing as she was asking Him to help her out.

Preacher said sometimes you just got to get on your knees when you prayed. She bet this was one of those times. She scooted over the side of the mattress, sank to her knees, and clasped her hands tight under her chin. "Dear God, don't be mad at me for scaring Mrs. Gibbons the other day. I'm kinda sorry, just not a whole lot 'cause she's such a crabby-pants. And she did call me a name. I don't know what kind of pickle she said I was, but I bet it wasn't a good one."

Allie squinted her eyes and pictured the scene, as if she needed to run it by God. That morning she'd stuffed Uffda's chew toy behind the davenport cushion. Her head had been so full of birthday party thoughts, she forgot she had it in her hand. Last time, she got in trouble for bringing it in the house. Mommy said the thing was ratty-looking and smelled like dog. It seemed like a good idea at the time—hiding it and coming back after the errand Mommy had sent her on. As soon as Auntie Esther and Mommy were busy hanging sheets on the clothesline, she figured the coast was clear. She pushed open the door from the kitchen and peeked into the parlor. Wouldn't you know it? That ol' Mrs. Gibbons sat right on the davenport—face scrunched-up, glasses slipping down her nose, head bobbing on her bony chest. Even in her sleep she looked crabby.

Allie stared at her, feeling nettled but not *naughty*. Then something came over her. With one hand, she covered her mouth to hold back a giggle. The next thing she knew, she found herself creeping across the frayed carpet to the piano and climbing onto the bench. She knelt in front of the black and white keys and raised her arms high over her head. Dare she do it? Mrs. Gibbons slept on.

Allie flattened her palms...leaned forward...waited a second...*whoosh*. She plunged almost headfirst, hands smashing into the keyboard with the full weight of her body. At the jarring explosion of sound, she about jumped out of her skin.

That was nothing to what Mrs. Gibbons did. She shot off the sofa with an ear-piercing shriek. Her glasses hurled toward Allie like they were launched from a slingshot. She ducked just in time. The glasses bounced off the wall behind her, clattered to the floor, and slid beneath the piano. Mrs. Gibbons landed on her feet with a thud, swinging her head back and forth. Her eyes were wild and frantic. When they settled on Allie, the gleam in those dark eyes made Allie shudder. *Maybe this wasn't such a good idea.*

Allie scrambled off the bench and tore around the corner to the alcove under the stairs. Her hands grabbed the sun-faded drapes, and she flung herself behind them. *Don't find me. Don't find me.* Allie held her breath when she heard the scuff of shoes on the floor. *Uh-oh.* She looked down. Her bare toes poked out under the drapery. Just as she glanced up, the drapes jerked open. There stood Mrs. Gibbons, chest heaving, face flushed.

She shook an angry finger at Allie. "I've known hooligans in my time, but this was downright wicked! How dare you!"

Allie cringed. Had she been wicked? Like in-the-Bible-wicked? But then Mrs. Gibbons called her that pickle-thing and her courage rose. "Well, you're a mean ol' warthog and I don't like you!" She stamped her foot for good measure.

Mrs. Gibbons' voice squeaked. "Your mother will hear about this, young lady." Her hands shook as she ran them through her hair.

Allie looked square in those glowering eyes. "And I'll tell her how I saw you sneak down the hall last night with cookies and bread under your arm. I bet you snitch food lots'a times when everybody's sleepin'. Then Mommy wonders where it is and sometimes doesn't have enough for the next day."

Mrs. Gibbons' eyes widened. She took a step back and smoothed her skirt. "Hold on now. Perhaps I—I was a bit hasty. There is no need for either of us to trouble your dear mother. We both know how hard she works, and there is always so much on her mind. We can relieve her of more worry. Don't you agree?" Her smile looked like a grimace. "The more I think about it, the more I see this was just a case of childish frolic." She held out her hand. "Shall we call it a truce and let bygones be bygones?"

Allie frowned at the outstretched hand, then raised her eyes to the enemy's face. *Ha. She looks awful shifty.* She gave her head a quick shake and skedaddled. When she reached the safety of the kitchen, she held the door open a crack to peer back into the parlor. Mrs. Gibbons wrung her hands, muttering something Allie couldn't hear. Then she spun on her heel. Sinking to her hands and knees, she crawled under the piano. Hunting for her glasses, Allie guessed. Allie closed the door and headed outside.

"Well, that's what happened." Allie stared at the ceiling. "Was I awful bad, God?" She clasped her hands tighter under her chin. "I'll try hard to be better. Like not calling her a warthog. Or knocking on her bedroom door and running away. Or hiding her pocketbook." A yawn snuck up on her—a yawn so big she thought she'd turn herself inside out. She scratched the same itch on her elbow. "'Kay. Amen again."

Allie crawled under the covers and sighed. It was hard for an almost-five-year-old to be good *all* the time.

# *Five*

Grace removed Søren's coat from the hook in the mudroom, clucking her tongue at the sight of dust on the shoulders. She opened the screen door and smiled at the girls sitting on the back porch steps. "What are you two up to?"

One pair of cornflower blue eyes and another of deep brown looked up at her. Allie spread her bare toes, curling them around the edge of the stair. "I told Lydie Sue it's almost my birthday and I'm gonna be five."

Allie's best friend beamed behind her freckles. "I'm already five."

"Yep. We'll be five at the same time." Allie clapped her hands. "Then six. Then more and more."

"Hey." Grace bent to brush back a few wisps of hair from her daughter's forehead. "Let's hold off on the more and more. You're growing up too fast as it is."

Allie scrunched her nose and shaded her eyes. "But six is okay, right?"

"When it gets here, six will be fine. In the meantime, five is perfect." Grace skirted around Allie. "Excuse me, ladies, may I sneak past you?"

When Allie leaned closer to Lydie Sue, Grace padded down the stairs, then strode across the yard to the clothesline. There, she held his coat close to her chest, sucked in a deep breath, and tipped her head back to gaze at the bold, azure sky. Today promised to be another July scorcher, but this midmorning mildness was a balm to her soul. She wished she could take Allie to the swimming hole when the heat struck, but by then supper would be underway, followed by cleanup and all the other chores. She had to prepare for washday; it would be here before she knew it. She needed to sort through Allie's clothes as well. She'd outgrown some, others—*Enough.* She'd think about all that later. She took a deep breath and shook the heavy coat several times. Pulling a stout whisk broom from her apron pocket, she tackled the dusty shoulders. A wrenching in her heart struck as she fingered the coat collar, but she pushed it aside and continued her task. She examined the coat front and back. Satisfied all was as it should be, she laid it over one of the lines and smoothed the sleeves. *An airing will do it good. I just need to bring it inside before Esther returns or I'll get one of her looks.*

A sharp bark, a brush of fur against her ankle, and a black, brown, and white blur that was Uffda raced past her, ears flapping in the wind. Grace reached to pet him. Too late. He hurtled around the side of the house. "Where in the world is he off to in such a hurry?"

Allie glanced her way. "He's chasing Lydie Sue's cat again."

Lydie Sue shrugged. "Rascal kind of teases him."

Grace headed toward them. "It's a good thing he never catches her because I'm not sure he'd know what to do if he did." She mounted the stairs, glancing back at the girls as she opened the screen door. "Have fun."

In the kitchen, golden cornbread sat in the warming oven, covered by a damp tea towel. Two fresh-baked cherry pies, crisscrossed with lattice crusts, lay stacked in the pie shelf. She'd reheat last night's ham and split pea soup later. Grace grabbed her mending basket, settling into the rocking chair near the back door where she could keep an eye on Allie and Lydie Sue through the screened window. She closed her eyes and leaned her head against the back of the chair, relishing this quiet time with both Esther and the boarders away for the morning.

She allowed herself a few moments of repose, lulled by the girls' happy chatter. Then she lifted her head and began to darn the heel in one of Allie's stockings. She glanced through the screen at the sound of the girls' coaxing voices. "C'mere, c'mere."

Geoffrey Chaucer sauntered to the top step and deposited his pudgy feline bulk between the girls.

"I like Geoffrey Chaucer." Lydie Sue played with the cat's ears. "He's a good ol' thing, isn't he?"

Allie planted a kiss on Chaucer's head. "He's the best."

Chaucer yawned, appearing indifferent to this clearly well-deserved tribute.

"My cat's a scalawag sometimes. The dogs around our place don't like her 'cause she chases them away. Just takes off after them lickety-split. Boy, can she run fast." Lydie Sue rubbed her nose and sneezed. "Does Chaucer do that?"

"I don't know for sure." Allie flipped her braid behind her back. "Bet he could if he wanted to."

Lydie Sue heaved a sigh. "The other thing about our cat is she scratches."

"Most likely got fleas," said Allie.

"Not that kind of scratching. I mean she scratches me, and I don't like it one bit."

"I'd thump her on the head if I was you. Bet she'd stop quick."

Grace smiled and shook her head. *Was I ever that young? That sure of life?*

"Maybe," Lydie Sue said. "My daddy's about fed up with her. He went to pet her yesterday and got scratched but good. Daddy liked to boot her out then and there, but Mama put a stop to it. She wants her to stay because she's a good mouser."

"Geoffrey Chaucer is a champion mouser."

"Zowie. A champion. My daddy'd like that." Lydie Sue stroked Chaucer. "Gonna live up Boulder Creek for a while."

"Your cat?"

Lydie Sue giggled. "No, my daddy. The mill's gonna send a crew out to find a lot of good trees. It's way too far to go every day. He'll live in a camp with a bunch of other guys."

Allie rubbed Chaucer's head. "My daddy lives in Heaven."

"Yeah? I wondered where he was."

"Uh-huh. He lives in Heaven. He just keeps his clothes here."

Grace's hands stilled.

Lydie Sue scratched her knee and looked sideways at Allie. "How come? Is he coming back?"

"No. Preacher said you can't come back if you go to Heaven. But we can go there to see those folks."

Lydie Sue sat up straight. "We can?"

"Yeah, 'cept we hafta die first so it's best to wait. Preacher said God knows the right time for everybody."

Grace placed one hand over her heart. Pain pricked, that familiar throbbing ache she buried deep inside. She squeezed her eyes shut. *I won't think about it. I won't.*

Lydie Sue pointed toward the clothesline. "Does your mama know he has to stay in Heaven?"

"I dunno. She sticks around home when Grampa and Auntie Esther take me to church. I was gonna say something, but she gets sad if anybody talks about my daddy."

"I bet Preacher would come tell her."

Allie gazed straight ahead, chewing her bottom lip. Then she looked at Lydie Sue and grinned. "That's a good idea. I'll ask him next Sunday."

Grace dropped her mending in the basket and jumped to her feet. She forced a smile as she thrust open the screen door. "Hey, girls. Anybody for cookies?"

"Yay!" Allie and Lydie Sue erupted off the step. They ran past her, leaving Chaucer in their wake. He flicked his whiskers and tail at the same time, then lay prostrate, no doubt needing to recover from the arduous task of being loved on.

Grace eyed him, took a longing look at Søren's coat on the clothesline, and turned to follow the girls, letting the screen door slam behind her.

***

Grace made sure both boarders had fresh water in their pitchers and clean linens on their bureaus before they settled in for the night. Izzy, wrapping her hair in cloth ties, regaled her with an account of the latest handsome gentleman who paid her a compliment at the café today. Her face lit with excitement as she told of his smile and shining eyes, but her expression fell when she said he left his second cup of coffee untouched as he rushed out the door to catch a train. Grace wondered if rushing out was because of the train or if the girl's giggling persistence had anything to do with it. If she were her sister or even a cousin, Grace might say something. But she reminded herself it wasn't her concern.

Then there was Mrs. Gibbons. Though she tried to sneak in and out before the whiny lady came to her room, no such luck. It was a good half hour before Grace could make her escape.

She took the back stairs into the kitchen in time to see her sister plunge Allie's foot into an enamel pan of sudsy water.

Esther looked at Allie with mock annoyance. "Did you leave any dirt outside?"

Allie giggled. "You're silly, Auntie Esther." She clasped the sides of the chair seat, swinging her free leg back and forth. "There's lots and lots more dirt out there."

"You could've fooled me." Esther glanced at Grace. "I've got her feet under control. I'll let you tackle her hands and face and anything else you deem necessary before she crawls between her sheets."

Grace held Allie's chin and lifted her face, turning it first one way, then the other. "Hmm...I *think* it's my daughter behind all this dirt."

"It's me, Mommy." Allie giggled again and swung her leg harder, which caused her toes to catch a dollop of foam, shooting it straight into Esther's face. Allie sucked in a breath. "Sorry, Auntie." But both Grace and Esther laughed, and Allie relaxed in her chair.

Esther wiped her sudsy cheek with her sleeve and carried the basin outside.

Grace poured warm water into a smaller enamel pan and grabbed a bar of soap and a washcloth. "Okay, let's see who we find in there." Grace was as gentle as she could be, but Allie still squirmed a few times when the cloth rubbed a little deeper into a patch of dirt that seemed ingrained. At last, Grace was satisfied and kissed Allie's nose. "There's my sweetie." Allie's skin shone with a pink glow. Damp tendrils of honey-gold hair framed her forehead and cheeks.

Her daughter's face might be clean, but her play dress? *Oh my.* "Show me your hands." Allie held them up. "What exactly have you been doing?"

"Well... First I helped Uffda find his chew-toy. I crawled way back under the porch 'cause he couldn't reach it. After that, Chaucer and me rolled in the dirt by the tree."

"*Chaucer and I.*"

Allie's eyes widened. "You, too?"

Grace smirked. "No. You're supposed to say *Chaucer and I,* not *Chaucer and me.*"

"'Kay. Chaucer and me—I mean I—rolled in the dirt by the tree."

"That explains everything." Grace moved to scrub Allie's hands.

Funny how this trivial act warmed her heart. She refused to see it as an irritation. No. She treasured this time—the dirt, the dress she'd scrub later tonight, the tangled hair that needed extra brushing. But Allie's giggle, her sparkling eyes, her uninhibited chatter—oh yes—she treasured this. She wouldn't miss it for the world.

Thirty minutes and one-hundred brush strokes later, a mostly clean Allie nestled in Grace's lap. They rocked in rhythm to the song of crickets serenading them through the open window. Grace reached for a book on the nightstand. "How about this one? Auntie Esther picked it up at the lending library. It's about a pigtailed cowgirl and her horse, Maude."

Allie stifled a yawn and nodded against her mother's shoulder.

"'Maude sped through the forest with the cowgirl leaning over her neck, hands clinging to the palomino's mane, red pigtails streaming behind her. Freckles on the cowgirl's nose stood out in the bright sun.'" Grace paused and held the book still.

Allie studied the picture, fingers tracing the image of the galloping horse and its rider. "How come they don't give the cowgirl a name?" Her chin jutted up as she looked at Grace.

"Maybe the author wants you to name her."

"Oh." Allie studied the picture again. "I think her name is Allie."

Grace stroked her daughter's arm. "Another Alice Ruth? What a good idea."

Allie shook her head. "Not Alice Ruth. She doesn't have the same grandmas as me to be named after. She's just Allie."

"Good thinking." Grace kissed the top of Allie's head and turned the page. "'Past the birch tree with its stark black spots against smooth white bark, past the pine tree with its cones littering the ground, past the fir tree with a frantic squirrel chittering at them from a low branch, on and on they ran. The cowgirl leaned further—'"

"Allie."

"Right. 'Allie leaned further over her horse's neck, urging Maude on. Was she afraid of the forest? Afraid of the horse's speed? Never. She loved them both. She loved the—'"

At the sound of the loud rap on the bedroom door, Allie gasped.

Grace sighed and lifted her head. "Yes?"

The door inched open until Mrs. Gibbons' face peeked through. "Mrs. Halstad? Oh, I regret to disturb you ever so much. You and your sweet little girl."

*Sweet little girl? I'm suspicious already.*

Mrs. Gibbons pushed into the room. "I wouldn't dream of interrupting. You know how discreet I always wish to be. But it's that bed slat, I'm afraid. It slipped off the frame again and, of course, the mattress is now tilted. I would adjust it myself if I dared but, well, you remember what my dear late husband said about my back."

Grace held up a hand. "Yes, Mrs. Gibbons. I'll be right there." Her sharp tone cut through the air.

Mrs. Gibbons froze. Her eyes flitted back and forth between Grace and Allie.

Grace stared at her until, for once, she seemed to get the message and backed out of the room.

"Mommy?" Disappointment flickered in Allie's eyes.

*That woman. Her poor dead husband. Her poor lame back. Her poor tilted mattress. Well, my poor brave Allie.* She snuggled her daughter close. "I'm sorry, sweetie. This can't be helped. And we'll never get a moment's peace unless I fix her mattress."

Allie breathed out a sigh and nodded against Grace's shoulder again. "I know, Mommy. She's kind of a trial, isn't she?"

Grace pulled her closer and chuckled. "I cannot disagree with you. How about you lie down on your bed with the book until I come back? I'll try to be quick like a bunny."

"'Kay."

Grace got Allie settled and headed for Mrs. Gibbons' room, determined to make this, if not the fastest visit in the history of mankind, at least the fastest visit in the history of this particular boarder.

Her efforts didn't matter a whit. She returned to find Allie fast asleep. The book lay near her hand, open to a picture of cowgirl Allie and Maude gazing out over a field of sunflowers. Tears pricked Grace's eyes as she collected the book, tucked the blankets under Allie's chin, kissed her cheek. None of this was fair. She hadn't asked for any of it. They should be a whole family enjoying the warmth and safety of Halstad House. Allie shouldn't have to share her with biddies, bills, or the business of running a boarding house. Grace sniffed and wiped her hand across her eyes. *Enough. I won't think about it now.*

In the kitchen, Grace found her sister at the counter, setting the oatmeal to soak in water and a bit of whey for tomorrow's breakfast. Esther motioned with her head to a steaming teapot and two cups on the table. Grace filled the cups and plunked into an oak chair. It wobbled under her weight. She added to her mental to-do list: fix chair legs. She eyed Esther over her teacup as she blew across the top. "I've been thinking about Allie's birthday gift."

"What did you come up with?" Esther covered the oatmeal and placed the pot in the warming oven. She moved to the table.

"I had hoped there'd be a little extra money this month." She replaced the cup on the saucer with a gentle clink. "Mary deciding not to come back until just before the start of school didn't help."

"You should have charged her over the summer. At least a partial payment to hold her room." Esther narrowed her eyes. "She took advantage of you."

"Maybe." Grace leaned into the chair back. "I suppose other places do that. It's hard to ask, though, when I've known her since grade school." She fingered the tablecloth. "There were other expenses too." She wouldn't mention what she owed on her account at the store.

Esther sipped her tea while Grace pondered her birthday options. The soft cooing of doves drifted through the window, wending through the silence. Grace took hold of her braid, running the tip across her chin and mouth in gentle strokes. Back and forth, back and forth—"Wait." Grace sat bolt upright.

Esther blinked. "Yes?"

Grace leaned forward, flattening both hands on the tabletop. "Buying her the roller skates is out of the question. What do you think about me giving her my old china-faced baby doll?"

"The one Grandma Browne gave you when you were little?"

"Yes. She's wrapped in a trunk in the attic. Her hair may need a little fixing up, and she only has the one dress. But I think it's still in good shape." Grace tapped the handle of her teacup. "Would Allie like it? Or would she think it's a dumb gift for a modern five-year-old?"

"I can't imagine Allie thinking *your* doll is a dumb gift. She'll be thrilled. I just know it." Esther set down her cup. "In fact, I haven't been sure what to get her until now. I have enough fabric at the farm to make a doll dress and matching bonnet—maybe even some booties." Esther's eyes shone. "It's perfect." She pushed her chair back and rose. "Grace, it's been ages since we've rummaged through your attic. This will be fun."

"Well, all rightie then." Grace scooted out from the table, joining her sister on the narrow back stairs. She loved it when she saw Esther's adventurous side. Even though their grandmother came to help out when Mama died, as a young girl Esther had shouldered a load of work and responsibility. And now, she still carried more than her fair share, all without a word of complaint. But Grace sometimes wondered if her sister ever longed for a life that included marriage and children of her own. She should ask Esther one quiet evening over a cup of tea. She should—but—selfishly, Grace knew she needed Esther's help to keep things running here, and, back at the farm, Dad depended on his oldest daughter every weekend. Grace shook herself. She wouldn't think about it now. She followed Esther up the stairs, their heels matching click for click.

# Six

The tiny second-floor landing offered the sisters three choices—to their right, a set of even narrower stairs would take them to the attic; straight ahead, a door opened onto a hallway and the house's main bedrooms; and off to their left, a small room lay tucked away by itself. Esther poked her head into the room. A treadle sewing machine stood against one wall, directly beneath a window framed with filmy white curtains. A cane-bottomed chair sat to one side.

Grace peeked around her. She gestured toward shelves filled with colorful fabric—two bolts of ordinary cloth, the rest a kaleidoscope of scraps. "Don't worry about fabric. If you don't have enough at home for a doll's outfit, there's plenty here. Help yourself."

"Thanks." Esther looked over her shoulder. "I still say this was pretty cramped quarters for a housekeeper. It must have been a dreary life."

Grace leaned against the doorframe. "From what Søren told me, the original owners were more concerned with proving they were as good as the Emmetts than providing swanky accommodations for the hired help." She gave a slight shrug. "The maids had it even worse upstairs." She crossed the threshold, sidestepping a shabby overstuffed easy chair and various baskets containing yarns, knitting needles, and crochet hooks. Leaning over the sewing machine, she raised the window to the top of the screen. The curtains stirred gently. "I'll leave this open tonight so we can get a cross breeze."

Back on the landing, Esther gave an off-hand wave at the door to the hallway. "Good thing the old skinflint decided spacious boudoirs were a must to keep up appearances. And five to boot."

Grace propped the hall door open with a sad iron. She glanced through, heaving a relieved sigh at the sight of an empty hallway and closed bedroom doors. "Everything is quiet. Let's go on up."

Esther had already begun to ascend the attic staircase. Grace followed behind, pressing both hands flat against the walls as she climbed.

On the third floor, they peered into the first two rooms. Esther made a *tsk-tsk* sound. "Barely big enough for a bed and dresser in either of them. Blistering hot in the summer. Freezing cold in the winter. How did the girls hired as maids do it? You couldn't pay me enough."

"Heavens to Betsy." Fanning her face with one hand, Grace moved to the tiny window in one of the rooms. "Let's open this and get some air moving. It must be over one hundred degrees up here." She shook her head. "I don't know how they did it either. Poor things." It took plenty of pushes and prods, but she finally managed to inch up the window. She wiped her hands on her apron and stepped into the large room that stretched the width and almost the length of the house, listening as Esther battled the window in the other small bedroom. She called over her shoulder. "I always hoped their lives weren't dismal, all work and no play. Maybe they were glad for a steady job."

With a screech, Esther's window slid open. She joined Grace and dusted off her hands. "Maybe on their days off they went home to their families where they laughed and poked fun at their boss with his highfalutin ways."

After they'd forced two stubborn windows in the massive main area open, Grace placed her hands on her hips and surveyed the room. Four steamer trunks either lined the walls or sat scattered amidst broken furniture, apple crates brimming with miscellaneous items, a spinning wheel with two missing spokes, and Allie's cradle and highchair.

Esther linked arms with Grace, scanning the dusty chamber. "I don't suppose you know which trunk it's in?"

Grace smirked. "Not exactly." She pointed to the nearest trunk. "It's either that one or the one just beyond it." She gnawed her lower lip. "Or the one in the corner or—"

"*Pfft.* In a word, no." Esther rolled up her sleeves. "Good thing we still have daylight coming through the windows. Let's get to work, sister-mine." She marched to the far corner and knelt before a black steamer trunk.

Grace chose the nearest trunk. Inside, clothes that had once belonged to their mother lay neatly folded. She'd forgotten all about them. Two white shirtwaists, a black ankle-length skirt, a flannel nightgown, several bloomers, stockings, and—"Esther, look at this." She held up a light-colored corset, somewhat faded by time, its whalebone stays faithfully maintaining the garment's shape.

Esther clucked her tongue. "I am *so* glad we don't have to wear those in this day and age."

"You and me both." Grace returned the corset to the pile. She rifled through the rest of the garments, then folded them back in place before closing the lid. She hoisted herself up. "It's not in this one. Any luck there?"

Head buried inside her trunk, Esther's low mumbles rose from within.

Grace moved on to the next trunk. One of its brown leather straps was ragged, the other split. Grace knelt and used both hands to lift the creaking lid. A soft gasp escaped her lips. She hadn't looked inside this chest since... On the left side, under a layer of tissue paper, her wedding gown rested in ghostly splendor. She fingered the creamy satin, hovering over the delicate pearl buttons she and Esther had sewn to the bodice with painstaking care. How proud she'd been to wear it as she stood beside her handsome bridegroom. How her heart overflowed with hopes and dreams—and love.

She smoothed the tissue paper back over her bridal finery, swaddling the gown like a mother with her precious baby. Then, she let her eyes roam to the stack of clothes on the right. Wedding clothes. *His* clothes. She touched the black wool jacket with wonder, remembering his crooked grin as she walked toward him on her father's arm. The jacket and trousers had been extravagant and too hot for a summer day. But he said she was worth it. Besides, they were only getting married once, so he was content to throw caution to the wind. She smiled when she picked up the stiff white collar that fastened to his shirt and chafed his neck. That was the only thing he complained about. "I'm all trussed up like a Christmas turkey." Even so, his eyes twinkled when he said it. Grace ran her fingers over the rough fabric. How had it been six years since their wedding? It felt like yesterday. It felt like forever ago.

A soft hand caressed her shoulder. She was surprised to find tears coursing down her cheeks.

"Grace?"

She looked into her sister's face.

"Love, don't do this to yourself."

Grace blinked and brushed her hand over her face.

"Look. I found the doll." Esther held up a baby doll with a china face, auburn curls gone awry, wearing a wrinkled calico dress with a torn hem.

Grace nodded. Her gaze swept the shadowy interior again. She wiped tears from her cheeks. *Enough. I won't think about it now.* She closed the lid with a firm hand. "Let's head back to the kitchen."

Esther stroked the top of Grace's hand. "Are you okay?"

Grace leaned her cheek against her sister's arm a moment. Then she patted the trunk, rose, and led the way downstairs.

"A little bird told me there's a brand new five-year-old in Emmett. Did I come to the right house?" At a squeal from the other side of the kitchen, Ethan peeked around Grace. He winked at her and stepped through the doorway in time to catch Allie as she leaped into his arms.

"Mr. Ethan!" She gave him a loud smacking kiss on his cheek, wriggled down, and grabbed his hand. "C'mon."

Allie tore around the table and skidded to a stop in front of her grandfather, dragging Ethan behind. "Grampa, this is Mr. Ethan." She spun her head around. "This is my grampa."

The gentleman rose from his chair.

"Hello, Mr. Browne." Ethan held out his hand to the white-haired, white-bearded man standing in front of him. "It's good to see you again." When Mr. Browne clasped his outstretched hand, Ethan felt the strength of a man accustomed to years of hard physical labor.

"Ethan, my boy, it's good to see you, too."

Allie drew her eyebrows together. "You know Mr. Ethan?"

"Oh my, yes." Her grandpa chuckled. "I've known your Mr. Ethan since he was a boy."

"Willikens."

"Gather around." Grace walked to the table with tea, coffee, and cups on a silver tray. Esther brought up the rear carrying a jug of milk, condensation droplets beading its sides.

"Coffee, tea, or..." Grace grinned at Allie. "Milk?"

Mr. Browne sat back down. Allie chose a chair beside him and patted the one to her right. "Sit here, Mr. Ethan."

He placed a hand over his heart and dipped his head. "Happy to oblige the birthday girl."

Grace and Esther spread everything out, poured the assorted beverages, and took their own seats on the opposite side of the round oak table.

Grace pointed at her daughter, a grin on her face. "All right, which do we do first? Presents or—"

"Presents!" Allie jumped up, upsetting her glass of milk.

Ethan grabbed it in time. "Always my preference."

Grace rose and retrieved four wrapped packages from an end table by the rocking chair. She handed one to Allie. "This is from Mr. Ethan."

Allie ripped the paper off of Ethan's gift. Her eyes sparkled. A small box appeared, and she made quick work of opening it.

She pulled out a whittled wooden horse painted the color of her hair. Caught mid-gallop, the horse's forelegs reached high as if in flight, its mane and tail tossed back by a wild imaginary wind. Allie's eyes widened. For a moment she sat without moving, then she hugged the steed to her chest. Her gaze moved to her mother. "It's Maude."

"Maude?" Ethan looked from one to the other.

"From a book we're reading." Grace laid her hand on her cheek. "It's perfect." Her eyes met his and a dewiness glinted in the afternoon light. She smiled and mouthed the words *thank you.*

Warmth spread through Ethan's chest. Wasn't it just like God to work behind the scenes, even arranging the tiny details concerning a little girl's toy horse?

"I love it, Mr. Ethan." Allie laid the horse on the table with tender care.

Mr. Browne's package came next. He'd wrapped it in plain brown paper tied with baling twine. Her name emblazoned the front in block letters. "Look Mommy. A–L–L–I–E. Like you taught me." Allie plopped the package in her lap and tugged at the snug knot, tightening it even more.

Mr. Browne pulled a jackknife from his pocket. He snapped the blade open, slid it under the twine, and slit it with one swift motion. "There you go, sweet pea."

Allie lost no time freeing her gift from its shackles. She shivered, gave a giddy laugh, and held it up. "A rabbit book. See? And they're wearing people clothes."

Grace leaned forward. "Wonderful. *Peter Rabbit* by Beatrix Potter. We'll enjoy that one."

Allie set the book next to Maude, grabbed her grandfather's hand, and kissed it. "Thank you, Grampa."

Grace handed Allie another package, this one wrapped in white tissue paper tied with a pink and white polka-dot ribbon. She bit her bottom lip and whisked a tendril of hair behind her ear. Ethan puzzled over the look on her face. Why in the world would she be nervous about this gift?

Allie untied the ribbon and ripped the tissue paper. She lifted the lid from a white cardboard box and peered inside. Clapping a hand over her mouth, she looked at her mother. "Willikens." Her eyes sparkled like sun on water.

A lovely baby doll lay in a sheaf of pale blue fabric. Allie lifted her out and cradled her in her lap. Blushing cheeks and a rosebud mouth adorned the doll's face. Blue eyes that opened and closed gazed at Allie. She wore a green-and-blue plaid dress with matching booties. Allie hugged the doll tight and rushed to Grace. "Oh, Mommy. Thank you, thank you, thank you."

Grace's features relaxed. "You really like it?"

She threw one arm around her mother's neck and kissed her cheek. "It's the best doll ever."

Grace ran a finger down the doll's cheek. "She was mine when I was a little girl."

"She was?" Allie pulled her head back to look at her mother. "I'll love her forever. What's her name?"

"Her name was Margaret. Sometimes I called her Meg. But you can name her anything you want."

"No." Allie bent to kiss the little china face. "Her name's Margaret. That's the one she knows." Allie climbed onto Grace's lap, snuggling Margaret in her arms.

Esther touched Allie's arm. "I see one more package here. Want to open it?"

Allie nodded.

Esther placed the last gift in front of her. "I'll hold Margaret for you."

"'Kay, but..."

"Don't worry. I'll take extra good care of her."

Allie ripped open the tissue paper, revealing a calico doll-sized dress, bonnet, and booties, plus a white flannel nightgown and cap. "Oh, Auntie Esther, are these for Margaret?"

"Yes. And I know for a fact they fit just right." She handed the doll back to a grinning Allie.

Allie's eyes swept the table. "This is the best birthday in my whole life." She leaned against Grace, looking, Ethan thought, like a cat in the cream.

Grace placed her mouth next to Allie's ear. "What do you say we bring out the cake?"

Allie's head shot up. "Yes!" She scooted down from her mother's lap.

Grace put her hand on Allie's head. "Why don't you put your gifts somewhere to make room on the table for everything?"

Allie placed the doll in the box, arranging the doll clothes, the *Peter Rabbit* book, and Maude around Margaret.

Ethan set the box on the floor while Allie hurried into her own chair.

Allie whispered to him. "Mommy made me a Swans Down birthday cake with pink frosting." She ran her tongue along her upper lip. "Mm-mm."

Ethan's eyes followed Grace. She walked across the kitchen holding a three-tiered cake complete with five glowing candles standing at attention on top.

"*Happy birthday to you, happy birthday to you...*" Everyone sang with gusto.

Allie wiggled in her chair, bouncing her heels against the legs.

Setting the cake in front of Allie, Grace rescued one wayward candle from toppling into the icing. "It's time for the birthday girl to make a wish and blow out her candles."

Allie scrambled to her knees and placed the palms of her hands on the table. She scrunched her face so tight, her eyes almost disappeared between her wrinkled nose and furrowed brow.

Ethan figured whatever she wished for must be a doozy.

Allie gave a quick nod, opened her eyes, smiled at him, and took a deep breath. Her cheeks puffed out, then deflated as a whoosh of air extinguished the flames.

Everybody clapped, whistled, stomped their feet, or ruffled Allie's hair.

Allie just beamed.

As soon as plates were filled, they dug in. For a few moments, the only sounds in the room were the ticking of the clock and murmured *yums* and *mm-hmms.*

"You've outdone yourself, Lily Grace." Mr. Browne's eyes twinkled as he raised his fork to her.

"Thanks, Dad." Grace raised her fork in a salute.

Mr. Browne took another bite, swallowed, then turned to Ethan. "How are things at the mill?"

"We're about as busy as we can be. Keeping up with the accounts has me on my toes every minute I'm there." Ethan swept his gaze around the table. "Speaking of *on your toes,* I witnessed quite a sight yesterday. During lunch hour, I watched some men at the log pond make a log jam. They move logs across the water and, boy howdy, those guys are so skilled they make it look like dancing. How they keep their balance while logs roll under their feet is a wonder. It's a dangerous job, and I'm glad to say we don't have any show-offs in the bunch. I could see the deep concentration on their faces. Man, I admire them."

Mr. Browne nodded. "I know what you mean. It takes a real knack to do that job without hurting yourself or someone else." He took a couple more bites of his cake, then shook his head. "I remember a time years ago when someone pretty near got a man killed because he was a show-off."

Allie looked up from her plate. "What did he do, Grampa?"

"Well, I happened to be at the mill loading boards in my wagon when I heard shouts. Another man and I tore around the side of the building. At the log pond, men on shore yelled at a man rolling a log. I could tell he was a master at it. His feet set up a rhythm to keep the log spinning in the water. But at the other end of the log, a young man grappled to keep up. It was obvious he was struggling. The first man made the log roll faster and faster until it was no surprise the younger man fell. I'll never forget the look of panic on his face right before he went under." Mr. Browne took a sip of coffee and shook his head again. "I've heard of men losing their lives in that kind of accident."

Everyone stared at him.

"What happened, Dad?" Esther set her teacup on its saucer.

"Fortunately, the young man survived. When a couple other men pulled him out, he sported a bloodied head and one broken arm from hitting another log. God watched out for him that day. He lost several weeks of work, but he was alive."

Grace clucked her tongue. "That's just awful. How could anyone do such a thing?"

"Mr. Emmett asked that very thing. He fired the man on the spot, experienced or not. The man pled his innocence, saying it was only a joke, that he meant to teach the younger man how to balance. But, you know, seemed to me there was a kind of gleeful spite on his face while he was doing it. I couldn't be sure, but I've always wondered if he did it on purpose." Mr. Browne helped himself to another cup of coffee. "Either way, it was no joke. A couple of men were so furious they thought he should've gone to jail. It was downright despicable."

Allie gasped. Her fork clunked to her plate. "Hey. That's the kind of pickle Mrs. Gibbons called me."

All eyes turned to her.

"What are you talking about?" Grace said.

Allie sucked in a breath. "Well, she called me that pickle thing when she caught me—" She swallowed. "—hiding behind the drapes."

Grace's eyes darkened. "Mrs. Gibbons called you despicable?"

Allie nodded. "I kind of scared her. On purpose. I was being a little bit naughty—just a little. Not like that bad man Grampa talked about." Her eyes filled with tears. "I don't have to go to jail, do I?"

*What?* Ethan started to rise, but one livid mama bear beat him to the draw.

Grace rushed to her daughter and wrapped her in a hug. "You are *nothing* like that man. Nothing at all."

"I should say not," chimed in an irate aunt.

Allie wiped her eyes and rested against Grace. She smiled at Ethan when he squeezed her shoulder.

An incensed grandfather cleared his throat. "I'd like to get my hands on that boarder of yours."

Ethan couldn't agree more. That Gibbons woman ticked him off. He had heard other stories about her and wished he could give her a piece of his mind.

"Don't worry. I'll have some choice words for her." Grace picked Allie up, sat down, and pulled her daughter onto her lap.

Esther rose. "Of all the odious—"

Grace looked at her sister. "I'll handle it." She cuddled Allie in her arms.

Ethan wished they could confront the boarder en masse, yet knew he had to respect Grace's wishes. But, man oh man, did he ever feel protective about this little one.

"I think we could all use a second slice of cake," Grace said. She kissed Allie's nose. "What do you think?"

In a short time, the afternoon returned to its sense of celebration with more cake, stories, laughs, jokes. Long before Ethan left, Allie's spirits had revived. She was back to her sparkling, precocious self.

Later, when he could finally tear himself away, Ethan gave Allie a piggyback ride to the kitchen door.

She scrambled down, threw her arms around his waist, and peered up at him with a huge grin. "I'm glad you came, Mr. Ethan."

"Thank you for inviting me." He gave her braid a tug. "Happy birthday again, five-year-old."

Allie squeezed him once more, then shot off to the other side of the kitchen.

"I'll see you out." Grace placed her hand on his arm. "Thanks so much for coming, Ethan. It made her day." She gave him a quick hug. "Come back soon, okay?"

Ethan placed his hat on his head and nodded. "See ya." Wild horses couldn't keep him away. He turned and hoofed it down the stairs.

# Seven

"But I'm not sleepy. And besides, I'm almost six." *And six-year-olds don't take naps.*

Mommy just said, "You've only been five for two days. Six is a ways off."

"Nuh-uh. *Farfar* and *Farmor* are coming for my next birthday. Six comes after five. So I'll be six."

Mommy bit her lip and tweaked Allie's nose. "Sweetie, *Farfar* and *Farmor* are coming for your next birthday *party* because they couldn't make it on your actual birthday. They're coming to celebrate your fifth birthday. You'll be five."

Allie frowned. "Again?"

"Not again. Still."

Allie stuck out her lower lip. "But when will I be six?"

Her mother counted off on her fingers. "We go all the way through summer, then fall when the leaves change colors, then cold, cold winter with snow and ice, then spring when the grass turns green, flowers bloom and birds sing, and then when summer comes around again you'll be six."

Allie sucked in a breath. "Willikens. I'll be five a long time."

Mommy ran her knuckles down Allie's cheek. "It'll come. Don't you worry."

"And when I'm six I get to go to first grade, right?"

"Yes, you will." Mommy blew out a little breath and got a kinda faraway look in her eyes. "Now, try to sleep at least a little while." She snuggled Margaret in the crook of Allie's elbow, tucked the blanket under her chin, and bent to kiss her forehead.

"'Kay." Allie squeezed her doll and sighed.

With her mother gone, Allie stared at the ceiling. She counted knotholes in the boards but stopped when she spied a cobweb in the corner. She shuddered, hoping no spider snuck up on her. Most critters were fine with her, but spiders gave her the willies. She closed her eyes tight and set her mind to falling asleep, hands clenched, toes pointed in rigid lines. After a slow count of ten, she let out the breath she'd been holding, relaxed her muscles, and opened her eyes. *What does Mommy do to fall asleep?* Allie glanced at the picture on the bedside table, smiling as she scooted Margaret to the other side of her pillow. With a gentle smack, she kissed the tips of her first two fingers, stretched her arm far out over the mattress, and touched the man's mouth. "Goodnight, sweetheart." She lay back on the pillow and closed her eyes again.

A minute or two later, her fingers tapped on the blanket, as if playing an imagined tune. Her eyes popped open. *I'm too full of awake to sleep.* With a grunt, she shrugged the cover aside, slid to the edge of the mattress, and threw her legs over. She walked to the bureau and began to finger the things lying on the embroidered dresser scarf. Her mother's favorite brooch looked pretty held against her bodice. Its elegant ruby in a silver setting contrasted with her plain brown dress. Setting that down, she picked up the boar's hair brush, pulling it through the curl at the tip of her braid a couple of times. She lifted the lid from the carved wooden box, peeked at the letters inside, and gently replaced the lid.

On the little table beneath the window, she spotted her paper doll cutouts. She sat cross-legged on the floor, spreading them in front of her. At first, she was content to dress them in the different outfits she, Mommy, and Auntie Esther had cut from magazines and the Sears 'n Roebuck catalog. But after a while it wasn't so much fun anymore. *I wish I could play dress up with Lydie Sue.* She glanced at Margaret. No. She needed someone who could walk around and make funny faces.

She fooled around with the paper dolls a few minutes more

until it dawned on her. She could play dress up with Uffda and Geoffrey Chaucer. They were boys, though. She didn't want to put girls' clothes on them. Then she thought of Daddy's things in the closet. They were boy clothes. She didn't think Mommy would mind *too* much and, maybe if she was real quick and real quiet, Mommy wouldn't even know.

She opened the closet door, and the smell of cedar chips hit her right away. Several shirts hung inside, and a coat dangled from a hook. Trousers, long johns, and neckerchiefs lay folded in neat stacks on a shelf. She could reach them if she stood on tiptoe. Beneath the shelf, a pair of boots and scruffy slippers sat side-by-side. Allie chose two red neckerchiefs, a brown-and-white striped shirt, and the slippers. Holding her treasures tight to her chest, she crept out the bedroom door, stopping to listen when she reached the landing. The muffled rattle of pans and dishes drifted up from the kitchen. Mommy and Auntie Esther must be getting things ready for supper or maybe making pies.

She gnawed her lower lip. *Better go out the front.* She side-stepped the squeaky places on the stairs and slipped through the door as quiet as a mouse. In the yard, Geoffrey Chaucer lay on a warm, flat rock sunning himself. He lifted his head a tad when Allie sat on the grass next to him.

She stroked his fur until he purred. "We're gonna have a grand time. You wait and see."

Chaucer flicked his tail, yawned, and stretched back on the rock. He suffered through Allie's decking him out in one of the neckerchiefs without getting tetchy at all, which Allie thought very gallant of him. When she appraised her handiwork, she clapped and said, "You are the handsomest cat in Emmett."

Just then Uffda sprinted around the corner of the porch and smothered her face with slobbery dog kisses. Allie giggled and clasped hold of Uffda's head, turning it toward Chaucer. "Look at that. See how elegant he is? Wouldn't you like to be elegant, too?" She took his renewed face-licking as a yes.

Tying the other neckerchief around his neck was not too

much trouble. The shirt was a different story. Slipping it on a dog full of wiggles and who wouldn't lend a hand—or leg—was no easy matter. Still, Allie put her mind to it, and at last it was done. She rolled the sleeves a half a dozen times to keep them from sliding down. The collar hung loose, but she hoped it would be all right. The slippers were a lost cause, being far too big, so she set them aside. All things considered, she was pleased with her real live dress-up dolls.

"Now we'll play house. Uffda, you can be the daddy."

Uffda cocked his head to one side, tail wags swishing the striped cotton fabric back and forth.

"Chaucer, who should you be?"

Chaucer yawned again, blinked twice, and carried on with his cat coma.

"How about if you're the grampa taking a nap?" Allie said.

The inert feline slept on, playing his part well.

She turned back to Uffda. "All right, let's make-believe we're going to the store. Come along."

The stylish Mr. Uffda seemed happy in his role, sticking close to Allie as she marched around the yard, with only a few side trips to sniff out curious smells here and there. All in all, Allie thought this the best idea she'd ever had.

That is, until calamity struck in the form of Rascal, Lydie Sue's cranky cat. The dog stopped in his tracks as she appeared. They faced off, eyes glaring. Then Rascal bolted across the yard. Before Allie could grab him, Uffda shot after her, his frantic barking filling the once quiet afternoon with a frenzied uproar.

"Uffda! No! Come back!" Allie sprinted after them, but it was hopeless. With Rascal in the lead, Uffda's hindquarters disappeared down the road, shirt sleeves working loose each time his feet hit the ground.

Allie shaded her eyes till they were out of sight, then walked back to Chaucer. "Uffda is so naughty."

Chaucer ignored her.

Allie plopped to the ground. A door banged shut behind her, and she froze.

"Allie?"

She lifted her eyes to the porch. *Uh-oh. Mommy.*

Grace descended the front porch steps. She glanced over her shoulder at her sister.

Esther stood on the veranda, one hand perched on the porch rail. "What was all the hullabaloo?"

Grace shrugged and walked onto the grass.

Allie got to her feet at a snail's pace, her face a picture of uncertainty. "Hi, Mommy." She bobbed her head toward Chaucer's prostrate form. "Isn't he handsome?"

Grace glanced at the cat, but turned her full attention to Allie. "Why are you out of bed?"

"I couldn't sleep and—and I thought I'd play dress up." Allie spread her arms. "That was a good idea, right?"

"Dress up?" Grace gazed at Allie in her dull brown everyday dress. She took a closer look at Chaucer and narrowed her eyes. "What is he wearing?"

Allie dropped her arms. She stared at her, wide-eyed. "A scarf."

Grace squatted to touch the neckerchief. She swiveled toward her daughter, feeling a mild panic inside. "Where did you get this?"

Allie scuffed one bare foot in the grass and wiped her hands on her thighs. "Well, I—it—" She sucked in a breath.

"Alice Ruth." Grace sat back on her heels. "Where did you—?"

*Whop!* A mass of slobbering, wriggling beagle collided with Grace, knocking her onto her backside.

"Uffda, what in the world?"

Uffda leaped up, smothering Grace's face with wild licks. She threw both arms around him, hoping to hogtie him into manageability. Knotted around his neck was a familiar red bandanna, now a dusty mess. Her suspicions rose and were confirmed when she grabbed the striped fabric attached to one foreleg. Søren's favorite shirt. "No." Grace gasped. She yanked the shirt from Uff-da's leg and untied the neckerchief.

Uffda gave her one last lick, then shot off to share his exuberance with Esther.

By now, Esther stood poised at the foot of the stairs, eyes glued on Grace and Allie.

Grace examined the shirt in growing alarm. Only two buttons remained; one sleeve showed a rip from elbow to wrist; the breast pocket hung from its bottom seam. Dirt and twigs covered every inch. Grief, sorrow, and something else bubbled within her. She buried her face in the shirt and burst out in a loud sob.

The something else grew. She let her hands fall to her knees and eyed Allie. "You took these from the closet?"

"I—I—I—" Allie dropped her gaze to the ground.

"Answer me."

Allie whipped her head up. Her voice came out in a faint whisper. "Yes, Mommy."

"How could you?" Grace clenched her jaws, inhaling through her nose. "Go to your room."

Tears streamed down Allie's cheeks. Grace, unmoved, could barely contain the urge to scream at her.

Allie reached a hand toward her mother. "I'm sorry, Mommy. I'm sorry."

Grace swatted away the outstretched hand. "I said go to your room."

Allie's breath caught on a sob. "Mommy?" She reached out her hand again.

Again, Grace swatted it away. She pointed to the house with a stiff arm. "Go. Now."

Allie whimpered. She darted past Esther, raced up the stairs, and disappeared through the front door.

Once more, Grace buried her face in Søren's shirt, buried her mind in Søren's memory. How could she bear it? A forlorn wail escaped her lips and settled into a pitiful keening. *Søren. Søren.*

A sudden crunch on the pathway intruded into her distress.

She looked up to see Esther, the compassion and understanding she'd always found in those amber-colored eyes replaced by a steely gaze.

Esther glared, her hands planted on her hips. "Lillian Grace, what were you *thinking*?"

Grace blinked. "What do you mean?"

"I mean your daughter. How could you treat her like that?"

"Are you defending her?" Grace sprang to her feet and faced her sister toe to toe, eye to eye. "Allie disobeyed. She had no business being out of bed. And she certainly had no business in the closet—let alone taking these." She brandished the torn shirt under Esther's nose. "Look at this. Look what she's done. No amount of mending will ever make it right."

"Mending?" Esther blew out a sharp breath and scowled. "Why would you mend it? Søren doesn't have a use for it anymore."

Grace wanted to shake her sister. Didn't she understand anything? "That's not the point."

"What is the point?" Esther crossed her arms and leaned closer. "Grace, you've got to come to grips with this. Søren is not coming back."

A stab of pain like a knife blade twisted in her gut. Of their own volition, angry words spewed out. "How could you know what it's like? You've never been married. You've never even been loved."

She may as well have slapped her. Esther reeled back, the color draining from her face.

A twinge of regret emerged in Grace when she saw tears swimming in her sister's eyes, but she pushed it aside. "Don't you get it? That's why these are so important. His clothes, the house—" She rubbed a grimy shirt sleeve against her cheek. "They're all he left me. They're all I have of him."

Esther shook her head. "He left you something far more important than *things*. He left you Allie."

Grace sputtered. "I—I know that."

"I don't think you do, Grace." Esther swiped a hand across

her eyes. "Without his clothes, you'd be okay. Hard as it would be, without Halstad House, you'd still be okay. But without Allie? Without her trust? Her love?"

"That won't ever happen."

Esther sighed. "Whatever you say, baby sister." She turned and trudged to the house without looking back.

Esther was wrong. This was different. Her daughter would always be here. Grace loved her, and Allie returned that love. She darted a look toward her bedroom. Allie stood with her nose pressed against the window. But as Grace caught her eye, she vanished. For a minute more Grace stared, willing her daughter to come back and smile at her. When no face appeared, another stab of pain hit her.

*Without Allie's trust and love?* In the midst of her churning emotions, a sudden stark clarity struck. What if Allie pulled away from her like she pulled away from the window? Grace clasped a hand over her mouth. What if Esther pulled away, too?

A fat robin chirped from an apple tree behind the garden, spread its wings, and flew over a thicket. Breaking into a stumbling run, Grace followed the flight of the bird. When she reached the thicket, she pushed the branches aside and found the path—the long-unused path to her special place.

She mounted the stone steps her husband had built against the hillside. When she reached the top, she stepped into the upper garden, once cared for by her own hands, now overgrown with weeds and thistles. Just as the thistles crowded out the green grass, the flowers, and the beauty of the garden, what weeds had she allowed to flourish in her heart, crowding out the beauty in her life?

Near the rambling lilac bushes stood her bench—the one Søren had lovingly crafted for her. Ignored all these years, it drew her now, a welcoming invitation to come, to rest, to forget, to remember. She lowered herself onto the wooden seat and surveyed the once-beautiful knoll, then raised her eyes to the Kettle River beyond and the July sky above. The river's gentle flow murmured in the distance, crickets whirred in the tall grass, the same fat robin sang from a trio of birch trees beside the bench.

She drew in a deep breath, filling her lungs with the scents of wild roses, fir, and pine. A stony barrier in her heart crumbled. A piercing light shone through. "Dear Jesus—" A sob escaped at the long unuttered name. "I've made a mess of things."

# Eight

Grace's heart stung at the sight. In the middle of the room, a dejected little girl sat cross-legged on the blue-and-brown braided rug. She cradled Margaret in her arms, her soft murmurs interspersed with sniffs and hiccups.

Allie swung her head around as the door clicked shut. Her eyes widened. Still clutching her doll, she made a beeline for the bed, leaped onto the mattress, and flung the cover over her head.

Grace had never felt unsure with Allie, not even when, as an untried nineteen-year-old, a newborn baby girl was placed in her arms. But she knew there was much at stake here. She sat on the edge of the bed and placed a hand on what she hoped was her daughter's head. "Allie?"

Choked sniffles.

"Sweetie?"

The blanketed form moved away from Grace's hand, but she plodded on. "I'd like it if we could talk."

Petite fingers gripped the edge of the blanket, pulling it down to reveal red, swollen eyes. "Am I still in trouble?"

Grace shook her head. "No, you're not in trouble."

"Is Daddy's shirt wrecked?"

Grace bit her lip. "I'm afraid it is."

Allie burst out from under the covers, hurling herself onto Grace's lap, throwing her arms around her neck. "I'm sorry, Mommy. I didn't mean to do it."

Grace held her daughter, stroking her back with one hand. "I know you didn't."

Allie continued to blubber. "Can you fix it?"

"No, sweetie, it's past fixing."

"But you loved that shirt." Her tiny shoulders shook against Grace's neck.

"I love you more." Grace enfolded Allie, rocking back and forth. "Shh... It's all right." The soft rat-a-tat of Allie's heart beat against her chest and Grace closed her eyes. *Help me make things right.*

Little by little the sobbing subsided. A muffled voice reached her ear.

"What?"

"You're squishing me."

Grace loosened her hold.

Allie pulled back to meet Grace's gaze, smile tremulous, lashes wearing a shimmer of tears. "You're not mad anymore?"

"No, I'm not mad. I just—" She cleared her throat and gave her daughter's cheek a hesitant touch. "Allie, I was wrong to speak to you the way I did. I'm so sorry. I wish I could take it all back." She tucked a stray curl behind Allie's ear. "I asked God to forgive me, and He has. Now I want to ask you. Will you forgive me?"

Allie's eyes grew round. "You talked to God?"

Grace nodded.

"I didn't think you knew Him. You know, not enough to tell Him stuff."

"I used to talk to Him all the time. And I want to do that again."

"Willikens."

Grace shifted Allie a bit. "But right now I want to ask you. Will you forgive me, sweetie?"

Allie's clear blue eyes met Grace's, earnest and somber, as if she recognized the significance of the moment. "Yes, Mommy. I forgive you."

Grace's own eyes brimmed with tears. She bent to embrace her daughter, cradling the back of her blonde head with her hand. Her voice came out in a shaky whisper. "Thank you, Allie."

Allie peeked at her mother through thick lashes. "I was naughty, too. Will you forgive me?"

Grace felt her grin spread. "Of course." She didn't deserve this, but oh how she cherished it. "Everything is forgiven all around."

"Yep." Allie rested her head on her mother's shoulder and fingered the collar of Grace's dress. "How come you stopped talking to God?"

How to explain so a five-year-old would understand? Grace took a deep breath, held it, exhaled. "When I received the telegram telling me your daddy died in the war, I closed off part of my heart. Instead of turning toward God, I turned away from Him."

"Were you mad at Him?"

Grace closed her eyes, remembering that day. "I guess I was. Yes, if I'm honest, I blamed Him for not bringing your daddy home safe and sound. I couldn't understand why. All the anger, all the sadness—I stuffed them deep inside of me."

"Why?"

"That's a good question. It sure didn't do me any good, nor anyone else for that matter. I wish I'd rushed to God years ago. I'm sorry I didn't."

Allie patted her mother's cheek and yawned. "But you did today."

"Yes, I did." Grace smiled. "Come on, sweetie." She slid Allie off her lap and back under the covers.

"I'm glad." Allie rubbed her eyes and yawned again. "Did a lot of soldiers not come home safe and sound?"

"Mm-hmm." Grace massaged her daughter's forehead, gentle circles across, down and around her eyes, back again.

"Mr. Ethan came home."

"Mm-hmm."

"I'm glad." Allie's eyelids grew heavy. "Daddy most likely wanted to come home, but I bet he's happy in Heaven. Don't you think so?"

"I do." And she did. An ache surfaced, but not the sharp horrible agony of earlier today. Was this the beginning of healing?

Allie's eyes closed. Her ragged breaths slowed, changing into a deep, steady tempo while a tiny pulse throbbed in the side of her neck. Grace leaned to kiss Allie's cheek. *Thank You, Lord, for this precious gift.*

After another kiss, Grace rose and stepped into the hallway. Her daughter's quick forgiveness was a miracle.

Esther was a different story. From the clatter of pots and pans emerging from the kitchen, she guessed the state of her sister's mind. Part of her wanted to escape back to the peace she'd just left, maybe even dive into bed and fling the covers over her own head. But she had amends to make. She straightened her shoulders, grasped the stair railing, and headed for whatever awaited her below.

Though the warm smells of fresh bread on the sideboard, cherry pie in the oven, and sweet clematis and wild roses outside the window infused the kitchen with a sense of coziness, the decided chill from Esther's corner of the world threatened to choke it out.

"Esther?" The parlor door swung shut behind her, coinciding with the slam of a cupboard. Grace's heart thudded as she stepped across the floor. "Esther?"

The hand placed on her sister's arm was brushed aside. Esther turned her back and began to chop celery with a vengeance on a much-stained cutting board.

Grace picked up a drab, discolored napkin, absently plucking at one frayed edge. "You have every right to be angry with me. Furious even. I said awful things to you." She took a deep breath, trying to keep it together. *Don't get emotional. Esther likes calm, straight talk.* "You've taken care of me my whole life. I'm not unaware of the sacrifices you've made, and I know I'd never be able to do all this without you." She spread her arms wide, then let them drop to her sides. "And I know—I know I hurt you—" *Stay calm. Try to explain.* She closed her eyes as a shiver crawled up her back. It was no use.

Words dammed up in her throat like the snarl of branches at the bend of a creek, until, *oh no,* one sob broke free, unleashing a torrent. Her hands flew to her cheeks. "Oh, Esther, can you ever forgive me? I am so, so sorry. I didn't mean it."

Esther froze. She set the knife down, turned, and studied Grace's face. Little by little, the hard look softened. Tears swam in her eyes as she held out her arms and wrapped her in a gentle embrace.

Grace buried her head on her sister's shoulder and wept.

Side by side at the kitchen table, the sisters nursed frosty glasses of fizzy homemade ginger ale. Esther's quick forgiveness and her willingness to restore peace to their relationship touched Grace deeply. But it also gave her a feeling of shame when she examined her own actions. Esther quietly lived out her faith. How often did Grace take that for granted while she herself allowed grief and selfishness to brew and fester? She stared out the window, lost in thought. Part of her feared God changing her, but the bigger part feared remaining the same.

But she'd made a start.

Esther's voice broke through her reverie. "Have you spoken to Allie?"

Grace pulled her gaze back into the room. She felt a slow smile on her lips. "Yes. She was heartbroken but quick to forgive. Like you." Her eyes met Esther's. "I asked God to forgive me, too."

Esther's steady amber eyes focused on her sister. "I knew something had happened. Tell me." She picked up her glass, leaving a damp ring on the red-and-white flowered tablecloth, and took a sip.

The time on the knoll—could she put it into words? "I climbed to my old special place. The place on the hill beyond the garden? I couldn't face it for so long. Too many memories. But this afternoon I felt drawn there." She glanced at her sister out of the corner of her eye. "I think God nudged me."

Esther lowered the glass onto her lap. "Did you go kicking and screaming?"

"More like out of desperation. What you said made sense, about Søren, Allie, Halstad House. I know you've said it all before, but for some reason, it got through my thick skull this time. It hit me—the possibility of losing her—" She clamped her lips together to stop the sudden trembling.

"I may have been a little—"

Grace gave her head a quick shake. "No. You were right. I don't know quite how He did it, but God somehow opened my eyes. I blamed Him for taking Søren away from me. I blamed Him for so many things. To be honest, I felt hopeless and trapped. I haven't been able to see past the hard circumstances." She sighed. "And the worst of it is that I figured I was justified. I don't know, maybe my life had been so charmed growing up, I never had to face tough choices—even though I assumed I did. For the first time, I had to face the fact that God is God. I don't have control over the universe. I have to let Him *be* God even if I don't understand."

"He has our best interest at heart. He promises that."

Grace nodded and took another drink of ginger ale. Its fizz tickled her nose, its sweet tang the taste of summer.

"Sounds to me as if a lot went on up there." Esther peered at Grace.

A lot? Yes. Facing the truth had brought pain, but something else, too. There was a small glimmer of—"Do you think maybe healing has started?"

Esther's lips curved into a grin. "Yes. You look different. Even your voice is different."

"Really?"

"Mm-hmm."

"I have a long way to go."

"Don't we all?" Esther set her empty glass on the table.

"Allie was dumbfounded when I told her I talked to God. *Willikens* was the exact word she used." Grace sighed. "Sad to think she'd be surprised about my talking to God." She shook her head. "Well, what's done is done. I can't erase those days."

"But it's a new day now."

"A new day." Hope stirred. "I like the sound of that." Grace settled into the back of her chair.

The ticking of the wall clock penetrated the silence. The muffled baying of a dog and the answering call of a woman's voice drifted through the window screen. Far in the distance, the deep, resonant whistle from Emmett's mill signaled a shift change and echoed off the ridge east of town.

Grace toyed with a droplet of water on her glass. "Do you ever wish you had a home of your own?"

Esther stared at her hands for so long, Grace wasn't sure she would respond. "If it's none of my business, you can just say so."

"Gracious. It's not that." Esther ran a finger around the rim of her glass. "Short answer, yes. Long answer, I want what God has planned for me. At thirty-five years old, that doesn't seem to be in His plan, at least not so far." She turned to Grace, tilting her head to one side. "We all have our dreams. We all have our heartaches. But I'm content. I know I'm where I belong. I'm needed, and I get to be with the people I love." She chortled. "That includes you, you know."

Grace grinned. "Was there ever anyone you were interested in?"

Several beats of the clock filled the quiet. "Promise you won't tell anybody?"

Grace gulped the last two sips from her glass and plunked it on the table. "Okay. Spill it."

"Do you remember Vince O'Connell?" A faint tinge of pink crept up Esther's cheeks.

"Vince O'Connell?" Grace shook her head. "His name doesn't ring a bell."

"I'm not surprised. He came around a few times when Søren first started courting you."

"Still, you'd think I'd remember him."

"Deary, you were so smitten, half the time I was amazed you knew if you were coming or going."

"What? I couldn't have been that bad."

"Believe me. You were."

How could she have missed something like that? "I'm sorry."

"Land sakes. Don't be sorry. I thought myself attracted to him for a couple of weeks. He started talking about marriage right away. At first I was flattered, but then I realized Vince was a whole lot more interested in *getting* married than he was in marrying *me*. In fact, on his third visit he brought up the subject, then in the next breath, he stumbled over my name."

"What a lunkhead."

Esther snickered. "Dad saw through him and sent him packing. I heard through the grapevine he was engaged to someone in Barstow less than a month later."

"Double lunkhead." Grace rubbed her cheek. "Were you sad?"

"I was more relieved than anything. I vowed to myself then and there I wouldn't marry anyone who didn't look at me the way Søren looked at you. That hasn't happened yet and, like I said, I'm content."

Grace felt tears brimming and took a deep breath.

Esther smiled, reaching to pat Grace's hand. "It's all good." She smoothed her skirt and stood. "How about we finish supper preparations?"

"Yep." Grace rose and turned to follow her sister.

*Pray for Esther's dreams to be fulfilled.*

She halted in her tracks. Where did that come from? God? But she'd only been back on speaking terms with Him for a few hours. Could she recognize His voice or was she just caught up in Esther's story? And, whoa, wait a minute. Her sister's dreams meant a home of her own. Grace knew it was beyond selfish, but could she pray for that, knowing she'd be on her own to run Halstad House?

*Well, You are God. I'm not. In for a penny, in for a pound.* She took another deep breath. *Please fulfill Esther's dreams, Lord.*

"Hey, slowpoke. You coming?"

*Thank You and amen.* She retrieved the glasses from the table and crossed the room to join Esther.

# *Nine*

"Ethan, my boy. How are you this fine morning?" A balding, gray-haired gentleman grabbed Ethan's hand, held it in both of his, and shook it like a pump handle. The strength of the man's grasp belied his years. The creases in his face gave testament to life's challenges. The sparkle in his eyes and the laugh lines at their corners revealed his unfailing humor.

Ethan returned his handshake. "Pastor Grant, it's good to see you."

"You, too, son." Pastor Elias Grant spread his lips into a grin broad enough to reveal a set of shiny false teeth and clapped him on the shoulder. "Your leg is well?"

"Yes, sir. If I get overtired, it acts up, but for the most part, it's fine."

The minister examined Ethan's face. "It looks to me like you came out the right side of a hard-fought battle. Let's get together soon. You've been busy settling in with your new job, but I'd sure like to have a sit-down chat with you. Catch up on things."

"I'd like that, too," Ethan said. "How about this week? Thursday evening maybe?"

Another broad grin. "Come by my house after work." The pastor looked over Ethan's shoulder.

Ethan glanced back and stepped aside to make room for a large family to greet the minister. Four copper-topped children trailed in single file after their parents. The youngest and last in line, a freckle-faced minx not more than three years old, wiggled his fingers at Ethan and stuck out his tongue.

Ethan crossed his eyes and stuck out his tongue right back. As he was about to mount the stairs to the church, a child's lilting laughter arrested him mid-step. He recognized that—

"Mr. Ethan!"

He set himself in the nick of time. A squealing figure in a straw hat flung herself at him, arms spread wide. She scooted onto the toes of his shoes, wrapped her arms around his legs, and pitched her head back to gaze at him from under the brim of her hat. She radiated the same winsome appeal that captured his heart the first day he met her.

"Guess what?" Allie said. Her eyes twinkled.

"What?" He laughed down at the precocious little charmer and tweaked her nose. When heels clicked on the boardwalk, he looked up. His knees turned to jelly. "Grace?"

Allie giggled and squeezed tighter. "That's what."

She strode toward him, a dream in her Sunday-go-to-meeting clothes. Her midnight blue dress, reaching halfway between ankles and knees, swayed to the rhythm of her gait. Some kind of snowy lace collar circled her neck, matching the trim on her blue felt hat. An ivory flower, petals rimmed in a rosy blush, hugged the front of the crown. She took his breath away.

Grace gave him a playful grin. "Hey."

"Hey yourself," he countered, smiling as he remembered the greeting they'd used when they were kids. Their good-natured teasing had evolved into a special exchange just between the two of them. He looked at her standing before him now. "This is the nicest surprise I've had in a good long while," he said. Aware of a frantic tug on his vest, he looked down again. Allie crooked her finger, so he leaned closer.

"Mommy talks to God now."

He eyed Grace. "I'm glad to hear it." He'd done his own talking to God about that very thing. His fervent prayer was that she would let go of her grief and reach out to the Lord. He knew how hard it could be, but he also knew the consequences of hanging on to pain and anger. Just as his wounded leg had needed to mend, so had his wounded heart.

He straightened and held an arm out to Grace. "May I escort you ladies inside?"

Grace glanced at the people entering the church and caught her lower lip between her teeth. "I hope no one has a heart attack when they see me walk through the door." The sweet refrains of "Blessed Assurance" drifted through the open windows. She smoothed the skirt of her dress.

"Hold up now." Pastor Grant rushed to them before they reached the first stair. He chucked Allie's chin. "Good morning, missy." His eyes reached Grace's and held them. "Grace Browne Halstad, it does my old heart good to see you. You are most welcome." He patted her cheek. "Most welcome."

Tears sprang to Grace's eyes. "Thank you, Pastor." She swallowed and licked her lips. "I'm afraid I wasn't very polite when you came to see me after..."

He held up his hand. "Water under the bridge. You are here now, God be praised. That's all that matters."

She blinked the tears away, took a deep breath, and smiled.

"You let this young man take you inside. We'll talk later." He turned to meet an older couple who sauntered toward him.

Ethan offered his arm again. "Shall we?"

She took his arm and he caught Allie's tiny hand with his free one. The song of a meadowlark in a nearby field mingled with the subdued piano music. The grassy scent of summer hung in the air. The morning sun warmed his back. He knew he was grinning like a crazy Cheshire cat as they climbed the stairs, but his heart was so full, he couldn't help it.

Why had she waited so long? She drank in the love and acceptance from the church family, the rich music of the hymns, the solid truth from God's Word. Like a parched wanderer in the desert who stumbles upon a hidden oasis, she soaked up every cool, refreshing morsel.

Halfway through the first song, Allie peeked over her shoulder, then spun around to kneel on the wooden pew, hands grasping its back. Grace turned to see Allie point at her, a wide grin on her face. She peered behind and caught Lydie Sue three rows away with a smile that matched Allie's. Next to her daughter, Ada Walters' face dimpled, and she gave Grace a slight wave.

"Allie."

Her daughter nodded and scooted onto her bottom, grin intact. She leaned against Grace and sang along whenever she knew the words.

> *He leadeth me, He leadeth me,*
> *By His own hand He leadeth me.*
> *His faithful follower I would be*
> *For by His hand He leadeth me.*

Hymn after hymn. Oh, how she'd missed this. Music held a special place for her. It soothed her, yet at the same time lifted her spirits like nothing else could. Memories flooded her mind. Hours spent in song with Esther while they sped through their work on Dad's farm and later at Halstad House. Countless hymns sung in this very church, both as part of the congregation and standing at the podium to sing a special with her sister.

Grace raised her voice in a strong soprano and smiled at Esther as she played the piano. To her left, Dad growled out a deep bass. On the other side of Allie, Ethan's tenor rang true. Someone down their row braved a warbled, dissonant attempt at alto. She found it lovely.

After twenty glorious minutes of song and a smattering of announcements by Ben Guff, Pastor Grant stepped to the podium and laid his Bible on the pulpit. He flipped through several pages and began to read. *"Who hath measured the waters in the hollow of His hand, and meted out heaven with the span, and comprehended the dust of the earth in a measure, and weighed the mountains in scales, and the hills in a balance? Who hath directed the Spirit of Jehovah, or being His counsellor hath taught Him? With whom took He counsel, and who instructed Him, and taught Him in the path of justice, and taught Him knowledge, and showed to Him the way of understanding?"*

He raised his head, gazing out over his congregation, his

voice somber yet tender. "The answer is no one. Brothers and sisters, these words from Isaiah chapter 40 should give us pause to reflect. God is the Creator of the universe. He is perfect in judgment and understanding, all knowing and present every-where—from our own little church in Emmett, Washington, to the vast reaches of space—beyond stars and planets and galaxies. He is God forever."

The minister leaned forward, his forearms on either side of the simple wooden stand. "He alone is God. He is the Almighty, the Creator, the Ruler of the universe. And yet He is also a very personal God, a Father who draws us to Himself." He turned to a different place in the well-used book before him. "Open your Bibles to Psalm 46 verse ten." He paused until the rustling of pages quieted. "*Be still, and know that I am God.* That's how the verse begins. Yes, know that He is God. But then what? Look at the first two words again. *Be still.* We can trust Him to be God, the kind of God the whole Bible reveals to us. Strong, loving, merciful, gracious, and so much more. Be still.

"Rest in the knowledge that He knows the past, present, and future. He has a plan, a good plan. A plan for the world. A plan for each and every one of us. You don't need to fret and stew. Be still.

"When life doesn't make sense and trouble strikes, let Him lead you. Let Him be God in your life. Be still."

Grace sat straight in her seat, eyes fixed on the minister. Her heart warmed as his sermon continued. God meant these words for her. Oh, she knew others would reap the benefits of this teaching as well, but surely, *surely* God meant these words for her. She reached into her pocket for a handkerchief and dabbed at the tears on her cheeks.

Allie peered at her. Grace smiled and patted her daughter's knee, then put one arm around her. Allie snuggled close as Grace leaned back, listening to the comforting words.

By the end of the sermon, the tears had stopped, but the warmth remained. She was surprised to see Pastor Grant give Ethan a nod before he sat down. Ethan headed for the front of the church. Ben Guff joined him, and they stepped onto the podium.

Ben bounced on his toes and beamed at everyone. "While Ethan grabs his gee-tar, guess I'll introduce our song. We're going to teach you a new one today. It's called 'This Little Light of Mine.' Soon as you pick up the words, sing along with us."

Ethan's guitar. Grace hadn't heard him play or sing for years. She loved the sound of his voice. And Ben. The postmaster and his wife had sung many a duet at church. Flo had passed away a year or so after Søren. Grace had no idea if, in his grief, Ben had sung much afterward, but she was happy to see him. The cheerful countenance she remembered was coupled with a quiet strength—a sure sign that he had weathered his storm well.

From the first strum, she knew they were in for a treat. Those first chords were gentle and sweet. The men sang the song like a ballad, their soft ebb and flow of melody and harmony spreading a blanket of peace over the room. Then Ethan glanced at Allie, winked, and took off a'runnin', as her dad would say.

> *Hide it under a bushel, no,*
> *I'm gonna let it shine.*
> *Hide it under a bushel, no,*
> *I'm gonna let it shine.*
> *Let it shine, let it shine, let it shine.*

Grace tapped her toes to the beat. Someone clapped along, and others picked it up. Verse after verse Ethan and Ben sang until everyone knew the words and joined in. When Grace's father stood, the entire congregation followed suit. On and on they sang.

At last Ethan strummed a final flourish. *Amens* and *praise the Lords* resounded. This was the icing on the cake to a service that brought Grace back to her roots.

Pastor Grant jumped onto the podium and raised his arms. "Let God be God in your life this week. And remember, let your light shine."

Hearty greetings and smiles abounded as parishioners gathered their Bibles, children, and whatnot, and headed toward the door.

"Hold up now." Pastor Grant jumped back on the podium. "I almost forgot. Several ministers in the area, me included, have heard of some needy families who live nearby. If any of you have clothing, bed linens, or canned goods to spare, let the elders or myself know. We'll arrange for them to be picked up and shared among those in need. Thank you ahead of time and God bless you. All right. Go enjoy the Lord's Day, brothers and sisters."

Grace lingered in the humble country church, warmed by the love of the people around her. Far from anyone having a heart attack at her long-overdue appearance, she was wrapped figuratively and literally in the welcoming arms of her spiritual family.

Allie was glad Mommy asked Mr. Ethan over for Sunday dinner. She wished Mr. Guff could'a been here, too. Maybe then they'd have more toe-tapping songs like at church this morning. But somebody else already invited him home. Oh, well. At least she had Mr. Ethan. She'd been quick to tell him Auntie Esther would make the biscuits, not Mommy. His mouth quirked up on one side when she said it, but she wanted to make sure he'd come.

They had creamed chicken over Auntie Esther's fluffy biscuits, green beans she'd helped pick from the garden yesterday, sliced tomatoes, and bread and butter pickles. Grampa brought his homemade cottage cheese. She didn't like it so much but ate it anyway so she didn't hurt his feelings. Allie loved Sunday dinners. And the best thing was dessert. Mommy had made apple pie last night. Her favorite. She wished they could have dessert every day, but Mommy said too much sugar wasn't good for little girls or anyone else. She ought to tell that to cranky old Mrs. Gibbons 'cause once Allie saw her snitch some pie.

Another favorite thing about Sunday dinners was that they were all together. Grampa brought Auntie Esther home after bein' at his place for a few days. Like always, it was just family around the kitchen table. They got to unwind, Mommy said. They'd sit around and talk or listen to Grampa read or play dominoes or checkers. And today was more special 'cause Mr. Ethan was here, too, just like family.

Then those biddies poked their noses in. Izzy said, "As I live and breathe," and made funny eyes at Mr. Ethan as soon as she saw him sitting with Grampa. Mr. Ethan got a funny look on his face, too, only different. Allie just bet Izzy liked Mr. Ethan, maybe a whole lot. But Dizzy Izzy and Mr. Ethan? Willikens.

And that Mrs. Gibbons. For a while, Mommy got run ragged taking stuff into the parlor. Back and forth, back and forth. Auntie Esther raised her eyebrows real high and told her she needn't jump at her every beck and call. Mommy said, "I know. I just want things to be pleasant today. I'll deal with it later."

Allie didn't know what Mommy meant, but right then she was busy showin' Mr. Ethan how to make Maude prance across the floor. He did a good job when she let him try. Someday she'd ask him to teach her how to whittle horses.

The biddies finally went up to their rooms. Everybody pitched in to clear the table. After they washed the dishes and straightened the kitchen, Grampa got the box of dominoes out of the cupboard. Allie watched Mommy and Mr. Ethan. He must'a told her a joke 'cause she started to giggle and gave him a little swat on his arm.

Allie smiled to herself and rubbed the end of her braid under her chin. That same happy, cozy feeling settled in her tummy. Yep. Mr. Ethan'd make an awful good daddy. She'd ask God about it again when she and Mommy said prayers tonight. 'Cept this part she wouldn't say out loud. Not yet.

# *Ten*

Grace was tempted to pitch a fit. Or toss the ledger straight out the window. If a grown woman couldn't—

"You better watch out. My mommy talks to God now!"

The slam of a door, the *thud, thud, thud* of running feet, and a tear-stained, red-cheeked Allie catapulted into Grace's arms.

"Heavens to Betsy. What is going on?" Her daughter trembled against her. Allie buried her face in Grace's apron, but muffled sobs escaped. "Allie?" Grace patted her shoulder, then bent to kiss the top of her head. "Sweetie, talk to me."

Allie pulled back to look at her mother. "She said somethin's wrong with my blood."

"What are you talking about?" This made no sense. "Who said what?" Grace smoothed damp hair from her daughter's brow.

"That ol' Mrs. Gibbons." Allie sucked air in through a hiccup. "She said my heart is black as night and pumps bad blood right through me."

Grace's hand stilled. Heat rose in her chest, and her stomach tightened. "Why would she say such a horrible thing?"

"She said I took her pocketbook. But I didn't! Not this time."

Grace eyed her daughter. "What do you mean, *not this time*?"

Allie stared at the floor. "I found it in the parlor one day. She was bein' mean to me so I hid it." Her head whipped up. "But I didn't *take* it. Not for keeps. Oh, and I scared her once and called her a warthog." Her voice sank to a whisper. "Am I bad? Like she said?" Tears swam in her eyes.

Grace fought to gain composure. She kicked herself for not dealing with her boarder before this. At her daughter's birthday party, she'd told everyone she'd take care of it. Well, she hadn't. She'd put it off far too long, and Allie had suffered for it. Money be hanged. This was the last straw. She sat down on a kitchen chair and pulled Allie into her lap. "Mrs. Gibbons had no business saying those awful things to you. They are lies, and I don't want you to believe them." She took a handkerchief from her apron pocket and dabbed Allie's eyes. "It sounds like you did some naughty things to get back at her?"

Allie nodded.

"The naughty things may have been what you *did,* but they are not who you *are.* God made you special. There's not another Alice Ruth Halstad in the whole wide world. He made each of us special. He also gave us the ability to choose to do good things or naughty things. Every day we can choose how we act."

"Sometimes it's hard. Like when Mrs. Gibbons is nasty to me," Allie said.

"I know." Grace rubbed Allie's shoulder. "But we can't control how someone else acts—only ourselves. To be honest, I've struggled with being nice to her, too."

"You have?"

"Yes. Now that I've let God back in my life it's been a little easier. I know His Spirit lives inside me, and I ask Him to help me."

Allie wiped her nose on her sleeve and laid a cheek against Grace's shoulder. "I'm sorry 'bout what I did. I just don't like her, Mommy. She's awful mean sometimes."

Mrs. Gibbons simpered and fawned around Grace. She knew on which side her bread was buttered. It was obvious she held no such qualms when it came to a little five-year-old. Well, Grace refused to allow her destructive, spiteful influence on Allie to continue. She pondered her next words carefully. "Do you remember when we read about God creating the world?"

Allie sniffed and nodded.

"When God looked at everything He'd made, He said it was

good. But when He looked at Adam and Eve, He said it was *very* good. People were the crown of His creation. The Bible tells us we are fearfully and wonderfully made. That's who we are." She gave Allie a gentle poke with her finger. "That includes you, kiddo."

Allie gnawed her lower lip. Grace could see the wheels turning.

"Is Mrs. Gibbons made like that? Like those big words you said?"

"Well—yes. But I don't think she lets God in her life. I also think that years and years of bad choices have turned her into a bitter woman."

"Willikens." Allie fidgeted on her mother's knee. "Do I have to tell her I'm sorry?"

Grace stroked Allie's cheek. "Normally I'd say yes, but I don't want you around her. You've told me you're sorry—how about if you tell God, too?"

"I did already. Some of it."

"Well, go ahead and do it all, okay?"

Allie clasped her hands and squeezed her eyes. "Dear Jesus, I'm awful sorry I did those naughty things. Like hiding Mrs. Gibbons' handbag and stuffing her stinky shawl behind the buffet. And I'm sorry I scared her with the loud piano crash."

Grace raised one eyebrow but kept her mouth shut.

"And pounded on her door and ran away. And...um...and for plugging my nose when she gets too close...and...um...I think that's it." Her eyes popped open, and she gave Grace a dimpled smile. All of a sudden she squeezed her eyes shut again and brought her clasped hands to her chin. "And I'm sorry she's a warthog."

*Close enough.* Grace could see her daughter's heart. She rested her chin on Allie's head. After a minute she took a deep breath and let it out. "I guess I'd better go talk with her."

Allie jumped down. "Don't let her grab you."

"Heavens to Betsy, why would she grab me?" Grace stood and removed her apron.

Allie pointed to her upper arm. "Like she did me."

Grace pushed back the sleeve of her daughter's dress, revealing bright red skin and what looked like finger marks. "Mrs. Gibbons did this?"

"Uh-huh. When she said those lies about my blood." Allie's eyes narrowed. "She grabbed my arm and shook me till my teeth rattled."

Grace plopped back into the chair. Her own blood boiled. She had to think this through and not go off half-cocked. This called for more than words, but what? The perfect plan came to her out of the blue. Like Allie said before, Mrs. Gibbons better watch out. Grace jumped up and grabbed Allie's hand. "Come on, sweetie. We have business to attend to."

Halfway to the post office, the clip-clop of horse hooves reached her.

"Grace!"

She shaded her eyes with one hand. Ethan rolled down the dusty street in a weathered buckboard drawn by his bay horse. She lifted a hand in greeting and waited, Allie by her side.

"Whoa." Ethan tugged the reins and wrapped them around the brake handle. He jumped down, grinning from ear to ear. "Hey."

"Hey yourself," said Grace.

"What are you two ladies up to this Saturday afternoon?" He tweaked Allie's nose and picked her up when she raised her arms. "Hi, kitten." He turned to Grace and his eyes narrowed. "I recognize that expression. You look like you're on a mission."

"I am. A mission to oust one of my boarders."

"A biddy got caught with her hand in the cookie jar?"

"I wish it was only that."

Ethan's smile vanished. "What happened?"

"Come with us to the post office, and I'll tell you all about it."

Ethan walked beside her, one hand on the horse's bridle, the other supporting Allie on his hip. He tamped his lips together when Grace gave him the details of Allie's encounter with Mrs. Gibbons and nodded when she explained her plan. He jerked his head to the right. "Is she back at the house?"

"Yes. I just need to make a telephone call. I'll head right back afterward."

At the post office, Ethan set Allie on her feet and tied the reins to the hitching rail in front of the building. Ben Guff's black model T Ford sat parked around the side.

Grace shaded her eyes again. "Would it be all right if Allie stayed with you while I make that call?"

"Sure. Then I'll go with you. I can think of some choice words I'd like to give Mrs. Gibbons."

Grace shook her head. "It's my responsibility. I can't run from it."

"I'm not asking you to run from it, just let me put in my two cents worth."

"No. I need to take care of it."

"I won't say much."

She shook her head.

"How about if I just watch the fireworks?"

"Ethan, no."

Ethan quirked his lips in a half-smile. "Good grief, woman. Has anyone ever told you you can be stubborn?"

"A time or two." Grace smiled. Then her eyes grew determined as she touched his arm. "I have to do this myself."

"Well, at least let me help escort her off the premises."

She pointed a finger at him. "Now that, I'll be happy to let you help with." She glanced at Allie, whose head had been swinging back and forth between the two of them. "Will you stay with Mr. Ethan while I go inside?"

Allie beamed.

Grace tucked a stray curl behind Allie's ear. She smiled at Ethan, pivoted, and strode to the post office door.

Grace watched the wagon lumber up the street. Ethan turned

to wave before he slapped the reins against the horse's broad rump, spurring Prince into a faster walk. She took her daughter's hand and stepped through their gate.

In the side yard, Allie skipped along beside her, blonde braid bouncing against her back. She laughed as a giddy outbreak of barks accosted them, followed by a dust-covered Uffda who ran frenzied circles around them until he plopped on the bottom step of the side porch, tongue lolling to one side. Grace raised her eyes to the second-floor windows before sitting down on a lower step.

Allie hunkered down in front of Uffda, rubbing and scratching his neck while he groaned and leaned into her hand. She looked at her mother when Grace cleared her throat.

"Allie, did you understand what Mr. Myers and I were talking about?"

"You're gonna kick Mrs. Gibbons out'a the house?"

"Yes. I want to explain why."

"You don't have to, Mommy. She's a stinker, and I'm glad she's going." Allie hesitated. "'Cept maybe it's not nice if I'm glad?"

"It's a little more complicated than that. I'll try to keep it simple. I told you that God can help us be nice to people even if we don't like them. But there comes a time when enough is enough. We don't just let someone keep doing wrong. We stand up and say *no*. That's what I'm doing now." She gave Allie a slight smile. "I'm sorry I didn't do it earlier."

Allie patted Grace's hand. "It's okay, Mommy."

Though she appreciated Allie's bigheartedness, her handling of the situation had been anything but okay. However, with God's help, she hoped to face things and right a wrong. She braced herself against the stair behind her for a moment, inhaling the scents of roses, freshly mown hay from the field behind Halstad House, and a hint of fall around the corner. With a quick prayer, she stood and brushed the back of her dress. "I'm going upstairs to talk with Mrs. Gibbons now. Like I said before, I don't want you to be around her at all. How about if you take Uffda to the backyard? You can play out there until I come to get you."

"'Kay." Allie jumped up and smacked her hand against her knee. "C'mon, Uffda."

Uffda zipped around the porch.

Grace reached for Allie's arm. "Remember, until I come for you."

Allie nodded and tore after her excited pooch.

The kitchen retained a calm stillness, enhanced by the steady rhythm of the wall clock and the flutter of lacy curtains at the open windows. The entire house echoed the quiet. Grace knew Isobel worked at the café this afternoon so Mrs. Gibbons was the only one upstairs. She squared her shoulders and pushed through the parlor door.

Her knock on the bedroom door elicited a muted "Come in." She stepped into the room where too-familiar smells assaulted her: stale air, unwashed laundry, and *eau de cologne*. She left the door open behind her. Mrs. Gibbons sat in a corner armchair, shoulders hunched over her bony bosom, looking like a whipped puppy. Something tugged at Grace's conscience until she remembered her sobbing daughter and the welts on her arm. "Mrs. Gibbons, I'm afraid we've come to an impasse."

The lady rose and wrung her hands. "Whatever can you mean, Mrs. Halstad? I do hope there has not been a misunderstanding with your dear daughter. I would never forgive myself if she misinterpreted anything I may have said. That can easily happen, of course, in one so young, as I'm sure you know. Why, my dear late husband used to say—"

"Stop." Grace took a deep breath. "We are way beyond misunderstandings and misinterpretations. I saw your fingermarks on my daughter's arm."

Mrs. Gibbons paled.

"You need to find other accommodations. You are no longer welcome here."

Mrs. Gibbons stammered. "I—I'm sure we can work this out. You must feel for the predicament that would put me in."

Her simpering voice grated on Grace's nerves more than

ever. "My mind is made up. I telephoned the boarding house in Orient. They have a room for you starting tonight."

"Tonight?" Mrs. Gibbons sounded like a screech owl.

"Yes. It is available for two or three weeks. After that, you will need to make other arrangements."

An astounding alteration unfolded before Grace's eyes. Her soon-to-be-ex-boarder transformed from a sniveling whiner to a vicious firebrand in a heartbeat. Mrs. Gibbons stormed to within inches of Grace and shot daggers at her with dark, piercing eyes. "You can't do this to me," she hissed.

Grace held her ground. "You have two hours to pack your trunk and your bags. Mr. Myers will be here at that time to load your belongings into his wagon and convey you to Orient."

Mrs. Gibbons spluttered, spraying Grace with drops of spittle. Venom shot out of every pore. "And you call yourself a Christian?" She pushed her face closer to Grace's.

Grace refused to budge. She held a fixed gaze on the lady until Mrs. Gibbons finally dropped her eyes and stepped back. "Two hours," Grace said.

Grace spun on her heels and walked out the door, heart pounding, a little nauseous, but imbued with a sense of victory.

True to his word, Ethan arrived two hours later, accompanied by Ben Guff. He found Grace and Allie in the kitchen rolling out pie dough. "Hey."

"Hey yourself."

"I brought reinforcements to help lug her trunk and anything else she has."

Ben grinned his happy-go-lucky grin and tipped his hat. "Ladies."

Grace dusted her hands and looked at Allie. "You stay here." She turned to the men. "I'll show you to her room. I gave her a refund of the rent money she'd already paid for the next two weeks. When her belongings are loaded, she can leave."

Ethan glanced at her. "Did you have her sign for it?"

"Yes. I gave her a copy of the receipt and kept the original."

"Good girl."

She guided them to the bedroom. The door flew open at her knock. Mrs. Gibbons glared at her, then pointed to a large brown steamer trunk, several carpet bags, and a mottled hat box heaped in the middle of the room.

Ben gave Mrs. Gibbons a nervous smile. "Ma'am."

She crossed her arms and stared out the window, ignoring all three of them.

That was fine by Grace. Ethan and Ben walked around her, and she was more than happy to leave them to this angry, malicious woman. She left the room and returned to Allie.

Fifteen minutes later, Ethan walked into the kitchen. "All set. Ben's in the wagon with her. Boy howdy, she said nary a word, but if looks could kill I'd be as dead as a doornail. She gives me the creeps." He studied Grace. "Are you all right?"

Grace bit her lip, regarding Allie who sat at the table with a picture book. She swung her eyes back to Ethan and shuddered. "I feel like I harbored a viper in my own home."

He caught her hands in his bigger ones. "But are you all right?"

She shrugged one shoulder. "A bit shaken. She was horrible. I've never had anyone look at me or speak to me the way she did. But I'll be fine." She gave him a smile. "God gave me the strength I needed."

He leaned forward until his forehead touched hers. "Lils."

They stood silent a few moments until he released her hands. "That is one biddy I'm more than happy to throw out. Guess I'd better get the show on the road."

"Ninety-eight, ninety-nine, one hundred." Grace set the brush on the table and commenced Allie's nighttime braid. She hummed a nameless tune as she plaited the sections of honey-gold hair in and out. Through the screened window came a soothing chorus to accompany her, the soft refrain of crickets, the tender cooing of doves, the mellow undertone of the wind in the pines. Allie smelled of fresh soap and a lingering scent of this afternoon's apple pies. Grace tied the end of the braid, leaned forward, and kissed the top of Allie's head.

Her daughter held Margaret in her arms. "The house feels different, Mommy."

"Different how?"

Allie shrugged. "Just different. Like when I have a bad dream and you wake me up and say it was only a dream."

"And you don't need to worry."

"Nope. 'Cause it's all better."

During the course of reading from *Peter Rabbit*, a lullaby, and newly established nighttime prayers, Grace mulled over what Allie had said. What was the difference? She felt it, too. When she tucked the coverlet under Allie's chin and kissed her good-night, one word surfaced: peace. That was the difference. Even Izzy, eating alone at the dining room table had appeared less nervous without the watchful eye of her fellow boarder hovering over her. Grace smirked. Less nervous, but no less dizzy. She had another story of an encounter with a handsome young man at the café. But Izzy was harmless, and her boy-craziness was not Grace's concern.

Grace vowed she would let God be God in the matter of future boarders. Even if money was tight—and she knew it would be—she'd ask Him before welcoming anyone else under her roof.

She smiled as she strode down the back steps to the kitchen. Esther would return from Dad's tomorrow. *She'll be thrilled to find an absent Mrs. Gibbons.* And Esther would be overjoyed to help Grace clean the lady's room on Monday. A tough job awaited them—scrubbing, scouring, mopping, dusting, airing everything out. She suspected they'd sing heartily while they worked. A sense of freedom enveloped her.

Grace glanced at the kitchen table as she made herself a cup of tea. Should she pull out the ledger and go over the books? She did need to figure out where she stood. She gnawed her lower lip. Nope. She'd deal with that later. Tonight she'd sit on the porch and revel in the peace, the freedom, and the music of nature. And thank God for it all.

# Eleven

Where in the world had she put it? She'd turned every bookshelf upside down and come up empty-handed. Esther had quizzed her about a special music book they used to play from. Though she hadn't seen it in years, it had to be somewhere. Probably in that notorious safe place everyone seemed to hide things, never to see them again. And like everyone else, she couldn't remember where that safe place was. Before ransacking the attic, she'd rummage through a couple of old leather cases tucked away in the back of her closet.

She crept through the bedroom, stopping to check on a napping Allie. Long lashes brushed the tops of her daughter's cheekbones. With each slow, steady breath, her chest rose and fell beneath the quilted coverlet. Grace itched to smooth a tuft of hair off Allie's forehead but thought better of it. Best not wake her.

The closet door opened without a creak, revealing a narrow enclosure bathed in muted sunlight from the tiny window on the wall. Grace ignored the clothes and shoes. At the back of the closet, she knelt in front of two wrinkled leather cases. Under the flap of the first case, a faded manila envelope lay atop an assortment of papers. Removing two, she raised them close to the window. One, Søren's high school diploma dated 1913, the other, hers from 1916. With a tenuous smile, she replaced them and rifled through the rest of the case. No book. She moved to the second case. Eureka and hallelujah. Right on top lay the music book. How it came to be in this unlikely place, she couldn't imagine. But she was thrilled and Esther would be, too.

At the door, Grace hesitated. She remained still a moment, then reached to touch Søren's fisherman's sweater, the one knitted by his sweet *mor*. The instant she touched the sleeve, memories flooded her mind, and tears sprang into her eyes. He'd looked so handsome in this sweater. So tall. So strong. So Norwegian.

A sob escaped her lips. She clapped trembling fingers over her mouth. She couldn't keep doing this. She had to stop. Wiping her eyes, she turned to leave.

*It's time.*

Grace froze. Her heart pounded and she whispered the word. "Lord?"

*It's time.*

God had said it was time and she wanted to be obedient. But she couldn't face it that night, nor the next morning. Now, as she knelt near the overgrown flower bed, Grace ripped a weed out of the sod. Knots tightened her stomach, more so her heart. *I have to be honest, Lord. I'm not ready.* Another weed landed in the pile. *It's been four years, but I'm just not ready.* Plop. Plop. More weeds on the growing pile. She wiped the back of her hand across her cheek and sucked in a deep breath. *Why is it so hard?*

The raucous caw of a crow in the pines clashed with the gentle buzz of a honey bee hovering in the yellow rose beside her. She grabbed a thick stalk with both hands and pulled. The muscles in her arms tensed when they met resistance. She pulled harder. The green-leafed enemy held fast. She doubled down, clenching her jaw. *Why. Is. It. So. Hard?* With a groan, she gave a powerful jerk. Tangled roots erupted from the ground, flinging dirt in every direction. She blinked it out of her eyes, spit it out of her mouth, threw the infuriating mass onto the mound.

Grace sank back on her haunches, wiping her forehead with her hand. "I know You are God. I'm not. If You say it's time, it's time." She yanked off the garden gloves and threw them to the ground. Her fists slammed against her knees. After a long minute, she lifted her eyes heavenward. She needed to do this but oh, her heart ached. Her voice grew soft. "Lord, would You help me?"

A hawk circled high overhead. Another honeybee joined the first, their buzzing a soothing hum as they flitted from one blossom to the next. The earthy scent of broken sod filled her nostrils. Grace closed her eyes, bowed her head, and waited.

Saturday, Ethan came up the walkway and let the gate swing shut behind him. He grasped the porch rail, but turned away from the stairs when a lilting soprano pealed from the backyard. Rounding the corner of the house, his heart skipped a beat. Grace strolled toward him, a basket of apples propped on her hip, a smattering of twigs and leaves caught in her hair, a rosy blush on her cheeks. Just like the sunburned, wind-tossed girl of his youth, eager to join him in another adventure at the drop of a hat.

She raised her eyes and pulled up short. "Hey."

"Hey yourself." He reached for the basket. "I needed to pick up a few things at the mercantile, so I thought I'd drop by to say howdy."

"I'm glad you did." Grace wrinkled that sunburned nose and waved him toward the stairs. "Come on. I'll see if I can rustle up a cookie or two."

They sat at the table, munching oatmeal raisin cookies and sipping black tea sweetened with honey. He loved this—the comfy kitchen, a cozy chat, and best of all, a smiling Grace sitting across from him. He could see changes in her. Eyes that held pain when he first came home, more and more showed a quietness and hope. He knew she still traveled the long road to healing, but at least she was on the road, not locked away in secret grief.

Outside the window, sunlight filtered through the clematis vine onto the porch floor, its lacy pattern moving inch by inch across the worn boards as Ethan and Grace talked.

"Where's Allie?"

"Napping. Finally." Grace broke off a piece of cookie. "I got a letter from my in-laws this morning. They can get away from the store for a few days next week and will come up on the train from Spokane. Allie was beside herself. She bounced around like a jumping bean for so long I decided to wear her out. I sent her outside to chase Uffda."

"And?"

"It did the trick. She's asleep upstairs. An added bonus—Uffda's asleep under the porch."

"Aha."

Grace picked up her spoon and traced circles on the tablecloth with the handle. "Ethan?"

"Mm-hmm?"

She raised her eyes and tipped her head a little to one side. "Would you mind coming over some evening and taking a look at the ledger?"

"Sure." He nodded and leaned forward, resting his arm on the table.

She wrinkled her nose and gave a slight smirk. "I try to stick to a budget, but somehow I run out of money before I run out of month. Maybe you could figure out what I'm doing wrong."

"I'd be happy to help out." Given the fact that Grace usually insisted the running of Halstad House fell to her, Ethan was surprised she asked. Surprised but glad. She carried so much on her shoulders. "When would be a good time?"

"Let's make it soon," she said. "I want to—" She turned at the sound of a horse whinnying and a wagon creaking. "Oh, that's probably Dad and Esther."

Ethan set his cup down. "Don't they usually come to town Sundays?"

"Usually. But Dad said he'd make some repairs on the back porch today." She brushed crumbs onto a small dessert plate and scooted away from the table. "There are enough repairs on this place to keep him busy every time he visits."

Grace moved to the stove and nudged the tea kettle closer to the firebox. She grinned as Esther came through the kitchen door. "Hello, big sister."

"How's my baby sister today?" Esther set a satchel against the wall and hung her hat on a hook.

Ethan deposited his cup on the counter and nodded to Esther. "It's nice to see you again. But if you ladies will excuse me, I'll see if I can give your dad a hand." He skirted past the sisters, slipped through the side door, and hustled down the stairs. He waved when he reached the bottom. "Mr. Browne, let me help you unload."

Grace's father looked up from the back of the wagon and flashed him a broad grin. Dressed in washed-out denim overalls with patched knees, a chambray shirt, sleeves rolled above his elbows, and a sweat-stained straw hat, Mr. Browne looked the picture of a hard-working country farmer.

After a firm handshake, Ethan grabbed a wooden toolbox and an MJB coffee can filled with a hodgepodge of nails, screws, nuts, and bolts. Mr. Browne slung three cedar boards over his shoulder, and the men circled the house.

When they'd plunked everything down on the porch, Ethan propped both hands on his hips. "Can I give you a hand?"

"I'd be glad for the help and the company." Mr. Browne winked and raised his voice. "I'm forever outnumbered by the female population in this family. We fellows have to stick together, you know."

"We heard that, Dad." Grace's laughter came through the open window right before her face appeared behind the screen. "You'd better show proper appreciation or the female population in this family may think twice about sharing the apple pandowdy we plan to make."

He held up his hands in mock surrender. "Point taken." He snatched off his hat and placed it over his heart. "I'm honored to be outnumbered by you two lovelies—three, counting Allie."

"That's better." Grace chuckled and disappeared from view.

Mr. Browne shrugged. "See what I mean?"

Ethan enjoyed working with this man. They ripped up three damaged boards and measured for their replacements. The Indian summer day had moved from a chilly morning to a perfect afternoon—blue sky, fluffy white clouds, moderate temperatures, a pleasant breeze. Behind the clamor of hammers and saws came kitchen sounds—the rich trill of the teakettle, the rattle of pots and pans, Grace and Esther's low chatter. Ethan pursed his lips and whistled the lilting melody of a ditty he'd learned as a boy.

Halfway through the job, Mr. Browne removed his hat and swiped the back of his hand across his forehead. "Heard a man from the mill ran into some trouble."

Ethan looked up from his hammer. "Do you mean Bob Bennings?"

"Don't know his name. Fellow's house burned down."

"Yeah. That was Bob Bennings." Ethan shook his head. "He rented a cabin on Sand Creek, he and his wife and three kids. They lost everything but the clothes on their backs. They were away for the day. When they returned, they found the cabin had burned to the ground."

Mr. Browne sucked air in between his teeth. "Do they have a place to live? How about clothes?"

"Mr. Emmett has a small house they moved into. It's right across the road from the mill. The boxes of clothes the church collected sure helped out. Plenty of kids' and women's paraphernalia, although Bob didn't fare quite as well." Ethan shifted to his other knee. "It's funny what sticks in a person's mind. Bob's wife had scrimped and saved egg money for months to surprise him with a work coat. She was so proud to give it to him. Wouldn't you know he didn't wear it the day of the fire and it went up in smoke with everything else. Boy howdy, she was fit to be tied. Cared more about that coat being lost than all their other stuff."

"Odd how that works," Mr. Browne said. He looked down at the approach of a feline visitor. "Here's the boss come to supervise." He scratched Geoffrey Chaucer under his chin.

The tabby sniffed the MJB can, the saw, and Ethan's boots. He twitched his whiskers and wound himself around Mr. Browne's leg before plopping onto the porch floor. From this supine position, he licked his paw for a few moments, but the exertion must've been too great. He laid his head down, body inert, and serenaded his subjects with a rumbling purr.

"Oho." Grace's father laughed and rubbed Chaucer's ears. "Guess he's done his bit. We'd best get back to ours."

By the time they'd put away their tools and swept sawdust and dirt from the area, sounds from the kitchen had stilled, replaced by the rich smell of apples and cinnamon.

The men leaned against the balustrade, admiring their labor. They looked up when the back door slammed. Grace and Esther appeared, Grace in the lead. She carried something in her arms, and Ethan's eyes widened when he realized what it was. He heard a quick intake of breath behind him.

Grace stopped in front of him. "Will you take this to your friend Mr. Bennings? We overheard you telling Dad about him." She held up Søren's tan coat, the one that always hung in the mudroom.

"I'd be happy to." He reached for it, studying her face. He couldn't quite read the expression in her eyes. Sadness? Resignation? Peace?

"All of Søren's clothes are still in the closet. If I work hard to box them up tonight, I might be able to load them into Dad's wagon and bring them to church tomorrow." Her voice caught. "You could take anything your friend might need. The elders can give away the rest."

Esther stepped beside her and placed an arm around her shoulders. "I'll help—if you'd like."

Grace gave her sister a shaky smile. "Thanks."

"Come here." Mr. Browne enveloped her in his brawny arms.

She nestled her head in the crook of his shoulder. "It's time, Dad."

Tears swam in his eyes. "I'm so proud of you, my little Lily Grace."

Ethan recognized the sting of tears in his own eyes. *Thank You, Lord.*

# Twelve

Grace's heart warmed as she listened to the conversation between Søren's parents and Allie. Like always, their visit proved bittersweet, bringing memories of Søren. But this time, the sweet took precedence over the bitter. She leaned back in her chair with a sigh. That had to be God's doing.

"Can you stay and go to church with us on Sunday?" Allie said. "We sing awful good songs."

"*Nei, min sønnensdatter,* my son's daughter, we must catch the train Friday to return home." Søren's father bounced her on his knee. "The store won't run itself."

"But we will come again for Christmas and stay longer." His wife's eyes twinkled as she looked at her granddaughter. "And we will make all the tasty Norwegian Christmas cookies." She turned her gaze toward Grace. "*Ja?*"

"*Ja.*" Grace touched her mother-in-law's arm. "I'm so glad you were able to get away for a couple of days. We miss you."

Ruth Halstad patted Grace's hand. "We miss you, too." She sat back and sipped tea from a delicate china teacup.

"*Farfar?*" Allie tugged his shirt sleeve. "You're my grampa, right?"

"*Ja.*"

"And my other grampa's my other grampa."

"*Ja.*"

"Then how come he isn't my *farfar,* too?"

"Ah." He placed his index finger along the side of his nose.

"That's our Norwegian secret. For Norwegians only." He shifted her so she was square on his lap. "It is time I told you our secret."

Allie's blue eyes grew round, her focus centered on her grandfather.

"*Far* means father in Norwegian. Your pappa was your *far*."

Allie nodded.

"And I was his *far*. That's two *fars*. I am your *farfar* because I am your father's father. You see? Father's father. *Far far.*"

"And grampa isn't my *farfar* because he isn't my father's father?"

"*Nei*, no, because he isn't Norwegian. I don't think he wants to be called a Norwegian name. But also, it is tricky. He is your mamma's father. Mother is *mor*. So he would be your *morfar*. Mother's father. *Ja?*" He put his finger to the side of his nose again. "*If* he was Norwegian."

Allie pointed to his chest. "You are *Farfar*. Father's father." Allie gnawed her lower lip. "*Mor* is mother. *Far* is father." She pointed to her grandmother. "I call her *Farmor* 'cause she's my father's mother."

"*Veldig bra*. Well done." He tickled Allie under her chin. "You are smart like your pappa and mamma both."

Allie's dimples emerged with her huge grin.

"*Ja*. My smart little granddaughter." *Farmor* reached for a red and blue flowered bag at her feet. "Allie, I have a surprise for you." From within, she pulled out a package wrapped in sunny yellow paper, tied with a yellow-and-white polka-dotted ribbon.

"A present?" Allie jumped down and scurried over.

"When we came for your birthday a few weeks ago, I saw how much you loved the coverlet I quilted for you." She held the package out to Allie. "I kept thinking of your little Margaret doll. Perhaps this is something you would like for her."

Allie ripped the paper from the package and pulled back soft, creamy tissue paper. Nestled inside lay a neatly folded rectangle of fabric. She held it by two corners, allowing it to fall open. "Look, Mommy. It's just like mine."

Grace fingered the doll-sized quilt. "It's exquisite." And it was. Vibrant hues of lavender, sky-blue, yellow, red, and forest-green against a white background mixed together to form an intricate Dresden Plate pattern, identical to Allie's full-sized coverlet. Sewn with Ruth Halstad's delicate stitches, this was a work of art. Like Allie's quilt, Grace imagined this, too, would become a family heirloom.

Allie threw her arms around her grandmother and kissed her wrinkled cheek with a loud smack. She nestled into *Farmor's* lap, resting her head on the sweet lady's shoulder.

Vegetable stew made with good beef stock simmered on the stove, its smell mingling with the sweet aroma of cardamom cookies Allie and *Farmor* had made that morning. The kitchen overflowed with quiet conversation, laughter, and reminiscing.

Late in the afternoon, the four of them gathered around the piano, Ruth Halstad on the piano bench. *Farfar and Farmor* sang several songs in Norwegian, their voices a little shaky these days yet still blending in perfect harmony. Allie leaned against her grandfather, toes tapping, a broad smile and dimples adorning her face. A vivid memory of Søren standing next to his father, singing these very songs, leaped into Grace's mind. The memory brought a smile—tremulous maybe—but not with pain and tears like before.

"I hope we do not disturb your boarders." Ruth turned a page in the songbook.

"Not at all. Miss Sommers is working at the café."

"She is the only one?" Ivar Halstad pursed his lips.

"Uh-huh." Allie hopped on one foot and flipped her braid behind her back. "Mommy kicked out the mean one."

He scratched his chin. "But one cannot be enough money to run this place—" He glanced at his wife before bringing his full attention to Grace again. "*Svigerdatter*, daughter-in-law, it is not good to have to worry about money. I do not say that you are, but one boarder? We have a little set aside. We can help if you have need."

Grace's heart swelled with love for these caring people. "I appreciate your offer, really I do. We're okay, though. We have enough to get by." At least she hoped they did. She still hadn't tackled the ledger. But her gut told her Halstad House was her responsibility. She'd press her nose to the grindstone and carry on. She had to. She suspected when her father-in-law said they had a little set aside, a little is exactly what he meant. She couldn't deprive them of that, much as she appreciated their generosity. "Besides, Mary Talbot will be back soon. That will make two." And maybe God would send another.

He took her hands in his smooth, strong ones. "You will ask if you need help? Do not take too much on your little shoulders. We love you. Always you are our son's wife who brought him much joy and gave to us our sweet Allie." He squeezed her hands once before releasing them. "*Ja?*"

"*Ja,*" Grace agreed.

He gave a quick nod and cleared his throat. "So. Enough talk of money. We have time for another song?"

Shortly before train time Friday morning, Grace and her mother-in-law packed a lunch for the Halstads' journey home.

"We will try to get away for five days at Christmas. If that is not too many?" Ruth wrapped cookies in waxed paper and placed them next to the sandwiches in her flowered satchel.

"You may stay as long as you like. You're always welcome." Grace handed her two shiny red apples, picked this morning from a tree in the garden.

Ruth put them in and closed the bag. "I forgot to mention. We heard from Einar Brevik."

Grace's head shot up. "Slimy Einar?" She gasped and clapped her hand over her mouth. "I'm sorry. I know he's your nephew. But Søren always—I mean, I—"

Ruth held up her hand. "No need to say you are sorry. He is the son of Pappa's sister, but I cannot like him. He was a shifty boy, forever blaming Søren for troubles he brought on himself. Pappa says he was dropped on his head too many times as a baby."

Grace giggled. "I only met him once. Søren said—" She shook her head. "Well, never mind what Søren said."

This time Ruth giggled. "I can imagine what my son said."

Grace remembered her husband's very words. Among other things, Søren always coupled the term *slimy* with his cousin's name—because the *ei* in Einar rhymed with the long *i* in slimy, and because slimy described his character. Søren figured the family would be better off only seeing Einar once every hundred years or so.

"Anyway, Einar ended his letter by saying he would see us at Christmas," Ruth said. "I do not put much stock in what he wrote. I only thought I would let you know."

The parlor door burst open. Mr. Halstad strode into the room with a rush of air and a hearty smile. "Mamma. You are ready? The train will not wait for us."

Three days before school was to start, Mary Talbot returned to Halstad House. She reappeared as inconspicuously as when she left at the end of last term. That first week Grace had to remind herself another boarder did, in fact, reside across the hall, next door to Esther's bedroom. They crossed paths at the dining room table when Grace served breakfast and supper, but Mary rarely lingered. Mornings, she left right after the meal for the half-mile walk to school, a burgundy satchel in one hand and two or three books in the other. Like clockwork, forty-five minutes after Mary departed, Grace heard the clanging of the bell announcing to the town of Emmett the school day had begun. Evenings, Mary disappeared to her room almost the moment she set her fork down. She dabbed the corners of her mouth with a cloth napkin, murmured a polite *excuse me*, and vanished.

Always pleasant, well-mannered, soft-spoken—when she spoke—Mary, Søren had said, was a mouse. Grace cringed at the word, but she couldn't disagree. Everything about Mary spoke of near invisibility. Her medium brown hair, worn in a bun, appeared rather mousy. Average height, no outstanding facial features, pale complexion, not fat, not thin. Mary tiptoed through life, Grace thought. Grace had known her since grammar school, yet she realized she didn't know Mary at all. Friendly, but not really friends. Mary had kept herself hidden. She still did.

And then something happened. Ethan came to supper.

"Pass the smashed potatoes, please." Allie grinned when Mr. Ethan set the bowl next to her, fluffy white potatoes with dabs of butter melting in pools on top. Golden streams trickled down the sides. Mommy plopped a spoonful on her plate next to a crispy chicken leg. She topped them both with a dollop of creamy gravy. Green beans and one of Auntie Esther's yummy biscuits, smothered in butter and raspberry jam, lay on the other side. Allie tucked her napkin under her chin and dug in.

"Ben's not coming for supper?" Mr. Ethan scooped beans onto his plate. "When will he be here?"

"About six-thirty," said Auntie Esther. "He had things to tie up at the post office. He'll grab a sandwich there and come over when he's done." She glanced at the clock. "That gives us plenty of time to eat, clean up, and deal with any interruptions from the biddies."

Mommy gave Auntie Esther a look, but Auntie Esther just shrugged.

Mr. Ethan smeared his biscuit with juicy, red jam and swallowed half of it in one bite. "Boy howdy, Ben is going to wish he'd been here for this meal. You ladies outdid yourselves."

After supper, Mommy, Auntie Esther, Mr. Ethan, and Mr. Guff meant to practice a song for church, with Mommy on the piano and Mr. Ethan on his guitar. Allie hankered for a toe-tapping one.

Every evening this week Mommy had run through her piano and singing parts. Then she moved on to other songs. Allie sat on the bench next to her and sang along with the ones she knew. Mommy even taught her a couple new ones and showed her how to play a little tune on the piano. Most times Dizzy Izzy sat on the davenport, sometimes with a book in her lap, sometimes just listening. She always smiled. Every once in a while, she patted out the rhythm on her knees with her fingers.

"I can't get over it," Mommy said. She came back into the kitchen after she checked on the bid—*boarders*. "Isobel and Mary don't need extra jam, butter, salt, pepper, or anything else. They are blissfully eating and chatting." She spread her napkin over her lap. "Well, Isobel is chatting. Mary is listening. But they seem content."

"Good," said Auntie Esther. "What a nice change—you can finish your supper before it gets stone-cold."

The grown-ups talked about this and that. Allie liked it. They laughed and every now and then teased each other. Not the mean teasing she'd seen some big kids do. Mommy told her to be careful 'bout that. It was only funny if the one being teased laughed, too. A real laugh, not fake. Tonight, everybody's eyes twinkled when they laughed.

After all the plates were licked clean—even Allie's—Mr. Ethan leaned back in his chair.

"Another piece of chicken?" Mommy held the plate out to him.

He shook his head and placed one hand over his stomach. "I couldn't hold another bite."

"You're sure?"

"More than sure, thanks." He set his napkin down and scooted his chair back. "Let me lend a hand."

Allie gathered all the napkins and chucked them into the brown wicker laundry basket. After that, she brought the dog dish and cat dish into the kitchen. Mommy scraped gooey oatmeal mush left over from breakfast into the bowls. A bunch of other stuff like dried bread crusts and table scraps went in, too.

Allie tugged on Mr. Ethan's sleeve. "It's my job to feed the aminals."

"That's a big responsibility. I'm sure your mother appreciates your help."

"Uh-huh, 'cause I'm awful good at it." She headed for the back door.

"Hang on." Auntie Esther scurried after her. "Let's give them a treat." She drizzled chicken gravy over the food mounded in each bowl.

Allie held tight when she carried the dishes outside. More than once Uffda had knocked them out of her hands. What a mess. He ran circles around her tonight, barking up a storm. But she held the bowls out of his reach. When she set his on the ground, he dove in, tail wagging to beat the band.

Chaucer sniffed his food when she laid it before him. He raised his head and blinked at her.

"It's got yummy gravy on it."

He turned his head and licked a paw, toes spread wide.

"I promise you'll like it."

Chaucer leaned against her leg and purred.

"Silly ol' thing." Allie hunkered down and scratched the top of his head. "You need some lovin', I bet." She rubbed under his chin and stroked his back.

His purrs grew louder. A couple minutes later, Geoffrey Chaucer twitched his whiskers and sniffed his food again. Only then did he dip his head and eat.

One last stroke and Allie bounded up the stairs. She walked into a tidy kitchen in time to see Mr. Guff stroll through the door.

He wore a red vest over his brown-and-green plaid shirt. His tan corduroy trousers were rumpled. Not handsome or tall like Mr. Ethan, barrel-chested, jolly Mr. Guff brimmed over with fun. His brows curved up in half circles that always made him look like he was surprised. He parted his reddish-brown hair on the side. Tonight it was slicked down. He wiped a couple drops of water off his cheek with the back of his hand and grinned. "How'do, folks."

"Hey," said Mr. Ethan. He leaned a broom against the wall in the nook by the door.

"Perfect timing." Auntie Esther hung a damp dishtowel over a rack by the stove and lifted up the tub of dishwater.

Mr. Guff hurried to her. "Let me get that."

She smiled and led him out the back door.

Auntie Esther patted Allie's head when they passed her on the way out.

"Evening, Miss Allie." Mr. Guff grinned and raised the tub. "Work before pleasure."

Just as they stepped back into the kitchen, Mommy poked her head through the parlor doorway. "All done in there. I hope you don't mind that I invited our boarders to listen if they care to."

"Not at all," Mr. Guff said. "They can tell us if we're any good."

Mr. Ethan grabbed his guitar from behind the table and reached out his free hand to Allie. "Come on, kitten."

In the parlor, Izzy had parked herself in an overstuffed chair near the window. Miss Talbot sat at one end of the davenport.

Mr. Guff said howdy to both of them and gave them big smiles. Then he joined Mommy and Auntie Esther by the piano.

Mr. Ethan set his mouth firm-like and walked right up to Izzy. "Miss Sommers, it's nice to see you again. Is work going well at the café?"

She giggled and simpered. "Oh, my. Yes, Mr. Myers. All is well in my world." She smoothed a hand over her messy hair. "I'm looking forward to hearing you sing."

Mr. Ethan dipped his head and turned to the teacher. "Mary, it's been a while. You're looking well."

Miss Talbot's face turned all pink. She stared at her hands in her lap, then peeked up at him. "Thank you." Her voice was barely a whisper.

Willikens. These biddies acted goofy. Allie plopped down on the other end of the sofa. Mr. Ethan headed for the piano.

Allie wanted to laugh when Mr. Ethan tuned his guitar. Mommy played a note on the piano. Mr. Ethan plucked a string, turned a key on the neck of the guitar, and the sound slid up, up, up, and down, down, down, then settled on just right. His eyebrows made a V, and he tilted his head every time he plucked. When all the strings matched the piano, he nodded and stood up straight.

Mommy opened the hymnbook. "Should we just begin and only work on parts if we need to?"

The rest of them said okay.

Piano chords lifted into the air. They took deep breaths, opened their mouths, and—

> *What a friend we have in Jesus,*
> *All our sins and griefs to bear.*
> *What a privilege to carry*
> *Everything to God in prayer.*

Even if it wasn't a toe-tapper, Allie loved that song. She liked to hear about talking to God. She clasped her hands together and listened.

On the second verse, Mr. Guff held up his hand. "I'm having trouble with the bass line there." He walked behind Mommy and pointed his finger at the page.

"Let me play it for you," she said.

Mr. Guff followed along. His voice dropped lower and lower. Allie could never sing that low in a month of Sundays. The lowest she ever got was when she ribbitted like a frog.

They practiced it three times.

"Got it." Mr. Guff walked back to stand by Auntie Esther.

They began again. Allie figured they were the best singers she'd ever heard. And she bet Mommy played the piano better than anybody in the whole world.

She glanced at Dizzy Izzy. The boarder stared at Mr. Ethan like he was a piece of chocolate cake with a cherry on top—good enough to eat. Her eyes looked funny whenever he came around. Not quite cross-eyed, but kind of squinty. She sighed a lot, too. Allie knew she liked Mr. Ethan, but he didn't treat her like someone special, so maybe it was okay. She hoped so.

Allie tipped back on the davenport and caught a glimpse of Miss Talbot. The teacher surprised her when she didn't hightail it to her bedroom like usual. She gazed at Mr. Ethan. Allie's tummy tightened. She leaned forward to get a better look. The corners of Miss Talbot's mouth tilted up in a half-smile. Her pale blue eyes had a dreamy look to them. Like when Mommy gazed out their window at a beautiful sunset. Allie narrowed her eyes. Yep, teacher zeroed in on Mr. Ethan. *Not another one.*

Allie swung her head toward the piano. Mr. Ethan winked at her. Then he smiled—right at Miss Talbot. Allie's heart ker-thumped. *Oh, no. Did You see that, God? Do somethin'. Quick.*

# Thirteen

Much later that night, in a quiet kitchen, Grace eyeballed the stitches on Allie's stockings. How many times could she patch the heels before she had to break down and purchase new ones? At least she knew how to darn stockings. That saved money right there. She'd have to hope for the best and—

"Oatmeal is set for breakfast." Esther closed the warming oven door. "Let's have a cup of tea before bed."

"Mmm. Sounds good." Grace placed the mending back in the basket. She raised her arms overhead and stretched before rising from the rocking chair. "I'll get the teacups. You can bring the kettle and tea tin."

Seated back at the table, Grace warmed her hands on the steaming cup. "This week we need to get the garden ready for winter. Every year I say I'll get plants pulled up as they die so it's not such a huge job." She took a sip and sighed. "But I didn't—again. It is what it is, though. Dad will probably come on Tuesday with his tiller."

Esther covered a yawn with one hand. "Pumpkins and squash are ready. When we're through with the garden, Northern Spies should be ripe. I thought it would be fun to can pie filling this year instead of just doing applesauce and drying the rest."

"Good idea. I'd better stock up on cinnamon and allspice so we don't run out in the middle of—"

They both jumped in their seats at a loud knock on the door.

"Land sakes," said Esther. "Who could that be this time of night?"

Ben Guff stood before them when Grace opened the door. He held his narrow-brimmed hat at his waist, fingers gripping it like a lifeline.

"Ben, come inside."

He stepped into the kitchen. In the glow of the oil lamp that hung from the ceiling, worry lines creased his brow.

"Are you all right?" Grace said.

Esther touched his arm. "Would you like a cup of tea?"

"No thanks." Ben swallowed hard. "I'm afraid I have bad news."

Grace's hand clasped her throat.

"I just got a telephone call from your dad's neighbor."

"Mrs. Jenkins?" said Esther.

He nodded. "She told me her son had gone over to talk to your dad about a calf he was selling and found him on the ground outside the house. Evidently, his feet got tangled up climbing down a ladder. He'd been there several hours—couldn't move because of the pain in his leg. He thinks it might be broken. Mrs. Jenkins called the doctor before she called me. She said as soon as we hung up she was leaving for your dad's straightaway. I thought I could drive you out if you'd—"

"Yes." Grace and Esther spoke at the same time.

"Won't take but a few minutes to get my car running. How about if I bank the fire in your kitchen stove before I go? Do you have a fire burning in the parlor stove, too?"

"What?" Grace ran a hand over her face. "Yes. Thanks. I'll go get Allie and pack a few things." She hesitated at the parlor door. "Esther. The boarders—"

Esther took her hand, pulling her into the other room. "You take care of Allie and yourself. I'll talk to the boarders. I'm sure they can get their own breakfast." She cupped Grace's chin with her fingers. "Let go of this concern. They are grown women. You are not shirking responsibility; you are going where you are most needed."

Tears filled Grace's eyes. She nodded and headed to her bedroom.

They made the trip to the farm in record time. Only a few people in Emmett owned automobiles, and Grace thanked God that Ben was one of them. He pulled up beside the doctor's Model T—a 1920 edition complete with glass windshield. Light from the kitchen window illuminated the back porch, its glow carving a hole in the darkness surrounding the farm.

In the backseat, Grace unwrapped a sleeping Allie from the heavy quilt she'd brought from home. "Sweetie?"

Ben jumped out and opened the car door. "Let me take her. No need to wake her up." He boosted Allie's limp form into his arms. She stirred, then nestled her head on his shoulder.

Grace gathered her overnight bag and the quilt and stepped out to follow Ben. Esther was already hurrying into the farmhouse. The gentle lowing of a cow in the barn broke through the hush and chill of the late October night, joined by the mellow hooting of an owl in the distance.

The kitchen of her childhood remained the same: wood cookstove with a cast-iron tea kettle on the back burner, a butcher-block worktable beside it, oak sideboard against one wall, wooden shelves holding dishes and pots and pans against another, and a round oak table surrounded by four chairs in the middle of the room. Lunch dishes cluttered the table. Remnants of an egg congealed on a plate.

Grace shook her head. That was unlike her father. He must have been in a hurry to take care of the task outside. Fear gripped her heart when she thought of how many hours he'd lain on the cold ground before Mrs. Jenkins' son found him.

"I'll go on into Dad's room." Esther hung her scarf and coat on a hook by the back door.

Grace nodded. She draped her outdoor garb next to Esther's, lit an oil lamp, and motioned for Ben to follow her. They made their way through the hallway to her old bedroom. "You can put her on the bed." She pulled back the covers to make room.

Ben laid Allie down. He stared at her for a moment before shifting his gaze to Grace. "Anything more I can do here?"

Grace shook her head.

"I'll head for your dad's room then."

Grace grabbed Ben's arm. "Thank you." She gave him a weak smile. "For everything."

Ben bobbed his head and stepped into the hall.

Grace slipped her daughter's arms out of her winter coat and laid it at the foot of the bed.

Allie's eyes opened a slit. "Are we at Grampa's?"

"Mm-hmm." After removing Allie's boots and setting them on the floor, Grace pulled the covers up and tucked them under her daughter's chin.

Allie yawned. "Can I see him?"

"In the morning."

"'Kay." Her eyes closed again. "My feet are cold."

Grace extracted one stockinged foot from under the covers and rubbed gently. She hummed a lullaby, watching Allie's face relax little by little. Once her breathing slowed and a slight *whiffle* flowed from the back of her throat, Grace rose and walked back down the hall.

Esther turned her head when Grace entered the room, lips set in a firm line, eyebrows drawn.

Dad's room seemed to shrink in size with the number of people crowded in. Ben stood next to Esther. Mrs. Jenkins sat in a chair by the window. The doctor leaned over the bed.

Grace stepped to her dad's side. This was not the robust man she knew. His pale face revealed hollow cheekbones etched with pain. Tears swam in her eyes. *He looks like a…no, I won't even think it.*

"It was a bad break." The doctor pulled his stethoscope away from Mr. Browne's chest. "I gave him laudanum. It may have eased things some, but the setting of the leg was difficult. He bore it well, though the pain must have been intense." He loaded his black bag with medical paraphernalia. "Now that you are here,

I'll take Mrs. Jenkins home and return in the morning. There's no more I can do right now. Hopefully, he'll sleep tonight. I know you'll keep a close watch on him."

He nodded to Mrs. Jenkins; she rose, and with that, they were gone.

Grace laid her hand on her father's forehead. "Thank goodness, no fever."

"We have that to be thankful for," Esther said. She straightened the covers around Dad's shoulders. "Well, there's no sense in all of us staying up. I'll take the first watch."

"I'll help for a while." Ben rubbed a hand across his face. "Don't think I could sleep just yet anyway."

Esther smiled and tipped her head to one side. "You're sure?"

"Yep."

"Thank you." She turned to Grace. "Why don't you try to get some rest? I'll wake you in a few hours and you can take over."

Grace hesitated at first, but saw the wisdom in Esther's plan. "All right. Be sure to wake me later. Don't wear yourself out."

At the doorway, she looked back over her shoulder. "Ben, I'll lay a pillow and blankets on the davenport for you."

She sat on the edge of her old bed to remove her shoes. She didn't bother to undress, just scooted under the covers and snuggled up against Allie. *Dear Lord, I know You are God and our lives are in Your hands.* Tears welled up and spilled over. *But please don't take Dad.*

With a shuddering breath, she settled into the pillow and closed her eyes.

Allie pulled back her grandfather's eyelid and peered inside. "Grampa, are you in there?"

A snort, a headshake, and Grampa opened his eyes.

Allie sat back on her haunches and grinned.

"Well, now." Grampa reached to give Allie's braid a gentle tug. "If it isn't my favorite granddaughter. When did you get in?"

"Last night. But Mommy said I had to wait till mornin' to see you."

"I'm sure glad you came. Doc says I have to lay up for a while because of this broke leg, so I can't even get out of bed."

Allie scratched her nose. "Who's gonna milk the cows and stuff?"

"Mrs. Jenkins' son will come to do chores. He's a good boy, that one."

"A little boy is gonna do all the chores?"

Grampa chuckled and shook his head. "He's a boy compared to me. No, he must be around forty by now."

"Willikens. He's old."

Grampa chuckled again. "If he's old, I must be ancient."

"How old is ancient?"

"Let's just say I saw the back side of forty a long time ago."

Muffled voices and the clatter of dishes drifted in from the kitchen. The screen door squeaked and slammed. Footsteps sounded on gravel.

He patted her knee. "All right, sweet pea, what should we do? You could tell me a story, we can look at the pictures in my Bible, or we could just sit here and gossip."

Allie wound a lock of Grampa's beard around her finger. "Preacher says gossip is a sin. I'm not sure what it means, but we better not do it."

"And Preacher is right." Grampa nodded. "I didn't mean *gossip* gossip, I meant talking about this, that, and the other thing."

"Hmm..." Allie flipped her braid behind her back. "Look at Bible pictures."

"Right you are." Grampa shifted to reach for the book on his nightstand. A gasp escaped his lips, and sweat beaded on his forehead.

"I'll get it." Allie jumped down and ran around to the night-stand. She grabbed the heavy Bible with both hands, climbed back on the bed, and studied his face. "Grampa?"

His eyes were shut tight. "Let me catch my breath." He took several deep breaths and let them out slowly.

Allie laid her hand on his arm. "Does it hurt somethin' fierce?"

"Something fierce." He took two more deep breaths. "But it's getting better." He sighed. "All right, sweet pea. Let's look at pictures."

Allie opened to her favorite Old Testament stories. Creation, Adam and Eve in the garden, the talking serpent who tempted them, Adam and Eve getting kicked out. A few pages further on, she squinted at the picture of a bearded Noah standing in an open doorway. Animals marched past him two by two. She pointed at the drawing. "Were you on the ark?"

Grampa grunted. "No. I may be ancient, but I'm not that ancient."

Allie turned more pages. They talked about some of the pictures, but just looked at others and moved on. She stopped at the one of Daniel in a pit, surrounded by great hairy lions. "He didn't even have to thump 'em on the head. God sent an angel to shut their mouths so they wouldn't eat him up."

"Yes. A miracle if there ever was one." He shifted again, gasped again.

Allie closed the book and set it aside. "Bad?"

"Mm-hmm." Grampa set his mouth firm and tight.

Sunlight streamed through the window and rested on Grampa's hands. Those strong hands of his could pick Allie up and swing her around in wide circles. They could chop wood. They could squeeze every last drop of milk from a cow like nobody's business. They could hammer nails and saw boards. But this morning they looked old. Blue veins jutted up in ridges through pale, wrinkled skin. His fingers curled in his lap like knobby twigs from the willow trees by the river.

Allie chewed her lower lip. "Preacher says Jesus can heal us. I'm gonna pray He will. 'Kay?"

Grampa nodded, his mouth still set.

Allie clasped her hands and squeezed her eyes shut. "Dear Jesus, Grampa's leg got broke and hurts him bad. Please make it all better. And make it so it doesn't hurt anymore. And make it so he can get out of bed and walk around." Her voice caught. "'Cause me and Mommy and Auntie Esther need him."

When she glanced up at Grampa, tears swam in his eyes, but he wore a happy smile.

Allie leaned in to rest her head on his chest. His white beard tickled her cheek. "I love you, Grampa."

"I love you, too, sweet pea." He put one arm around her and pulled her close.

"Good morning." Grace stepped into the room, a tray balanced in her hands. "Do you think you could eat some oatmeal mush? I have buttered toast, too." It melted her heart to see Allie snuggled up with her grandfather. But she hoped she hadn't tired him. Grace studied Dad's face. Though he looked better than he had last night, the creases in his face were deep—telltale signs of pain.

She set the tray on the nightstand and smiled at Allie. "All right, missy-moo, Auntie Esther has your breakfast on the table. How about you scoot on in and eat. We have to head home soon."

"'Kay." Allie kissed her grampa's cheek before jumping down and scampering out the door.

The jostling of the bed triggered a gasp and clenched fists from Dad.

"Esther will be right in with some white willow bark tea. Maybe that will help a little with the pain." Grace placed a hand on her father's forehead. Still no fever, thank the Lord. "Dad?"

Mr. Browne's white cotton nightshirt rose and fell as he breathed in and out in slow steady breaths, eyes shut tight. He gave a faint nod. A horse whinnied in the corral, a dog barked, chickens cackled. "Ought to be outside taking care of things."

"That'll come soon enough. Right now you need to rest and heal." Grace picked up a damp washcloth from the tray and wiped Dad's face and hands with gentle strokes.

"Feel like a baby," he said.

Grace just smiled.

The door opened and Esther walked in holding a steaming brown mug. "Good morning." She set the mug on the bureau and came to stand next to Grace. "How about if we get you situated so you can try a little breakfast? We can plump up your pillows, and you can sit up."

The task turned into an ordeal despite Grace and Esther being as gentle as they could. Dad sucked air in through his teeth, and sweat glistened on his forehead before they finished and eased him back on his pillows.

Grace grabbed the washcloth and wiped his face again.

Esther held the mug to his lips. "Try a sip. Maybe it will take the edge off."

He managed three sips before waving the tea away.

"The doctor will be here soon. I'm sure he'll bring more laudanum with him," said Esther.

Dad grimaced. "Heard about people getting hooked on that and I sure don't want to. Besides, I feel funny when I take it."

"It will only be for a day or two, until the worst of the pain goes away." Grace touched his cheek and grinned. "Please tell me you're going to be compliant and not cranky."

He sputtered, but his mouth broke into a smile. "Yes, ma'am."

Esther turned to Grace. "I'll help Dad with his breakfast while you get ready to go. Allie should be about done, and Ben went out to get the car started. He'll come on Saturday to pick me up and take me back to Halstad House. I'll talk with Mrs. Jenkins about staying with Dad until Sunday afternoon. That way I can help you out on Saturday. And we have that quartet to sing for church."

Heavens to Betsy, was that just yesterday evening they practiced? So much had happened since then, it seemed like ages ago.

Esther placed a hand on Grace's arm, her eyes running over her sister's face. "There's a lot to do for one person. Will you be okay to handle it yourself?"

"I'll have to be." Grace leaned down to kiss her father's cheek. She smiled at Esther, even though uncertainty threatened to run amuck. "Don't worry. It'll be fine."

At the door, she turned and pointed a finger at her father. "You behave. Do what the doctor says."

His eyes showed a little of their usual twinkle. "With Esther bossing me around, don't think I'll have much choice."

# Fourteen

"Okay, boots by the stove, coats and scarves hung in the mudroom. As soon as I have wash water on the stove, I'm off to clean bedrooms."

Allie scurried after her mother as she pulled aside curtains to let the morning light in. "I can help, Mommy. I'm a good helper."

"You are a good helper."

Allie peered up at her with sparkling eyes and a wrinkled nose.

"Let's do this. You lend a hand with the biddies' bedrooms. When we're done it will be time for lunch and then your nap."

Allie giggled and put her hand over her mouth.

"What's so funny?"

"You called them biddies."

A flush crept up her cheeks. Esther always called them that, but she rarely did, even when sorely tempted. "I meant to say boarders."

And bless them, those boarders had left the kitchen ship-shape. They'd even stoked the fires before they headed off to work. Two less things to do on top of today's long list of chores. Speaking of which, she'd better get crackin'. She added more firewood to the kitchen and parlor stoves before heading outside to the well with two empty pails.

Once water was heating, Grace lugged the broom, dust mop, and a bucket of soapy water upstairs. Two cleaning cloths protruded from her apron pockets. Allie carried the dustpan and a lamb's wool duster.

"We'll tackle Miss Sommers' room first." Grace pushed open the door. She had to say this for her: Isobel might be flighty, but she kept a tidy room. They stripped the sheets, wadding them up and leaving the pile in the hallway, then retrieved fresh sheets and pillowcases from the hall linen closet. After unfolding one of the sheets, she leaned over the bed.

"Make it fly!" Allie stood with hands clasped.

Grace whipped it up with a snap. The sheet spread out, fluttered, and glided over the mattress.

Allie giggled and clapped. "When I get bigger, I'm gonna do that."

"Yes, you will." Grace tucked the sheet in, stretching the ends to make tight corners. "For now, how about you take the duster and run it over the bureau and table legs and the windowsills? We can sweep and scrub the floor afterward." Allie scampered off while Grace finished making the bed. She wiped the cloth over the nightstand, picking up a book that lay there. Grace glanced at the title. *The Duke's Revenge.* Though she wasn't familiar with it, she suspected it was one of those novels Pastor Grant warned about. As boy-crazy as Isobel was, getting her ideas of what constituted a gentleman from this kind of book was a bad combination. No mere man could ever live up to such unrealistic expectations. Isobel was in for a real disappointment. Grace shook her head. *Okay, back to work.* She set the book aside, glad again that Isobel was not her concern.

Right. One down, one to go. They stepped across the hall. Oh my. Grace surveyed Mary's room and clucked her tongue. Clothes, books, and general clutter littered the floor, the bed, and the bureau—much worse than the usual disarray.

"Willikens." Allie scrunched her nose. "Do we hafta clean all this?"

They'd clean it, all right. But tonight she'd have a talk with Mary about at least tidying up. Grace refused to do this every week. Heavens to Betsy, they had their work cut out for them. After changing sheets, straightening messes, dusting, sweeping, and mopping, Grace called it good. "Whew." She placed her hands on her lower back and stretched. She rubbed the palm of her hand over her forehead and turned to her daughter. "Come on, missy-moo. Time for lunch."

They set off downstairs, Allie trudging along with the duster trailing on the floor. By the time they reached the kitchen, Allie's feet were dragging.

"You sit up to the table while I put sheets to soaking." Grace sprinkled soap flakes into a tub and poured in hot water from the oversized pot on the stove. One set of sheets followed. She stirred them into the water with a stout stick.

*Bless you, Søren, for purchasing this modern contraption before you left.* Two tubs—one for washing and one for rinsing—rested on a sturdy wooden stand with a hand-cranked wringer in between the two. She remembered the days of lifting hot, dripping sheets out of a tub, twisting them to get the water out, and burning her hands in the process.

That done, she carried bread and cheese to the table and sat next to Allie. "Hungry?"

Allie nodded, stifling a yawn.

Grace said a quick prayer and sliced the lunch fare onto their plates. "You were a big help today."

"Mm-hmm." Allie gave her a half-smile and chewed, resting her head on her hand.

She'd ignore the *no elbows on the table* rule this once. "You dusted and scrubbed and swept right beside me."

"Mm-hmm."

"It was a lot of work, but we got it done." Grace poured Allie's milk.

"Mm-hmm."

"I know the boarders will appreciate clean rooms."

"Mm-hmm."

"More cheese?"

"Mm-hmm." Allie's eyes sank to half-mast and she jerked her head up after it slipped. She switched hands and leaned her cheek into the new one.

Grace dusted off crumbs and stood. "Come on, sweetie." She

picked up her daughter. After nestling her head against Grace's shoulder, Allie didn't move a muscle. Grace hummed a simple tune as she carried her through the parlor, up the front stairs, and into their room. Allie was sound asleep before Grace had tucked the covers under her chin.

Two sets of sheets to wash, rinse, and hang on the line in the frosty air. Parlor, dining room, and alcove to dust-mop, carpets to sweep, furniture to polish, rag rugs and tablecloths to shake out over the porch railing, kitchen floor to mop. *Focus. One thing at a time.*

Two hours later, Allie appeared in the middle of the parlor cleaning craze. "Want me to help?"

"Nope." Grace squeezed her daughter's shoulders. "Put on your coat and boots. Uffda is in the backyard looking for someone to play with. You skedaddle."

Allie grinned and skipped past her mother and into the kitchen. The door slammed, and Allie's laughter joined excited barks.

Both boarders returned in the late afternoon and retreated to their rooms.

Time drug on, but finally, chores completed, Grace headed for a cup of tea. She settled into the rocking chair and leaned her head against the back. With a deep sigh, she closed her eyes and sipped the hot, sweet liquid. Allie's giggles and shouts drifted into the room. *She deserves some fun after the day she's had.*

"Supper!" Grace planted her feet flat on the floor, jostling the cup, and spilling tea in her lap. Heavens to Betsy, she had nothing started. A quick glance at the clock alerted her to the time crunch. In forty-five minutes the boarders would seat themselves at the table, expecting a hot meal.

Just then Allie skipped into the room. "What's for supper? My tummy's making noises."

"I forgot to get anything going." Grace grabbed a cloth and dabbed at the front of her apron. "I know we have jars of stewed chicken in the pantry. They'll cook up into good gravy, and I'll bake biscuits to pour it over. We have green beans, pickles, and sliced cheese. Yep, we're all set."

She rushed to the pantry and came out with three jars of chicken to find her daughter scowling. "What's wrong?"

Allie stood in the middle of the kitchen, nose wrinkled. "You're gonna make biscuits?"

"Well, yes. Needs must, you know. If the gravy is creamy and tasty enough, maybe nobody will notice the biscuits." She glanced at the clock again. "Or maybe they'll turn out this time."

"I don't know." Allie chewed her bottom lip.

At the sound of a horse blowing, Allie dashed to the side door and peered through the window. "Mr. Ethan!"

"Whoa." Ethan pulled on the reins, removed his hat, and wiped a rough sleeve across his forehead. The chill air cooled his sweat-soaked scalp. He slid from the saddle and patted his horse's neck. "Just about toppled me, boy. That on top of working on the floor today about did me in."

Prince swung his head toward Ethan and nickered.

"Apology accepted." Ethan eased his full weight onto his leg and rested against the saddle a few moments. He looked up. The lights from the kitchen at Halstad House illuminated the porch in the growing dusk. Rubbing his thigh lessened the pain and when he mounted the steps he was able to smile back at the beguiling, golden-haired charmer peeking at him from the side door window.

She threw open the door and rushed to him with outstretched arms.

"Hi, kitten." He folded her into a hug.

She grabbed his hand and pulled him inside, chattering a mile a minute. "Grampa fell off a ladder and his leg got broke and it hurts somethin' fierce and Mr. Guff drove us in his car and brought us home after breakfast and I helped clean the biddies' rooms and Mommy did the rest 'cause I fell asleep and she forgot to fix supper and now she has to make—biscuits." This last word was said with a grimace.

Ethan glanced at Grace. "I stopped at the post office, and Ben told me about your dad's accident. I'm sure sorry to hear it. Ben said he'd go out every evening to help with chores. I'll join him two or three times a week, too."

Tears shimmered in her eyes, and Ethan's stomach clenched. She looked worn out—loose chestnut strands had escaped her braid, a wet spot soaked her apron, and furrows crossed her forehead.

But she smiled and held out her hand. "Thank you. I'm glad you came."

He took it and rubbed his thumb across the top. "What can I do to help?"

Allie tugged his sleeve. "Can you make biscuits?"

"Allie." Grace pursed her lips, but her eyes twinkled. Her gaze shifted to him. "It's no secret mine won't win any prizes. We'll simply smother them with gravy."

He grinned and hung up his coat and hat. "A cranky army cook taught me how to throw together some mean biscuits. I'd be glad to whip up a batch."

"Really?" Grace beamed at him.

"Yes, ma'am. Lead me to the flour and lard."

"You bet." She waved him toward the counter.

A half hour later—ah, right on time. Ethan could hear the boarders' voices in the next room just as he pulled the biscuits out of the oven. He slid the baking sheet onto the worktable.

Allie gasped. "They look like Auntie Esther's."

He slipped one lightly browned, fluffy biscuit onto a small plate and cut it in two. After spreading butter and honey on one half, he handed the plate to Grace.

She took it and sniffed. Glancing at him, she picked up the buttery biscuit and bit into it. She closed her eyes. "Mmm..." A sigh escaped. "It's so unfair." Leaning forward, Grace gave him a quick kiss on the cheek. "But my boarders will be thrilled. Thank you, good sir."

Ethan felt as light as his biscuits—a man who had just conquered the world. He placed the rest of the biscuits on a platter and followed Grace and Allie, each carrying steamy bowls of stewed chicken gravy and green beans, into the parlor. After the tiring day he'd had, his limp may have been pronounced tonight but who cared?

"I won't be long," Grace said.

"No problem." Ethan sat in the rocking chair. "I'll rest here while you take care of Allie."

Allie jumped into his lap and threw her arms around him. "G'night, Mr. Ethan. I'm glad you came."

"Me too, kitten." He tweaked her nose. "Sleep tight now."

"All right, missy-moo. Bedtime." Grace took her daughter's hand and led her through the parlor door.

By the time she returned to the kitchen, Ethan, relaxing in the rocker, had his feet up on a chair in front of him. She grinned at the sight of his socks. His right big toe stuck out for the world to see—or at least her. Skin peeked through a hole in the heel of his left sock.

When the door thudded shut, Ethan looked up. "All set?" His feet hit the floor, and he stood, stretching his arms overhead.

"Nice look." Grace pointed to his feet.

He glanced down. "I have three more pairs like them back at the bunkhouse." He smirked. "I may have to wear two sets at once this winter so the holes don't line up."

"Bring them next time. I'll darn them for you."

"Boy howdy, I won't turn that down." He gave her braid a slight tug. "C'mon." He headed to the kitchen table. "I sure got a charge out of Allie telling me about her *aminals* tonight."

Grace grinned and scooted a chair up. "I know it's silly but I'm hanging on to her saying *aminals* for animals and *elk* for her egg yolk as long as I can. She's growing up fast enough as it is."

"It's not silly. I think it's endearing." Ethan gave her a wide smile and rolled up his shirtsleeves. "I'm ready if you are."

Grace tapped her fingers on the table. "I shouldn't even ask you to help with this. You've done so much already—what with getting the garden ready for cold weather. I know it's my responsibility. Maybe you could just give me a few pointers?"

"Grace, I'm glad you asked me when I was here the other day. And I'm happy to help. I'm a bookkeeper, remember? I do this all day long. Besides, that's what friends do. Help each other."

"I know." She loved that she could count on him. She just didn't want to shirk her duty. "I guess I feel like I'm not living up to my end of the bargain if I can't handle this side of things." She shrugged one shoulder. "They're only numbers, right? They shouldn't intimidate me so much."

Ethan gave a snort. "What would intimidate *me* is if you did everything perfectly and never needed help from anybody. Quit worrying." He rubbed his hands together. "Let's get started."

Grace walked to the sideboard and pulled a ledger, pencils, and paper out of the top drawer. She laid them in front of him and sat again, chewing her fingernail. "Ethan?"

"Hmm..?" He picked up a pencil.

"Promise you won't scold?"

His gaze met hers. "Scold? I'm amazed at everything you do here. How could I find fault with—?" His forehead creased. "Did Søren—?"

Grace nodded. "It's almost the only thing we ever argued about." She jerked her head. "Not that I blamed him. I was hopeless at trying to balance the budget." She breathed out a soft sigh. "Still, I hated to be reminded of it."

Ethan pursed his lips and ran his fingers through his hair. "Søren loved you."

"Oh, I know. He just wasn't crazy about my mathematical skills." And she'd hated feeling inadequate. Well, no sense dwelling on it. She rose from the chair. "How about I make us some tea while you look at the ledger?"

"Sure." Ethan picked up a pencil and opened the book.

Grace pulled the teakettle forward to the hot end of the stove. She busied herself gathering cups, saucers, and the tea tin. She raided the cookie jar for a handful of oatmeal cookies. When everything was ready, she set it all on the table.

Ethan didn't even look up, just grunted and scribbled away.

Grace grabbed a pile of cloth napkins from a cabinet drawer and brought them back to the table. She studied each one, separating those that needed to be mended. Every once in a while, she glanced at Ethan, but then continued her task since he was absorbed with his.

Almost an hour later he set down the pencil and rolled his shoulders. Two of the papers in front of him overflowed with figures.

Grace fingered the stack of napkins. "Well?"

"There were some arithmetic errors, but those are easy to fix. Don't worry about them." Ethan picked up the pencil and tapped it against the ledger. "I'm more concerned about the actual budget. It will be tough to keep Halstad House afloat doing what you've been doing. Not for lack of trying, but lack of funds. If you—"

"But I have to keep it afloat." Grace's heart lurched, and her chest tightened. "I have to make a home for Allie and myself. Halstad House is our security." Tears stung the back of her eyes.

"Whoa. Let me finish." Ethan scooted his chair closer. "I said *doing what you've been doing.* I have a couple of ideas. You can turn this around. There's hope, Grace."

She flopped back in her chair. *Thank heavens.* "Ideas I am open to. What do you have in mind?"

"For one thing, how long has it been since you raised your rent?"

"I never have." She squirmed in her chair. "It's hard to ask..."

"You make a cozy home for your boarders, but it's a business. The sister of a fellow I work with boards in Orient. I know for a fact they charge five dollars a month more than you do. That one little thing would make a big difference."

"But five whole dollars? You don't think they would bail if I raised my prices by that much?"

"Not at all. Like I said, you make a cozy home for them. I'm willing to bet they would pay more to keep living here." Ethan set the pencil next to the others, lining them up in a neat row.

"Okay. If you think it would help, I could do that. And then things would be all right?"

"Almost. Not quite."

Her shoulders sagged.

"I have another idea, though."

She tilted her head to one side. "What?"

"You need a boarder to replace that horrible woman we booted out. Another boarder at full price would allow you to pay off your account at the mercantile and even be able to put a bit away for emergencies."

She could do both those things. "Boarders don't grow on trees, though. And I told God I wouldn't let anyone else move in unless I sensed He was guiding them here."

"Good plan. Why don't we pray for the very boarder you need?" He held out a hand to her.

She smiled and took it. "All right."

"Thank you." Grace gave Ethan a quick hug at the door a little while later. "There's hope, right?" She'd only asked him a dozen times.

"Yep. There's hope." He flashed her a grin, moss-green flecks glinting in his hazel eyes.

"Here." She handed him a cookie wrapped in a napkin. "One for the road."

Ethan stuffed it into his coat pocket and reached for the doorknob. He stood a moment, then let go and met her gaze again, rubbing the back of his neck. "I don't want to overstep my boundaries but—"

"But?"

"Have you forgiven him?"

Grace wrinkled her nose. "What do you mean?"

"Have you forgiven Søren for scolding you about the whole budgeting issue?"

"But he was right. I made a hash of things."

"That's not the point. Søren was imperfect like the rest of

us. I'm sure you two would've worked it out but—be honest—did you, do you feel some resentment? And has it maybe colored the way you see yourself? At least in the area of money and figures?" He squeezed her hand.

Grace glanced at the floor. She remembered those arguments. Hated the way she felt afterward. Hot tears pricked her eyes when she looked up. She bit her lip and nodded.

"Listen, I'm an expert on letting resentment eat away at me. *And* on believing a lie that the enemy of our souls pitched at me."

"You? What happened? May I ask?"

Ethan gave a sharp nod. "In the hospital back East, I spent most of my time flat on my back. One day I overheard two nurses talking. One of them said she felt sorry for that poor cripple in bed eight." His stare cut straight through her. "I occupied bed eight."

Grace sucked in a breath. "Of all the nerve. I'd like to tell them a thing or two."

When he grinned, a dimple appeared in one cheek. "That'd be a sight to see." He chuckled and shook his head. Then his face sobered. "I believed that lie for quite a while. I felt sorry for myself and resentful to boot. But God got hold of me. I needed to forgive those nurses." Ethan blushed. "And some other folks I'd let myself feel resentful toward. Then I had to face the lie I believed, reject it, and grab hold of God's truth. I am not a cripple. No matter what happened with my leg, I am whole, complete in Him." He gave her hand another squeeze.

Grace surmised the struggle Ethan must have gone through, not just physically, but in his mind and spirit, as God led him on that journey. Strong and whole—yes, that was Ethan.

"Maybe this isn't quite as dramatic, but it's the same idea. I'd hate to see you sidetracked by it." He slapped his hat against his thigh. "Right. Enough sermonizing. Just think about it. I'll head over to Ben's now." He turned and disappeared out the side door.

# *Fifteen*

Grace finished her nighttime routine and sat on the edge of the bed. Allie lay fast asleep in her trundle bed, her smooth, even breathing spreading a calm into the room that echoed within Grace. She closed her eyes. *Ethan is right, Lord. I didn't want to admit it, but I have felt resentful toward Søren, even angry. What he said hurt. I figured he thought I was thick-headed when it came to numbers. I do need to forgive him.* She laid a hand on her chest. *Lord, I forgive Søren for the things he said.* She picked up his picture and ran her finger across his face. "We don't have the chance to work it out, but I forgive you, Sweetheart. And I let it go. Right now." She placed the picture back on the nightstand.

*Lord, I'm sorry for believing the lie that I am dumb with arithmetic. In Your Word You say that You have not given us the spirit of fear but of power, love, and a sound mind. So the truth is I have a sound mind. That's how You made me. Even if I'm not a mathematical genius, I can learn what I need to know.*

She smiled and wiped away a tear. "I like that."

"While I'm at it, Lord," she whispered, "please touch Dad's leg. Strengthen him. With Ben driving to the farm every evening to help out and Ethan riding with him two or three times a week, I know Dad will be thankful chores are getting done. But it will be hard on him to lay in bed day after day when he'd rather be working with them."

She glanced over at a sound from Allie. Just a snuffle. Allie rubbed her nose in her sleep and rolled over. Grace lifted her eyes to the darkened window. Stars glittered in the inky sky. She took in a deep breath, savoring the stillness in the room and in her heart.

She paused a moment before pushing herself off the bed. Walking to the bureau, she surveyed the familiar items, then removed the lid from the wooden box. Her fingers trembled as she took out the top letter. Was it time? If she opened it there'd be no more letters to look forward to. It would mean the end of... something. She peeled back a tiny slit from one corner of the envelope. Her fingers stilled. No. Not yet. Maybe when—

She gasped. "Heavens to Betsy, I forgot to set the oatmeal for breakfast." She dropped the letter in the box, replaced the lid, and rushed out the door.

Just as Grace placed the oatmeal in the warming oven, the parlor door squeaked open and Mary Talbot's face appeared.

"Mary?" Grace closed the warming oven door. "Hi. Were you needing something?"

Mary stepped into the kitchen. She glanced at Grace, then lowered her eyes.

Grace took a close look at her boarder. She couldn't decipher the odd expression on her face. "Is everything all right?"

Mary nodded. She clasped her hands together, released them, brought one up to swipe a loose curl from her eyes. She glanced at Grace, looked away again.

*She acts like she's about to face a firing squad.* Grace walked over and touched Mary's arm. "Please, sit down."

Mary sank into the nearest chair.

Grace chose the one next to her. "Can I help in any way?"

Mary peeked at her, looked away again. She sniffed. "I—I'd like to ask you something."

"Of course."

Mary met her gaze and held it this time. "Are—are you and Ethan Myers a—a couple now?"

Grace shook her head to clear it. That was the last thing she'd expected to hear. "A couple?"

Mary bobbed her head.

"Ethan and I are good friends. We've been the best of buddies since school days. But a couple? No."

"I thought now maybe he wanted to be. I think he did even when we were young." Mary snickered, but Grace found the sound devoid of humor. "Just like every other boy in school."

"I doubt that very much." This was by far the most peculiar conversation she'd ever had with Mary. She shifted in her chair. "Why do you ask?"

Mary stared at her clasped hands. When she looked up, her eyes held an expression Grace could not decipher. No tears, no sparkle—just a dull hardness. "My father thinks I should make a play for Ethan," Mary said.

Grace's stomach clenched. The thought of Mary and her father discussing Ethan in such a cold, calculating way brought Grace's protective instincts out in full force. "A play? What do you mean? Are you interested in Ethan—in a romantic way?"

Mary shrugged one shoulder. "He's better than most men, and I don't want to teach school forever. He has a steady job. He has always been easy to get along with." She shrugged her shoulder again.

This conversation was getting stranger by the minute. Grace fingered the edge of the table cloth. "There's a whole lot more to being a couple than that. A lasting relationship needs love and respect—mutual love and respect, among other things."

Mary sighed. "I'm not fooling myself. No one has ever shown the slightest interest in me, but my father says now that Ethan is—like he is—maybe I stand a chance. So I should make a play for him."

Grace frowned. "Now that Ethan is like he is?"

"I thought he was always just about perfect. But now that he's damaged, well, he might consider—"

"Damaged?" Grace sat bolt upright. "What are you talking about? Do you mean because he limps when he's overtired?"

"His leg—yes. Of course. But my father says the boys in

the war came back damaged in the head, too. He called it shell-shocked."

*Lord, would it be a sin to haul off and smack her?* Grace contemplated sitting on her hands to keep them from doing just that. "I don't know where your father got his information but for *your* information, Ethan is not damaged. He may have been wounded in the leg but his recovery is near-complete." She steadied her breathing. "He is by far one of the smartest, kindest, most selfless, godly men I know, and he deserves someone who sees his worth and values him for it."

Mary dipped her head. "I didn't mean to upset you." She stood, opened her mouth, closed it again. "I'll head to my room now."

Grace remained seated after the door shut. "Make a play indeed. She could never make Ethan happy." She rubbed her stomach, trying to calm the knots that threatened to overtake any composure she'd experienced earlier. "Who does she think she is? Ethan damaged? Ha." She slapped her thigh and jumped to her feet. "Of all the loathsome, contemptible—she's no better than those nurses he told me about." She shoved her chair under the table. "Well, Mary Talbot, all I have to say is this: *Don't get your hopes up.*"

# Sixteen

"You're what?" Grace's jaw dropped.

Esther beamed. "Ben and I are getting married Christmas Eve."

Married? Grace plopped onto the chair next to her sister and stared. "When did—I mean, how did—Esther, Christmas is only five weeks away."

"I know, I know."

"When did this happen? You haven't said a word."

Esther studied Grace's face. "Don't be miffed. I haven't meant to be secretive. It sounds strange, but I didn't know myself until this week. Ben and I have gotten to know each other better when he comes to help on the farm. But a few days ago, it was as if my eyes were opened. I saw him in a different light."

"A few days ago?" What was Esther thinking? This was going way too fast. She couldn't stand the thought of her sister having her heart broken because of hurrying into a marriage. "Don't you think you're rushing it?"

Esther shook her head and took Grace's hand. "No, I don't. Please be happy for me."

Grace inhaled to steady herself. "Do you love him?" The sparkle in Esther's eyes startled her. She'd never seen that look before.

"I do." She breathed in a sigh and covered her cheeks with her hands. "I didn't know it could be like this."

*Heavens to Betsy, my always-in-control, level-headed sister is smitten.*

"What about Ben? Does he feel the same?"

"Yes, he does." Esther's smile lit the room. "He said he knew first. He talked to Dad right away."

Grace raised one eyebrow. "What did Dad say?"

"He's over the moon." Esther chuckled and brushed a hand across her eye. "Maybe he'd given up hope."

"But why rush into a wedding so soon?" Grace leaned forward and squeezed Esther's knee. "There's plenty of time. Maybe in the summer? Please. Be sure."

Esther shook her head again. "At twenty-four, you may think you have all the time in the world. But I'm thirty-five and Ben is thirty-seven. We don't feel like we are rushing things. God brought us together, and we're ready to start this new journey. Why wait?"

Grace leaned back in her chair. She tugged and straightened her apron to give her hands something to do. "I don't know what to say."

"Say you're happy for me. Say you think it's wonderful. Say you'll help me plan my wedding. My Christmas wedding."

Without warning, her prayer for Esther popped into Grace's mind. For her dreams to be fulfilled. *Is this from You, Lord? I just didn't think You'd answer so fast.* She took a deep breath. *You are God. I'm not.*

Her gaze met Esther's. The wounded look in her sister's eyes coupled with her hopeful appeal brought the sting of tears to Grace's own. What was wrong with her? "I'm sorry." She shifted in her seat. "Of course I am happy for you. And I think it's wonderful. And I will most *definitely* help you plan your Christmas wedding."

The relief in the room was palpable. Esther's smile returned. "Ben talked with Pastor Grant last night. He's thrilled. He offered the use of the church, but I'd rather have it here at Halstad House. Would that be too much trouble? I know the Halstads are coming from Spokane for Christmas and—"

Grace held up her hand. "I wouldn't have it any other way." A wedding at Halstad House. This could be fun. There hadn't been a wedding here since—well, she wouldn't think about that. This was about Esther. And Allie would be beside herself.

"What will you wear?"

Esther waved a hand in front of her as if shooing away a pesky fly. "My best organza will be fine. I might see about ordering a new hat from the mercantile. A simple one, maybe with netting peeking over the brim."

*You have a gown.* The statement careened into her thoughts, leaving her almost winded. Her gown? Did God want her to give her gown to Esther? Her heart tightened. How could He ask her to let go of another part of her past with Søren? And this—her wedding gown? Grace drew in a breath and gazed out the window. The sun's rays highlighted the clematis and wild rose vines. Chaucer sprawled across the top porch rail, his bulky orange form contrasting with the dull colors of the vines, prepared for their winter sleep. Beyond, the garden lay ready for its own season of rest. The calm tableau quieted her heart. Somehow it felt right. Hard, but right. *Jesus, help.* She could do this for Esther.

"How about my wedding gown?"

Esther froze. "Oh. No. I couldn't."

"Why not?"

"I know how special it is to you and rightly so. Plus, Allie may want to wear it someday."

Grace smiled at the thought. "If she does, how much more meaningful to wear the gown worn by both her mother and her aunt?"

"But it's your wedding dress."

"And you're my sister."

Esther brought one hand up to her throat. "You're serious?"

*Jesus, help.* Grace nodded.

Esther straightened in her chair. "It would need to be altered. I'm broader across the beam than you are. Maybe Ben could haul the sewing machine to the farm so I could work on it in the evenings."

Grace shook her head. "I'll do it. I'm sewing several things for Ada in exchange for her husband making sure the house is ready for snow and cold weather." She grinned. "Halstad House may be my responsibility, but I am not eager to crawl up on the roof and check shingles or clean the chimney myself."

"I'm overwhelmed," Esther said. She slapped her hands on her lap. "But if for any reason you change your mind, just say so." She pointed her finger at Grace. "And I mean it, sister-mine."

Grace pushed herself off the chair. *For Esther.* "Come on. Let's take the gown out of the trunk."

---

What was that? Allie could see Mommy in the dark bedroom. She sat next to her on the bed, tickling her chin. Allie yawned wide and rubbed her eyes. "Is it morning?"

Mommy patted Allie's arm. "First snow."

Allie gasped and threw back the covers. She shot out of bed like a jack-in-the-box, almost knocking her mother to the floor. She'd waited her whole life for this.

Mommy giggled and grabbed Allie's hand. "Let's get Auntie Esther."

Allie shivered against the chill as they padded across the room. *Squeak.* They froze at the sound of the door hinges, and a sharp cough from the bedroom next door. Izzy.

Allie's heart fluttered.

Mommy stood still a minute, then gave Allie's braid a gentle tug. "Okay. Shh...no biddies allowed."

Allie bet she didn't even know she said biddies and not boarders.

They crept across the hall like burglars. Even in the dark Allie made a beeline for Auntie Esther's room. Just as Mommy lifted her hand to knock, Auntie Esther pulled the door open.

She held a glowing lantern in one hand. On her head, pin curls peeked out from under a red-flowered scarf. She grinned and gestured with her free hand. "First snow. Come on, ladies."

The three of them set off in their flannel nightgowns and bare feet. Shadows flickered on the wall like prancing fairies as they tiptoed down the front stairs.

A hush greeted them when they stood on the front porch, the silent song of falling snow. A soft layer of white coated the yard and seemed to call Allie's name. Last year Mommy held her the whole time because four-year-old feet would get too cold. But five-year-old feet were a different story.

Auntie Esther set the lantern on the porch.

Mommy looked at them with a twinkle in her eye. She bent her knees and crouched down. "Ready. Set. Go!"

They scampered down the stairs, squealing when their feet touched the crunchy, frozen grass. They threw their arms in the air and twirled round and round, dancing, laughing, singing a silly little tune they made up on the spot. "First snow, first snow. We love you, first snow."

Auntie Esther caught Allie's hand with one of hers and Mommy's with the other. Mommy grabbed Allie's free hand. They spun in a circle with their heads thrown back. Allie stuck out her tongue to catch icy snowflakes that looked like frosting and melted as soon as they landed.

Yippy, yappy Uffda streaked around the corner of the house. He bounded in frenzied loops around them, snapping at the snow in wild abandon. He ran smack dab into Auntie Esther's leg, almost sending her flying tail over teakettle. She laughed so hard she snorted.

Allie's teeth chattered, and Mommy grabbed her waist, swinging her around in one last twirl. Allie's legs flew straight out.

Mommy had to catch her breath. "All right, missy-moo. Time to go in before we turn into icicles."

They hightailed it up the stairs. Auntie Esther snatched the lantern, and they made a mad dash for the warm, welcoming kitchen. Steam rose from milk heating in a pan on the stove. Wool socks, one of Allie's other nightgowns, and soft blankets hung on a drying rack set up at the side of the cookstove.

Mommy dressed Allie in newly-roasted clothes, rubbed her feet, wrapped her in a toasty blanket, and tucked her into the rocking chair. "Snug as a bug in a rug." She kissed Allie's forehead and pulled back to smile at her. "Hot cocoa coming right up."

Mommy and Auntie Esther changed into fresh clothes, and all three of them sat draped in blankets. They warmed their hands on the mugs, sipping creamy hot chocolate.

Allie's feet had been red and cold, cold, cold, but not anymore. She felt comfy-cozy all over—way down to her tummy. *First snow.* She sighed. "Mommy?"

"Mm-hmm?"

"This is the most best day ever."

Grace's stomach tightened just looking at her to-do list. No sooner did she complete one task and cross it off than two more pressing needs leaped onto the tally. She closed her eyes and rolled her shoulders. These last weeks had been crazy with Christmas and wedding preparations. And spending time with Allie? Ha. Except for their first snow frolic, that was almost non-existent. She'd even had to shorten their bedtime routine because of her creeping exhaustion—much to Allie's disappointment. Anxiety and guilt poked their sneaky little heads into her overcrowded schedule, curling their lips like unruly troublemakers. She'd been telling herself if she could get through until Christmas, she'd have time to breathe.

Lydie Sue's coming today was a godsend. Even so, her daughter's dejected expression this morning pricked at her conscience. She had to do something. She scanned the list again. One item leaped out at her—one they could do together.

She peeked into the parlor. Allie and Lydie Sue lay on their tummies under the piano, knees bent, ankles crossed, chattering away. A hodgepodge of toys surrounded them—paper dolls, Maude the horse, Allie's doll Margaret, and the floppy, red-haired Raggedy Ann Lydie Sue brought with her.

"Girls?" Grace stepped into the room. "Would you like to help me gather things for the bridal bouquet?"

"Yeah!" The girls scampered from under the piano and came running. Allie threw her arms around her mother.

Grace pulled Lydie Sue into the hug. "Take your toys to the bedroom, and meet me in the kitchen, okay? I'll get our coats and hats and boots ready."

Grace piled their winter gear into the rocking chair. Just in time. How could two wee five-year-olds sound like a herd of wild elephants bounding down the back stairs? She hoped Isobel and Mary, tucked away in their rooms, weren't disturbed. Oh well, they could plug their ears if they were.

Allie led the way through the backyard to the steps leading to the upper garden. "Don't worry, Mommy. If any bears are up there, I'll thump 'em on the head."

"That's a relief."

"Zowie." Lydie Sue grabbed Grace's hand. "Do you got bears?"

"Never fear, honey. We're safe as can be."

Lydie Sue's forehead creased, and she tightened her grip.

Four inches of snow covered the ground. Ethan had not only shoveled the front and sidewalks yesterday, but cleared this path, too. *Thank you, Ethan Michael Myers.*

When they reached the top, Grace brushed snow off the wooden bench and set an empty basket on it. She clapped her mittens together, sending snow flying. "Okay. We are looking for small pinecones and holly sprigs." She walked to the closest fir tree, examining the layer of white glaze covering its evergreen branches. Bare ground, sheltered by a canopy of lower boughs, lay beneath. "Look here." She waved the girls over. "These are perfect." A scattering of small, tightly packed cones littered the hardened earth. "You two gather some while I scope out the holly."

Lydie Sue swiveled her head left and right. Her forehead relaxed, and she dropped to her knees next to Allie. Both girls giggled, shoveling cones into their pockets as fast as they could. Pockets bulging, they scampered to meet Grace back at the bench.

"Lots of holly by the big cedar stump," she said.

"'Kay!" Allie and Lydie Sue tossed cones into the basket and turned to cross the knoll, kicking clouds of snow high into the air with the toes of their boots.

"Make sure the leaves are green and the berries bright red," Grace called after them.

She determined to send that confounded list to the back of her mind and enjoy this break. She took a deep, bracing breath and let herself revel in the moment.

In no time at all, the basket overflowed with greens, reds, and browns, all sprinkled generously with white. Grace inspected their plunder, shaking loose snow from cones before replacing them. "Nice work, ladies. Now..." She looked at their shiny faces and bright eyes. "It's playtime!"

They romped. They threw snowballs. The air rang with shrieks of laughter.

This reprieve might be short-lived, but it was welcome just the same.

An hour later, Allie and Lydie Sue sat at the kitchen table devouring the last of their egg salad sandwiches. Grace's wicker basket, filled with Christmas bouquet finery, sat near them on the table. Botheration. So did the to-do list.

"Yoo-hoo." Esther appeared at the back door.

"Auntie Esther!" Allie's eyes and cheeks glowed. "We're havin' egg smash sandwiches."

Grace held up a plate. "Would you like one?"

"No thanks. I just finished lunch with Ben." Esther hung her coat and scarf on a hook and removed her galoshes, setting them by the stove. She walked to the table and fingered the basket's contents. "What's this?"

Grace glanced at the girls. "Shh..."

They clapped hands over their mouths, blue and brown eyes dancing.

"It's a surprise." Grace picked up the girls' empty dishes and stacked them on the counter.

"Aha," Esther said. "Well, I learned years ago not to ask too many questions before Christmas."

Grace untied her apron and slung it over a kitchen chair. "All right, missy-moo. Why don't you and Lydie Sue get your dolls and a couple of books? You can take a rest in the parlor. Auntie Esther and I will be up in the sewing room."

Allie and Lydie Sue raced to retrieve their toys.

Grace and Esther followed them up the back stairs. On the landing, the girls ran straight to the hallway leading to the bedrooms while Grace and Esther turned into the former housekeeper's quarters. Fabric packed every available space in the room, along with multiple spools of thread, scissors, packets of needles, and paper patterns. A half-finished plum-colored skirt hung by wire strung from the ceiling.

"Welcome to semi-organized chaos," said Grace. She removed her satin wedding gown from a white bed sheet and handed it to Esther. "I think this will be the final fitting. Then you are all set." She shrugged her shoulders. "As far as the dress goes, that is."

Many tucks, pins, and seam adjustments later, Esther scrutinized Grace. "You look tired, baby sister."

"Hold still." Grace placed the last pin in the bodice, leaned back, and blew out a breath. "The girls and I just had a nice respite. But everything's hitting me again. I feel like the wearies are nipping at my heels."

"You're overworking."

"There's just so much to do. It's never-ending."

Esther stepped out of the wedding gown and slipped into her taupe-colored everyday dress. She cocked her head at Grace. "The wedding is six days away."

Six days. All-out panic surfaced.

"Why don't I stay here until then? I could help out," Esther said.

Grace shook her head. "With Dad's leg still bad, he needs you. I feel guilty enough that I can't do anything to help at the farm. I'd feel even worse taking you away, too."

Esther's eyes quizzed her. A muscle in her jaw tensed. "What's left to be done?"

"First off, like I told you before, I bartered with the Walters for work I needed done here at the house. Since Harv only works for the mill seasonally and Ada has the store covered, he took the time to check the roof shingles and replace a handful. He's cleaned the chimney, changed out first floor screens with storm windows—everything I wanted done before the worst of winter hits. In exchange, Ada commissioned me to do several sewing projects. I still have two left. All the projects are to be Christmas presents. So I'm committed to finishing them this week. And late nights when everyone is in bed is my only uninterrupted time."

Esther sighed and lowered herself into the lumpy easy chair. "Between those jobs and altering this gown, you're all but tied to the sewing machine."

"I need to let out the seams in Allie's best dress." Grace wrinkled her nose. "And lower the hem an inch or so. I haven't finished decorating for Christmas either. Mom and Dad Halstad are due on the three o'clock train this afternoon, and I'd hoped to have it all done before they arrived." She forced a smile. "I want so much for everything to look festive for Christmas and for your wedding. This is the first Christmas in a long, long while that I've made much of an effort. I want it all to be perfect."

"Maybe perfection is too high an expectation. You're just one person, Grace. And besides these extra tasks, you still have your regular chores. No wonder you're worn out."

"What can I say? For some reason, my boarders still expect meals and clean rooms." All of a sudden, Grace let out a whimper and covered her face with both hands.

"Grace!" Esther jumped up and wrapped her sister in a hug.

She would not blubber. She may be overwhelmed, but she could hang on. Right? Grace leaned into Esther's shoulder and wiped away one stray tear. "I'm okay really—or at least I will be. It's just that Allie deserves a special Christmas. You deserve a special wedding. I want it for you both." She heaved out a huge breath.

Esther leaned back to meet her sister's gaze, her jaw set firm. "You are definitely worn out."

"Am I just being a whiny baby?" Grace pulled an embroidered hankie from her pocket and blew her nose.

"Nope," Esther said. "And just to be clear, I'm staying tonight, tomorrow, and tomorrow night."

"But Dad—"

"Ben can talk to Mrs. Jenkins. I'm sure she'll stay."

"But..."

Esther narrowed her eyes. "I'm staying."

Grace sputtered. "I shouldn't let you—"

"I'd stay anyway. Besides which—"

"They're here!" Allie's shout reverberated from downstairs. "And they brought lots'a presents!"

"Heavens to Betsy." Grace grabbed Esther's hand. "Come on."

Silver-haired Ruth and Ivar Halstad, cheeks rosy from the cold, stood by the piano in the middle of a mountain of valises, satchels, totes, and a bulging gunnysack with brightly colored packages peeking over the brim. Ivar held a beaming Allie on his hip and gestured with his hand, coaxing Lydie Sue to join them. She looked at him from under lowered eyelashes and rubbed the toe of her shoe against the carpet.

Grace walked straight to Ruth and enveloped her in a hug. "I'm so glad you're here. Merry Christmas."

"*God jul.* Merry Christmas." Ruth leaned closer to whisper in Grace's ear. "And I'm sorry."

Grace tilted back. "What do you have to be—"

"Well, if it isn't sweet little cousin Grace."

Grace's eyes shot to the door, and her stomach dropped. *Slimy Einar.*

# Seventeen

She didn't mean to. She didn't *want* to. It happened anyway. The moment Pastor Grant uttered those timeless words, tears coursed down Grace's cheeks.

"Dearly beloved, we are gathered here in the sight of God and these witnesses to join this man and this woman in holy matrimony." The minister stood before a tree trimmed with popcorn and cranberry garlands and a colorful collection of Christmas ornaments. Lighted candles flickered on the windowsills, their golden flames mirrored in the frosted panes, set against a backdrop of the dark winter evening. Dressed in a black suit, the elbows of which were worn to a shine by years of use, Pastor Grant held a small book in his hands but rarely glanced at its pages. "Who gives this woman to be married to this man?"

Dad straightened his shoulders. "I do." His voice rang clear and strong. He kissed Esther's cheek. With a smile and a nod, he placed her hand in Ben's. Leaning heavily on his cane, he made his way to the front row seat next to Allie.

"You did good, Grampa." Allie patted his arm. When a few titters emerged from behind her, she twisted around and put her finger to her lips. "Shh…" She turned back to her grandfather and gave him a big grin.

He draped his arm across her shoulders.

Esther and Ben faced each other, hands joined. Grace saw Ben mouth the words, "I love you." Unshed tears filled his eyes.

Grace's heart swelled at the adoring look he gave her sister, the look Esther had waited so long for. But no matter how hard she tried, Grace couldn't prevent the memories from flooding in. Another wedding. The same satin gown. A nervous young couple standing in front of the parlor window. An adoring look from a beloved face. Søren. Her chest tightened, her pulse quickened. *Lord, help me make it through this without falling apart.* She took a deep breath and exhaled. She'd already missed Ben's response to the minister.

Pastor Grant shifted to Esther. "Esther Rose Browne, wilt thou have this man, Benjamin Robert Guff, to be thy wedded husband, to live together after God's ordinance in the Holy Estate of Matrimony? Wilt thou love him, comfort him, honor and keep him, in sickness and in health, and forsaking all others keep thee only unto him as long as you both shall live?"

"I will."

Vows. Rings. The kiss. The announcing of Mr. and Mrs. Benjamin Guff.

The ceremony was beautiful. The ceremony was agonizing.

Grace spotted Allie at the cake table again. Adorable in her fancy white dress with frills at the collar and pleats on the skirt, she stood on tiptoe holding her plate out to Izzy. Izzy. Who would have guessed that Isobel Sommers knew her way around a cake? The unexpected baker and decorator had insisted on making the wedding cake. And what a creation it was. Exquisite. Scrumptious.

Seven flowered china plates loaded with seven kinds of traditional Norwegian Christmas cookies lay scattered over the table as well. Izzy scooped a piece of the elegant cake onto Allie's plate, smiled, and walked to the parlor. Allie plopped a number of cookies next to her slice.

Oh dear. This would not do. Grace walked toward the table, but pulled up short as Pastor Grant approached her.

"Grace." He took her hand and squeezed it. "Halstad House looks beautiful. You outdid yourself. The tree—lovely, absolutely beautiful. And the unusual wooden crèche on the buffet. Where is it from? I suspect a story behind it."

"Søren sent it from France when he first—" She struggled to get out more words. "When he first—" She bit her bottom lip.

The pastor's eyes softened. "I'm sorry. We don't need to talk about it now." He tightened his grip for a moment, then placed a hand on her shoulder. "Healing will come, my dear. I promise."

Grace nodded.

"Yoo-hoo."

At the sound of a voice, Pastor Grant looked behind him, then back to Grace. "I'll talk with you later." He patted her arm and stepped away as Esther and Ben drew near.

Esther threw her arms around her sister, hugging her tight. "Everything was perfect. Everything. The decorations. Your music before the ceremony. Dad walking me down the aisle. The cake. Can you believe it of Izzy? The bouquet. Who would've thought pinecones, holly, crocheted snowflakes, and ribbon could be transformed into something so gorgeous?" She looked at her groom. "And Ben." She grabbed his hand.

Ben stood behind Esther, his characteristic grin wider than ever. "Isn't she a beautiful bride?" He wrapped his arm around Esther's shoulder and kissed the top of her head. His gaze traveled over the parlor, and a chuckle escaped. "Lookie there. Those women have Ethan wedged between them so tight he looks like a sausage in a bun."

Grace followed his gaze. In the middle of the davenport, sandwiched between Isobel and Mary, Ethan looked ready to bolt. Poor guy. Dad sat at one end of the sofa, observing them with a smirk on his face.

Grace turned back to the newlyweds—eyes only for each other, Esther vibrant in the silky gown, Ben looking grand in his new brown suit. Memories stabbed at Grace's heart anew. *Focus.*

Esther gave her a quizzical look and patted her shoulder. "The photographer is ready to take pictures. Why don't you grab Allie and have him take a picture of the two of you?"

"I'd like that." She scanned the room again. "If I can find her.

Will you excuse me?" She made her way toward the last place she'd seen her daughter. With each step, emotion threatened to overtake her. *Hold on.*

Allie wasn't at the goodie table.

Surprised at the force of emotions surfacing, she pushed through the door and into the kitchen. If she could get away from the crowd long enough to pull herself together, she'd be fine. Just a few blessed minutes alone. In the quiet room, she leaned against the worktable, taking slow breaths in and out. Søren's face drifted before her closed eyes. She lifted a shaky hand and rubbed her forehead. "Breathe—"

"Here you are."

Grace opened her eyes and froze. Søren's face disappeared—replaced by that of the last man she wanted to see. Even the sound of his voice made her skin crawl. "Einar. I didn't know you were here."

He walked toward her, an over-bright smile plastered on his face. "I snuck in the back about halfway through the ceremony." He extended a hand to her, frowning when she stepped out of his reach. He hid it right away behind another showy smile.

His eyes traveling over her gave her the heebie-jeebies. She may have only met him a couple of times, but no one could ruffle her feathers as fast as he could. Einar should have been a handsome man. Grace supposed at first glance he was. He wore a snappy three-piece pin-striped suit. His near-black hair, slicked straight back, accentuated high cheekbones and a wide jaw. He should have been handsome. But those eyes. They changed everything. Pale gray, almost lifeless. Weren't the eyes the windows of the soul? She didn't even want to think about what lay hidden inside his soul.

"I regret that I haven't been back this week to see you. I meant to, but my business associates outside of Emmett had things for me to attend to." Einar moved closer. "I've been remiss in seeing you and for that, I apologize." He placed a hand on his chest. "But I wanted to see you before I leave tomorrow, cousin."

"We are not cousins."

"No, but family, surely we are family. And as family, please know you can call on me if you ever need anything. Running Halstad House with all its responsibilities must be difficult for a young woman alone. I would help in any way I can."

"I'm hardly alone. Dad is nearby. Esther and Ben are across the street, and Ethan Myers comes by regularly."

"Ah. Yes. Ethan. Still, if you should ever need me, I am more than willing to help." He reached out his hand again and snagged hers this time. "I noticed tears during the ceremony. Doubtless it brought back memories of your own wedding. The loneliness you must feel after Søren's tragic passing—" He shook his head and made a *tsking* sound. "I sympathize, Grace." He shifted his feet. "You know, I have always held a great fondness for you, and I—"

"Stop." Grace wrenched her hand from his. Heavens to Betsy. "Don't speak that way."

He opened his mouth, closed it with a snap, and held his hands up in mock surrender. "As you wish, but it has been four years. Time to move beyond your grief."

*As if I would ever turn to you in that regard, you weasel.* This was too much. "Excuse me. I need to get back to my guests. And I don't wish to continue this conversation."

Einar clutched her arm before she could walk away. Her eyes met his. She glimpsed cunning and something else she couldn't name. Malice? She'd been annoyed with him all along; now she had an overwhelming urge to slap that stupid grin off his face. Before she put the thought into action, she pulled away. "Excuse me."

He let his hand drop and turned as the parlor door opened.

"Esther said you were looking for Allie?" Ethan strode into the kitchen, his eyes swinging between the two of them. "She and Lydie Sue hid under the table, scarfing down cookies like nobody's business. Don't worry. Esther put the kibosh on that." He placed a hand on Grace's shoulder. "Everything all right in here?"

The corners of her mouth curved up a tad, and she nodded. "Yes. Einar is just leaving."

Einar scorched Ethan with his eyes. When he switched his gaze to Grace, they mellowed somewhat, but the coldness lingered. "Think about what I said. Anything I can do—you only need to ask." He extended his hand. When she tensed, he let it fall to his side.

"I'll be happy to see you to the door," Ethan said.

"Don't trouble yourself." Einar pressed his lips together. "I can find my own way." He gave Grace an abrupt bow and pivoted on his heels. His hat and coat hung from a hook on the wall. He retrieved them, mashed the hat onto his head, threw on the coat, and let the door slam behind him.

Grace lay flat on her back, a puddle of melancholy staring into the darkness. A blissfully quiet house should have calmed her after the flurry of the day's activity and the crush of high-spirited guests. Instead, her mind raced. Nothing would be the same. Esther married. Just she and Allie now. A pang gripped her heart, a fist closing tighter and tighter. Could she do it by herself? Even after Søren died, Esther was there to pick up the slack. Now she would—

"Mommy, my tummy hurts."

Grace rolled to the side of the mattress.

"Mommy!"

A bark-like sound erupted, and Grace shot out of bed. The smell hit her as she lit the lamp. The evidence lay splattered on Allie's nightgown, sheets, and blanket. Grace gagged. She hated that smell. The times this had happened before, Esther had volunteered to take care of the mess. Tonight Grace had to be the grown-up. She steeled herself and brushed tendrils away from Allie's clammy forehead.

"It's comin' again!"

Grace grabbed the bowl from under the pitcher and held it

in front of her daughter. Round two spewed into the bowl. Grace gagged once more.

Allie shuddered and whimpered. "It's too yucky."

"I know, sweetie." She shifted Allie to a sitting position and wiped the muck from her mouth and chin. "Let's get you cleaned up." She grabbed a fresh nightgown for Allie and one for herself. Who knew what state the one she wore would be in once this was through? Carrying her daughter, she made her way to the kitchen.

A quick bath and clean gown for Allie, still green around the gills. Trips up and down the stairs to retrieve soiled bedding and a malodorous bowl. She plopped the wadded sheets, pillowcase, and blanket into the washtub to soak and added Allie's grubby nightgown. The bowl, she scoured till it shone. Finally, her own nightgown joined the sheets in the wash water. After a quick scrub, she donned a fresh one. Back upstairs to make Allie's bed, her feet dragging. One more trip to fetch Allie.

"Rock me?"

Grace nestled Allie on her lap and set the rocking chair in motion with a push of her toes.

"How come my tummy did that?"

"I think you ate too many sweets, and your tummy isn't used to it."

"I'm not gonna eat sweets ever, ever again."

"Mmm..."

Allie rested her head on Grace's chest.

Grace would sing a lullaby if she had the strength. She had none left. A tub full of reeking bedclothes called her name. She couldn't cope with it tonight. She winced at the thought of facing that revolting sight tomorrow morning—Christmas morning no less—but exhaustion engulfed her like a heavy mist.

In no time, Allie's breathing slowed, settling into a gentle flow. Grace laid her head against the back of the chair. Images paraded across her mind. The wedding, memories of Søren, Esther's joy, her own heartache. She thought she'd come so far. Had she been kidding herself? It felt as if she was back to square one—the pain, the grief, the loneliness. How could she bear it? She closed her eyes, then rose and laid a sleeping Allie in her trundle bed, snug under sheets smelling of a hint of cloves.

Sitting on the edge of her own bed, Grace picked up Søren's picture and placed it on her lap. She ran her fingers over his likeness, but the once familiar comfort evaded her. Those smiling eyes were not real. He wasn't there. She set his picture back on the nightstand.

*Be still, and know that I am God.*

Grace slipped under the covers and tugged them up to her chin. "You are God." All the same, she couldn't stop the tears. She tried to wipe them away, but gave up. With a shuddering sigh, she buried her face in her pillow and wept.

# Eighteen

The only explanation was God. She wasn't the same girl who had cried herself to sleep the night before. Grace awoke, if not brimming with hope, at least filled with an assurance she hadn't felt in ages. *Be still, and know that I am God.*

She stretched her arms over her head and got to her feet. Allie's soft, even breathing soothed her as she dressed in the dark. Even the thought of tackling the contents of the washtub didn't dampen her spirits. She'd set her Christmas cinnamon roll dough to rise, then take care of that task.

In the kitchen, she lit the hanging lamp and added wood to the cookstove, ignoring the tub for the moment.

*"Angels we have heard on high…"* Grace sang with a hushed voice while she measured, sifted, kneaded. A knock at the kitchen door interrupted her labors.

Ethan poked his head around the door. "Hey."

"Hey yourself."

"Merry Christmas. I saw the light and thought I'd pop over to see if you needed any help with Christmas breakfast."

Her hands thick in dough, Grace motioned with a lift of her chin. "Come on in."

Ethan hung his coat, hat, and scarf on the hook by the door and deposited his overshoes near the stove. He rubbed his hands together. "What do you need me to do?" He pointed at the washtub. "I suspect that's high on your list."

"I'm not sure you want to attack that. Allie was sick last

night. I got her and her bed cleaned up, but was too tired to deal
with things in the washtub."

"Poor baby. Too many—"

"Sweets? Most definitely."

"I can take care of this while you continue with the cinnamon rolls. I hope that's what you're working on anyway."

"I am." She brought her shoulder to her cheek and rubbed
away an itch. "Are you sure you want to tackle that mess?"

"Someone has to do it. Might as well be me."

"I accept." She grinned. This was no time to be stubborn and
insist it was her responsibility. "You'll probably get a special re-
ward in Heaven for that job."

Ethan chuckled and shook his head. "I'll settle for a cinnamon roll or two. Where is a bucket to empty this out? And the
other washtub and the stand with the wringer?"

"The stand is on the back porch under an old blanket. Everything else is in the mudroom." She flipped the dough and rubbed
that same itch with the back of her hand. "I have water heating.
It must be close to a boil by now."

Ethan headed out the back door, returning with a bucket. He
made several trips emptying the tub.

Grace leaned forward to peer out a window. Ethan walked to
the very back of the yard and poured the bucket's contents into
the far corner. "Bless him, Lord."

When the tub was drained of most of the water, Ethan
washed out the bucket and took it outside. He came back in with
the stand and second washtub. Once that was set up he began
pouring hot water over the bedclothes. "Soap flakes?"

"Second shelf in the mudroom."

He retrieved the box and sprinkled soap into the water. "I'd
better get rinse water heating." Off he went again.

She heard the clunk of the bucket as it knocked against the
door or maybe the wall. After a few minutes, the hand pump at
the well began its rhythmic thumping. She glanced at his coat on
the hook and galoshes by the stove. *He must be freezing in his shirt
sleeves and leather boots.*

His cheeks were rosy, his ears red, but he didn't complain of the cold when he came back into the kitchen and emptied the rinse water into the pots. He made four more trips. "Okay, here we go. Or almost." He looked around the stove area. "Plunger?"

"Mudroom. Very back corner. Might be hiding behind something."

Once he found it, he set to work. Up and down with the plunger, suds rising to the surface, sheets and nightgowns roiling round and round.

Grace transferred the large ball of dough into the brown stoneware bowl that had been her mother's. She set it to rise on the counter by the stove, covering the bowl with a cotton tea towel. Then she turned to clean the butcher-block worktable. "Wasn't that wedding cake Isobel made something else?"

"It was. I could hardly believe she decorated it herself. I guess she has hidden talents."

"It's too bad she's so boy crazy."

"That's what's going on? At least she's harmless."

"I wish the same could be said of Mary."

Ethan looked over at her. "What do you mean?"

Oops. She hated gossip. Should she tell him what Mary said? No. It'd be embarrassing for both of them. "I think she's going through a phase or something. Just keep an eye on her when she's around."

Ethan raised an eyebrow and resumed plunging. After a few minutes, he turned to her again. "I'm moving this week."

Grace's head shot up. Her heart skipped a beat. "You're leaving Emmett?"

"No." His eyes held a question. "I'll be renting a house on Second Street from Dell and Doris at the Bluebird Café. I'm pretty fed up with living at the bunkhouse—too much like being back in the army." He gave her a crooked grin. "Loud snoring and smelly socks hung over the radiators." He gave the laundry a swish. "When I was at the mercantile and Ada mentioned the Blues had just lost their renters, I scooted to the café as soon as I could. They were delighted to get another renter so fast and evidently I passed muster because they had me sign a lease then and there."

Relief flooded Grace's mind. "I've walked past it, of course. What's it like inside?"

"Good condition. Two bedrooms, a kitchen, a front room. And it's furnished. There's a small corral and barn for Prince and a lean-to for my wagon. Everything I need. I'll be close enough to help Ben with a couple projects he has planned. Close enough to help out here, too." He pointed a finger at her and grinned. "And no argument from you, young lady."

Funny. She couldn't think of a single argument. She gave him what must have been a silly smile and shook her head.

Ethan walked to the stove, picked up a pot of steaming water, dumped it in the empty washtub, and did the same with the second pot. "Will you want these rinsed twice?"

She nodded.

Off he took to the backyard for more water to heat. When he returned, she handed him the long wooden tongs she'd retrieved. With them, he grabbed the first thing that came out—Allie's nightgown. He held it up to the rubber rollers and cranked the handle. The rollers grabbed the fabric, squeezing it between them. Soapy water ran back into the first tub. The nightgown moved through until it dropped into the opposite tub filled with clear rinse water. He continued with the other items. "So did Einar give you much trouble?" He swirled sheets in the wash water.

"He apologized for not seeing me earlier in the week, then proceeded to tell me how hard it must be to run Halstad House by myself and how lonely I must feel. He gives me the creeps."

"Hmm..." Ethan's hands stilled, and he lifted his eyes. "I don't trust that clown."

"He annoyed me mostly. Although at the end, he flat out made me mad."

"Like I said, I don't trust him." The expression in his hazel eyes deepened, sending her a message as clear as his words. "Be careful if he comes around again, okay?"

"I will." She wrung out the wet cloth and hung it near the stove. "I just hope we've seen the last of him."

"Yeah." Ethan shook his head and returned to wringing sheets this time.

Just then Allie stepped through the parlor door, barefooted, dressed in her nightgown, and rubbing her eyes. She grinned when she saw Ethan.

"Merry Christmas," Grace and Ethan said at the same time.

Allie yawned and scratched her arm. "Are you making cinnamon rolls?"

"Yes," Grace said. Allie's color looked normal. In fact, she looked like she had bounced right back. "You said you weren't going to eat sweets ever again. Are you sticking to that?"

"Do you think a few bites'd be okay?"

Grace chuckled. "I imagine a few bites won't hurt. Say, Mr. Ethan has some big news."

Allie turned her attention to Ethan.

"I'm moving next week," he said.

All the color drained from Allie's face, and her chin trembled. "But I don't want you to go." She ran to him and threw her arms around his waist.

Ethan glanced at Grace. "I'm not handling my announcement well this morning." He hunkered down and pulled Allie into a hug. "Kitten, I'm not leaving town. I'm moving closer to you, actually. I'll be renting a house about four blocks from here."

Allie leaned back and studied his face. "Really and truly?"

"Really and truly." He returned his gaze to Grace.

She felt almost giddy. "I guess the Halstad women want you to stick around."

Allie lifted her cheek for *Farmor's* kiss.

"*God jul,* my sweet *barnebarn.*" *Farmor* always wore her hair in a braid wrapped around her head like a crown. But today a black beanie lay right in the middle. Colored stitches zigged and zagged and made curlicues all around the hat.

Allie eyed the shapes. "It's beautiful."

"*Farfar* gave it to me this morning. Very special Christmas present," *Farmor* said. "My mamma, she had one just like it." *Farmor* gripped her hand, and they moved to the table.

Allie grinned when Mommy set a platter of cinnamon rolls down. "Come and get it. Breakfast is ready," she said. Mommy told everyone where to sit. She even asked the biddies to eat in the kitchen so they wouldn't be alone on Christmas morning. Allie didn't mind too much 'cause she had Mommy, Mr. Ethan, Grampa, *Farfar*, and *Farmor* there. The biddies seemed happy to eat with them—'cept when they didn't get to sit by Mr. Ethan. They both frowned. Oh well. He sat on one side of Allie. Grampa sat on the other.

Allie was awful glad that right before the wedding, Uncle Ben had packed Grampa up and brought him to his place. That way Auntie Esther could take care of him 'til his leg got all better. When Uncle Ben and Auntie Esther took off for their honeymoon, Mr. Ethan came to stay with Grampa. They were just across the street and she could see them both any time she wanted. Well, mostly.

Grampa said a blessing, then dished Allie's egg, bacon, toast, and a small piece of cinnamon roll onto her plate.

Good thing her tummy felt better 'cause the cinnamon roll tasted yummier than ever. Mommy was the best cook in the world—long as you didn't count biscuits. And Mommy knew just how Allie liked her fried egg—so the gooey yellow elk ran all over the plate. "After breakfast, we get to open presents, right?" Allie said.

*Farfar's* fork stopped in mid-air. "That is what is under the tree?" The corners of his mouth turned up, and his eyes twinkled. "I thought I saw a box or two when I walked past."

Allie shook her head. "There's 'bout 'leventy-seven."

"That many?" *Farfar* chuckled. "*Ja*, we must open them after breakfast."

Allie could hardly wait.

Grace loved this. Her favorite holiday spent with her favorite people. She'd breathed a sigh of relief when Einar hadn't shown up uninvited. After his appearance last night, she'd been a little afraid he might. But everything was just right this morning. Well, almost. Esther and Ben wouldn't return for a couple of days. And Isobel and Mary were not technically family, but she couldn't bear the thought of them sitting alone at the big dining room table while the rest of them enjoyed a cozy Christmas breakfast in the kitchen. Then she'd invited them to join the family in opening presents and, though they'd hesitated, she'd insisted, knowing there was at least her own gift for each of them. The two bi—boarders had appeared thrilled to join them. They'd spent an inordinate amount of time staring at Ethan. And Isobel overdid the giggling whenever he made a humorous comment. Oh well, like she'd said all along, Izzy and her boy-craziness weren't her concern. *Right, Lord?*

For the first time, a tiny sliver of doubt pricked her conscience. Hmm... Well, she'd think about it tomorrow. Right then she had a squirmy daughter who looked like she was going to jump out of her skin. Time for presents.

An hour later, it looked as if a tornado had ripped through the parlor. Ribbons, twine, crinkled paper, and empty boxes littered the floor. One and all admired the gifts spread on their laps.

Ethan had outdone himself with his whittling. For Allie: a beautiful doe and fawn. For herself: a young woman with a braid down her back, arms spread wide. "She looks like you, Mommy," Allie had said.

In return, Grace had knitted him two pairs of wool socks—toes intact.

The Halstads had given her a polished maple Lazy Susan for her kitchen table. That would come in handy. And Dad presented her with a beautiful lace shawl.

Grace had raided her gift drawer. She had a habit of stashing away a few things as she made them or ran across a bargain too good to pass up. After a crocheting kick when she'd come across some extra white cotton yarn, she'd been able to give the boarders each a crocheted doily and Mom Halstad a crocheted collar for her shirtwaist. At the mercantile, Ada said she had extra cash left over from her sewing projects. So she bought shaving cream, a mug, and a brush for Dad Halstad and a pair of suspenders for her father.

The two dads laughed when they discovered they'd given each other the new 1923 Farmer's Almanac.

Allie had drawn pictures for everyone. Some were hard to decipher, but loved just the same. And Allie's gifts? Oh, my goodness. In addition to Ethan's doe and fawn, Grace had knitted her a winter hat and mittens and bought a child-sized china tea set embellished with delicately painted flowers. *Farfar* and *Farmor* gave her a doll bed just right for Margaret. And the piece-de-resistance: roller skates from her grandpa. Allie was chomping at the bit to try them.

Mid-afternoon, Grace took Allie's hand as everyone linked theirs around the overflowing dining room table.

"*Min svigerdatter*, my sweet daughter-in-law, has given this old man permission to lead us in the blessing. Let us sing the table prayer, *ja*?" Mr. Halstad regarded each person. "If you do not know it, the tune is the same as the 'Doxology'. The words are different than our traditional Norwegian table prayer, but we have sung this one for many years. So?" He hummed the starting note.

All but Isobel and Mary joined in.

> *Be present at our table, Lord.*
> *Be here and everywhere adored.*
> *These mercies bless and grant that we*
> *May strengthened for Thy service be.*
> *Amen*

"Oh, can we do it again?" Izzy asked. "I think I can follow along this time."

They broke out in song once more, Izzy shadowing, a beat behind at times, but making a valiant effort. Even Mary chimed in on a couple of the lines.

Izzy clapped her hands together. "I love it. It's beautiful."

"*Ja*," said Mr. Halstad. "*Veldig fint.* Very fine."

Grace viewed the food spread before her. Lots of preparation had been involved, but working with Mom Halstad had been a joy and when she saw each smiling face, she experienced a sense of real contentment. Ham, mashed potatoes and gravy, sauerkraut and sausage, baked beans, green beans with bacon, cranberries and lingonberries, sourdough rolls... My goodness, what a scrumptious combination of Norwegian and American fare. She was glad, though, that the Halstads left the lutefisk at home. Søren had loved that stuff, but she gagged whenever he'd opened a package of the smelly fish.

Allie swallowed a bite of ham. "When is Auntie Esther coming home?"

"She and your uncle Ben should be back the day after tomorrow," Grace said. "Remember, they'll be living at the house connected to the post office, not here."

"I 'member. And that's why Mr. Ethan is staying there now. 'Cause they're gone and Grampa doesn't want to be alone."

Dad snorted. "And he's helping me out with this confounded leg." He glanced at Ethan and gave him a thumbs up. "But I admit I'm enjoying his company."

"And I, his," said Ethan. "We've become quite the partners in crime."

Ruth turned her eyes to Isobel. "Wherever did you learn to decorate a wedding cake as you did? For one so young, you have a wonderful gift."

The young woman blushed. "Thank you. My father's sister has owned a bakery in Spokane for years. Father and Mother were usually busy during the day so instead of going home to an empty house after school, I'd go to Aunt Ellen's bakery. At first,

I just enjoyed the smells and looking at her goodies. Then when I was about ten, she started to teach me how to bake. 'Don't let Dizzy Izzy get in your way,' Father would tell her. But I think she enjoyed it. I know I did." Izzy dabbed the corners of her mouth with her napkin. "I took to it like a duck to water. By the time I was fourteen, we moved on to decorating. That was my real love. Wedding cakes are the biggest challenge, but they're worth it."

Allie wiggled in her seat. "It was the most beautiful wedding cake ever."

Izzy beamed.

"So Spokane is where you grew up?" Grace's dad smeared butter on another sourdough roll.

"Yes. I graduated from Lewis and Clark High School two years ago."

"And how is it you ended up in little Emmett?" Dad took a bite of his roll.

Izzy blushed again. "Father and Mother had a chance to take an extended trip to New York City. They didn't want me to—that is—we all thought it best if I stayed behind. Aunt Ellen got sick about then so staying with her was out. Doris Blue at the café is an old school chum of Mother's. Mother wrote to her, and Mrs. Blue agreed to hire me on." Izzy's hands fluttered, and she smoothed back her disordered coiffure. "But it's a good place to work, and as you know," she looked at Grace, "Mrs. Blue arranged for me to get my room here at Halstad House." She looked down at her lap, then raised her head and gave everyone a nervous smile.

How sad. Nineteen years old and on her own with parents too busy for her. A memory from last week sprang into Grace's mind. Izzy had just returned from her shift at the café. Grace always set the boarders' mail on the small wooden table by the front door. Izzy's face glowed when she saw a letter addressed to her. She almost skipped up the stairs, letter in hand. When Grace served supper that evening, Izzy's eyes appeared red and swollen. Had the letter held bad news from her parents? Maybe telling her they were still too busy to see her at Christmas? If so,

Grace was even more pleased that she'd invited the boarders to join them.

When dinner was over, Mom Halstad brought out a platter loaded with the seven sorts of Norwegian cookies. A few held their stomachs and said they couldn't eat another bite. But they dug in anyway.

Ruth pointed to a cone-shaped cookie wafer. "Allie, this is called what?"

"Crummy kaka."

"Good. *Krumkaker.*"

Allie pointed to one with a fluted edge. "Sand buckets."

"*Ja,* good. *Sandbakkels.* Do you know another?"

"That one's fat mans."

"*Bra,* good. *Fatigmann.* You know more?"

Allie shook her head.

"Let me try." Grace pointed to a rectangular cookie with a delicate design on it. "That one is *Goro.* Then *Serinakaker, Pepperkaker,* and...I always forget this one. Don't tell me." She bit her lower lip. "*Berlinerkranser?*"

"*Ja. Veldig bra.* Well done. It is a long time to remember so many names."

Cookies were sampled. Grace allowed only one for Allie. *No repeat of last night, please.* As she rose to clear the table she looked at Isobel and Mary. "We'll gather around the piano to sing Christmas carols shortly. You are welcome to join us."

"*Ja,*" Ruth said. "We would like it very much."

Both boarders nodded, grinning as they gathered up their plates and flatware.

Grace wondered if she should shield Ethan from the impending boarder ambush or leave him to his own devices. Well, he was a big boy, and she'd be at the piano. She'd keep a sharp eye on Mary, though.

# Nineteen

January blew in a foot and a half of snow, temperatures that hovered just below freezing, and ninety-five pounds of answered prayer.

At the jingling of the doorbell, Grace leaned the carpet sweeper against the wall. "Coming."

The face that greeted her when she opened the front door radiated delight. "Have I found Halstad House?" A diminutive gray-haired woman with sparkly greenish-gray eyes grinned at her. She held a carpetbag in one hand, a pocketbook in the other. "An obliging man at the depot directed me this way."

"Yes, this is Halstad House." Something about the woman evoked an inexplicable desire in Grace to gather her in her arms, give her a big hug, and invite her for tea.

"My name is Mrs. Mae King, and I am hoping you have a room available."

Grace couldn't stop staring. What was it about her? When Mrs. King shivered, Grace came to her senses. "Heavens to Betsy. Come inside." Grace opened the door wider. "Let me take your valise." She set it by the piano. "How about your coat and scarf?"

Mrs. King handed her a red wool scarf. "I'm a bit chilly yet. I think I'll keep my coat on a while longer."

Grace couldn't help herself. She refrained from the hug but—"Would you care for a cup of tea?"

"That would be lovely."

Grace ushered her into the kitchen and gestured to a chair at the table. "Please sit down." She moved the kettle forward on the stove. While the water heated, she retrieved her best china teacups, saucers, and matching teapot from the cupboard. The cookie jar held oatmeal raisin cookies baked yesterday. By the time she poured, Grace had a lovely setting of cups and saucers, cookies, and tea spread at the table. She was going whole-hog and felt almost giddy.

Mrs. King surveyed the room. "Your home is lovely. I've always thought kitchens were the coziest rooms in the house, and it's certainly true here."

"Thank you." Grace sat across from her guest. She swiveled the Lazy Susan so the sugar bowl and creamer were in front of Mrs. King.

Mrs. King touched the maple wood. "A charming piece."

"It was a Christmas gift from my hus—my late husband's parents."

Mrs. King nodded and took a bite of a cookie.

They chatted about the snow, the cold, the train ride. After Grace poured more tea, she raised her eyes. "Where are you from, Mrs. King? And what brings you to Emmett?"

"I've been living in Seattle with one of my daughters." Mrs. King set her cup in its saucer and gave her a sweet smile. "Both my girls live there, but Emily has a little apartment attached to her house. That's where I stay. I've been visiting a dear friend in Spokane and when it was time to go, instead of buying a train ticket for Seattle, I felt a nudge from the Lord to head north."

A nudge from God? "He sent you here?"

"Yes. I stopped at the boarding house in Orient, but the same nudging said to keep going. The moment I stepped into your parlor, I knew this was where I was supposed to be. God lives here."

Tears stung Grace's eyes. *God lives here.* "How long do you think you'd want a room?"

"For a few weeks, I'd imagine. Maybe a few months."

"Your daughters won't worry about you?"

"Not at all. They're used to my ways. And I can always count on them to be praying for me." Mrs. King dabbed her lips with a napkin. "Do you have a room available?"

"Yes. The corner room is vacant. It's furnished, of course."

"I didn't think I'd heard wrong."

Grace shifted in her seat and inhaled. "Mrs. King, please don't be offended, but I had a bad experience with a former boarder, and I promised God I would pray before accepting anyone else. I'd like to give you a yes right now but—"

"Bless your heart." Mrs. King touched Grace's hand. "I wouldn't have it any other way." Just then the good lady stifled a yawn. "Goodness. Excuse me. This morning started quite early."

"You must be tired." Grace brushed crumbs from her fingers and rose. "Let's do this. You rest upstairs in the corner room. In fact, join us for supper and stay the night. Surely God will have shown me what to do by then."

Mrs. King stood and scooted her chair under the table. "Are you certain?"

"I insist." Grace gave her a grin.

"Lead on." Mae returned the grin and followed Grace through the parlor door.

"Allie, why don't you fill this bowl with bread and butter pickles? Then you may take the pickle bowl and the butter dish to the dining room table. That would be a big help." Grace placed a small china bowl on the kitchen table and stayed a moment to make sure her daughter could handle the job.

Allie's tongue protruded from between her lips as she forked pickles from the jar to the bowl. Task completed, she headed for the dining room with two dainty dishes and a broad smile.

Grace returned to the cookstove to finish the last touches on supper. A quiet rap caught her attention.

"Knock, knock." Esther poked her head around the open door. "May I come in?"

"Well, if it isn't Mrs. Guff. Get over here and give me a hug." Grace wiped her hands on a tea towel and clasped her sister in a sweet embrace. "Come sit for a few minutes."

"Auntie Esther!" Allie burst through the parlor door and

threw her arms around Esther. She looked up into her aunt's face. "Guess what? We got a new boarder. I haven't seen her yet, but Mommy says she's nice and loves God and has gray hair. So she must be old."

Esther tugged Allie's braid. "How old do you suppose she is?"

Allie chewed her lower lip. "She's prob'ly 'bout seventeen."

"Hmm..." Esther smoothed a stray curl off Allie's forehead. "Your mommy is twenty-four, and I'm thirty-five. We're much older than seventeen."

"What if she's forty? Willikens. She'd be real old." Allie took her aunt's hand and drew her to a kitchen chair.

"Tea?" said Grace.

Esther shook her head. "No thanks. I need to get back soon to get our supper on the table."

"Why don't you and Ben and Dad come for supper? I have a pot of beef stew simmering, sourdough bread, and sliced cheese. There's plenty for everyone. That way you can meet our new boarder. I think you'll like her. Her name is Mrs. Mae King, and she stole my heart. She's just the sweetest thing."

Esther shook her head again. "I'm anxious to meet her, but let's not overwhelm her with the whole clan just yet. So how did she find Halstad House?"

"God sent her."

Esther pulled Allie onto her lap. "I've got to hear this story."

"I'll give you the short version right now." Grace scooted into the chair next to her sister. "It was pretty amazing. After a visit with a friend in Spokane, she sensed the Lord telling her to head north rather than go home to Seattle. She stopped at the boarding house in Orient first, but again sensed Him urging her to keep going. She told me the moment she stepped into Halstad House, she knew this was where she was supposed to be. She even said, 'God lives here.'"

Esther's eyes widened. "My goodness."

"I know," said Grace. "I wanted to say yes then and there. However, a while back Ethan and I prayed God would send just the right boarder. And I promised I would pray about anyone who came looking to board. I took her up to the corner room to rest, came back to the kitchen, sat in the rocking chair, prayed, and prayed some more. No audible voice, no Scripture popping into my mind. But I got such a peaceful feeling inside. I know we don't live our lives governed by feelings, but this was different. I honestly believed it was from the Lord. His peace. I still believe it."

"Goodness. I can't wait to meet her."

Grace and Allie joined the boarders for supper. Grace sat next to Izzy with Allie on her other side. Mary and Mae King sat across from them.

"Mrs. King, this is my daughter Alice Ruth. She prefers Allie." Grace ladled stew from a large bowl on the table into a soup bowl and handed it to Izzy. She picked up another bowl and ladled more stew into it. "This is Miss Isobel Sommers and next to you, Miss Mary Talbot."

"I met Miss Sommers and Miss Talbot while you were still in the kitchen." Mae accepted the steaming bowl Grace handed her and set it on the table. "Two enterprising young women, bless their hearts. Miss Talbot touches the lives of children every day. Miss Sommers touches the lives of those she comes in contact with at the café."

"Just call me Dizzy Izzy like everyone else," Izzy said.

Mrs. King gave her a dazzling smile. "I would rather call you Isobel. It's such a beautiful name."

Izzy's face took on a thoughtful look. "Mrs. Halstad calls me Isobel, too. You know, I think I like that."

Grace paused a moment. She realized that though she tried to call the young woman Isobel, she thought of her as Izzy more often than not. She'd make an effort to change that.

Mrs. King shifted her gaze to Allie. "I am happy to make the acquaintance of this young lady. And you would rather I called you Allie?"

"Yes, please." Allie buttered a slice of bread.

When everyone was served, they bowed their heads while Grace said a blessing.

Allie swallowed a bite of bread and lifted her eyes to Mrs. King. "Are you a gramma?"

"Indeed I am. I have four granddaughters. The oldest is nineteen. The youngest turned sixteen last summer. So no little ones anymore. But I love all my girls dearly."

Allie sighed. "I sure could use another gramma. Lydie Sue has two of 'em, and I only got one."

"You only *have* one," said Grace.

"Yeah and one more would make me happy for sure."

Mrs. King winked at Allie. "If it's all right with your mother, maybe I could be a sort of honorary grandma."

"An ornery gramma?" Allie's forehead creased.

Mrs. King laughed and shook her head. "No, no. An honorary grandma means even if I'm not in your actual family, I could still act like a grandma." She looked at Grace.

"I think that would be just fine." Grace squeezed Allie's shoulder. "How about that?"

"Goody." Allie took another bite of bread, leaving behind a smudge of butter on her upper lip.

Casual conversation and the clinking of cutlery ensued. Everyone seemed as taken with Mrs. Mae King as Grace was. Charming and genial, she brought a new spark of life to the house.

Mrs. King regarded Grace. "Do you have a church in Emmett?"

"Oh yes, and we love it. Pastor Grant is a wonderful Bible teacher."

Allie chimed in. "And we got the best singing."

"We *have* the best singing," said Grace.

Allie nodded. "Uh-huh. Mommy and Auntie Esther take turns playin' the piano. And sometimes Mr. Ethan brings his guitar. Then we sing real toe-tappers."

Mrs. King glanced at her housemates. Both had perked up at Ethan's name. "Do you young ladies attend the church as well?"

They shook their heads.

Chagrin seized Grace's heart and mind. Why had she never invited them? "Please come with us this Sunday. We'd love to have you."

Isobel's whole countenance brightened. "I'd like that." She sat up straight and smoothed her skirt.

"I will need to check my schedule," said Mary. "But if I am free I will certainly join you."

Grace felt relief flood in. *Forgive me for not asking them before, Lord. If they come, please touch them.* And she meant it. She'd never heard them speak of Jesus. They needed Him just as much as she did.

"Pass the pickles, please," said Mrs. King. "They are delicious." Her eyes gleamed as she looked at Grace, and she gave a slight nod of her head.

Warmth spread through Grace, as if she'd just been given a benediction. Maybe she needed to see things a little differently at Halstad House.

Several nights later, Grace sat in the rocking chair with Allie on her lap. Heated air from the parlor below rose through the floor vent making their bedroom comfortable and warm. She tied the leather string to the end of Allie's braid and set the brush on the table. "Before we read, let's hear your memory verse for Sunday School."

"'Kay. God is—"

*Thud.*

Allie sat bolt upright. "What was that?"

Grace shook her head. "I'm not sure. Sounds like it came from Miss Sommer's—"

*Thud. Eek!*

"Heavens to Betsy, what's going on?" Grace scooted Allie

off her lap. "I better check that out, sweetie. You can look at the pictures in the book while I'm gone."

She headed out of their bedroom and knocked on the door. "Miss Sommers? Isobel? Is everything all right?"

"Get away!"

Grace blinked. *What?* "You want me to get away?"

"No. Not you. Come in, come in!"

Grace inched the door open and peeked inside. Isobel stood on the bed, hopping from her right foot to her left. One hand covered her mouth; the other, at the end of a rigid outstretched arm, pointed across the room.

Grace closed the door behind her. "What's wrong?" Her gaze shifted in the direction Isobel indicated. The curtained window, the oak bureau and mirror, an overstuffed brown chair. All as it should be. "I don't see anything unusual." All of a sudden, from the corner of her eye, she caught movement—something bolting out of a pool of darkness and skittering across the floor straight at her. Without thinking, she shrieked and jumped on the mattress next to her boarder. Her breath came in gulps. But she flushed and placed a hand on her chest when she got a good look at the object of all the ruckus. "A mouse?"

For crying out loud, it was only a mouse. What was she doing acting so silly? "I have a basket in my room. I'll get it and trap the mouse underneath. Then I can dispose of the crazy thing." She moved to step down.

"No." Isobel clutched her arm and pulled her back. "Crazy thing is right. Something's off with that mouse. I tried to trap it, and it came at me like a maniac. That's when I dove for the bed."

"Really? Hmm..." Grace bit her bottom lip and peered around the room. "Well, it's nowhere to be seen now. I'll make a dash for it."

Isobel gaped at her. "Be careful."

Grace jumped to the floor, took two steps, shrieked again, and hopped back on the bed. Good grief, Isobel was right. The mouse was crazy. And relentless. Grace watched the demented vermin run under the bureau again. "This is ridiculous."

"Yes," said Isobel. "But that critter is screwy."

Just then the door squeaked open, and Allie peered inside. "Mommy?" She stepped into the room and closed the door. "What's that?" She pointed at a dark streak headed for her.

"Quick! Up here!" Grace jumped down, snatched Allie's arm, and flew back onto the mattress, dragging her daughter with her. "A deranged mouse."

"A strange mouse?" Allie whipped her head toward the animal. "Want me to thump it on the head?" She started to hop down, but Grace grabbed her.

"No."

Okay. What should they do? In spite of the circumstances, the whole thing tickled her funny-bone, and Grace couldn't help grinning. "Well, this is a fine kettle of fish."

Isobel grinned back and sat down. "Now what?"

Mother and daughter plopped down next to her. Grace ran the tip of her braid back and forth under her chin. After a few moments, she looked up. "I'm going for the big guns."

Isobel's forehead creased. "What?"

"You'll see." Grace's gaze shifted to Allie. She sat on her backside, knees bent, arms wrapped around her legs. Tiny wiggling toes peeked out beneath her nightgown. Allie glanced at Grace, all dimples and smiles. *The little scamp is having the time of her life.* Grace took hold of her daughter's chin. "I'm going downstairs. You stay on the bed with Miss Sommers."

"'Kay."

"Promise?"

Allie nodded.

Grace removed her slippers and crept off the mattress. Sure enough, the mouse made a beeline for her. She threw a slipper at it, tossed the other on the bed, and dashed to the door, grabbing the lantern on her way out.

Ten minutes later, she came up the back stairs lugging the big guns—her inert orange-and-white tabby. Chaucer slouched against her, front paws and head resting on her shoulder. Grace supported him with one hand under his rump while the lantern swung from the other.

When she passed Mrs. King's room, the door popped open. "Are you girls all right?" Mae King wore an ankle-length flannel nightgown with a shawl draped over her shoulders. Her gray curls shot out every which way. Allie might consider Mrs. King old, but the mischievous glint in her eyes told Grace she was up for an adventure.

"Come on." Grace gestured with her head. "We're on a mouse hunt."

"I'm in." Yep. The glint intensified. "Let me take that." Mrs. King clasped the lantern and followed Grace down the hall.

When they reached the bedroom, Grace opened the door a crack. "We're here. Where is it?"

"Back under the bureau," Isobel hissed.

Grace and Mrs. King had no sooner stepped into the room when the crazed rodent dashed out. Chaucer turned his head and tensed.

"Here goes," Grace said.

She deposited the cat on the floor. He immediately went into stalker mode. The mouse stopped in its tracks. Grace swore it studied Chaucer, maybe wondering if it could take him. Not a smart move.

Her normally slothful feline transformed before her eyes. He crouched, his tail swinging from side to side. A low growl emerged from deep in his throat. Then, quicker than lightning, he pounced. The mouse disappeared into Chaucer's mouth, all but its tail, which stuck out from between the cat's lips. Chaucer's whiskers twitched. The next thing Grace knew, the tail followed suit, slurped up like a noodle. One whopping big gulp. One outrageous mouse swallowed whole.

"Ew!" was the collective cry.

Grace clapped her hand to her cheek. "Heavens to Betsy."

"As I live and breathe." This from Isobel.

Allie, on her hands and knees, stared wide-eyed. "Willikens."

Mae patted Grace on her back. "Bless his heart."

Geoffrey Chaucer licked his chops.

Do cats smile?

# Twenty

Willikens. There were so many of them they took up the whole pew. Allie sat on Grampa's lap, combing his beard with her fingers. It looked kind of scruffy. Mommy sat next to her, then Miss Izzy—oops, she liked to be called Miss Isobel now—then Miss Talbot, then Mrs. King, and then Mr. Ethan at the very end.

Everybody had to fly around getting ready for church this morning on account'a breakfast was late on account'a the fire had gone out in the stove. Allie 'bout froze. But they made it on time, and she felt snug and warm now.

She glanced at Miss Isobel. Big round eyes stared straight at the preacher. Down the row, Miss Talbot's were round too 'cept she looked mostly at Mr. Ethan. Allie wished she'd stop doin' that.

"Let's open with a word of prayer." Pastor Grant closed his eyes and raised his hands. "Our gracious heavenly Father, we come to You as Your children..."

Allie stole another peek at Miss Isobel. Eyes squeezed tight, hands clasped just as tight, she looked like she meant business.

Miss Talbot bowed her head, but Allie could tell her eyes weren't shut. They were aimed at Mr. Ethan still. Wonder if he could feel them boring into him like a—

"Allie, this is prayer time. Close your eyes now." Mommy was whispering in her ear. How did she know Allie was peekin' unless she was peekin' too? Allie sighed. Mommy knew everything.

"Can you stand for the singing, Grampa?"

"You can count on it. May take a little longer, but I'll make it." Grampa leaned forward and grasped the back of the pew in front of them. With Mommy and Allie's help, he stood. He smiled down at Allie and patted her head, but his face twisted for a second. Allie knew his leg still hurt. Guess she'd better pray some more.

Auntie Esther played the chords for the first song. "What a Friend We Have in Jesus." Allie loved that song. She liked to think about Jesus being her friend.

Uncle Ben moved to the podium. "Turn to page forty-five in your hymnals and let's sing like we mean it." He waited a couple of minutes while pages rustled, then grinned real big. He waved his hand in time to the music.

*What a friend we have in Jesus,*
*All our sins and griefs to bear...*

They sang three more songs—a couple of them toe-tappers. Then Pastor Grant came back up front. He laid his Bible on the stand and flipped through a handful of pages. When he found his place he scanned the crowd. "Brothers and sisters, I feel compelled this morning to review the gospel that Scripture lays before us. The gospel—the good news—a simple message. Simple in the design set forth by the God of the universe. Yet it cost our Savior everything and, if we choose to follow Him, costs us everything as well."

Pastor told about Jesus dying for our sins and getting put in a rich man's tomb and rising up again after three days. Allie looked around while Pastor Grant carried on with his preaching. She couldn't help looking at Miss Isobel, who used to be Dizzy Izzy. Tears streamed down her cheeks. She gave no notice of anything else. Just zeroed in on the pastor.

When she prayed last night, Mommy had asked God to touch Isobel and Mary. Looks like He was touching Miss Isobel for sure.

Miss Talbot was a diffcrent story. She fiddled with the cuff of her sleeve and squelched a yawn. If she thought Mr. Ethan'd be impressed she had another think coming.

Allie took a closer look at Mr. Ethan and Mrs. King. They stared at the preacher, and tears swam in their eyes. Allie turned to Mommy. Her eyes glistened with tears, too.

Allie's heart did a flip-flop. Maybe she'd better pay attention to Pastor Grant her own self. Willikens.

<hr>

"You, sir, are spoiled." Grace scratched Chaucer's neck. An intense purr emanated from deep in his chest, sending vibrations up her fingers like the tremors of Ben's Ford traveling at a breakneck speed of fifteen miles per hour. "I'm not complaining, mind you. You've earned your bed in the house with your nightly mouse patrol."

Chaucer stretched and slumped to his side.

Grace shook her head. "Sorry but..." She placed her hand under his tummy and tugged. "On your feet. Time to go outside."

Chaucer yawned, rose from the hearth, and followed Grace through the mudroom and out the back door.

Uffda, no doubt overjoyed to see his long-lost companion, bounded toward Chaucer. They performed their daily ritual of touching noses, after which Chaucer sat to give himself a morning spit-bath while the keyed-up canine ran circles around him.

Allie and Mae, all smiles, strolled into the kitchen when Grace returned. Allie, in a brown wool dress, a blue ribbon tied to her long braid, carried a sheet of paper. "This is for Mr. Ethan." She held it up for Grace's inspection. "I know he likes horses. So I drew this. It's Prince. He's eating strawberries."

"Aha. Strawberries."

Mae draped her beige knit sweater over the back of a chair. "Allie told me you are visiting that dear boy this morning—giving him a welcome to his new home. What a wonderful idea." She sat and opened her pocketbook to place two envelopes inside. "Where are my fellow boarders?"

"Isobel is working all day at the café." Grace retrieved a large basket from the cupboard. "Mary said she'd be gone the whole day, too. I think she's calling on friends."

Mae nodded and snapped her pocketbook shut. "I have a quick stop at the post office, but I'll walk as far as the mercantile with you, if you don't mind." She glanced at the basket. "Is there anything I can help you with?"

"Would you give Allie a hand rolling up her picture and tying it with a ribbon? No fold marks that way. I'm heading to the root cellar for a few minutes." Grace carried an empty two-quart glass jar with her. When she returned, eggs suspended in liquid filled the jar three-quarters full. She set the jar in the basket.

"Is that water glassing?" Mae gestured to the jar. "Did you use pickling lime?"

"No. Ada Walters ordered hydrated lime for me. It's much cheaper than the pickling lime and works just the same." Grace walked to another cupboard and looked over her shoulder at Mae. "I have enough lime to preserve farm fresh eggs for years."

She returned to the table with a jar of last summer's raspberry jam and put it in the basket.

"What can I get, Mommy?" Allie danced from one foot to the other.

"A pound of butter from the icebox. There is one wrapped on the bottom shelf."

Allie made a beeline for the icebox.

"My hands are free," said Mae.

Grace handed her the cookie tin. "Ginger molasses cookies. Would you put a dozen in a paper bag? Bags are in the bottom drawer out in the mudroom." She pointed to the back door. "There's a built-in cupboard out there."

Mae headed for the mudroom.

Grace grabbed a loaf of bread from the bread box, wrapped it in a barely damp tea towel, and set it in the basket. Allie brought the butter, Mae the bag of cookies. Grace added them to the hamper. "Okay." She surveyed their bounty. "What do you think? Fresh eggs for breakfasts, bread, butter, jam, cookies—"

"My picture!" Allie grabbed her drawing and handed it to Grace.

"Heavens to Betsy, the most important thing!" Grace gave

it a special place by the raspberry jam. "All set?" She looked between Allie and Mae. They both nodded. "All right, ladies. Bundle up. Let's head across the street."

The familiar jingle of the bell above the door heralded their arrival. "Hi, Auntie Esther!" Allie grabbed the edge of the counter and bounced on her toes.

Ben and Esther stood behind the counter, sorting magazines and newspapers.

Grace set the basket on the floor and stepped to her post office box. A letter lay inside. Hmm... No return address. She stuffed the letter in her coat pocket. "Good morning, Mrs. Guff. Allie and I are off to take Ethan a housewarming gift." She pointed to the basket.

Esther leaned over the countertop. "He'll be thrilled." She gave Grace a half-smile, her eyes twinkling. "Good for you, sister-mine."

"How is Dad this morning?"

Esther's face went from a smile to a frown in a split second. Her forehead creased. "He had a rough night. His leg kept him awake for much of it. But he's resting now."

"Is this normal? What does the doctor say? Is it—" Grace glanced at Allie. She'd run around behind the counter and was busy helping Ben. She lowered her voice. "Does he think Dad's leg will be like this the rest of his life?"

Esther shrugged. "He doesn't really know. But—" Her face brightened. "I firmly believe God is still in the business of miracles."

Grace latched onto that thought. Yes, God was still in the miracle business. She'd cling to Him and keep praying.

Mrs. King walked toward Ben, setting her pocketbook on the counter and removing her two letters.

Ben swung Allie up in his arms and whispered in her ear.

She plunked two stamps down in front of Mae. "Four cents, please."

"Yes, ma'am." Mae laid the letters on the counter. She dug in her coin purse, pulled out four shiny pennies, and handed them to Allie. "Thank you, little postmistress." Her gaze traveled to Ben. "I'm writing my daughters about the adventures their mother is experiencing in snowy Emmett. Bless their hearts. They pray for me faithfully and say they will try to come for a visit in the spring."

"Goody," Allie said. "I wanna meet them." She slid to the floor.

Mae turned to Grace. "Are you ready, my dear?"

"Yes." Grace took Allie's hand and picked up the basket. "We'd better skedaddle. Tell Dad hello."

"Okay," Esther said. "See you soon." Ben and Esther returned to sorting the piles on the counter.

At Walters' mercantile, Grace approached Ada and handed her an envelope.

The shopkeeper wrinkled her forehead. "What is this?"

"A little more to pay against my account." Grace smiled. A lightness spread through her, like the sun's rays peeking through the clouds. It wasn't enough to pay off everything, but enough to make a dent. She spoke with Ada for several minutes. They chatted about church, about the snow and ice, about Ada's new recipe for roast chicken. When another customer came into the store, Grace called Allie away from her examination of the candy jars. "Time to go, missy-moo." They left Mae perusing the mercantile shelves. "We'll see you back at Halstad House," said Grace.

"Welcome to my humble abode." Ethan swung the door wide and beckoned Grace and Allie to enter with a sweep of his hand.

"Mr. Ethan! We brought you oodles of goodies." Allie gave him a hug before peeking behind him. "I like your house." She took off her galoshes and set them by the door. "Wait'll you see what all we got."

Behind her Grace stomped snow off her boots.

"Here, let me take that." Ethan reached for the basket.

"Gladly." Grace handed it over. "Somehow it doubled in weight on the way."

He placed the basket on his kitchen table. Their coats and

scarves he hung on a rack by the front door. "Well, this is it." He rubbed his palms on his thighs. It wasn't as if he had built this house, so why did he feel nervous about what they thought of it?

In the front room, two overstuffed chairs sat near the wall, a curtained window between them. On either side, end tables each held an oil lamp and a smattering of books.

Grace walked further into the room. "What are you reading?"

His Bible lay on one table, a pen and paper next to it. On the other, a Sherlock Holmes mystery, *The Hound of the Baskervilles*, rested next to a volume of Robert Browning's poetry. Grace picked up Arthur Conan Doyle's book, then Browning's. "Hmm...very eclectic." She gave him a soft smile. "I'm impressed."

"Look in the basket, Mr. Ethan." Allie had climbed onto a wooden chair at the kitchen table. She fidgeted like an anxious schoolgirl awaiting the results of an exam.

"Alrighty. What do we have here?" He glanced back at Grace. She grinned and stepped to the table.

He pulled out the jar of eggs and raised his eyebrows. "A science experiment?"

Grace laughed. "It kind of looks like one, doesn't it? Those are fresh eggs preserved in hydrated lime. It's called water glassing. Keep the jar in a cool dark place. Take out however many eggs you need, rinse them well with fresh water, crack them like normal, and fry them up or use them in baking. I made small batches and checked a couple eggs a month or so ago. They seemed fine, but in case you crack one open and it smells bad, just toss it. They should be good, though, and will keep all winter until Dad's hens start laying again."

"Ingenious. My mother never did this, so it's new to me."

"Keep looking, Mr. Ethan." Allie pointed to her drawing. "That's the most 'portant."

He unrolled the paper and whistled. "Is this Prince?"

"Uh-huh. He's eating strawberries."

"Aha. Strawberries." Ethan winked at Allie. "It looks just like him. Thank you, kitten."

Allie beamed. "There's more."

He emptied the items from the basket one by one. "I'll break-fast like a king. Eggs, bread, butter, jam. I have some bacon to throw in." He held up the paper bag. "And cookies for dessert." He set everything on the kitchen counter. "I'll put it all away later. But first, how about the grand tour?"

His bedroom held a bed with a plain metal frame. Even though the only colors in the room consisted of an oil lamp trimmed out with images of red roses in full bloom and a gold-and-brown granny square quilt, the effect was homey, not drab. A nightstand, a pine bureau, a well-used steamer trunk, and hooks on the wall for clothes completed the decor. Everything was neat as a pin.

They walked into the second bedroom next. It was spartan, to say the least. A simple wooden chair pulled up to an equally simple wooden table. That was it. But Allie gasped when she saw what lay on the table. Unfinished figurines spread out across the tabletop.

"Willikens. All your whittling."

"They're beautiful." Grace touched a small sculpture of a bear, her fingers gently stroking its back.

The smile she gave him warmed his heart. "Thanks. It's nice to have a place set aside to work." He shrugged. "That way I can close the door if I make a mess and don't have to trip over things. Hey, how about some tea or cocoa? And maybe a couple of those cookies you brought."

"Yeah!" Allie darted out the door.

Ethan and Grace trailed behind.

Grace rummaged through the cupboard Ethan pointed to and found a small flowered plate. She placed a few cookies on it and set it on the table while he prepared their hot drinks. Then he pulled a box of dominoes from a shelf. The three of them sat at the table, warmed by sunshine streaming through the windows, enjoying the game and each other's company.

After several games, Ethan set the dominoes on their ends in a circle. He let Allie touch the first one. She erupted in laughter as one after another fell.

"Again!"

He was happy to do as he was told.

Two hours flew by—much too fast for his liking. But he couldn't hold back time.

Finally, Grace stood. "As wonderful as this has been, we'd better get home."

They donned their outdoor garb, Allie chattering about his house, the games, and the goodies they brought.

When they said their goodbyes, Ethan watched them walk down the boardwalk, raising his hand in farewell when they turned to wave at him. He sighed and sauntered to the kitchen to tidy up. The house seemed a little forlorn.

*Lord, what do I do with all these thoughts?* He picked up the dishes and placed them in a small enamel tub. He blew out a breath. *I guess I'll go one step at a time and keep trusting You.*

Prince whinnied from the barn, and he smiled to himself. "Okay, Myers. No time to feel sorry for yourself. Get back to work."

Grace was back in the kitchen after putting Allie down for her nap before she remembered the letter in her coat pocket. She opened the envelope and flipped the missive over to see the signature. Her breath caught. Einar.

*What does he want?*

It was all too clear what he wanted. Apologies abounded in the first paragraph. Perhaps she misunderstood his motives? He hadn't meant to offend. The second paragraph made her skin crawl.

I wish to convey my fond affection for you. I have always held strong feelings for you but, of course, had to curb them when Søren was alive. Now that he is gone...well, dear Grace, please tell me I might have a chance to win your heart. I plan to revisit Emmett in a few weeks. May I hold onto the hope that we can spend some time together?

Grace could read no more. She felt tainted just holding the paper. "What a loathsome man. Slimy doesn't begin to describe him." She opened the firebox in the cookstove and threw both letter and envelope into the flames.

Would she really have to deal with him again?

# Twenty-One

Grace stirred the stew and moved it to the back of the stove to simmer. Ethan and Allie sat at the kitchen table, Allie drawing another picture for him, Ethan scanning Grace's ledger so they could go over it later.

The side door opened, and Mae walked through, giving them a wide smile. "Brr...beautiful sunshine, but that wind has a decided nip to it."

Ethan stood. "Mae, it's good to see you."

"You, too, my dear boy. Look." She waved two letters in front of her. "I heard from both my girls today. I can't wait to read these." She turned to Grace. "Your sister sends greetings and... these." She handed her a tin container. "One dozen biscuits."

"Yum!" Allie twirled her crayon.

"You just saved everyone from a fate worse than death—my biscuits." Grace glanced at Ethan. "Although with 'our dear boy' here I probably would have put him to work."

Mae slipped out of her galoshes and placed them near the stove. "While I was at the post office, Esther invited me into their house. What a charming place they have. She asked me back for supper this evening, and I accepted her kind offer." Mae unwrapped her red knit scarf. "I wanted to let you know I won't be here."

"That should be fun. She's a wonderful cook." Using a hot pad, Grace removed the lid from the tea kettle and added more water. "Did you see Dad?"

"Yes. Saw him and spoke with him. His color is better today,

I think. And he walked around a little more than the last time I saw him. I could tell the leg bothered him, but I'm glad he's pushing himself a bit." She stepped to the table and leaned over Allie. "What a lovely drawing."

"It's for Mr. Ethan. He likes my pictures. This one is his new house." She raised her eyes to Mae. "I could draw you a picture if you want."

"I'd like that very much. Bless your heart." She patted Allie on the shoulder, then moved to the parlor door.

"Lunch will be ready in a half hour," Grace said.

"That will give me time to read my letters. I'll see you then." The door swung shut behind her.

Grace's eyes had followed Mae as she retreated through the parlor door in her stockinged feet. "She is such a blessing." She shifted her gaze to Ethan. "Not just because of the extra rent money—though that helps of course. But she's the perfect combination of a fun-loving nature and a saintly mindset. I want to be like her when I grow up."

Allie raised her head. "You are up."

"Thanks, sweetie. I think."

She and Ethan exchanged smiles.

Ethan could watch her all day. Grace looked so cute in her red-and-white checkered apron, her chestnut braid swinging back and forth as she strode between the stove, worktable, and cupboards. Next to him, Allie worked on her drawing. Her tongue peeking out from closed lips must have helped.

Grace looked over from chopping vegetables at the butcher-block table. "I just read an interesting article about our entry into the war. It concerned the Zimmerman message. I remember hearing of it before, but just the basics. I know it was sent from Germany to Mexico and that British Intelligence intercepted it. Didn't some people think it was a hoax?"

Ethan nodded. "At first. It wasn't until the German Foreign Minister admitted the telegram was genuine that everyone's eyes were opened. That admission coming a month after Germany re-sumed submarine warfare was the catalyst. President Wilson's fight to keep our country neutral was a moot point then."

Grace shook her head and made a *tsking* sound. "Govern-ments and wars." Her voice cracked. She cleared her throat. "Did Germany really think Mexico would attack us?"

"From what I understand, they figured if Mexico at least kept us busy, we'd be too preoccupied to ship supplies to England. It would've made it tough for the British to keep fighting. Germa-ny threw in the incentive of Mexico regaining all the land in the Southwest they'd lost in the Mexican-American war back in the 1840s." He glanced down at Allie's drawing and smiled. "Mexico decided against it, but the damage was done as far as Germany was concerned. About two weeks after Zimmerman came clean about the coded message being authentic, that and the sinking of the Lusitania, Congress declared war on Germany."

Allie looked up. "What's a cold message?"

Ethan tapped the end of her nose. "Coded message. It's a message that has a secret code. It's used when somebody wants to give someone else information or tell them a secret, but they don't want anyone else to understand what they're saying." He smoothed a wisp of hair off her cheek. "In this case, the Germans used number patterns instead of words. Once the British figured out which letters matched the numbers, they could read what the message said. In other words, they decoded it."

"So secret codes are bad? They start wars?" Allie scratched her nose with a crayon, leaving behind a brown streak.

"Not always. They can be harmless and fun, or they can be used to warn people. So they can be good, too." Ethan scooted his chair closer to her. "Secret codes can be words, numbers, hand signals, flags, anything, as long as the other person knows the code."

"Like what?"

"Well, I remember one my dad and I had. When I was a youngster, our family sat together at church. Our minister was famous for l-o-o-o-n-g sermons. Long was bad enough for a young boy, but I found them boring as all get out. I confess when I got bored, my mind wandered. Sorry to say I used that time to think up ways to pester my older sisters. They sat between my dad and me, so I couldn't be reached by the long arm of the law—my father. In the heat of the moment I'd forget to mind my P's and Q's, so he came up with a solution: a secret code."

Ethan rested his elbows on the table and entwined his fingers. "If I acted up too much, he'd catch my eye and tug on his earlobe. Once I saw that tug, I knew I was in for it. It meant a trip to the woodshed when we got home."

"Willikens." Allie's mouth formed a perfect O.

"You can say that again. I straightened up right away. Maybe no one else knew what that tug meant, but I sure did."

Allie brushed the end of her braid slowly back and forth under her chin, chewing on her lower lip. Then her eyes fastened on him. "We need a secret code."

"We do?"

"Uh-huh. Me and you and Mommy. For big stuff. Something just for us." She wrinkled her nose. "But let's don't do ear tugs."

"Or woodsheds?"

"Huh-*uh*." She gave an exaggerated shiver.

"Gotcha." Ethan closed the ledger. "How about this? If your mom needs help for something important—say she has a fresh batch of cinnamon rolls and can't find anyone to eat them—you use our secret code, and I'll come running."

Allie scratched her leg. "Cinnamon rolls are kinda 'portant. But what if a bear snuck in the kitchen?"

Slow nod. "I can see where that would be important."

Allie's eyes brightened. "Or the roof blew clean off?"

"Y-e-s, that, too."

She scooted to her knees, placing her hands flat on the tabletop. "Or if the river got all turned around and rolled straight through town." She blew out a breath. "*And* floated our house down Main Street?"

Ethan's mouth twitched. "I don't know what I was thinking. Those things hadn't crossed my mind. But it's best to prepare for any emergency." He placed one arm around the back of her chair and locked eyes with her. "You're right. We need a secret code."

"Goody." Allie clapped her hands. "So what's our secret code?"

"Let's put our thinking caps on."

Her face dropped. "I don't got one."

"Oh, yes you do. It's a pretend cap. It means thinking up ideas." One elbow on the table, Ethan cradled his chin in his hand. "This is the tricky part. It has to fool other people but not make them think we're up to something. Plus it has to be simple enough for us to remember."

Allie cradled her chin in her hand, too.

"Let's use words instead of signals."

"'Kay."

They sat a few minutes.

"Come up with anything yet?" Ethan said.

She shook her head. "Nuh-uh. This is hard."

He stared at the ceiling, then slapped his thigh and swung his head to her. "I've got it. When I was ten, I had a dog named Sargent. My job was to take care of him. Because sometimes I'd forget, my mother always reminded me. She'd say, 'Have you fed Sargent yet?' Or 'brushed him yet?' Whatever I'd forgotten. How about this? If your mom needs my help, she'll say, 'Allie, have you fed Sargent yet?' People who don't know you would see you have a dog dish in your yard. They'd never suspect Sargent didn't live here. What do you think?"

"That'd work." She swung her gaze to Grace. "Mommy, can you 'member that?"

Grace planted one hand on her hip. "Allie, have you fed Sargent yet?"

"Good job. Then I hightail it to find Mr. Ethan."

"Who will come to chase away any bears or put the roof back on." He felt himself beaming.

Grace laughed and pointed straight at him. "Or eat cinnamon rolls."

"That, too." The warmth in his chest grew as he watched

his favorite girls. He was ready and willing to fight for them—against bears or any other disaster thrown at him, rivers and roofs included.

Grace and Mae sat on the davenport in the parlor, the clicking of knitting needles a soothing duet in the quiet. Grace had pulled a small table close. It held two china cups and saucers, steam rising from both, a teapot covered with a blue, white, and yellow tea cozy Ruth Halstad had given her, a small jar of honey, and a miniature silver cream pitcher. Allie, tucked away in her trundle bed, slept. Isobel and Mary had retired to their rooms earlier.

"It's wonderful to see God working in Isobel. Bless her heart, I already see changes in that young woman," said Mae.

"I agree. I haven't heard her gushing over a single handsome gentleman she's met at the café. That in itself is quite a feat. You know, beyond providing for her as a boarder, I've been glad her life wasn't my concern—not like she was family. Hmm. That sounds awfully calloused when I say it aloud. Still, it is heartening to see the changes in her." Grace counted the stitches in her last row. Satisfied, she began the next.

The duet continued.

"Her prayer was genuine, and God is faithful. Like all of His own, He will persevere in transforming her into the image of Jesus." Mae laid her knitting next to her. She bent to stir a dollop of cream and a scant teaspoon of honey into her tea, then relaxed back against the sofa. "Are you sure she isn't your concern?"

Grace spun her head toward Mae. "What do you mean?"

"Well, not in the sense that she is your responsibility. That is God's. And her parents, I fear, have not undertaken to guide her. But that's water under the bridge right now. God will be her guide—a true Father. As for you, maybe He has brought her into your life to reach out to her. I can tell she looks up to you."

"Me? But I have a long way to go in my own relationship with God. And I'm certainly not a good Bible teacher."

"That's not what she needs you to be. Between the Holy Spirit, the Word, and Pastor Grant, those bases are covered. No, I think she needs you to be her friend, to show her that she is valuable. You don't have to fix her or preach to her. Ask God to show you little things you can do to support her or lend a helping hand."

A twinge of guilt hit her when she realized she'd been so wrapped up in her life, it had never occurred to her to reach out to Isobel as a friend, not just a boarder. It was a new thought. "I could do that." She nodded. "Yes, I'll ask God to show me those little things."

Mae patted Grace's hand. "Good girl."

Grace fixed her eyes on her yarn and kept them there for a good five minutes. She wanted to bring up something that had weighed on her heart for so long. Something she'd not been able to talk with anyone about. "Mae?"

"Hmm?"

"Did God make it happen? Søren dying, I mean."

Mae sighed. "I don't have all the answers, dear one, but I've known grief and loss also. I am on a journey of faith just as you are, and I have learned a few things along the way. Though God is sovereign, I do not believe He *made* your husband's death happen. For reasons we don't understand, He *allowed* Søren's death. I believe there is a difference." Her eyes softened. "And in His sovereignty, He can take even the most painful things in our lives and somehow turn them into good, just as He promised in His Word. He can give us beauty for ashes. Again, we don't understand how. We see the moment; He sees the whole—eternity past through eternity future. He promises *weeping may tarry for the night, but joy cometh in the morning.*"

Tears sprang into Grace's eyes. She slipped her gaze to Mae again and gave her a tremulous smile. "It is better, but still hard."

"I know, dear. But this is not the end of your story. God promises to make all things new." She shifted in her seat. "One thing I have found helpful is to practice thankfulness. Instead of ruminating on painful circumstances, losses, or what could have been, I try to focus on God's provisions. I'm not talking about denying our grief or sorrow. In the throes of our reeling emotions, we can often only cling to Him and cry out for help. He understands. He walks us through the dark valley. But somewhere down the road, we are able to see a glimmer of hope—no matter how small. At that point, we can begin to thank Him for little things. I call it my thankful list. It reminds me I really do have things to be thankful for. You can do the same and teach Allie to do it also."

"What a wonderful idea." Grace knew Mae was Mrs. King, but there didn't seem to be a Mr. King. She spoke only of two daughters, their husbands, and four granddaughters. The grief and loss she spoke of must be the pain of widowhood. "Well, I am thankful for Allie. And Esther and Ben. Dad, too."

"And your young man, Ethan?"

Grace grinned. "He's not my young man, but I am definitely thankful for his friendship."

"What else?"

"Being able to get a few debts paid off. Boarders." She shot Mae a huge smile.

"And Halstad House? Many women who lost husbands in the war were not so blessed. They had to move back in with their families—or if they had none, were left homeless."

"Yes. Even though it can be a struggle to make ends meet and to keep things running, I am thankful for Halstad House. A home for Allie and me."

"I would also encourage you to spend time in the Word every day if possible. As busy as you are, even if it's only for a brief time, you'll be feeding your soul and mind. I find it vital to keep me on track."

Grace nodded slowly. "Before I go to bed would work. Allie is asleep, chores are done, and the house is quiet." She fixed her eyes on Mae. "I can add your encouragement to my thankful list."

<hr/>

She may as well begin as she planned to carry on. She sat in the rocking chair, the oil lamp's warm glow lighting her Bible. Allie's smooth, steady breathing calmed her. She removed the bookmark and read from where she had left off last week. Proverbs 3. When she reached verses five and six, the words seemed to leap off the page. *Trust in Jehovah with all thy heart, and lean not unto thine own understanding: in all thy ways acknowledge Him, and He will direct thy paths.* Her heart stirred. "Thank You. Lord, help me to trust You."

She managed ten minutes of reading until the words blurred on the page. She placed the bookmark in the Bible, closed it, and set it on the table. Yawning, she leaned back and shut her eyes. And recited her thankful list.

# Twenty-Two

*N*o, *no, no. Not Einar.* Wash day—the hardest day of the week—
and *he* showed up. Grace had begun her day at 4:00 to get
a head start before breakfast. Mary and Isobel were gone for the
day. Grace had peeked in to see Mae and Allie ensconced in the
parlor on their hands and knees playing with Maude and the
whittled doe and fawn. Margaret, with her smooth porcelain face
and unblinking eyes, sat propped against a piano leg supervising
the whole affair.

Grace had the kitchen to herself. She was dealing with the
weekly mounds of linens—sheets, pillowcases, towels, and washcloths. Washing, scrubbing, wringing, rinsing, more wringing,
and hanging them outside in the cold, all while hauling buckets
of water from the well and boiling it on the stove.

She blew out a breath. Einar stared at her through the window in the side door, giving her that insincere smile that turned
her stomach. Much as she wanted to, she couldn't ignore him.
She opened the door. "Einar. I didn't know you were in town."

"Grace. It's nice to see you." Those pale gray eyes roamed
over her from head to foot. Twice. "Beautiful as always."

His look made her skin crawl. Besides, she knew she looked
like the wreck of the Hesparus—wild tendrils of hair bursting out
from under her red bandanna, cheeks no doubt flushed crimson,
sleeves rolled up revealing unladylike work-toughened hands,
her oldest dress and apron wet and stained—beautiful indeed.
Could she get away with slamming the door on him?

Too late. He stepped into the room.

"I don't really have time to visit. I'm in the middle of laundry as you can—"

Einar held up a hand. "No need to entertain me." He hung up his coat and hat, but gave only a cursory swipe of his boots on the throw rug. He walked to the stove, tracking snow and water in his path.

She sighed.

"May I help myself to a cup of coffee?" Einar rubbed his hands together over the cookstove.

"I don't have any made up."

"Tea then?"

"Einar, really I—"

The corners of his mouth turned down. "I came all this way in the cold. Surely you can grant me a few minutes."

Grace bit her bottom lip.

"We can have a nice, cozy chat. Just the two of us," he said.

*Drat the man.* Well, the sooner they talked, the sooner he'd leave. "Five minutes is all I can spare."

His smile broadened, and he sat down in a kitchen chair.

Grace moved to sit across from him.

"Tea?"

She stopped mid-step. Her stomach tensed, but she walked to the cupboard and pulled out one mug.

"You'll join me, won't you?"

She grabbed a second mug and in short order had fresh tea on the table. Only then did she seat herself.

"Isn't this comfortable?" Einar inhaled and leaned back into the chair. "I don't suppose you have any of your delicious cookies handy?"

"Sorry. I won't bake until later this week."

"Doesn't matter." He looked around the room. "I'm surprised Søren didn't put out the effort to modernize in here. This could be a nice place."

Grace stiffened. "Søren was a good provider."

Einar frowned and shook his head. "Now, now, Grace. I'm not criticizing my cousin. I'm only thinking of you."

She licked her lips. As much as it galled her, she chose to ignore the condescension in his voice.

After a sip of tea, Einar pointed to the pile of laundry on the floor next to the washtub. "You work too hard. You'll wear yourself out if you're not careful. I'd hate to see you lose your youthful bloom."

*Lovely thought. Thanks for mentioning it.* Grace brought her mug to her lips. She caught herself jiggling her leg, a sure sign she wanted this over—fast. She stilled it before she spilled her tea.

After taking several more sips, Einar set his mug on the table. "Did you receive my letter?"

Grace nodded.

"Good. I want to apologize again. I am truly sorry if I insulted you." He flicked a piece of lint from his trouser leg. "However, I have an excuse for my conduct. Two actually." He leaned forward. "Let me explain. First of all, as I wrote, I have held feelings for you for years." When Grace shifted in her seat, he held up one hand, index finger pointing to the ceiling. "Hear me out, Grace. I could say nothing before, but now...well, I have hoped that we could come to an understanding. As I said, you work too hard. I could make your life much easier at Halstad House. Imagine what it would be like to have people waiting on you hand and foot. I know you'd like that."

How would he know what she'd like? And she didn't care for where this conversation was headed. Her heart beat faster. "Einar—"

He rushed on. "Secondly, I confess I was hit by jealousy. I got the impression Ethan Myers thought he had the right to protect you—though why you would need protection from me is a mystery." He raised both hands palms up. "I admit I am as susceptible to the green-eyed monster as the next man, particularly when it comes to you."

"This is ridiculous." She plunked her mug on the table. "You have no need to be jealous."

Einar arched his brows.

"That's not what I meant to say. No one has any need to be jealous. I am—or rather I'm not—" She brushed her hair away from her forehead.

"So you and Ethan aren't engaged?"

*Engaged?* She drew in a deep breath. "Ethan has always been—"

Einar's eyes bored into her.

Why did those eyes rattle her? "Ethan is...that is to say, he's my—or rather he's not—" This wasn't coming out right. And she felt like she'd just thrown Ethan under the horse cart.

Einar steepled his fingers and slouched into the back of the chair. "I knew you'd never be so imprudent. What could Ethan Myers possibly offer you?" He studied her for a moment, then moved as if to take her hand. "It gives me hope."

Grace yanked her hand back before he could grab it. Hope was the last thing she intended to give him. Heavens to Betsy, what was wrong with her? She didn't seem able to put two intelligent words together to make a coherent thought. She clasped her hands in her lap. "Einar, I don't want to give you any false hope. I don't think of you in that way."

His eyes narrowed. "It's my job to convince you otherwise."

Her heart thumped against her ribcage. Years ago, Grace had seen a magazine article containing a photograph of the author's butterfly collection, each lifeless insect pinned to a board, wings spread in a macabre caricature of flight. She'd found it morbid. Now, she found their plight too real. Pinned.

Though Einar's eyes revealed the same dullness she'd seen before, something else glinted there. Did he enjoy seeing her discomfort? She wanted him out of her house. She jumped to her feet and spluttered, "I have to get back to work."

A vein throbbed in Einar's temple and his nostrils flared. "I took time out of my busy schedule to see you. The least you could do is to be hospitable." He pressed his lips together and took a deep breath.

She could almost see him tamp down his emotions.

He rose and straightened his collar. "Well, I've given you plenty to think about." His toothy smile appeared.

She wanted to slap it off his face.

Einar waggled a finger at her and spoke in a ridiculous sing-song voice. "I won't give up. You know what they say about a man in love."

Grace didn't know and didn't care. She stared at him, both hands tightening into fists.

"All right." He dropped the sing-song. "I'll say no more now. I'll save it for later—when you're not so busy." He sauntered to the door, taking his coat and hat from the hook and flashing his sickening smile again. "I'll be seeing you."

When the door shut behind him, Grace shuddered and brought her hands to her cheeks. *Argh... What a tiresome man.* She squared her shoulders, strode to the washtub, and grabbed a pillowcase. She attacked it as if it were the offender, scrubbing so hard her knuckles were in danger of drawing blood.

A half hour later, with her muscles aching and sore, Grace was down to two sheets and two pillowcases in the rinse tub. Once they were wrung out and hung outside, she'd only have the towels and washcloths left.

A knock at the door. *That man had better not be back.*

Ethan poked his head inside.

Oh, good. She greeted him with a smile. "Hey."

"Hey yourself." He grinned, waving an envelope. "I was at the post office, and Ben entrusted me with this letter for Isobel."

"Just put it on the table. I'll move it to the front hall when I'm done here." Grace wiped her forehead with the back of her hand. "Are you playing hooky from work?"

"No." Slinging his coat and hat over the wall hooks, he bent to unlace his galoshes, but zeroed in on Grace hovering over the washtub. He wiped his boots on the throw rug, checked the bottoms, wiped again. "Mr. Emmett sent me into town to pick up some parts at the mercantile. Harv said they should be delivered in an hour or so. Ada said more like two or three. We'll see who's right. But Boss said to hang around till they come in, so here I am."

He walked to the cookstove and picked up two buckets from the floor. "Be right back." When he returned, he poured water into pots on the stove. Then he helped Grace wring out one of the sheets. "How's your dad doing?" He pulled the sheet from the roller bars and dumped it in the waiting laundry basket.

"Esther said the last couple of nights have been rough. The pain kept him awake. He hates to wake her, but it's been bad enough that he's been forced to. She and Ben took turns alternating hot and cold packs on his leg and supplying him with white willow bark tea and soda crackers. He refuses to take any more laudanum."

"I'm sorry to hear it's been so tough. Don't give up, though. We'll keep praying."

"Thanks." Grace rubbed the side of her neck and cranked another sheet through the wringer.

Allie and Mae's voices drifted in from the parlor. Outside the kitchen window, two chickadees hopped along the porch railing, darting back and forth through the clematis vine. The fire crackled in the cookstove, spreading its warmth through the room.

Ethan threw her a sideways glance. "I wanted to warn you that Einar Brevik is back in town."

Grace caught his gaze. "He was here earlier insisting on talk and tea." She placed her hand over her heart. "He declared his undying love for me."

A muscle twitched under Ethan's cheekbone.

She grabbed a pillowcase with the wooden tongs and lifted it to the roller bars. "I wanted to punch him."

"What a piece of work." He shook his head. "I wouldn't trust him as far as I could throw him."

"He gives me the heebie-jeebies. I can't figure him out, and I don't want to."

An odd look crossed Ethan's face. "Steer clear of him. Like I said, I don't trust him."

"I'll do my best."

A few minutes later, Ethan picked up the wicker laundry basket full of clean, wet sheets and pillowcases. "Do you need fresh water for the towels?"

"No. This is fine."

"Gotcha. I'll hang these outside." He took off for the backyard.

Grace plunked the towels and washcloths into the suds, grabbed the plunger, and set it in motion. Up, down, up, down. By the time Ethan had returned with an empty basket, she was cranking the last load into the tub of clear rinse water. She glanced up. "Let's hang these inside on drying racks."

"Point me to the racks, and I'll set up while you wring out that load."

"They're in that little nook between the stove and the side door."

An old quilt, folded several times, lay nestled against the stove's rock hearth. Ethan toed it. "I assume this is the illustrious Geoffrey Chaucer's bed?"

"You bet. He's earned a place inside at night. You heard about our mouse adventure, didn't you?"

"Oh yeah." Ethan's muffled voice came from the nook.

"We haven't had another one, as far as I know. It's fine by me, but Allie is disappointed. Chaucer's prowess was impressive, to say the least."

Ethan prepared the wooden racks, fitting the ends together. "Believe me, if I have a mouse infestation—"

"Hey, we had one mouse."

"Well, if I have one or an infestation, you'll find me at your door, hair standing on end, shaking in my boots, begging to borrow your one-gulp champion."

Grace hooted. "Somehow I doubt that, but I'm liking the picture it conjures up." She hauled the basket over. "You know, mister, I was very brave. Didn't shake in my boots once."

He tipped his head toward her. "Thought I heard something about shrieking and jumping on the bed."

"Hmm...guess there was that." She giggled.

Two pairs of hands made quick work. In less than ten minutes, Grace hung up the last washcloth. She placed her hands on the small of her back and stretched. Before she could grab the now-empty laundry basket, Ethan took it from her.

"Why don't you sit down?"

Grace shook her head. "I need to clean everything and put things away. Then get lunch ready."

He pointed a finger at her. "You sit. I can take care of clean-up."

"But..."

He raised an eyebrow and pulled the corners of his mouth down. "Sit."

She sat. "All right. I feel like I'm shirking my responsibilities, though."

"Yeah, I've been wondering about that. Laying around all day eating chocolate bonbons..."

Grace sputtered and broke out into a full-fledged laugh. When she caught her breath, she wiped tears from her eyes. "Silly boy." She moved a stool in front of the rocking chair and put her feet up. *Ah...*

Ethan set down the basket and stepped to the cupboard. He took out a china cup and saucer, scooped tea leaves into a mesh tea ball, set it in the cup, and poured just-boiled water over it. He added a dab of honey and laid the cup and saucer on the little table next to her.

"Thanks." She smiled at him. "For everything."

He frowned at the two mugs on the kitchen table.

Grace wondered if he suspected one belonged to Einar.

He picked them up and placed them in the white enamel dishpan after throwing their left-over contents into the slop pail. Turning to the washtubs, he rubbed his hands together. "Better get crackin'."

Grace drank about half her tea, comforted by its sweet warmth and by Ethan's sweet gesture. She glanced at him and laid her cup down. Leaning back and closing her eyes, she let the dull background clatter lull her. *Night and day. Those men are as different as night and day.*

Grace woke to find that Ethan had gone, leaving a spotless kitchen behind him. "Bless him, Lord." She stood and rolled her neck and shoulders. Time to slice bread, cheese, and the last of the ham. Maybe open a jar of peaches?

Giggles erupted from the parlor.

"Hey, you two," she hollered. "Lunch in five minutes!"

# Twenty-Three

Allie sucked in a breath. "Uffda, be careful." He barked and moved forward, but she grabbed the scruff of his neck and pulled him back. "Stay." He plopped his rump on the ground. She knelt in the snow, slipped off her mittens, and tossed them down.

Uffda snatched one and darted away.

"Hey. Give that back!"

Uffda's tail-end disappeared around the corner.

Allie sighed. "Mommy isn't gonna like that." She turned her eyes back to a small yellow blossom peeking through a tiny patch of green. With bare fingers, she pushed away damp blades of grass and...*easy does it*...picked the flower. "Willikens," she whispered. Cradling it in both hands, she ran for the house.

Mommy opened the back door after Allie had kicked it three times with her booted foot.

"Look what I found."

Mommy put a hand to her cheek. "The first buttercup. Beautiful. It's so delicate and dainty." She kissed the top of Allie's head and closed the door behind them. "Why don't you show Auntie Esther while I find a tiny cup to put it in?"

Allie headed for the kitchen. "Look." She held the teensy flower up. "From our very own yard."

"Land sakes, first of the year." Auntie Esther grinned wide. She sat at the kitchen table with a cup of tea and a plate of ginger cookies in front of her.

Mommy brought over a wee glass bottle with water in it.

Allie set the buttercup inside. She propped her elbows on the brown-and-yellow plaid tablecloth and stared.

Mommy and Auntie Esther stared, too.

"Spring's on its way," Mommy said. She touched Allie's shoulder. "Come on, let's get your coat and boots off. Auntie Esther has something to tell you."

"'Kay." Allie took off her coat and scooted into a chair.

Mommy knelt to untie Allie's boots. She gazed at her daughter's red hands. "Where are your mittens?"

*Uh-oh.* Mommy made those mittens. Allie's tummy tightened. "Uffda ran off with one. My hands were too full. The other one's outside."

"Hmm..." Mommy's mouth got a little firm. "Well, I'll see if I can find them in a bit. Right now—" She glanced across the table. "Esther?"

Auntie Esther held out her hand. "Allie, come sit on my lap."

Allie scrambled up and looked in her aunt's eyes. They shone like stars, all bright and twinkly. "What are you gonna tell me?"

"Something wonderful." She smoothed a loose curl from Allie's face and tucked it behind her ear. "I'm going to have a baby."

Allie gasped. "A baby?" She threw her arms around Auntie Esther's neck and hugged her. Hard. "Is it a boy or a girl?"

"We won't know for quite a while. Not until after your birthday. Probably sometime in the fall—October."

"Willikens. Is that forever away?"

Auntie Esther draped her arm over Allie's shoulders. "These things take time."

Allie nodded and chewed her bottom lip. "Will your tummy get bigger and bigger and then the baby pops out?"

Mommy and Auntie Esther looked at each other and grinned.

"Well, it's kind of like that," said Auntie Esther.

Allie bobbed her head. "I saw a calf get borned at Grampa's farm. Bossie's tummy got this big." She spread her arms as far as they would go.

Auntie Esther snorted. "I hope I don't grow as big as a cow, missy. And I definitely want to be in my own bed, not on a barn floor."

"Oh, Grampa put straw down."

"Still... Well, we won't have to worry about that for months."

Allie leaned her head on her aunt's shoulder. "A real baby. It'll need someone to play with. I can help. I'm a good helper."

"That would be nice."

Allie sighed. "I wish Mommy would have a baby."

"Maybe someday." Auntie Esther slipped Allie's braid behind her back. "She needs to be married first."

"Oh yeah. She's gotta have a husband." She tipped back so she could look into her aunt's face. "You know that big black bull in Mrs. Jenkin's field? Grampa said he's the baby calf's daddy. He kept hanging his head over the fence, gawking away at Bossie. He must'a snuck out'a the gate one night so they could get married."

Auntie Esther cleared her throat.

Mommy's face turned kind of pink. "Yes, well..."

Allie kissed her aunt's cheek. "I can't wait for the baby." She jumped down and took another gander at her buttercup. All sorts of glad filled her up inside. She skipped to the parlor door.

But Mommy's whisper was still in earshot. "Heavens to Betsy, Esther. I don't know if I should thank Dad or chew him out."

March pried winter's grip loose, sending a warm Chinook wind and three days of rain to melt away the snow. All that remained were a few small drifts on the shaded north side of the house. Sights, sounds, and smells of spring emerged. Just this morning Allie had bounded onto Grace's bed as the sun peeked through the window.

"Mommy, the birds are singing hallelujah!"

Even the mud and all the extra clean-up it entailed couldn't dampen Grace's spirits. This bright new season had always invigorated her. Today was no exception. Now, with night approaching and the day's chores almost complete, she headed up the back stairs carrying newly-laundered linens.

"Miss Sommers? Isobel?" Grace rapped her knuckles on the door.

"Come on in."

Grace opened the door to find Isobel at the oak bureau, attacking her face with a washcloth like a crazed warrior. Suds spewed over her cheeks, forehead, the bodice of her dressing gown, and the throw rug beneath her. Her ever-disheveled hair flew every which way.

*Oh my. Esther would have a conniption fit if she saw her rubbing her skin raw like that.*

"I brought fresh towels and washcloths."

"Thank you. Just set them on the bed." Isobel continued her ablutions.

*A conniption fit to be sure. Well, it's not my concern what she—* Grace pulled up short. Wait. Was this one of the little things Mae spoke of? She chewed her lower lip. Well, the worst that could happen was she'd get tossed out on her ear. "You know, I could give you a few pointers on the best way to wash your face if you'd like. But if you'd rather I minded my own business, just say so."

Isobel grabbed the towel and wiped the soap from her eyes. "If my skin could look like yours, I'd be thrilled."

"Really?"

Vigorous nodding. "I've always admired it. I thought scrubbing would make mine smooth and clear like yours."

Grace moved forward. "Actually, I don't use soap on my face."

"You're kidding." Isobel threw the washcloth in the sudsy water as if it had suddenly burst into flames.

"Why don't you wring out the washcloth and set it aside. Then dump the soapy water in the slop bucket and refill the bowl with fresh water from the pitcher. While you rinse the soap off, I'll tell you how I learned to care for my face. And my hair, if you're interested."

"Yes." Isobel's eyes lit up like a child's on Christmas morning.

Grace sat on the edge of the bed. This wasn't so bad. "I'm not sure if you knew, but my mother died when I was born. Esther was only eleven, so Dad's widowed mother moved in to help out. She lived with us for nine years. I wasn't interested in learning about any of this stuff, but by the time Grandma Browne passed away, Esther was almost twenty and she had learned a lot. In turn, she taught me Grandma's secrets when I got older."

Isobel dried her face with a hand towel. "But if you don't use soap..."

"Ah—secret number one: cold cream. Ada sells it at the mercantile, but I usually make my own. It works just as well and saves money. Before bed, I splash my face and neck with warm water, then pat it dry—never rub—with a soft hand towel. Then I work cold cream into my skin with my hands—gentle strokes. I wipe it off with a tissue or a soft damp washcloth and rinse with clear water until the cream is gone. Now comes secret number two: cold water. Esther says to splash my face with water as cold as I can stand. She does it ten to twelve times every night. I confess I fudge about that number at times. But I try to do at least five. Esther says the cold water tightens the pores. The last step is cold cream again. I smooth it over my skin and, voila, I'm done. Grandma told Esther to always go to bed with a clean, moist face. It will pay off as we age. I remember Grandma's lovely skin, so it must have worked for her. And Esther's is the same."

"It's working for you, too." Isobel gave her a slow nod. "I'll pick up cold cream right away."

Grace pushed herself off the bed. "Be right back." She ran downstairs, then to her room, returning with a dollop of cold cream in a small glass container and a pint-sized mason jar filled with water. She walked Isobel through Grandma's arsenal of beauty secrets. Only once did Isobel falter. The jar of water Grace brought from the icebox was just that—icy. At the first splash, Isobel squealed and reared back. Grace giggled and patted her shoulder. "I know. But as Louisa May Alcott says, 'Let us be elegant or die.'" From the small jar she scooped out a bit of cold cream. "Smooth this over your face."

A few minutes later, after Isobel's task was complete, Grace turned her toward the mirror. "You have beautiful skin. Look."

Isobel blushed. She swiveled her head from side to side. "It looks so much better, Mrs. Halstad."

"Please. Call me Grace."

"Grace. I really like it." She turned away from the mirror. "Now, how about my hair? It's a disaster."

"Grandma Browne's hair secrets coming up." She walked to the bed and sat down. "Come sit by me." She patted the spot beside her.

Isobel lowered herself to the bed.

"Brush your hair every night with Grandma's secret method. Use a soft-bristled boar's hair brush. This is a special kind of brushing—to spread the oil from your scalp clear down to the tips of your hair. One hundred strokes."

"One hundred?"

"Yes. Slow and gentle, going over one section before you move on. First, the top while you're sitting or standing, then lean over and work from underneath." Grace fingered Isobel's hair. "It will bring the shine out. Because my hair is long, I braid it before bed so it doesn't tangle. Yours being shorter, I'd recommend pin curls."

"I pin my hair up every night or tie it with rag wraps. But it frizzes when I brush it out in the morning."

"Try using a wide-tooth comb or just finger-comb it. That's what Esther does. Gentleness is the key." She leaned closer to examine Isobel's hair. "You have enough natural wave to make it lay nicely, I think. If you'd like, I can come to your room in the morning and help you comb it out."

"I'd like that."

"And on Saturday evening we can go over Grandma's hair washing secrets."

Isobel beamed.

Grace jumped to her feet. "Well, I'd better take care of my own routine." She waved as she reached the door. "Sleep well."

By the time she returned the next morning, Isobel had

cleaned her face—ten cold splashes included—and smoothed cold cream over her skin. She was just removing the last pin curl.

"Let's finger-comb it," Grace said. She demonstrated how to do it so it didn't frizz the hair.

Isobel finished the job.

"I was right," Grace said. "I can see the natural waves. Look how it lays."

Isobel peered into the mirror. Tears sprang into her eyes. "Oh my. Thank you, Mrs.—thank you, Grace."

"You're more than welcome." She followed her instincts and leaned in to give Isobel a hug.

At breakfast, Allie stared at her tablemate. "Willikens, Miss Isobel. You're beautiful."

Mae's eyes twinkled. "She's right. You look lovely, my dear."

Isobel looked down at her lap. When she raised her head, a smile tugged at the corners of her mouth.

# Twenty-Four

Giggles and groans. Plenty flitted around the dining room table, along with a squeal from Allie when she'd earned ten more points.

Grace tweaked Allie's nose. "You're getting altogether too good at this, young lady."

Allie beamed. "Me and Miss Isobel are tied."

They turned the dominoes blank side up and shuffled them around the tabletop.

More giggles and groans continued until Isobel plopped down her last domino. She held up her hands. "I'm out."

A frantic inspection of tiles showed no more plays. Grace tallied the final points. "Isobel, you're the winner."

"What? I never win at games."

Mae chuckled. "Bless your heart, you did this time."

"Good job!" Allie clapped and bounced her heels against the chair legs. "We were real close, but you won fair'n square." She jumped down. "Mommy, can I go outside and play?"

Grace nodded. "I'll call you when lunch is ready."

Allie hightailed it out the door as Mary Talbot strolled in.

"Mary," Grace said. "You missed a rousing game of dominoes, but come join us anyway."

"No thanks." Mary slipped out of her boots and laid her valise by the front stairs. "I have things to do. I'll just brew a pot of tea to take to my room if you don't mind."

"Of course not."

Mary padded to the kitchen.

Isobel regarded Grace and Mae with puzzled eyes. "Something strange happened last night."

Mae tilted her head. "Yes?"

"When I went to bed, I picked up one of the books on my bedside table. *The Stranger's Shadowy Secret.* I started to read, but didn't make it more than a page when I felt kind of funny, like I was fidgety inside. That's the only way I can describe it. And the words didn't catch my attention like they normally do. In fact, I found them pretty sappy. I set the book back on the nightstand, blew out the light, and pulled the covers up to my chin. The fidgety feeling went away. I closed my eyes and slept like a baby all night long." She caught Mae's eye. "What do you think it means?"

"This is wonderful." A look of delight crossed Mae's face. "I believe the Holy Spirit spoke to you."

"What?"

"I suspect those books you've been reading aren't what you'd care to read aloud to either of us?"

"Gracious, no. But they seemed exciting before. What changed?"

"You did. You are a new creature in Christ. He's transforming your mind, making you what He always intended you to be."

Isobel's eyes widened. She breathed in a deep breath. "Do you mean God Himself communicated with me?"

"I believe He did. Not in an audible voice, but He got His point across." Mae's eyes twinkled.

"As I live and breathe." Isobel placed a hand on her chest. "God took the time to speak to me. Me." A tear trickled down her cheek. She wiped it away with her finger.

"Dear one, He is your Father. Your Heavenly Father who is always there. He promised to never leave you or forsake you."

"He promised?" Isobel's forehead lifted so high her eyebrows disappeared under newly coiffed bangs. "My Heavenly Father."

Grace rubbed her arm. "I don't know about either of you, but I have goosebumps."

"Something else happened. This morning at the café, a gentleman came in for breakfast. He was really handsome and took the time to talk to me. He even asked me to join him. A few weeks ago, I'd have been in a tizzy and acted like a silly schoolgirl. This time I didn't. I felt as cool as a cucumber. I thanked him, but said I needed to get back to work."

Grace wanted to jump up and down and shout hallelujah or at least clap Isobel on the back. She did neither, only said, "I'm so proud of you."

Mae's eyes twinkled again. "As I said, God is transforming you."

"As I live and breathe." Isobel looked at Mae. Her brows furrowed. "I have a question."

The kitchen door opened. Mary stepped into the parlor, holding a tray with a teapot and cup and saucer in her hands. She smiled as she sauntered past the table.

"I still have a strong desire to marry," Isobel said. "Is that wrong?"

Mary's steps slowed.

"Oh no, my dear." Mae shook her head. "I believe that is from God as well. Unless it changes, you can trust Him to lead you." She gave Isobel a gentle smile. "He gives us instructions from His Word we must heed, though. But they're not burdensome. They are for our protection."

"What kind of instructions?"

Mary's footsteps hesitated, came to a full stop.

Grace grinned. *Good. She's getting Mae's teaching even if she didn't plan to.* Mary hadn't mentioned anything about Ethan for a good long while. Grace hoped that was a thing of the past. Grace admitted she struggled from time to time when she thought about their conversation, but she did have an honest desire for Mary to know Jesus.

"The most important as far as marriage is not to be unequally yoked. I'll look up the reference and show you this evening," Mae said.

Isobel's forehead creased. "What is unequally yoked?"

"God instructs you to marry a Christian man. Not one who

just claims to be a believer, mind you, but who shows it by his life, his pursuits, his words. What misery you'd find being married to someone you couldn't share the most important part of your life with—your faith in and love for God. You would be unequally yoked."

"That makes sense. And I can understand how it is for my protection. Would you both..." Isobel cleared her throat. "Would you both pray that I will do that? I mean, not run after just anyone but, well, I guess follow where God seems to be leading? And to discern if a man is a true believer?"

"Of course we will." Two sets of heads bobbed.

Mae placed her hand on Isobel's. "Make sure that he is growing closer to God and of course, that you are, too."

Mary resumed her walk through the parlor and up the stairs.

Just then Allie's head poked through the open parlor window. "Hey, Mommy."

Uffda planted his front feet on the windowsill and barked.

"What is it, sweetie?"

"That Einar man is coming up the road. He's riding a horse. Looks like he's headed here." She and Uffda pulled away from the window and ran across the porch toward the back steps.

*Einar.* Grace's face fell. Her heart sank.

Mae's mouth tightened. "I don't trust him. I think he's up to no good. Would you like us to stay with you?"

Isobel nodded with vigor. "We sure will."

"No. Thank you, though." Grace took a deep breath to calm her heart. "I got so frazzled when he came before I must not have made myself clear. I need to do that this time. I want there to be no doubt of my feelings, or rather my lack of them as far as he is concerned. And will you pray for me? That I'll be as—as—"

"Cool as a cucumber?" Isobel grinned.

"Yes. And that I can make myself crystal clear."

Mae rose. "Isobel dear, let's take the back stairs up to our rooms."

The two of them headed for the kitchen.

Mae swirled around, pointing a finger at Grace. "We'll be

praying for wisdom and God's protection. If you need us, don't hesitate to call."

They disappeared through the door.

A horse's whinny, footfalls on the front steps.

*God, give me strength.*

Einar's face appeared at the front door window. His smile could curdle milk.

Grace squared her shoulders and marched to the door. "Einar. Come in."

"Grace, lovely as ever." He strode into the room like a man on a mission. After taking off his hat and overcoat, he dumped them in her arms.

She draped them over the front stairs banister.

His smug gaze roamed the room before settling back on her. Dressed in a brown-and-white plaid suit, a white shirt with a starched collar, and a dark brown vest, Einar no doubt would shine as a dapper young man in the big city.

Grace found him ostentatious, overdressed for a country town like Emmett.

He looked down at her, his voice dripping with melancholy. "I fear things were left in some confusion the last time I was here. Household duties had you preoccupied. Perhaps you got the wrong idea, or perhaps I didn't make plain my thoughts or my heart. Either way, today I've come to clear things up and offer you something I'm convinced will make you very happy."

"We do need to talk. I want to make things unmistakable with—"

He held up a hand. "Wait. Let me have my say. You'll understand then."

Grace gave a quick nod. She led the way to the dining room table and seated herself.

Einar parked himself in the chair next to her, eyes boring into hers. "Will you listen without interrupting or jumping to conclusions?"

Grace took a couple of calming breaths. She leaned against

the chair back. "As long as you will do the same for me. Listen to what I have to say. Respect any decision I make."

His gaze flickered over her face. "Fair enough. I can be generous, especially since I am certain you'll be won over."

Grace clasped her hands in her lap. "All right. Go ahead."

Allie's laughter and Uffda's excited barks drifted through the window. Those everyday sounds plus the knowledge that Mae and Isobel prayed for her upstairs quieted her thudding heart. Anchored her.

Einar smoothed his already slicked-back hair. "I told you of my feelings for you. Now I want to show you in a tangible way." He reached inside his suit coat, slipping out a green package tied with a darker green bow. He laid it on the table before her. "This is for you. A token of my deep affection."

Grace stared at the package.

He pushed it closer. "Go ahead. Open it."

Grace ran her fingers over the paper. As smooth as satin. Curious as to what lay inside, she untied the ribbon and opened the package, careful not to rip even a corner. She gasped and put a hand her throat. Her gaze whipped to Einar.

He smiled and dipped his head.

An elegant necklace rested on creamy white fabric, a gold heart studded with six perfect rubies. "It's exquisite." Grace touched the jewels, then clasped her hands back in her lap.

"Try it on." Einar moved as if to stand, but Grace shook her head. Sitting again, he leaned closer to her. "This is what you could expect if you were my wife."

"Wife?"

"Wife." Einar leaned closer still. "I want to make your life easier. I want to take care of you and your little Annie."

Grace's eyes narrowed. "*Allie.*"

"What?"

"Her name is *Allie.*"

"Of course, of course. Slip of the tongue is all." He inhaled a deep breath, sat back, crossed his arms, then crossed one leg over the other. "I have money to shower you with gifts like this.

Money enough to provide a better life for you. No more boarders. No more scrimping to make ends meet. No more long days of work, work, work. I could afford to hire a couple of servants to work for you." Confidence oozed from him. "I think we should get married as soon as possible. What do you say?"

She didn't even hesitate. "I say no."

"No?" He tugged at the hem of his vest with crisp movements. Lines creased his forehead.

"No."

His nostrils flared. "After all I offer you?"

Grace sighed. "It's my turn now."

Einar uncrossed his arms and tapped his fingers on the tabletop.

"I will not marry you, Einar. Be clear on this. I know what it is to love someone enough to marry them. It takes a special kind of love, not to be taken lightly. I do not feel that way about you, nor do I see my feelings ever changing." She shook her head. "No, I will not marry you."

His feet hit the floor with a thud.

"Remember, you said you would respect any decision I made," Grace said.

"I didn't expect such a foolish one, though."

Glancing at his face, she wondered how she ever thought his eyes devoid of life. They sparked now. Something sinister lurked there.

His lips pressed together in a tight frown, forming deep creases around his mouth. "You are refusing me?"

"I am refusing you." Grace wiped damp hands on the skirt of her dress.

The sound from deep in his throat could only be described as a growl. He grabbed the package, wrapped it loosely, and stuffed it inside his coat. "I won't be repeating my proposal." He jumped to his feet. "You may never receive another. Most certainly not one as good as mine. You'll waste your life at Halstad House, probably wither away into a frumpy old widow." He waved his hand at her when she started to rise. "Don't bother. I'll see myself out."

At the door, he slung his overcoat over his arm, not bothering to put it on. He slammed his hat on his head. His violent moves almost toppled the lamp on the hall table. It tipped, but righted itself. He slammed the door and was gone.

Grace sat in a daze. *Just like that, it's over?* She'd said what she needed to say. Done what she'd needed to do. *Thank You, Jesus.* She placed her hands on her cheeks, almost giddy. *Thank You.* She stood, ready to call her prayer warriors down to share the news.

*Yip.*

"Hey!"

Thumping sounded on the porch. Grace rose, but before she could get there, Allie's blond head disappeared down the stairs.

*What in the world?* Grace dashed out the door.

Einar stood by his horse, jamming the green package into a saddlebag. He raised his eyes toward Grace. "That mangy mutt of yours..."

The mangy mutt lay in a whimpering heap five feet away.

"You hurt Uffda!" Allie rushed to Einar and gave his leg a swift kick.

He grabbed her shoulder. "Why you little..."

"Let go of her!" Grace ran toward them.

With a snarl, Einar shook Allie and shoved her backward.

She crashed into her mother.

Grace caught her and steadied her. She glared at Einar. "Don't you ever, *ever* lay a hand on my daughter again."

"Yeah! And not my aminals neither!" Allie shook her fist at him.

The front door slammed. Mae and Isobel appeared like avenging angels—heads held high, arms crossed, eyes glowing.

Chaucer rounded the corner of the porch and padded to Uffda's side, hunkering down in the dirt, body flat against the ground.

The dog roused himself. Shaking his head, he turned to Einar, yipping and lunging at him.

"Uffda!" Grace snapped her fingers.

He vented throaty doggie grumbles, but complied, sitting at her feet. Chaucer followed.

Einar scorched Grace with his eyes. "I suggest you learn to control your beasts. And your kid."

"And I suggest you climb on your horse and ride out. You are not welcome here."

"And don't come back." Allie stomped her foot.

"Allie, go up on the porch, sweetie." Grace steered her toward the steps.

Allie trudged up the stairs to Mae and Isobel.

Grace pivoted and met Einar's gaze. His menacing gaze. "I mean it. You are not welcome here. Ride out."

"With pleasure." His words spewed venom. He snatched the horse's reins from a short hitching rail. The horse reared back with a whinny and Einar yanked the reins. "Hold still, you brute."

Low growls emanated from both Uffda and Chaucer as they lay near Grace.

Einar climbed into the saddle. "You've seen the last of me, Grace Halstad. I hope you're happy." He jerked the reins, wheeling his horse around. With a violent kick to the animal's side, they bolted away.

Grace shaded her eyes, staring after him. Once he'd disappeared from view, she headed for the porch and lowered herself to a stair before her legs gave out. Mae and Isobel placed their hands on her shoulders. Allie laid her head in Grace's lap.

Chaucer and Uffda ascended the steps. Chaucer leaned his head against her thigh, purring as she stroked his back. Uffda whimpered and pressed his nose to her knee.

"How are you doing, buddy?" She scratched under his chin, and he licked her fingers.

Grace tucked a loose curl behind Allie's ear. "And how are *you* doing, sweetie?"

"I'm okay."

Grace laid her hand on Allie's head. "Did Uffda bite Einar?"

"Huh-uh." Allie raised herself up and pulled one bent knee close to her chest. "He lifted his leg and wee-weed on him."

Grace sputtered, caught her breath, sputtered again. A sharp laugh burst out. She buried her face in her hands, letting laughter have its way. Snickers behind her spurred on more laughter. At last, she sat up straight, wiping tears from her eyes. She patted Uffda's head. "Good dog."

"We showed him, didn't we, Mommy?" Allie grinned and rubbed Uffda's neck with long, even strokes. "He won't come back, I bet."

*Lord, may it be so. I see a wickedness in him.* "How about we go inside now? I want to put arnica on Allie's shoulder. And after that donnybrook, I think we could all use some sustenance." Grace took a last look down the road before she rose. *Lord, please keep him away.*

# Twenty-Five

"Mm...mm." Grace ran her tongue across the spoon, smacking her lips when she'd licked off every morsel of frosting. "Best ever. You were a big help."

Allie dipped her finger in the bowl and brought the last creamy, chocolatey bite to her mouth. "Yummy."

"Are you up for visitors?" Esther held the side door open while she poked her head inside.

"Absolutely." Grace scooted her chair back.

Esther stepped into the kitchen, a package tucked under her arm. "Look who I brought with me."

"Grampa!" Allie rushed to meet them.

Grace grabbed her arm. "Hang on. Let's not knock him over."

Dad moved into the kitchen, breathing hard, balancing himself with his crutches. "Sweet pea, your old grandpa is a little out of breath. And still kind of unsteady on his feet. How about I sit down and you hop up on my lap?" He lowered himself into a kitchen chair and leaned his crutches against the table. He grimaced when Allie climbed onto his lap, but his lined face slowly relaxed.

Grace and Esther exchanged glances.

Allie placed her hands on either side of Dad's face. "Does your leg still hurt?"

He nodded. "Afraid so."

Tears sprang into Allie's eyes. She rested her head on his chest, stroking his snowy beard.

Grace gestured for Esther to sit. "You're still looking a little green around the gills. Let me get tea for us and milk for Allie. She and I just finished frosting a chocolate cake. What do you think? Want to try some?"

"This morning sickness is for the birds." Esther frowned. "It's sure put a damper on eating. Unfortunately, it's not only in the mornings." She sighed. "Maybe I could try just a bite."

Grace placed everything on the table. She patted Esther's arm. "It will be worth it. I promise."

"I know." Esther tipped her head. "Keep reminding me when I complain."

Dad snorted. "Well, I don't have morning sickness. What I will have is a whole piece of chocolate cake, thank you very much."

Allie leaned into the tabletop. "Me neither. And me, too."

Esther brought a small forkful of cake to her mouth, sniffing when it reached her nose. She blanched and set the fork back on her plate. "Maybe not today after all. I'll stick with tea. It goes down well. My energy is better; it's just this food thing." After two or three sips, she placed her package on the table. "I brought something to show you. They were delivered this morning." She pulled out a dozen sepia-colored photographs.

Grace bent over them. "Your wedding pictures." She sorted through them one at a time, oohing and awing over each one. "They are so beautiful, Esther."

Allie jumped down. "Can I see?"

"Whoa. Wash your hands first. No sticky frosting fingers touch these." Grace grinned and covered the photographs with both hands.

Allie skipped to the kitchen counter. When she returned, she kept her hands behind her back and peeked at the photographs. "Willikens. You look like a fairy princess."

Esther planted a kiss on Allie's cheek. She reached over and extracted the bottom picture, holding it in front of Grace. "This is one of my favorites."

Grace gazed at the photograph of Allie and her. She brought her fingers to touch their images. "It's lovely."

"And it's yours." Esther's smile lit her face. "My wedding gift to you. For giving me such a beautiful wedding."

Grace held the picture for Allie to see.

Allie bent closer. "Hey. We look kinda like fairy princesses, too." She lifted her eyes. "Don't you think so, Grampa?"

He swallowed his last bite of cake. "Yep. You take after my side of the family." He winked at Grace and Esther. His eyes twinkled like the dad of old.

Then the twinkle faded, and he cleared his throat. "I have some news and you may not like it, Lily Grace."

Grace glanced at Esther.

Her sister shrugged one shoulder.

"I sold the farm to Tom Jenkins."

Grace gasped and brought a hand to her throat. "You sold it?"

"Daughter, this leg isn't healing like it ought to. It's been months, and I'm still on those confounded crutches." He blew out a breath and leaned against the chair back. "Anyway, Tom wanted to buy it. The time seemed right."

Grace placed her hand on his arm. "You just took me by surprise." She blinked hard to hold back the tears.

He tugged her braid. "I know, honey. I'll miss it, too."

She swiped at a tear that had spilled over. "But where will you live? You know, Esther's old room is still empty. You're welcome—"

"No," Esther piped in. "He's been using our spare bedroom and we won't need it for quite a while even after the baby comes. We'll shuffle things around and Dad can move in there."

"Thanks for your offer, Lily Grace." He patted her hand and gave her a tender smile. "But I'm not up to navigating those stairs of yours." His smile broadened. "And I doubt you'd want me lolling around on your davenport all day long and disturbing your boarders."

Grace inhaled and blew the breath out. *Lord, help me to accept this change. I know it's best for Dad.*

"Got a question for you, though." The twinkle was back in

Dad's eyes. "Are you interested in the chickens? If you are, you'd better get 'em while the gettin's good."

She squared her shoulders. Now, the chickens. Aha! Could she ever use them! "You bet I am. I'll have to fix up the old chicken coop in the back corner of the yard. It'll take work, but I definitely am interested in being able to step out the back door to gather my own eggs."

"I figured so. I know how many you go through since I've been your supplier for years. How about Bossie?"

Allie had been quietly listening to their conversation. Now, she jumped up and hopped on one foot. "Bossie, Mommy, Bossie."

Grace shook her head. "I'm afraid not. The chickens are one thing, sweetie, but milking the cow morning and night, seven days a week, is too much work to add."

"'Kay. But anyway the chickens will be fun." Allie switched to hopping on the other foot.

"I didn't think you'd want her," Dad said, "but I thought I'd ask anyway. I know how much milk you go through every week, too. Maybe you can work out a deal with Tom."

Grace sighed. "We'll cross that bridge when we come to it." Another weekly expense on the horizon.

Dad and Esther had been gone over an hour. Allie napped upstairs. Grace sat at the kitchen table. Her heart ached at the thought of no more farm in the family. She knew it made sense. It was too much for Dad to handle alone, especially with his leg like it was. But still... She rubbed a hand over her face. So many changes. She supposed she should grab the ledger and determine how paying for milk every week fit into the budget. They used a lot of milk every day. Plus she needed extra to make butter and cheese. *Lord, I can't think about it now. It makes my head spin.*

The parlor door opened, and Mary inched into the room. "Are you busy?"

"Not at all. Come sit with me. Would you like a cup of tea? We have chocolate cake."

Mary shook her head and sat next to Grace. She looked at her lap. When she raised her eyes to meet Grace's, a slight smile played on her lips. "I'd like to pray that prayer that makes one a Christian."

Grace's heart leaped. "Oh, Mary, that's excellent." She glanced at the wall clock. "Mae should be home in an hour. Or we could run down to the church when Allie wakes up. Pastor Grant is likely there. Either of them could show you the right verses and lead you in a prayer."

Mary shook her head. "I'd like you to do it."

"Me?" Grace's heart fluttered, and she had to wipe suddenly sweaty palms on the skirt of her dress. "I've never done it before. They'd be so much better."

Mary shifted in her seat. "Please?"

Grace swallowed. Hard. *Help.* "All right." She rested her forearms on the table and folded her hands. She closed her eyes for a couple of moments, trying to gather thoughts. *Okay. Here goes.* "You've heard of John 3:16, right?"

"Yes."

"*For God so loved the world, that He gave His only begotten Son, that whosoever believeth on Him should not perish, but have eternal life.* You and I are part of the *whosoever.* We all are."

"What does that mean, part of the whosoever?"

"I don't know the Bible references. I can look them up tonight and write them down for you. But I'll try to remember. All of us have sinned. The Bible says we have fallen short of the glory of God. And it says the wages of sin is death. God sent His Son Jesus to pay the price for our sins since we couldn't. He reached down to give us that free gift, but we have to come to Him." Heavens to Betsy, did that make any sense?

Mary looked hard at her, eyes unblinking. "You mean we have to meet Him halfway?"

"Not halfway." She was making a muddle of this. "He came

the whole way. We just have to believe it and ask Jesus to forgive us. We have to receive the free gift He's given."

Mary stared out the window.

Chaucer lay sprawled across the porch rail where a beam of sunshine fell on his tawny fur.

*Lord, I maybe haven't said everything clearly, but would You speak to her anyway?*

Mary turned back to Grace. "Will you help me?"

Grace's heart raced. This was the thought that unnerved her. What if she didn't do it right? But she squared her shoulders. "I'll say the words and you repeat them after me, okay?"

Mary bowed her head and closed her eyes. She brought clasped hands under her chin.

"Dear Jesus..."

"Dear Jesus..."

"I need You."

"I need You."

Word for word, Mary followed Grace's prayer. "Forgive me. I know I've sinned and I can't pay the price for my sin. But You already have. Please come into my heart. Make me Your child. I want to belong to You now. Thank You. Amen."

Mary looked up. "That's it?"

"The Bible says *As many as received Him, to them He gave the right to become children of God.*"

"So I'm a Christian now?"

"Did you mean everything you prayed?"

"Yes, but I don't feel any different."

Grace cringed a little. "I don't really know how that works. Maybe it takes time? But it would be good to start reading your Bible. Do you have one?"

"Yes. It was my mother's."

"Good. And talk to God just like you talk to your friends. And I hope you'll come to church, too. Pastor Grant is a good Bible teacher." Grace laid her hand on Mary's arm. "I don't mean to overwhelm you, but sometimes in the evenings we sit around the dining room table while Mae talks about the Bible or things she's learned. We'd love to have you join us."

"Maybe." She looked at Grace again. "So I'm a Christian now?"

"Yes. You've been born again."

Mary stood. "Thank you. I think I'll go to my room and see if I can find Mother's Bible." At the parlor door, she glanced back. "Thank you, Grace." Her footsteps tapped across the parlor and up the stairs.

Grace blew out a breath and laid her head on her forearms. *Jesus, if I made mistakes, would You right them?*

At supper that evening Mary told the others about praying with Grace and how she was a Christian now.

Isobel whooped and ran around the table. She threw her arms around Mary. "I'm so happy for you. Hey, we're sisters now." She turned her eyes toward Mae. "Right?"

Mae grinned at them both. "Yes. Sisters in the Lord, seeing as how you are His children. Oh, Mary, I am happy for you, too. It's the best step you can take in your life. God will guide you on your journey. He will always love you, never leave you or forsake you. You are His now. I am delighted."

Mae took a peek at Grace and gave her a quick nod.

Relief flooded in, calming her stomach as well as her mind. After supper cleanup, she might ask Mae to help her find those verses. She ought to write them down and keep them in her Bible, in case anyone else wanted her to pray with them. But she had to confess she hoped it wouldn't be for a while. It was a scary business.

But worth it.

Allie slept in her trundle bed, her breathing soft and gentle as her chest rose and fell. Doves cooed outside the bedroom window. Esther's homemade candle glowed on the bureau, its vanilla scent diffusing throughout the room. Grace held the photograph of Allie and herself. She gazed at it and smiled. Then she placed it beside her and shifted her gaze to Søren's framed photograph on the nightstand. His handsome face, the face she knew so well. Would it begin to fade from her memory if she didn't see it every day, every night?

*It's time.*

She took hold of his picture and laid it on her lap. Her chin trembled as she ran her fingers over his image. "I will always love you, Søren Ivar Halstad. Always." She inhaled a shuddering breath. "But I have to move forward. For my sake and for Allie's. You were a good husband. Thank you for leaving us Halstad House. I'll try not to let you down."

She slid his photograph out of the pewter frame and placed it on the mattress. Her fingers left a small smudge on the glass. After wiping it away with the hem of her nightgown, she slid the picture from Esther's wedding into the frame. Allie and Grace. Her heart warmed. You know, they did look a little like fairy princesses. She placed the picture frame back on the nightstand.

From the bottom drawer of her bureau, she drew out a leather photograph album. She flipped through family pictures until she came to an empty page. Here she placed Søren's photograph, fitting its corners into tiny slits in the thick black paper. She smoothed it out, stroking his face again, her eyes pricking with tears. Then she closed the cover and set the album in the drawer.

When she stood, the letterbox caught her eye. She lifted the lid—his last letter still unopened on the stack. *It's probably time for that, too.* She touched the envelope. No. She couldn't do it. Not yet. She replaced the lid and blew out the candle.

# Twenty-Six

"Hey, you." Grace clapped a hand to her cheek. She treasured this unexpected time with Allie, even if she was getting trounced.

Allie giggled and jumped Grace's last two checkers. "Crown me."

"I would if I had anything left to crown you with. You win. Again." She pushed black checkers toward her daughter. "How did you get so good?"

"Uncle Ben showed me stalogy."

"*Stalogy?*"

Allie nodded and gathered checkers into piles, red in one, black in another. "You know, where you figure everything out."

Grace furrowed her brow. "You mean *strategy*?"

"Uh-huh."

"When I try strategy, I get as far as the first move, then draw a blank as to what comes next."

Allie giggled. "That's how come I win."

Grace snorted. "Hmm... When Auntie Esther and Uncle Ben get back from their little vacation, I may have some words for him."

Allie reared back, scrutinizing her mother. "You're not really mad, are you?"

"Pfft. Not at all. In fact, I'm proud of you."

"Me, too."

"I like how your mind works. I bet you'll be especially good at arithmetic. Just like your daddy."

"And Mr. Ethan?"

Grace blinked. "Yes, like Mr. Ethan, too." She rubbed her hands together. "All right, missy-moo, set 'em up for another round. I've got a good feeling this time."

An impish grin danced across Allie's mouth.

Grace had seen that same grin on Dad many times over the years. Funny how that worked.

When Allie finished setting up the board she looked up. Her smile faded. "Look, Mommy." She pointed to the kitchen door.

Grace couldn't believe it. What was *wrong* with that man? He had some nerve showing up here again. She squeezed Allie's shoulder and strode from the table as Einar opened the door and stepped into the room. He fumbled with the doorknob.

"I meant it when I said you are not welcome. You need to leave." Grace parked her hands on her hips.

"Ah now, Gracie-girl, don't be like that. Just let me get this confounded door closed." He muttered under his breath. "Got a mind of its own."

Something was wrong. Very wrong.

The door swung wide, banging hard against the wall. He grabbed it, slammed it shut, and cackled like a lunatic. "Knew I'd get it." His face sobered as he brought his eyes to her face.

Grace felt a tingling in the back of her neck. Evil had slunk into the house, clinging to Einar like smoke to a jacket left near the campfire. No dapper young man today, not with his shirt untucked in places, stains on his shirt front suggesting a spill and hasty mop-up, and his jaw sporting a coarse stubble.

He swiped away a speck of spittle from the corner of his mouth. A belch escaped, adding the reek of liquor to body odor.

Liquor? But prohibition was in effect. Where did he get it? A stab of fear raced up Grace's chest and lodged in her throat. She'd seen Einar angry. Would liquor fuel that anger? She might be naïve about it, but she'd heard stories. She staggered back, putting distance between them.

He looked past her. "And there's our little Sally. Gonna be a beauty like her mama." He tottered forward two steps, stumbled, righted himself.

Allie's saucer-like eyes tracked him.

Allie. Grace's precious, precocious daughter who was afraid of nothing except spiders. Until today. Until Einar. She had to get him out of the house.

But Allie first.

She walked to the table and took a deep breath. "Everything is all right, sweetie."

Allie blinked, her face ashen. She stared at Einar and licked her lips.

"Allie?" Grace clasped her daughter's shoulder.

Allie swung her head.

An oath and a dull crack from behind her startled Grace. A potted plant lay on the floor, dirt scattered all around. Einar swore again. "Who put that thing there?" He kicked the shattered remains of the clay planter, and it rolled under the kitchen range. He lost his balance, but righted himself again.

*Think, Grace, think.* She gnawed her lower lip. *Yes!* She turned back to Allie. "Have you fed Sargent yet?"

The glaze in her daughter's eyes faded, replaced with a quick gleam. She shook her head.

"Why don't you do that now?"

Allie scooted off the chair, dashed through the mudroom, and down the back-porch stairs.

Grace rubbed her upper arms, her gaze darting after Allie as she rounded the corner of the house and disappeared.

"Yeah, she needs to feed her doggy." Einar wiggled his eyebrows. "And it gives us time alone."

Alarm bells exploded. Her stomach lurched. She straightened her spine, pulling herself up to her full five-foot, four-inch height. "Get out of my house."

"Well now, I'll get out when I'm good and ready." He held up a hand, palm out. "Don't worry. I'm not gonna propose again. I just thought we could be...friendly-like." He stepped toward her.

She backed away.

"No need to be afraid of me, Gracie-girl." He took two more wobbly steps toward her.

She backed away three.

"Woman, can't you hold still?"

The glint in his eyes spoke volumes. He was throwing down the gauntlet. Was this a game to him? She took three more steps backward, her eyes scanning the room. If she could put the table between them, unsteady as he was on his feet, she could dash to the parlor door and out to the front porch. He'd never catch her.

He latched on to her arm. "Oh no you don't. I see what you got in mind."

She shook loose from his grasp and backed into the counter. Something poked her in the back. She reached behind her—and felt the handle of her heavy cast-iron skillet. She gripped it and brought the pan in front of her, clutching the handle with both hands.

"You gonna fry up some eggs for us?" He threw back his head and cackled again.

That cackle did it. She refused to give way to fear. She squared her shoulders and inhaled a deep breath, bringing the skillet up and over her shoulder, brandishing it like a batter at home plate. "I'm giving you fair warning, Einar."

"You gonna lambast me? You and what army?" He took another step toward her. "And besides, sweet little Gracie wouldn't—"

*Whack!*

Sweet little Gracie walloped him.

Einar spun and fell to his knees. He managed to catch his upper body on the seat of one of the kitchen chairs. "You trying to break my arm? It's gonna be black and blue tomorrow for sure."

"I warned you. Now, get out."

He glanced at her, then the skillet. "You're crazier than a loon." He pushed himself up, struggling to stand upright. "I'm gettin'. I'm gettin'." He staggered toward the door.

She followed at a safe distance. When he turned to look at her, she raised the skillet.

Einar threw open the door and careened down the porch

steps. The picket gate clicked behind him as he headed for his horse, stumbled, ended up on his hands and knees.

Grace stood on the landing, skillet held high. She glanced up the street. Ah, welcome sight. Ethan, carrying Allie in his arms, ran down the boardwalk.

When he reached them, he hoisted Allie over the fence. "Stay put."

Allie plopped her little behind on the grass, watching Ethan's every move.

Einar had a good two inches on Ethan, but it didn't matter. Ethan grabbed Einar by the seat of his pants with one hand and the scruff of his neck with the other. With one mighty heave he tossed him into the saddle, grabbed the reins, and flung them at him.

Einar snatched them. "You can have her. She's nuttier than a fruitcake." He wheeled his horse around. "But you tell her from me, she'll live to regret this."

"There've been enough of your threats. Ride out of here, Einar Brevik." Ethan slapped the horse's rump.

The horse bolted, nearly unseating Einar. It was a wonder he stayed in the saddle. They galloped toward the bridge that crossed the Kettle River.

Ethan, breathing hard, mounted the stairs, his limp pronounced. "Lils, are you all right?" He took her by the shoulders. "Did he hurt you?"

She shook the skillet under his nose. "If he ever sets foot here again I swear I'll—"

"Whoa. What say we put that down before you brain me?"

Grace lowered it to the porch floor.

"Did he hurt you?"

She shook her head. "I chased him off." She pointed to the skillet. "With that."

Ethan pressed his forehead against hers, his chest still heaving, his hands shaking. "Girl, you do beat all. No pun intended." He raised his head and looked toward Allie, holding out his hand.

She ran up the stairs and catapulted into his arms, burying her head in his shoulder. "He scared me."

"I know, kitten."

Grace placed a tender hand on Allie's cheek. "You were so brave, sweetie. And you remembered the code."

Allie gave her a tremulous smile.

Ethan tweaked her braid. "You know, that whole code thing was a brilliant idea. You were right, we needed it. Worked like a charm."

Allie clasped Grace's hand. "Mommy was brave, too. She chased that mean man away."

"She did indeed." Ethan trailed a knuckle across Grace's cheek.

Grace smiled and blew out a breath. "And I hope I never have to do anything like that again."

Allie raised questioning eyes to Ethan. "Are we still brave even if we feel kinda scared inside?"

"Oh, kitten." He kissed her nose. "That's when we're the most brave."

Grace closed her eyes as a slight breeze blew wisps of hair across her cheek. *Thank You, Lord.* She stood a few moments longer, grateful for Ethan's strong presence, with Allie nestled safely in his arms. When her heart rate had returned to normal, she wiped her forehead with the back of her hand. "Well, I've got some cleaning to do in the kitchen. Einar kicked a potted plant and scattered dirt all over the place."

"I'll give you a hand," Ethan said. He walked to the door and held it open as the three of them stepped back into Halstad House.

Supper over, kitchen cleaned, Ethan gone, Allie asleep, Grace sat in the rocking chair. The Bible on her lap lay open to Psalm 91. *He that dwelleth in the secret place of the Most High shall abide under the shadow of the Almighty.*

She leaned back and closed her eyes. "Thank You for Your protection."

"Mommy?" Allie stood next to the rocking chair.

"Why are you awake?"

Allie's lower lip trembled. "I had a bad dream."

Grace set the Bible on the table and patted her lap.

Allie climbed up and hugged Grace close.

"What did you dream about?"

"I don't 'member. But it was bad."

Grace kissed the top of Allie's head. "We're okay, sweetie. We're okay." She rocked her daughter and hummed a lullaby.

Coyotes yipping to the moon serenaded them. Their song, borne along by the breeze, calmed her. It brought back memories of lying in bed as a young girl on the farm, listening to the hushed howls, as they soothed her and lulled her to sleep.

Allie's breathing slowed.

Grace kissed the top of her head again. "We're okay, sweetie." She closed her eyes and leaned her head against the chair back. "We're okay."

# Twenty-Seven

March and April vanished in a flurry of chores, projects, and responsibilities. May arrived, bringing beautiful weather, but also the reminder that she'd soon need to get the garden in on top of all her other work. Grace often felt like she met herself coming and going in the busy rush. She tried to keep up with Bible reading and prayer, reciting her thankful list, time with Allie, church, visits with Dad and Esther...but a disquiet plagued her. An itch she couldn't scratch. She tried to ignore it, but it only got worse. What was wrong with her?

One morning she slid loaf pans into the oven. She checked the firebox and got clean-up underway.

The back door slammed. "Mommy, I fell down." Allie limped into the room, tears leaving muddy streaks on her face. "It hurts awful bad."

Grace knelt beside her daughter. Allie's knee, scraped and packed with gravel under the skin, dripped blood down Allie's leg and on to her bare foot. "Oh, sweetie, sit down and let me clean this up."

"Will it hurt?"

"I'm sorry. Getting the gravel out will hurt, but we have to clean it so it can heal. Can you be brave?"

Allie gave a half-hearted nod.

"I'll place a warm wet cloth over the scrape. You stay here while I get more water from the well."

Bucket in hand, Grace descended the back porch steps. Uffda

ran after her. "Good gracious. You stink to high heaven. I assume you had a run-in with a skunk?"

He tried to jump on her.

"Don't you dare, you smelly thing." She waved the pail at the dog, then walked to the pump and filled the bucket.

Returning to the kitchen, Grace poured a portion of the good, clean well water into an enamel pan and added steaming water from the kettle. Careful not to slosh any liquid on the floor, she carried the pan to where her daughter sat waiting, then grabbed a clean cloth and a bar of soap and began to clean Allie's knee. Gentle as Grace tried to be, Allie still whimpered. Finally, when there was no trace of gravel, Grace wiped the area with hydrogen peroxide, rinsed it well, dabbed the knee dry, spread calendula cream over it, and wrapped it in a bandage. "Let me see your hands."

Allie whipped them behind her back.

"Sweetie, you probably caught yourself with your hands. We need to clean them, too."

Scraped and bleeding, the palms of both her daughter's hands revealed gravel lodged under the skin. Grace went through the same cleaning routine. When she'd finished, Allie looked frazzled and worn out. Grace could relate. She felt the same way.

"I'll heat up chicken vegetable soup for lunch. Soup and crackers."

They ate in silence.

Lunch over, Grace lifted her daughter and ascended the stairs to their bedroom. "After your nap, you'll feel better."

"Can you rock me?"

"Sure." Grace pulled Allie close and set the rocker in motion. She sang a lullaby, then hummed several tunes until Allie's breathing slowed to a steady rhythm. After laying her on her bed and covering her with a light blanket, she made her way back to the kitchen.

Was that smoke she smelled? *The bread!* Smoke trickled from around the oven door. "Oh no." When she opened it, a thick cloud of smoke gushed out. Four loaves of bread lay inside, black, crusty, and ruined. Coughing, she yanked them out, ran to the side porch and flung them down on a table. "Like it or not, everyone will have to settle for biscuits tonight."

Still coughing, she threw open windows and doors, waving a towel frantically through the air for several minutes, trying to chase the smoke outside. Then her eyes alighted on the jumble left behind after doctoring Allie. "Right. Clean this first." She rolled her shoulders and set to work.

She put the kitchen back in order. Now she could tackle the major job. The one she'd earmarked for today. Ten chickens and one cranky rooster arrived in a week and a half. The chicken coop repair loomed, and she'd determined to do it herself. How hard could it be? She retrieved Søren's leather work gloves, a heavy hammer, and a can of various-sized nails from the tool shed, then stood before the coop. A fierce storm shortly after Søren left had damaged one side. A severed branch from the maple tree had sideswiped the roof, knocking shingles off and leaving that portion of the roof sagging. Part of the wall had fallen; the other part remained attached to the roof—but just barely.

The branch first. Grace seized one end and pulled. Crabgrass had grown around it, gripping it tightly. She fetched a garden hoe and chopped at the tangled mess. And chopped. And chopped. Throwing the hoe aside, she gave the branch a mighty yank. It broke free, but in the process, a limb jabbed into one of the window screens and punched a huge hole in it.

"Great."

Out of the blue, Uffda, wrapped in the foul stench of skunk, darted out from under the lilac hedge and proceeded to run circles around her, yipping the whole time. She tried to ignore him as she worked, but between tripping her up and the intense smell, her patience snapped. "You're driving me crazy." She found an old rope in the tool shed, tied one end around the dog's neck and the other around the maple tree.

Uffda didn't appear any too happy with the situation. His yips turned to sharp barks.

"Uffda, stop it. Do you have any idea how annoying that is?"

He kept barking.

"Evidently not."

She turned back to the coop, chewing the inside of her cheek. "If I hoist up the roof and brace it, that should help." She found two long boards. Pushing up the roof was easier said than done, but she stuck with it. When she finally managed to get one side up, she slipped a board under and moved to the other side. Her muscles strained as she struggled to lift that side. When she slipped the second board under the edge of the roof, straightaway she saw the problem. The beam thing had come loose from the corner post, jutting out from the nails meant to secure it.

She took off the leather gloves and tightened the bandanna on her head. Reaching to grab the corner post and give it a shake, her hand landed on a yellow jacket, which promptly stung her. She whipped her hand away, sucking air in through her teeth. *Jella-waspers,* Dad called them. Their sting hurt like the dickens, he said. He was right. Sitting on the fallen branch, she popped the end of her finger in her mouth to soothe it, holding her breath against the burning pain.

To further complicate matters, a blur in the shape of Lydie Sue's cat Rascal dashed through the yard, right past Grace's feet. Grace whirled her eyes to Uffda. He'd gone crazy, lunging, jumping, barking harder.

Grace sprang to her feet. "Uffda, no!"

Too late. He broke free from the rope and bolted after Rascal. Running past her at full speed, he clipped the bottom of one of the boards she'd set to brace the beam. Down it went. In her scramble to grab it, the board slid through her gloveless fingers. Splinters stabbed into her palms.

The roof sagged again.

Barely containing the urge to scream and stomp her foot, Grace called after Uffda. "Bad dog." She plopped onto the branch and set to work removing splinters with her fingertips. The tightness in her chest increased. "Stinky dog."

The weather turned muggy. A lone fly buzzed around her face and landed on her cheek. She brushed it away with the back of her hand, only to have it return. Then a speck of dirt lodged in her eye. "Arggh... If it isn't one thing it's three others." She blinked and blinked, but the stubborn speck remained. She pulled a hankie from her pocket. Dabbing her eye with it finally did the trick. Speck gone, she gritted her teeth and rubbed a hand over her face.

*Come on, girl. Buck up. It's your responsibility. You can do this.*

Gloves went on. Hoisting the roof back up proved harder this time. Her shoulders and arms ached, her muscles quivered. But she succeeded and braced it with the boards. Okay. Attaching the beam to the corner post came next. She knew she'd need to stand on something to reach it. She tramped to the kitchen and brought back a step-stool.

The challenge of pulling out spent nails made her arms clumsy, but she persevered until every last one lay on the ground. She took a deep breath and closed her eyes. *If I can get this part done, I'll put the wall up later.* She climbed down from the stool, secured a handful of nails in her apron pocket, and climbed back up again. Hopefully, the nails would be long enough to go through the side of the beam and anchor it to the post. Grace hammered with heavy strokes. The first time she hit her thumb, she gasped. The second time, she caught her breath, removed the glove, and stuck her thumb in her mouth. The third time, she swiped tears from her eyes.

At last, she stepped down and surveyed her work. *Looks good.* She gingerly removed the boards and slowly lowered the roof to set it on the beam. *Seems okay.* Grace tested the corner post with a slight push.

*Screech.* The beam ripped loose from the nails, and the whole shebang fell again. The roof sagged even lower this time. She almost cried.

"I can't do this."

A clap of thunder caught her by surprise. Dark, smoldering clouds, in a sudden rush to eject their burden, dumped water on the earth as if a huge bucket had been overturned. She threw her hands up and dropped to her knees. This time she did cry. Her shoulders shook as she broke into sobs. "This is your fault, Søren. You left me. Left me to fix everything on my own. To handle all the finances, the boarders, the cooking and cleaning, to make all the decisions. Everything. You left me with all the responsibility. But I can't do it." She beat her balled fists against her thighs. "And you left me to deal with your stupid, stupid, slimy cousin." Her voice rose. "He just won't stay away. He is a vile man. He scares Allie and he scares me."

Her fingernails bit into the palms of her hands. "I'm so angry with you. You left me." She buried her head in her hands, rocking back and forth while the rain beat down.

# Twenty-Eight

"I really thought I could do it." Grace swiped a hand across her cheek and stared out the window. The dreary, overcast sky mirrored her frame of mind.

"You aren't invincible, you know." Esther set two cups on the table and bustled back for the teakettle. She began pouring boiling water into the tempered teapot.

Grace roused herself, realizing she was letting her pregnant sister wait on her. She started to rise. "I should be doing that so you can rest."

"Sit down." Esther waved her away and brought the pot to the table. She lowered herself into the chair next to Grace and took a deep breath. "You can't do everything, sister-mine."

"I know. It just feels like I'm supposed to." Grace rubbed her forehead. "I don't know what's wrong with me."

Esther held the teapot lid in place with two fingers while she tipped the spout over Grace's cup, filling it with steamy, dark liquid. "Well, while you try to figure that out, how about if you let Ben and Ethan fix the chicken coop?"

Grace sighed. "I'd appreciate it."

"Good. Because I've already asked Ben, and he talked to Ethan. They'll be here early tomorrow morning."

Grace's eyebrows shot up.

Esther held up her hand. "And don't get all snippy with me. I have several crates of noisy hens and a cranky rooster scattered around my backyard. They are eager for their new domicile and, frankly, so am I." Esther gave her a mischievous grin. "So I played the bossy big sister card."

She knew her smile was half-hearted, but Grace patted Esther's hand and shrugged one shoulder. "It's okay. Thanks."

It made perfect sense, and Ethan and Ben were willing. They'd helped her countless times before, and she was always grateful. What *was* wrong with her? She sighed again. Well, for now she'd ignore the grouchy feeling squeezing her insides and think about a sound, solid chicken coop housing her new egg-producing brood. And she wouldn't have to endure splinters or smashed thumbs to make it happen.

*Wham!* The peal of a hammer smacking wood pierced the tranquil Saturday dawn, sending a covey of quail, plumes bobbing, scurrying under the lilac bushes.

Hands on his hips, Ethan surveyed the damaged chicken coop and looked over to Ben. "No wonder Grace couldn't secure the beam to the corner post."

Ben glanced up. "What'd you find?" He stepped away from the nesting boxes he'd been building and wiped his forehead with a blue bandanna.

"The beam is splintered on that end." Ethan pointed to one corner. "Probably from storm damage. There's no way any amount of nails would've held it. Glad I brought an extra beam and boards from the lumberyard. The whole thing needs to be replaced."

Ben set the hammer down. "Hang on. I'll give you a hand."

The two men trooped to the wagon, fetched the lumber, and toted it all back to the coop. It took a while for them to prop up the roof, but once they had it stabilized, they removed the old beam.

Ethan measured a cut in the new beam to fit over the corner post and reached for his saw.

"Let me know when you're ready to put it up." Ben returned

to forming nesting boxes, and the peal of his hammer pierced the morning again.

By the time Allie hollered from the back porch that lunch was ready, the coop stood fit for occupancy, complete with new rafters where needed, new skip-sheeting on the damaged side, and shingles to replace those lost or broken. Ethan fastened the corner of the last screen over a window. "All right and tight. I defy any fat hen to fly the coop, so to speak."

Ben laughed. "Hey. Good one, Myers. And I defy any varmints to break in and wreak havoc."

They headed inside.

After a long morning of labor, Ethan wondered if he'd ever fill up, but at last, he leaned back from the table and rubbed his stomach. "Boy, that hit the spot. Body and soul are on speaking terms again. Thanks for a great lunch." He rose and took his plate and flatware to the counter. "We'll tackle the chicken run now. I brought enough wire and screen so we can cover the top to keep owls and hawks from swooping in." He frowned when a silent Grace stared at her plate. "Grace?"

She looked up and blinked. "What?"

He glanced at Allie whose watchful eyes peered at her mother, eyebrows scrunched. His gaze back on Grace, he cleared his throat. "We'll put a screened top over the run to keep out owls and such."

She nodded. "Fine." Rising, she held out a hand to her daughter. "Time for your nap." Without looking back, she led Allie to the corner stairs.

Ethan and Ben glanced at each other before Ben stood and deposited his plate, knife, and fork on the counter as well.

"She must be tired," Ben said.

"Must be." Ethan ran a hand through his hair. That wasn't like Grace. His chest expanded as he inhaled. "Well, should we attack the run? Then we can go to your place, grab the crates, and introduce the brood to their new home."

"Back off, Mr. Meanie." This afternoon that old rooster act-ed downright cantankerous. Allie was ready this time. She wore knee-high garden boots and Mommy's two-pocket apron. She'd rolled it three times around her waist so it didn't drag to her an-kles and make her trip. But best of all, instead of an egg basket, she carried a broom.

The rooster eyed her, cocking his head to one side. A scary noise came from low in his throat.

"You mind what I said." Inside the run, she neared the coop door.

That's when he made his move. With a squawk and a leap, wings outstretched, he launched himself. Those claw-looking things on his feet pointed directly at her.

Allie shivered, but held her ground.

*Swoosh!* She swung the broom to scare him away.

'Cept he flew right into the sweepy-part and ricocheted backward like a giant hand had snatched his hind end. That bad-tempered banty sailed through the air with his legs and wings stretched straight out in front of him, and big, round eyes marked him the most startled rooster as ever was. When he land-ed, he shook his head and dropped his wings close to his body. Then he swiveled his head around, looking this way and that, like he couldn't figure out how he got back to where he'd started from.

"Willikens." Allie opened the coop door and stepped inside. After she came out, with three eggs in each pocket, the rooster eyed her but hightailed it to a corner. "Good boy." She unbolted the screened chicken run door, made sure to lock it behind her, and headed for the house.

In the kitchen, everyone gathered for their after-church din-ner. Grampa sat in the rocking chair, his leg propped on a stool. Mommy and Auntie Esther rushed around doing the last-minute stirring and mixing. Mrs. King, Miss Isobel, and Miss Talbot fin-ished setting the big round table. Uncle Ben poured water into everybody's glasses.

Mr. Ethan gave Grampa a cup of coffee and winked at Allie.

"I peeked out the window. Good job with that old rooster. I don't think he'll give you any more trouble. You showed him who's boss."

Allie grinned and held her chin high. She placed the eggs in a bowl and the bowl on the counter.

At dinner, everybody laughed and chatted 'cept Mommy. She did a lot'a sighing and just picked at her food.

All of a sudden she stood up. "I think I'll go outside for a bit."

Mr. Ethan stood, too. "Want some company?"

Mommy shook her head.

He laid down his napkin. "I could—"

"No!"

Everyone stopped talking and looked at everyone else. Miss Talbot stared back and forth between Mommy and Mr. Ethan. She sat up straighter in her chair.

Mr. Ethan's eyes widened, and he swallowed hard. He opened his mouth, but nothing came out.

Mommy walked through the mudroom and out the back door. She crossed her arms and held her elbows.

Allie looked at Mr. Ethan. *God, don't let Mommy be mad at him forever. I want him to be my daddy somethin' fierce.* She raced to the window and watched her mother climb the steps to the upper garden. Uffda ran after her, but she must'a yelled at him 'cause he slunk down and laid his head on his paws.

Allie didn't like the way the room felt. It wasn't comfy-cozy like normal.

Mrs. King stood up fast. Her voice was bright. "Well girls, let's clean the kitchen and then play a game of dominoes."

Ethan was flummoxed. Grace had seemed kind of off for a while now, but she'd never acted like this before. He knew he should stay and help, but he couldn't. Not right now. He walked out the side door and leaned against the porch rail, gazing up the street. He inhaled a deep breath of fresh air, exhaling it slowly.

*What is going on, God? Is there something I'm not seeing? Not hearing?* He rubbed the back of his neck. *Please show me.*

He turned at the creaking of the side door. Mary stepped through and closed it behind her, curling and uncurling her fingers, a sheen of perspiration dotting her forehead. She pulled a hankie from the cuff of her sleeve and blotted it away.

"Are you on your way out somewhere?" Ethan asked.

"No." She cleared her throat. "Actually, I came to talk to you."

"Me?" She and Isobel didn't act like vultures anymore, for which he was glad. In fact, he admired the changes he'd seen in Isobel. But Mary, somehow he still felt nervous around her. He could be a gentleman, though. He pulled out a chair. "Won't you sit down?"

She slid into the chair. Before he could sit she popped back up. "I'd like to stand, if that's all right."

"Uh, sure. Is there something I can help you with?"

Mary ran her tongue across her lips and blotted her forehead again. "There's something I want to tell you."

Ethan dipped his head. "Okay."

"Not too long ago Grace helped me pray the prayer."

"The prayer? Oh, you mean you asked Jesus into your life?"

"Yes. Grace showed me how."

"Mary, that's wonderful." Ethan leaned back and grasped the top of the railing. "A whole new world is opening for you. We at the church will do everything we can to help you grow in your walk with the Lord. I know Pastor has some great books that explain things to new believers."

"So I'm a Christian now."

Ethan gave her a slow nod. "Yes. Yes, you are."

"So you wouldn't be unequally yoked."

He cocked one eyebrow. "What are you talking about?"

"I heard Mae tell Isobel not to be unequally yoked." Mary wet her lips once more. "But I'm a Christian now and you wouldn't be. So, we—we could get married."

"Married?" Good grief. No way had he seen this coming. "What put that into your head?" He'd better nip this in the bud.

"I've never given you the slightest indication that was my desire, have I?"

"No." Mary flapped her hand in front of her face. "But my father urged me to try, I mean to go after, well, to..." She stared at him, her eyes pleading. "He can be pretty persuasive, and he urged me to pursue you. He said you were one of our boys come back from the war and I could overlook certain things."

Ethan shook his head. "Mary, slow down. I don't know what you're talking about. None of this makes sense."

"Father says you all came back damaged in one way or another, but I could live with most of it."

Ethan jerked his head back, muscles going rigid. Damaged? A coldness settled in his belly. A vivid picture of two nurses came to mind, pitying the poor cripple in bed eight. Damaged. No! He straightened his spine. He was God's man, complete in Him, whole.

Mary spluttered. "You know, I've seen for years how you look at Grace, how you looked at her today. But she doesn't love you. I thought maybe you could settle for me."

The well-aimed kick in the gut found its target. "Surely she didn't tell you that?"

"As good as. We've gotten friendlier over the last few weeks. One day I asked her if she and you were a couple and she said although you'd always been good friends, you weren't a couple." She cleared her throat once more. "It amounts to the same thing."

He lowered his head, staring at the porch floor, then raised it as a horse and buggy clip-clopped down the street toward the bridge. His shoulders drooped. Hope wavered. He gave a half-hearted shrug and returned his gaze to hers. "Settling—as you call it—is not the answer, Mary. I won't do it. Nor should you. Somewhere there's a girl who won't see me as damaged."

Mary flinched.

"A girl who sees me as whole and even a pretty wonderful guy." He shook his head. "You can stop looking in my direction, though, and you can tell your father there will never be anything between us in that way. I'm sorry."

At least she had the decency to blush. Red crept up her neck and into her cheeks, forming rosy splotches against her sallow skin. "If that's the way you feel."

"It is."

She covered a cough with her hand, sighed, and walked the length of the porch toward the front door.

Ethan rubbed his palm over his chest. He strode back into the kitchen. "Folks, I think I'll head home."

Allie ran to throw her arms around him. "We still have Sunday morning cinnamon rolls, and we're gonna play dominoes. Don't you want to stay?"

He gave her braid a gentle tug. "Another time, kitten." When she stepped back, he spun on his heel and walked out the door, the pressure of everyone's stares following him. He stuffed his hands in his pockets and, head bowed, strolled up the boardwalk in the direction of his house.

The next three days brought on a hard-fought battle and demanded hours on his knees. Hours of pleading. Hours of crying out to God. Hours of listening. But at last, after a final *Thy will be done*, with disappointment, weariness, and uncertainty vanquished, peace flooded his soul. He rose a courageous warrior. Faith stronger. Fully surrendered to his Savior. Committed to the purpose God's still small voice whispered in his ear. *Come what may, care for Grace and Allie. Protect them. Defend them. Love them.*

With the boarders in their rooms and Allie asleep, Grace poured herself a good strong cup of tea. She couldn't pinpoint the cause of her discomfort. No, that wasn't true. She knew the cause; she just didn't know what to do with it. The vexing itch deep in her gut persisted. When the side door opened, she jumped, sloshing hot tea on the back of her hand.

Esther and Ben walked into the kitchen followed by Dad on his crutches. Esther marched straight to her and placed a hand on her arm. "You are coming to Wednesday night service with Ben and me."

"No, I'm not. I need to stay here with Allie."

Dad leaned his crutches against the table and sank into the rocking chair. "I'll remain here, Lily Grace. It'll do you good to go."

Grace narrowed her eyes at Esther. "I'd rather not."

"That may be, but you're coming with us."

Grace sucked in a deep breath and clenched her jaw. "You are being a bossy big sister."

"Yep. Sometimes that's my job." Esther crossed her arms and stared at Grace.

Grace tried to stare her down, but gave up and dropped her eyes. She knew her sister well. Esther would never give up. "All right, all right. I'll go. Just let me grab a sweater."

Esther pointed with her chin. "There's one on the back of that chair."

Grace snatched it and turned toward them.

"Don't forget your Bible."

Her Bible lay on the Lazy Susan. She snatched it, too.

On the walk to church, Esther linked arms with her sister and spoke in a hushed voice. "You're in agony. You're struggling with something."

Tears stung Grace's eyes. "I know." She let out a slow sigh. "I thought I had come so far. Now I find that deep down I'm angry with Søren for leaving me to take care of everything alone." She glanced at Esther. "And that makes me feel guilty. Am I a bad Christian? Do you think God is disappointed in me?"

"Oh, honey, no." She patted Grace's arm "Maybe God will speak to you tonight."

The first two hymns, sung acapella, calmed her. Then Pastor Grant stepped to the podium and asked them all to turn their Bibles to Hebrews 12:15. "This verse speaks very clearly about the danger of harboring bitterness. It can take root, troubling our own lives and then spreading to trouble those around us," he said.

Grace swung wide eyes on her sister.

Esther whispered, "I didn't know what he was going to teach on."

"Honest?"

Esther crisscrossed her heart with her finger.

Pastor Grant leaned over the podium. "Brothers and sisters, as is our custom for Wednesdays, the teaching will be short so we can spend time in prayer. But tonight I want to look at the importance of God's words on forgiveness and unforgiveness. We, as His children, must grasp these truths and allow Him to transform us.

"Bitterness and unforgiveness steal our joy. They leave us stuck. They can eat us up and hold back the power of God in our lives. We all experience hurt. Sometimes we feel betrayed. Sometimes we feel abandoned. Those feelings can be the seeds of bitterness."

The preacher's words tugged at Grace's heart.

"We must choose our next steps carefully. If our hearts harbor those feelings, if we don't deal with our hurt by the grace of God, they can take root. Hold a finger in Hebrews, but flip over to Ephesians 4:26. *Be ye angry, and sin not: let not the sun go down upon your wrath: neither give place to the devil.*"

Grace caught her breath. She wanted no part of the devil in her life. *Oh, God, help me.*

Pastor continued. "The tricky part is, sometimes we know what we're doing; but sometimes we don't realize we've stuffed the hurt down deep. We don't realize bitterness has taken root. That's when we need to call on God to reveal it to us. And don't think you can pull up that root yourself. Look again at verse 15 in Hebrews 12. Read that phrase *the grace of God.* Only His grace can free us and restore our joy. Yes, we need to repent of hanging on to the hurt and resentment. Yes, we need to forgive the person who has hurt us. We need to release them into God's hands. It's not easy. Forgiveness is costly, but it's worth it. Let God exchange bitterness for forgiveness. In His own mysterious and miraculous way, He pulls out the root Himself and sets us free.

"First the root of bitterness springs up to trouble *you,* but then *many* are troubled. There's the rub. It festers. Back in Ephesians 4, we are told to put away wrath, anger, clamor, evil speaking, malice. I believe these are the fruits of bitterness.

"We've talked before about the fruits of the Spirit found in Galatians chapter five. Love, joy, peace, longsuffering, kindness, goodness, faithfulness, meekness, and self-control.

"Which fruits do you want to define your life?"

He closed his Bible. "One day I'll do a full sermon on this. For now, ask God to reveal any unforgiveness. Go to Him with it." He looked to their pew. "Ben, will you come lead us in two more hymns? Then we'll begin prayer time." He raised his eyes to the small congregation. "While Ben makes his way up, I'll share a few requests. Ada Walters heard from her sister in Vermont. Their mother lives with her and has developed pneumonia. Ada asks for prayers for healing. Continue to pray for Esther and Grace's father, Mr. Browne. His leg is weak and he still must use crutches." Pastor Grant creased his brow. "And I have heard disturbing news. Even with Prohibition in effect, rumors of a bootleg whiskey operation in our little community have reached me. Pray that the evil will be exposed and the perpetrators dealt with."

Grace's stomach lurched. She remembered Einar's last visit and his frightening behavior. But before she could give it too much thought, Ada and Harv Walters joined them in one corner of the sanctuary where Ben had set up a circle of chairs. After several minutes of sharing requests, the five of them united in sweet prayer, bringing everything to the Father.

The sun had long ago sunk behind Emmett Ridge by the time they left the church. On the walk home, Grace linked arms with Esther. "Thank you for inviting me tonight."

Esther smirked. "Inviting you?"

"Well, insisting I come. I needed to hear everything Pastor said." She hesitated a moment. "During prayer time, I didn't share my whole heart with the group—some things were too personal. I need to talk to God about them when I get home."

Esther squeezed her arm. "I'm glad, sister-mine."

Ben peeked around his wife. "Me, too."

Grace filled her lungs with good, clean, pine-filled air. Yes. Talking to God about harboring unforgiveness might be a little scary, but she couldn't go on like this. She longed for His freedom and joy. Tonight she would pray, laying everything before the Lord, until she had that freedom and joy back.

# Twenty-Nine

*Ninety-eight, ninety-nine, one hundred.* Grace set the brush on the table and began Allie's braid.

Allie yawned, wrinkling her nose. "Are you still mad at Mr. Ethan?"

Her hands stilled. "Did you think I was mad at him?"

"Uh-huh."

"No. I'm not mad." She finished the braid and fastened the end with a leather tie. "Guess I kind of acted mad at everybody."

Allie leaned back and stared at her mother. "Yeah, but you're nice again. I'm glad."

*Ouch.* Scripture was right. An unforgiving spirit affected not just her. It sprang up and troubled those around her. She kissed the tip of Allie's nose. "I'm sorry I acted like a grouchy old bear with a toothache."

"That's okay." Allie opened their nighttime storybook, yawned again, and nestled against Grace.

An hour later, back in the kitchen, Grace stirred the ingredients for a special coffee cake. Baking it tonight meant one less thing to do in the morning. At the last minute she decided to double it. She increased all the ingredients, but when she opened the icebox, the egg bowl held only one. Great. That meant a trip to the chicken coop. The hens, undisturbed by the move from the farm, had been popping out eggs with gusto. Well, three was all she asked for tonight.

She lit a lantern and strode across the yard. All quiet inside the dark coop, barring the sporadic gentle burbles emanating from low in the chickens' throats. Led by the circle of light from the lantern, Grace made her way to the nesting boxes. She slipped her hand under the first hen. One egg. Sliding it out, she placed it in one of her apron pockets. The next two held chickens, but no eggs.

All of a sudden, an eerie feeling overtook her, as if someone was watching her. She swung the lantern toward the door. No one had followed her in. She shrugged and moved on. Next box, another egg. She slid it into her pocket.

The eerie feeling intensified. The skin on the back of her neck tingled, and she pivoted to throw light in the corner. Nope. Not a single boogeyman. This was unnerving. *One more and I'm out of here.* She placed her hand under the next hen. Oh good, an egg.

The uncanny sense of being watched hit her with such force her heart raced. She lifted the lantern and gasped. Illuminated by the flickering lantern light, that surly, insufferable rooster stood on the nest box next to her, razor-sharp talons wrapped around its edge. Merciful heavens, the red cox-combed beast stared at her, eyeball to eyeball, hers wide and still, his flitting left and right—no doubt weighing his plan of attack. Panic surged through her. He may kowtow to Allie, but he had no such qualms with Grace. He intimidated her to no end. *Lord, remember how You sent an angel to Daniel in the den to close the lion's mouth? I sure could use one now.*

With slow, even moves, Grace pulled the egg from under the chicken and slid it into her pocket. Now for the getaway. She dare not turn her back on him. Visions of his flying through the air and landing on her shoulders, ready to tear into her, flooded her mind. Lantern held aloft, she backed away, taking unhurried baby steps.

The burble from the rooster was not gentle and calming like the sweet hens. More like a warning shot leveled at fool-hardy trespassers. He hopped to the floor, ruffling his wings, then made a bee-line for her.

She shrieked as she bumped into the door. Frantic, she fumbled behind her to grab the handle. She threw the door open, scooted through, and slammed it behind her. Trembling but heaving a sigh of relief, she wilted against the door. Ridiculous for a grown woman to be scared witless by that creature. She needed to conquer her fear. And she would. As she pushed off the wall, an image of Einar popped into her head, bringing with it the same sense of foreboding she'd just experienced inside the coop. Hmm... Another fear she'd have to conquer? Well, she wouldn't think about it now. She shook the mental picture away and stepped out of the run.

She latched the gate and squared her shoulders, smiling as another thought popped into her mind. "Score one for you this time, buster. But just you wait." She'd look to God for courage... and her five-year-old daughter for advice.

Grace drew in a deep breath. The first week of June and right on time. The fragrant scent of locust trees in bloom enveloped her like a cocoon, covering her with a feeling of quiet and calm. Pale peach-tinged clouds floated above the darkening mountains across the river as the sun dipped over the horizon. A chorus of crickets sang their night-time vespers. The perfect evening. She expected Ethan any time. She'd wait for him on the porch and maybe they could soak up every moment of this magical setting before retreating to the kitchen to attack the ledger.

His whistled rendition of "Skip to My Lou" heralded his arrival. He grinned and gave her a quick wave as he mounted the stairs.

Seeing him dressed in blue denim dungarees and a white cotton shirt, his jaw freshly shaved, Grace was struck with how handsome Ethan actually was. When he removed his hat, she noticed stray water drops clinging to the hairline above his temples. Had he cleaned up just for her? She patted the chair beside her. "Let's sit out here for a while."

"Suits me." He placed his hat on a nearby table and sank into the chair, stretching his long legs and clasping his hands in his lap. "Ah." He exhaled a sigh. "Just what the doctor ordered."

A comfortable silence lay between them.

After a few minutes, Grace leaned her head back. "Do you smell the locust trees?"

"Mm-hmm. Nice."

"It's one of my favorite smells." The breeze swept a loose curl across her eyes. She tucked it behind an ear. "How about you. Do you have a favorite?"

"You mean besides the aroma of your cinnamon rolls baking?"

"Well, that's everybody's favorite." She gave him a sideward glance. "What about a close second?"

"Yep. The clean scent in the air after a summer rain."

"Mm..." She nestled deeper into her chair. "Okay, favorites game. Favorite animal?"

"No contest. Horses. Someday I'd like to have a place out of town where I could have a few—even breed them."

"You always did love horses."

Ethan turned his head. "How about you?"

"Don't tell Uffda or Chaucer, but rabbits are my favorite."

"Rabbits?"

"It might be because I've never actually raised them, but they're so cute and cuddly. I read an article about a lady who raised Angora rabbits. Evidently, Angoras grow a new coat of fur regularly. When they do, their old coats are no longer attached to their skin. The lady combed the fur right out, spun it, and knitted or crocheted beautiful, soft mittens and baby booties. I could do that."

"Yes, you could."

Grace sighed. "Maybe someday. Okay. Favorite color."

"Green. Yours?"

"Blue. Favorite folksong."

"I know it's the saddest song in the world, but I love 'Danny Boy.'"

Grace eyed him. "That makes me tear up whenever I hear it. Mine is 'The Skye Boat Song.' How about favorite hymn?"

"'Fairest Lord Jesus,'" Ethan said.

"'This is My Father's World,'" Grace shot back.

He crossed his legs at the ankles. "Favorite birdsong."

"What?"

"You know, prettiest song sung by what kind of bird?"

She didn't even have to think about that one. "Meadowlark."

Evidently he didn't either. "Red-winged blackbird."

Just then the rooster crowed, his clamor cutting into the evening's serenity.

Grace and Ethan looked at each other and burst out laughing.

"He's vying for a spot on our list," Grace said.

"Well, besides having his days and nights mixed up, he doesn't have the finesse of a meadowlark or red-winged blackbird."

"Definitely not. Poor thing."

Ethan straightened his shoulders. "Moving on. Favorite cookie."

"Oatmeal raisin."

"Yum. Mine, too. You know what they say about great minds."

"Absolutely." She thought a second. "Favorite flower."

"Peonies." Ethan smoothed a dark curl away from his forehead. "Like my mother had next to the house when I was growing up."

"I remember those. They were lovely. I imagine she was sad to leave them behind when you moved from your farm into town."

"I don't know about her, but I cried like a baby."

Grace chuckled. "You did not."

"You're right. I didn't. Just trying to impress you with what a sensitive guy I am."

"Mine are a darker pink than hers were, but feel free to come gawk at them anytime you want."

He dipped his head. "Thank you, ma'am. Your favorite flower? Yellow roses still?"

"Yes. Something about them always brightens my day. Okay. Next favorite. Vegetable."

Ethan scrunched his face. "I suppose I have to choose one. Not Brussels sprouts, that's for sure. Carrots, I guess."

"Mine is green beans. Fruit next."

"Hmm..." Ethan scratched his jaw. "I'm going to go with apple."

"Red or yellow?"

"Yes."

Grace giggled. "All right, you can have both because I have two favorites. Raspberries and watermelon."

"Wait." He yanked his legs in and sat up straight. "I'm changing to watermelon. I forgot about them." He pulled his eyebrows into a V. "I hope I don't lose points for changing."

"You goof. Change away."

Chaucer ambled over and plopped down between them, purring when they reached to pet him.

Grace clucked her tongue. "You interrupted our game, but I think we're done. And in case you heard what I said about rabbits, don't get in a kerfuffle. I still love you." Her eyes lifted to Ethan. "I planted a few watermelon seeds in the garden. Hopefully, this summer will be long enough and hot enough for them to mature."

"I can already taste them and feel the juice dripping down my chin. So your garden is in?"

Grace nodded. "Yes. Mae and Isobel helped Allie and me plant everything. They are even giving us a hand with the weeding and watering. We had a good time that day—laughing and singing. You know, they feel a whole lot more like family than boarders."

"Mary didn't help?"

Grace shrugged one shoulder. "Mary moved out last weekend at the end of the school term."

Ethan twisted to look straight at her. "She's gone?"

"Yes. It was kind of an awkward conversation when she told me she was leaving. Awkward and sad. She said she couldn't stay in Emmett."

"I think you have me to thank for that."

"What? How so?"

"Don't ask." Ethan leaned back in his chair again.

Grace had to bite her tongue to keep from asking. "Okay." Why in the world did Ethan think he was responsible? "The saddest part was when she said she wasn't sure she wanted to be a Christian anymore, that praying didn't work. I couldn't think of the right words to say so I didn't say much. Mae tried to talk to her later, but her mind was made up. And now she's gone. So... one less boarder makes finances tight again. But Esther says Ben will go out to the farm in a couple of days and bring Bossie back to their place. I won't have to buy milk anymore. That will save money."

"Is this a lead-up to diving into the ledger?" He placed both hands on the arms of his chair.

"No." She averted her gaze. When she looked back at him she swallowed, trying to moisten her suddenly dry mouth. She pressed a hand to her stomach in hopes of curtailing the jitters. "I'd like to talk with you about something."

"All right." Ethan rubbed his palm down his pant leg before dropping his hand to Chaucer again. "Shoot."

"A while ago God showed me something I was holding inside, something I wasn't even aware of." She cleared her throat. "All this time I harbored resentment toward Søren for leaving me alone to deal with Halstad House, raise Allie, and provide a home for us. I know he didn't do it on purpose, but knowing it in my head didn't alter how I felt. I think I didn't want to face it. That resentment slowly turned to bitterness without me realizing it. Then Pastor Grant spoke about the effects of bitterness and unforgiveness. It was hard to hear and a little scary to admit and talk to God about it. But I knew I had to. Pastor showed us the passage in Hebrews where bitterness not only affects us, but springs up and affects those around us. Like ripples on a pond. That was happening more and more. Usually, I did okay, but often I just felt...peevish is the best way to describe it, I guess." Grace gave Ethan a weak smile. "I'm so glad I brought it all to the Lord. And even though it was hard to see, I'm glad God showed me what had been stewing in my heart all along. I asked Him to forgive me for hanging onto that resentment and to heal the wounds I felt deep down. And I asked Him to restore my joy. I know His forgiveness is always there; I just needed to give up what I held onto and accept what He offered. Forgiveness, peace, freedom." Her chest rose as she breathed in. "It's also changed how I see Søren. I always thought he could do no wrong. Maybe he's more real, not way up on a pedestal." Grace whipped her head toward him. "I don't mean that in a bad way... I just meant..."

"It's okay. I know what you mean."

Ethan's eyes held an expression she couldn't quite read, but it reassured her.

"I can see the difference in you," he said.

"You can?"

"Uh-huh."

"Well, Allie told me I was nice again."

Ethan snorted. "I wouldn't put it quite like that because I think you're always nice, but you definitely seem happier."

Grace chewed her bottom lip. "There's something else."

Ethan nodded. "Okay."

She cleared her throat again. "I asked God for forgiveness and I apologized to Allie and Esther, but I..." She reached down and took his hand from Chaucer's head. Her chin quivered. "Here you are my best friend and I about snapped your head off. I'm sorry for being rude and ill-tempered. You didn't deserve it. Then when you didn't come around for several days I worried that I'd ruined—"

"Hey." He squeezed her hand. "No worries, Lils. I already forgave you. But if you need to hear it..." He locked eyes with her. "I forgive you. It's all good."

Relief flooded in. "Thank you," she whispered.

The breeze rustled the locust blossoms, carrying their fragrance anew. Grace nestled into her chair again and squeezed his hand in return.

# Thirty

"Done." Grace hung a damp dishtowel on the rack, its red and brown embroidery outlining a bonnet-clad girl under the word *Wednesday*. Wiping her hands front and back on her apron, she glanced out the window when the familiar clip-clop of a horse's hooves and the creak of a wagon passed the house. White lace curtains flapped in the back window. A hummingbird flitted among the rambling wild roses and her clematis vines that twined around porch posts and railings. Though at times she felt overwhelmed running a boarding house, not today. Her eyes roamed the room, from the gleam of the wooden floor she'd polished yesterday on her hands and knees, to the cookstove with fresh blacking. She gave a deep sigh. Funny how a spick-and-span house could fill her with a sense of well-being, but it always did.

As soon as Allie came in from the chicken coop, they'd head to the post office. She looked forward to a long-overdue visit with Esther and Dad.

The back door slammed. Allie waltzed into the kitchen, her eyes glowing. She held up a basket. "Lookie. I got seven whole eggs."

"That's wonderful." Grace took the basket. "Those chickens are certainly earning their keep."

"Uh-huh. And they're layin' eggs, too."

Grace grinned. She brought the clean egg bowl from the worktable and laid the eggs in it one by one. "No trouble with the rooster, I take it."

"You mean Fred? Nope."

"Fred?"

"Uh-huh. I named him that."

"What made you think of that name?"

"He just looks like a Fred."

"Aha." Grace placed the bowl on the worktable. "All right, let's wash up and head across the street."

"Yeah!" Allie rushed to the counter while Grace poured water into a basin.

When they were both clean as a whistle, Grace held the door while Allie scurried under her arm. In the middle of the street, Grace took Allie's hand and swung it back and forth. "I guess Fred is a better name than the one your Auntie Esther picked."

"What did she name him?"

"Stew meat."

Allie stopped in her tracks. "Willikens."

The bell over the post office door jingled when they entered. Allie raced through the doorway. "Uncle Ben!"

Ben looked up from sweeping the floor and beamed. "Good morning, you two." He wrapped Allie in a hug, then tossed her high in the air.

Giggles erupted from the five-year-old.

"Are you staying a bit?" he asked. At Grace's nod, he gestured toward the rows of mailboxes. "You've got something in yours." He stepped behind the counter, poked his head through the entry to their house, and called out for his wife.

Grace thanked God for Ben. Not only had he proven to be a good friend to her and an attentive uncle to Allie, he had shown himself a kind, loving husband to Esther; no doubt he'd be a great father. Grace had watched her no-nonsense sister blossom over the months they'd been married—she was more carefree, a little softer around the edges. And in another four months, Esther would experience the incredible joys of motherhood.

Esther's smiling face appeared. "Perfect timing. I just pulled biscuits out of the oven. I have fresh butter and honey. Any takers?"

"Me." Allie wiggled down from Ben's arms.

"Just let me grab our mail first." Grace opened her box and pulled out a white legal-sized envelope. She examined the return address as she walked toward her sister. "Guenther Law Offices, Spokane, Washington. Hmm...addressed to Mrs. S. I. Halstad. Well, that's me, but I've never heard of Guenther Law Offices."

Stepping from the post office into Esther and Ben's kitchen was like stepping into a different world. While the post office's simple interior designated it as a place of business, Esther's kitchen imparted a cozy, cheerful, sit-right-down-and-make-yourself-at-home quality. Tan curtains with blue flowers matched the table cloth covering her square oak table. A large braided rug in various shades of brown dotted with denim blue lay underneath. Lovely tatted lace borders lined the edges of the open shelves where Esther kept her dishes. Today, the sun's rays streamed through a window, dispersing light as it hit a cut glass creamer. Like a prism, it cast a tiny rainbow onto the table.

Dad sat in a chair, leg propped on an ottoman, buttering a steaming hot biscuit.

"Grampa!" Allie ran to him, clutched the arm of the chair, and rocked on her heels.

He grinned and set the biscuit and knife on a china plate. "If it isn't my favorite granddaughter and her charming mama." He hitched Allie onto his lap.

"Hi, Dad." Grace planted a kiss on top of his head. She stood next to him while she ripped open the envelope. After scanning the contents, she frowned and plunked down onto a kitchen chair beside him. *What in the world?* She rubbed her forehead and reread the lawyer's words. *This can't be.*

"Lily Grace?" Dad laid his hand on her arm. "You're as white as a sheet. What's wrong?"

"This letter. It makes no sense."

"Grace?" Esther laid the baking pan on a small butcher-block table and scooted into the chair across from her. "What is it? What does the letter say?"

"It says..." Grace sucked in a shaky breath. "It says that Mr. Guenther is an attorney representing Einar Brevik. His *client* alleges that Søren borrowed money from him to purchase our home and he used Halstad House as collateral." She shook her head. "He also says that he reviewed Einar's claim and researched courthouse records. He found everything to be legitimate."

"Poppycock." Esther waved a hand in front of her face. "I don't believe a word of it. Let me see that." She reached across the table and snatched the letter.

"I don't believe it either," Grace said. "Søren had no use for Einar and he certainly wouldn't have trusted him with any business dealings. He always said..." She glanced at Allie who had crawled into her grandfather's lap and stared at Grace wide-eyed. "Well, never mind what he said."

"Pfft." Esther smacked the letter onto the table, jostling the creamer and teapot. "And according to this, you have to vacate the premises? Of all the odious, loathsome—"

Grace cleared her throat, tipping her head toward her wide-eyed daughter.

"Sorry," Esther whispered.

Allie jumped to the floor and tugged on her mother's sleeve. "Did that Einar man do somethin' bad?"

Grace smoothed the worry from Allie's brow. "I think he's trying to pull the wool over our eyes. But we'll figure it out. Don't fret."

The kitchen door opened, and Ben's voice called out, "Look what the cat dragged in." He and Ethan, all smiles, breezed into the room.

Allie ran to Ethan and grabbed his hand. "That mean Einar man is tryin' to put some wool in our eyes." She scrunched her nose.

He gave her a blank look and shifted his gaze to Grace.

She offered him a lopsided grin. "She means he's trying to

pull the wool over our eyes." Grace motioned for Allie to sit on her lap.

"Here. Read this." Esther leaned over the table, her apron stretching tight across her rounded belly. She thrust the letter at Ethan.

Ethan examined the letter. Ben looked over Ethan's shoulder, but had to dart back to the other room when the post office bell jingled. Ethan muttered as he read, and his nostrils flared. When he looked up at Grace, his eyes flashed. "This is utter rot. Søren would never—"

"I know. But what do we do? Ignore it because it's ridiculous?" She toyed with Allie's braid.

Ethan shook his head. "No..." He rubbed his thumb along his jawline. "I rode into town with the boss and a man named Corelli. God must have orchestrated the timing. Corelli is the attorney for the mill. Right now he and Mr. Emmett are having lunch at the Bluebird Café. I'll run over and ask if he'd come take a look at this when they're through."

"Mommy?"

Grace cringed at the sight of Allie's over-bright eyes. She feared her daughter had picked up on the tension blanketing the room. She brushed stray wisps of hair from Allie's temple. "I'm sorry if all our talk scared you." She kissed her forehead. "Don't you worry. We'll get it taken care of and everything will be right as rain. Okay?"

"'Kay." Allie touched Grace's cheek.

"Well, there's no sense worrying about it." Esther rubbed her stomach. "We'll wait to hear what the attorney has to say." She rose and placed more plates and knives on the table. "In the meantime, let's eat these biscuits before they get stone cold. And when he does get here, Allie—" She pointed a finger at her. "You and I can go see how Bossie is doing instead of listening to a bunch of boring old grownup talk."

Grace shot a smile Esther's way.

An hour later, Grace poured Mr. Corelli a cup of tea. "Would you care for a biscuit with honey?"

He eyed the plate of biscuits, fresh from the warming oven, and sighed. He shook his head. "I shouldn't. Just finished a big meal, you know." He lifted the teacup to his lips, sipping as he perused the letter from Einar's attorney.

Mr. Corelli reminded Grace of a walrus—minus the tufts, of course. Portly, almost corpulent, with wide-set eyes, a broad, flat nose, and a massive salt-and-pepper mustache with sides that hid his jaws, the attorney inspired confidence in her, despite his comical appearance. He wore a tailored black suit with a red-and-green plaid vest. A gold watch chain hung from its small pocket. At first glance, his lackadaisical expression gave her the impression he was half asleep, but on the second and third glances, she changed her mind. His eyes revealed intelligence and a keen mind.

He replaced the cup in its saucer. Propping his elbow on the table, he rested his chin in his hand and tapped a finger against his cheek. "Hmm..." He looked from one to the other, Grace, Dad, Ethan, Ben. "Hmm..."

Dad shifted in his chair. "Well?"

Mr. Corelli sat back, reached for a biscuit and smothered it with butter and honey. "The letter appears genuine. Guenther presents a solid case."

Grace laid a hand on her chest. "But, Mr. Corelli, my husband never would have done this. He always spoke of how thankful he was to own the house outright."

Dad snorted. "And if he'd been in need of money, Einar Brevik is the last person he would have approached."

"Even if Einar *were* the last person, Søren never would've taken a nickel from him," Ethan said.

Grace nodded. "It's true."

The attorney held up his hand. "I believe you. I'm only telling you what I see here. I have suspected Mr. Guenther of being involved in a few questionable deals, but nothing has ever been proven. And he *is* a board-certified, licensed attorney." He wiped the corners of his mouth and his mustache with a napkin. He glanced at the plate of biscuits again, then shook his head. "But, young lady..." He smiled at Grace. "There is an easy solution to this dilemma."

"Praise the Lord." Grace slumped in her chair. "And what is that?"

"Produce to the courts the documents showing that Halstad House belonged to Søren outright and therefore to you."

Grace felt a flush creep across her cheeks. The documents. Ah, there was the rub. "Søren took care of all our business affairs. I don't have a clue where any documents might be. I've never run across them amongst the ledgers and papers I deal with." She stole a look at Ethan.

He shook his head. "I've never seen them either."

"Unfortunately, this is quite common." Mr. Corelli clicked his tongue. "Well, don't worry. We'll go one step at a time. I'll examine the courthouse records while you hunt for those documents at home. Deal?" He held out his hand to Grace.

She shook it. "Deal."

He checked his pocket watch and snapped it shut. "I must go." Rising, he looked at Grace. Walrus features or not, his eyes exuded compassion and concern. "Don't worry. We'll sort this out."

"Wait." Ethan rubbed the back of his neck. "I think you should hear this."

Mr. Corelli sat back down.

"I hesitated to say anything because I only heard this second-hand, actually, maybe third-hand. But it may shed light on what Einar's up to."

All eyes turned to him.

"Tell us what you know, son," Dad said.

"A fellow I work with—someone I've always found trustworthy—told me he overheard a conversation between two men the other day. He was at the livery stable and at first he didn't pay them any mind. Then he heard them speak of some pretty shady dealings. They had no idea he was there, and he was afraid to move in case things turned ugly. The men talked about some gang mixed up with bootleg whiskey. They buy it in Canada since it's not under prohibition, smuggle it across the border, and sell it here on the black market. They mentioned Einar's name more than once."

"Brother." Ben rubbed the back of his neck. "Do you suppose they're the business associates Einar comes to see?"

"Hard to say." Ethan shrugged a shoulder. "But I wouldn't be surprised. Anyway, they laughed about Einar trying to sweet talk some lady." His face flushed when his eyes met Grace's. "They said Einar had found the perfect place to cache the liquor and to conduct his business, less than five miles from the border." Ethan inhaled. "He was trying to get his hands on a large white residence right here in Emmett."

Grace's breath caught in her throat. "Halstad House."

Lying in bed later, Grace tried to calm her fears. She'd come up empty-handed today in her search for legal papers. Tomorrow, she'd scour the place from top to bottom. All of a sudden Søren's parents came to her mind. She should write to them in the morning. Maybe Dad and Mom Halstad had some idea where to look. Yes. She'd write first thing.

She snuggled deeper under the covers. Surely God would not let her lose Halstad House. The very thought was absurd. She stared into the darkness. The night-blackened room usually wrapped her in a snug cocoon where she lay sheltered, protected. Tonight, a somber unease hovered. She pulled the blanket up to her chin. She was His child, and He was Almighty God. He would never allow such a thing to happen.

Would He?

# Thirty-One

"I've looked everywhere, Esther. Even ridiculous places like empty crocks in the root cellar and the same trunks you and I tore through searching for my old doll." Grace tilted the spoon above her teacup, watching amber-colored honey drizzle into the dark liquid. "Allie insisted on helping. I've been so preoccupied with the document hunt I'm afraid she's been stuck with the short end of the stick as far as my attention. After so many times of me turning down her pleas to play or go swimming or for a walk, maybe she figured ransacking the house with a befuddled mother was better than nothing."

"And has she been a help?" Esther topped off her tea.

"Yes and no. She brought every scrap of paper she found for me to peruse. I had no idea the number of recipes, laundry hints, and grocery lists I've left lying around. I kept reminding myself her heart was in the right place no matter how distracting it was. It's a moot point now, though."

"What do you mean?"

"We found a spider. Or rather, it found us. I pulled a box away from the wall up in the attic and exposed one of those oversized freakish spiders with hairy faces. The ones that look like they're staring at you?"

Esther nodded.

"It startled me so much I jumped back, but Allie's shriek liked to have raised the dead. She shinnied up me like a terrified bear cub scrambling up a tree. How I kept my balance I'll never know. I've seen that girl handle snakes and all sorts of creepy-crawlies with no qualms at all. But throw a spider into the mix and she comes unraveled. I can't say I blame her with this one. Nightmarish-looking is an understatement. Now she leaves the ransacking to me and scampers around with Uffda, Chaucer, and sometimes, Fred."

"Fred?"

Grace grinned. "Stew Meat to you."

"Land sakes."

Grace splayed her hands out on the tablecloth and bent to rest her forehead on them. When she sat back up, she groaned. "I'm making light of things but..."

Esther touched her hand. "I know, sister-mine."

"I've come to a dead end." Grace rubbed a hand across her face. "If Søren was here right now, I'd give him a piece of my mind. What in the world did he do with those papers?"

Esther walked to the stove and retrieved the kettle. "You know, I've been thinking. Maybe Søren didn't store those papers here at all since you don't have a safe. His folks must have one at their store. That would be a natural place for him to keep them." Esther refilled the teapot with steaming hot water, then returned the kettle to the stove.

That made sense. Grace laid her spoon on the saucer. "You may well be right. I should have telephoned them instead of writing, but I figured the documents would show up before they wrote back. Well, it's been two weeks." Her stomach tightened. "*Two weeks*, Esther. I only have two more weeks before—"

"No panic allowed." Esther lowered herself back into her chair. "Yes, it's been two weeks. Which means their letter ought to be here any time."

As if on cue, Ben peeked his head through the kitchen door. "Flipped the closed sign at the post office and ran over here right away." He held out an envelope.

Grace jumped up and grabbed it. "Thank heavens." She ripped it open and pulled out one thin page. Her heart sank at the first sentence.

"Well?" Esther asked.

"The Halstads don't have any documents or any idea what Søren did with them."

"What?" Esther took aim at a wet spot on the tablecloth, stabbing it with her napkin. "I thought I had found the answer."

"Me, too." Grace plopped into her chair. "It was a good thought." Now what? She kneaded her forehead between her thumb and fingers. She had to come up with something.

Esther poured another cup of tea when Ben scooted into the chair next to her. "Do they say anything else in the letter?"

Grace scanned the page. "Just that to make sure, they rummaged through their safe and the office desk. Nothing from Søren."

The wall clock ticked. Uffda barked in the backyard. Fred crowed.

Esther blew out a deep breath. "No matter. We're not licked yet. There's always Mr. Corelli. I bet he's found something by now."

Grace refolded the letter and slid it into the envelope.

"What I want to know is why Einar pursued this in the first place." Ben scooted his chair closer. "It's almost as if he knew you didn't have the papers."

Grace shrugged her shoulders, then glanced at Esther when she cleared her throat.

"It's my fault," Esther said.

"What?" Grace couldn't believe that.

Esther leaned back in the chair, her eyes holding an appeal as she looked at Grace. "A few days ago I remembered something that happened last Christmas. You and I were in the kitchen joking about your bookkeeping organization, or lack of it. I asked if you'd kept all the records straight from the start of the boardinghouse four years earlier. You said, 'Four years ago? I don't know where half my stuff is. Ethan has to help me keep things straight from two weeks ago.' We got a good laugh over that, but when I turned around, I saw Einar stepping from the kitchen into the parlor. He must have overheard our exchange and took a chance."

Ben toyed with the handle of his teacup. "I wouldn't put it past him."

"I'm sorry I opened my mouth," Esther said.

Grace rose and kissed the top of her sister's head. "The fault is Einar's, not yours." She flipped her braid behind her back and squared her shoulders. "Okay, okay. Two dead ends. So now we wait to hear from Mr. Corelli."

Didn't people tell stories of God coming through at the last minute? *Please, God. The last minute is approaching like a freight train.*

Two days later, Grace stood over Esther's kitchen table, help-ing her sister measure cushy green flannel for baby blankets. Dad snoozed in a nearby chair, head back, mouth agape, snoring in an uneven rhythm. She and Esther looked up as the door from the post office swung open. Grace caught her breath.

Three silent men strode into the room—Ethan, Ben, and Mr. Corelli.

Grace tried to gauge the attorney's frame of mind by the ex-pression on his face, but he gave away nothing. She and Esther scooped up the pile of fabric and dumped it on the sideboard.

Chairs scraped against the plank floor as Ben and Ethan pulled out seats for the ladies. Dad snorted and sat up with a start. Everyone scooted up to the table, fidgeting in the ten-sion-choked air.

"Well?" Grace's stomach clenched, and her heart hammered against her rib cage.

Mr. Corelli shook his head.

Esther gripped her sister's hand so tightly Grace was afraid she'd cut off the blood flow.

"I searched. I talked to countless people. I checked the re-cords." Mr. Corelli shook his head again. "If Guenther has done something shady, he is covering his tracks well. Ethan tells me you have not found any documents?" He pursed his lips and gave her a hopeful look.

"No," Grace whispered. A heaviness settled in her chest. She rubbed her arm with her free hand to chase away the goose-bumps. The attorney's eyes conveyed such sympathy, her own filled with tears. "We were hoping you..."

"I am so sorry, Mrs. Halstad. Without that proof I can do nothing. Every T has been crossed. Every I dotted. All the records filed state that Halstad House reverts legally to Einar Brevik if the debt is not paid."

*It can't be.* Grace stared down at her lap, the pressure in her chest as intense as Esther's grip. Struggling to take deep, even breaths, she lifted her eyes to Mr. Corelli. "So that's it? It's over?"

"I'm afraid so. My hands are tied." He tugged the knot of his tie, twisting his head left and right. He pulled his gold watch from his vest pocket and stood. "I wish..." His gaze traveled around the room. "Again, I am more sorry than I can say." He shook his head one last time and clicked his tongue. With that, he left the kitchen. A minute later, the bell over the post office door jingled.

Esther squeezed Grace's already squished hand. "You and Allie can move in here."

Grace leaned toward her sister. "Thank you." She rose on legs so shaky she had to steady herself against the table. "I should get home."

Everyone but Dad jumped to their feet. Ethan's chair tipped, landing with a thud. "Stay here."

"We'll go with you."

"You shouldn't be alone right now."

They all spoke at once.

She held up her hand, palm out, looking from one to the other. She needed time to think. She needed time to pray. "I'm not shutting you out. Honest. But just for a while I'd like to be by myself."

The burning sensation of anxious eyes on her back trailed her as she walked away.

She stepped onto the boardwalk. From the barn, Bossie's lowing, soft and mournful, reflected her heart. "It's done," she whispered.

The next afternoon, Grace sat in the dining room with Mae and Isobel. She should have said something earlier. Given them time to prepare. But she'd been so sure everything would work out. Grace reached both hands across the table, catching first Mae's hand, then Isobel's. "Where will you go?"

Isobel paled. "I—I don't know."

Mae pulled her hand from Grace's and wrapped an arm around Isobel. "But God knows."

Isobel turned to Mae, a question in her eyes.

"You can count on it, my dear," Mae said.

Isobel took a deep breath. "Yes. Yes. I read Proverbs 3:5 and 6 just this morning. God said He will direct my paths." Little by little, color returned to Isobel's cheeks. Her smile to Grace may have been tenuous, but it was genuine. "Don't worry about me. God is still God, right? I may not know where I'm going, but I'm on my way."

Mae glanced at Isobel, then Grace. "I could return to one of my daughters, although I don't sense the Lord releasing me from my stay in Emmett." She rubbed Isobel's shoulder. "Who knows? Maybe we'll be roommates somewhere."

"That would be fine by me," Isobel said.

Mae smoothed the tablecloth in front of her. "We'll be fine, Grace. What about you? How are you doing?"

Grace wanted to smile and say she was trusting God. That all was well. Why was she still fighting an uphill battle? "I thought I had come so far in my faith."

Would she ever trust God with no reservations? She sighed. Now she could add guilt to the other emotions rampaging within her. "I prayed and prayed. I was so sure God would..." She ran a hand across her cheek. "I don't understand why He allowed this. The house Søren bought. Allie's home. My home. Our future. Our security." She flicked away a tear from her cheek as if it were a pesky gnat. "I know the Bible says God is with me, but sometimes it doesn't feel that way."

Mae fixed her gaze on Grace. Her eyes held love and compassion. No condemnation. She stroked Grace's arm. "You *have* come a long way. Even if you don't realize it." She rested her forearms on the table, linking her fingers together. "When we pray, His answers may not look like what we expected. That doesn't mean He isn't there. He is in every moment—no doubt working behind the scenes where we cannot see. I confess I don't understand why this has happened either. But now is when walking by faith comes in. He says that all things work together for good to those who love God."

"Walking by faith comes easy to you." Grace blushed as she detected the peevish tone that had slipped out.

Mae chuckled, though a hint of sadness lurked behind her smiling eyes. "Oh, no, my dear. Faith is most always hard-won. I certainly struggled along the way." She looked between the two young women. "Should I tell you some of my story?"

Their silence prompted a slight nod from her. She closed her eyes for a few moments.

Gathering her thoughts? Or praying? Grace suspected the latter.

Mae opened her eyes. "When my husband and I first married, I enjoyed what I considered our picture-perfect life. Cliff worked at an insurance company. Selling policies came naturally to him. People loved him. He made good money, and we furnished our home with nice things—nothing grand, but very tasteful. Though I loved our home and our life, I made the dreadful mistake of pushing my husband to work harder, maybe become a partner in the business.

"Cliff did not take kindly to my urging. He tired of what he called nagging. I called it helping him to meet his untapped potential. Years later I realized God called it being a contentious wife—which Proverbs describes as a continual dripping.

"Anyway, in eight years I gave birth to three beautiful children. Sarah the oldest. Emily two years later. Five years passed before our last baby arrived. Our precious son, Charlie."

A son? Grace had heard Mae speak of her daughters many times, but never a son.

Mae lifted a sad smile to them. "I became so caught up in raising the children, at first I missed the signs that all was not well. When I did notice the strain on Cliff's face, his stooped shoulders, and frequent sighing, I questioned him. He always said everything was fine—until one night he came home hours late, weaving into the room, slurring his words, reeking of liquor. He plopped onto the davenport and told me business had been slow. He had lost two of his clients and his boss had reprimanded him. He blamed me for the turn of events, saying my constant nagging made him lose his confidence. Staring at my husband, I wondered if I *had* contributed to it. I told him how sorry I was and vowed never to nag him again.

"It made no difference. He lost another client and, finally, his job. He began drinking more, staying out late, berating me when he returned home. He would sober up for a while and land a new job. Every time, I hoped things would be better. But something always happened at work, and he started drinking again and blaming me. As the children grew older, he found blame with them also, especially Charlie. His blaming and bullying worsened as years went by. He never raised a hand to any of us, but, oh, his words could be so cruel. Even so, I convinced myself that as a submissive wife I needed to stay to help my husband. I kept silent about what went on at home when speaking with friends or my family.

"Meanwhile, more and more, Cliff bruised our souls with his harsh words. And to my shame, I allowed it to continue.

"The year Sarah graduated from high school, my husband died in a trolley-car accident in downtown Seattle. At the funeral, Charlie looked at me with cold, bleak eyes and said, 'I'm glad he's dead.' He never spoke of his father after that."

Mae closed her eyes and clasped her hands as if in prayer. For a moment she sat, silent and still, then she inhaled and looked at them again. "I took in sewing to make ends meet. Sarah got a job at the soda fountain in a store close by. My parents helped as they could. When someone invited me to a small community fellowship near our home, I decided to try it. I'd attended a large, popular church off and on, but would come away feeling empty and discouraged. What a difference I found in that humble little fellowship. The pastor spoke the truth in love. He brought the Bible to life, hitting a chord with me almost every Sunday. God became real to me there.

"Sarah and Emily joined me and the Holy Spirit brought deep healing to all three of us. However, no matter how I pleaded, Charlie refused to come."

Grace's eyes stung. She laid a gentle hand on Mae's arm. Isobel squeezed Mae's shoulder.

Mae sighed and nodded. "Somehow, and I know God is the only answer, Sarah and Emily came through that time heart-whole. They both married caring, committed Christian men and are blessed to see their own children walk with the Lord. How I thank God for that.

"Charlie was a different story. Bitterness and resentment grew, eating away at him. One day I returned home from the market to find Charlie gone, along with a satchel, some clothes, and a little food. He was fifteen years old." Tears swam in her eyes. "I haven't seen or heard from him since that day.

"After all these years, the wound can still sting, even though I know God has forgiven me and continues to restore me. I pray for my sweet boy every day. I have learned to trust God for the good things, the bad things, and the impossible things."

Grace wiped away the tears streaming down her cheeks.

Isobel didn't bother to wipe hers away, just let them fall.

Grace stood and walked around the table. She put her arms around Mae and Isobel, resting her head on Mae's gray curls. "We'll pray for Charlie, too."

"Lord, I don't want to harbor resentment and bitterness again." Grace's whispered words mingled with Allie's even breathing and the familiar night-time chorus of crickets chirring, an owl hooting, and doves calling to each other. She rubbed the palm of her hand over her heart and choked on a sob. "I'm not God. You are. I may not understand, but I give Halstad House to You. Even if my emotions are reeling, I choose to trust You. I choose to believe You'll direct our paths—Allie's and mine. I don't know what's around the next corner, but You will hold our hands and guide us. You promised it in Your Word so I'm going to hang on to that promise with all my might."

A breeze flowed in through the window, bringing the sweet scent of woodbine. The flame in the oil lamp flickered. Grace leaned forward and blew a puff of air down the lamp's chimney. In the dark, she crawled under the covers, closed her eyes, and waited for the night's song to lull her to sleep.

They were in God's hands.

# Thirty-Two

It made perfect sense. Ethan was sure she'd agree. Almost sure. Grace could be kind of stubborn sometimes. He'd thought the idea through from every angle and as long as he worded it right—yes, she'd agree. His boots tapped against the faded boardwalk. He drummed his fingers on the legs of his brown corduroy trousers, humming a nameless tune.

"Mr. Ethan!" Allie collided with him and squeezed his waist. "We're goin' to the mercantile."

Mae and Isobel brought up the rear, Mae clothed in lavender, Isobel in turquoise blue.

"Good morning." Mae smiled, eyes twinkling, the embodiment of everyone's favorite grandma.

"It's nice to see you," Isobel said. She sidestepped a broken board.

Allie tugged Ethan's sleeve. "Look what Mommy gave me." A shiny copper penny lay nestled in her hand. "I can get a peppermint stick or some lemon drops."

"Yum." Ethan hunkered down in front of her. "Your mother is home?"

"Uh-huh. She said she could have a piece of quiet if I went with Mrs. King and Miss Isobel."

Mae laid her hand on Allie's shoulder. "She was teasing you."

"I know. She had her teasing smile on."

Ethan tweaked Allie's braid and rose. "I'll let you get to it then. Don't want to keep that candy waiting."

"Have a pleasant day." Mae turned in the direction of the mercantile with Isobel at her side.

Allie hugged him again. "Bye."

"Ladies." He tipped his hat as they sauntered away. This was providential. Ethan had hoped to catch Grace alone so they could talk in private.

He found her in the kitchen, elbow-deep in linens. He'd never seen anything so fetching. Her apron covered her frock; a red bandanna tied around her head kept the hair out of her face; that chestnut-colored braid he loved hung almost to her waist. Man, what he wouldn't give to feast his eyes on this vision every day in his own kitchen.

"Hey," he said.

"Hey yourself. Come on in." Grace placed her hands on the small of her back and stretched. "Would you mind setting this box with the ones over there?" She pointed to the wall next to the side door where four stacks of boxes stood like sentinels.

Ethan threw his hat on a chair. "You bet." He hoisted the box of linens and planted it on top of the closest stack.

"Gracious. I'm ready for a break. How about if I get a bottle of ginger ale from the root cellar? Want to split it? We can sit out on the back steps and visit awhile."

"Sounds good to me. Need any help?"

"No. I'll only be a minute."

Ethan walked through the mudroom and out the back door. Seating himself in the middle of the stairway, long legs crossed at the ankles, he leaned back and rested his elbows on the step behind him.

In the chicken run, hens the color of hard-baked brick pecked at the ground, accompanied by soft clucks. The rooster, in more flamboyant colors, strutted around his kingdom, keeping his brood in line.

Ethan had been as stunned as Grace when it became clear she had to relinquish Halstad House to Einar. He'd run the gamut of emotions—anger, confusion, sadness, resignation. However, today, contentment descended on him like soft spring rain. His life could be on the verge of a major change. One he'd hankered after for a long time.

"Here you go." Grace handed him a glass of fizzy golden ginger ale. She sat next to him and took a sip. "Mm..."

"Good stuff." Ethan smacked his lips. "Do you plan to make more this year?"

"We'll see. Esther, Ben, and I could do it—maybe once things settle down."

"You can recruit me, too."

Grace gave him a half-smile.

Geoffrey Chaucer lumbered up the stairs, flopping to his side between them.

"Hey there, mister." Grace scratched him under the chin, setting off his internal motor. Rubbing her hand down his back, she turned her gaze to the garden. "I hate to miss our fall raspberries. They have such a great flavor. It looks to be a bumper crop, too..." She sighed. "Oh well."

Here was the opening he needed. He brought his knees up and set down his glass. "How are you doing with all this?"

"Up and down, I guess." She tipped her head. "At times I feel such confidence that everything will be all right. Other times, panic sneaks up on me like a bad dream. I break out in a cold sweat trying to figure out what direction to take. We can't live with Esther forever." Grace wrinkled her sunburned nose. "But underneath those ups and downs, I know God is working even if I can't see it. A few nights ago Isobel said, 'I don't know where I'm going, but I'm on my way.' I'm right with her."

Uffda trotted around the corner of the house. The moment he spied Ethan, he sprang up the stairs and leaped onto him, tail wagging in circles while his tongue slathered Ethan's cheek.

He pushed him down onto his lap and rubbed the top of the dog's head. "Good boy." Uffda scooched until he lay prone across Ethan's knees, tongue lolling, tiny groans escaping.

Ethan's eyes met Grace's. "I have a solution for you. About which direction you should take."

"You do? I'd love to hear it."

Why was his mouth so dry all of a sudden? He took another sip of ginger ale and swallowed. "You and I should get married."

Grace's eyes widened. Her mouth fell open. She blinked and locked eyes with him. "What are you talking about?"

"We should get married."

"I heard that part. I'm just wondering where it came from."

"It's logical, the smart thing to do." Wasn't it obvious?

"Oh, is it now?"

He recognized the expression on her face, the one eyebrow uplifted thing. "Don't go all stubborn on me. If you'll listen to reason..." He wiped sweaty palms on his pants legs.

She narrowed her eyes. "How is it the smart thing to do?"

"You have to move out. This would provide you with a place to go."

"Hmm..."

"You could bring your animals."

"Ethan..."

He rubbed the back of his neck. "I'm not doing a very good job of explaining. Let me try again."

"Good idea." She set down her glass and laced her fingers together.

"Okay." He drew a deep breath. "Like I said, you have to move. This gives you a home—you and Allie. All your animals can come. And—" He thought he'd prayed this through. Maybe he should've prayed a little more, but anyway, he hoped the next point would convince her. "You and I get along. You said yourself that I'm your best friend. Well, you're mine. What better reason to get married?"

She shot him a look that didn't bode well. "I received just as good an offer from my sister."

He scrambled to pull his thoughts together. "Yeah, but this would be your own place, not hers. You could do what you want, like change curtains or whatever."

"So..." Grace raised a hand to count on her fingers. "I should marry you because I need a place to live, you and I get along, my animals can come, and I can change the curtains?"

"Kind of, yes." Except it sounded better in his head. "One more thing." Heat crawled up his neck. "You and Allie can share the second bedroom."

A blush appeared on Grace's cheeks. "Good of you."

He gave a nervous laugh. "Hey, look at my side. I get to be a knight in shining armor and rescue a damsel in distress."

"Aha." Grace shook her head. "In other words, you're offering me a mercy marriage?"

Ethan sputtered. "That's not what I'd call it—exactly."

She stood and brushed off the front of her apron. "No thanks." She turned toward the back door.

"But—I—"

Chaucer rose and stared at him.

Ethan stared back. "What?" He felt a headache coming on.

The tabby slipped down the stairs. Ethan swore he held his nose in the air. "You've got to be kidding. The cat is taking Grace's side?" This whole thing did not go as planned. Maybe he should've left off the rescuing a damsel business. Where did that come from anyway? He'd blurted it out without thinking.

When he let go of Uffda, the dog took full advantage of his freedom. He erupted into a licking frenzy, covering Ethan's face with drool. As the screen door banged behind him, Ethan called over his shoulder, "At least your dog likes me!"

"Hi, sweetie." Grace patted the cushion beside her.

Allie scrambled onto the sofa. She scratched her knee and swung her bare feet back and forth. "Whatcha doin'?"

Grace held out a photograph for Allie to see. "I'm supposed to be packing knickknacks, but I ran across a cigar box with pictures in it and got distracted."

Allie took the photograph from her mother. "Who's this?"

"Your daddy's Uncle Sven and Aunt Miriam in front of their store in Spokane. This was before *Farfar* and *Farmor* took over the store."

"They look nice."

"I've heard they were very nice."

Allie set the picture in the box and took another. "How 'bout this one?"

Grace glanced at the photo. "I don't know." She flipped it over, but nothing was written to enlighten them on who the man plowing a field could be. "I'll have to see if Grandpa knows. Or maybe *Farfar* does. We can ask him next time they visit." She retrieved another picture, studying the little boy squinting into the sun, holding a string of fish.

Allie's heels kicked against the davenport's wooden frame. "Mommy?"

"Mm-hmm..."

"Do we hafta move to the poor farm?"

"What?" Grace dropped the picture into the box. "Why would you think that?"

"Lydie Sue's brother said we hafta go to the poor farm 'cause we're poor now. He said the poor farm is an awful place. They make everybody work in the fields all day long—with no breaks. Some people drop dead 'cause they're plumb wore out. They only feed them bread and water and give them one blanket to sleep on the floor." Allie's eyes held a question.

Grace's pulse quickened. She pulled Allie onto her lap, kissing her forehead. "Harv Jr. doesn't know what he's talking about. We are not going to the poor farm. We're moving in with Auntie Esther, Uncle Ben, and Grandpa, remember?"

"I told him that, but he said they'd pro'bly kick us out. Then we'd hafta go to the poor farm anyway." She leaned into her mother. "I didn't really believe him. He can be a stinker. But I had to know for sure."

Poor farm indeed. Grace wondered how two good-hearted people like Harv and Ada could have produced such a rapscallion for a son. It was beyond her. Allie said he teased his sisters without mercy. He'd done more than his fair share of teasing with Allie.

Grace wrapped her arms around her daughter and propped her chin on Allie's head. "There is a poor farm outside of Colville.

People who have no money or jobs and no place to go move there until they can get back on their feet. They work in the gardens, and I suppose there may be fields. But I'm sure the folks who run the farm are kind and do their best to make everybody comfortable."

Allie scrunched her nose. "No bread and water?"

Grace turned Allie around and tickled her ribs. "No doubt they have bread and water, but they go along with farm-fresh meals. And I bet they sleep in real beds, too." She cupped her daughter's cheek in her hand. "We'll be with Auntie Esther for a while. But as soon as I find a job, we can get a place of our own." She tweaked Allie's nose. "It'll be an adventure."

"I like a'ventures."

"Well, there you go."

"Yoo-hoo."

Grace and Allie looked over the back of the sofa. Esther made her way from the kitchen, cradling her rounded belly with her hands.

"Auntie Esther!" Allie jumped down and rushed to her, placing her ear on Esther's tummy. "Is the baby moving?"

"Baby is sleeping, I think." Esther rested a hand on the back of Allie's neck. "He has his nights and days turned around. He kicks off and on throughout the day and after supper he starts doing somersaults."

Allie lifted her eyes. "Tell me if he kicks, 'kay? I wanna feel it."

"Okay."

Allie turned to Grace. "Can I go outside 'n play?"

"*May* you go outside and play?"

"May I go outside and play?"

"Yes, you may."

Allie darted to the kitchen. With one hand on the door, she pivoted. "We're not goin' to the poor farm, Auntie Esther." She pushed the door open and disappeared.

"What was that all about?"

Grace shrugged. "News travels through this town faster than a prairie fire."

"Ah. What do the gossips have to say?" Esther slid onto the sofa.

"I'll tell you later."

Esther pulled an envelope from her apron pocket.

"What do you have there?" Grace asked.

"The return address is Guenther Law Offices. I thought you'd want to read it right away."

Grace stared at the envelope, trying to guess what lay inside. "I doubt they've changed their minds." Taking it from Esther, she opened it and scanned its contents—one type-written page, terse, to the point. "A not-so-friendly reminder. They take possession next Wednesday." She dropped her hands into her lap and shifted toward Esther. "I don't want to be here when they come."

"And you don't have to be. We'll make sure you've moved to our place by then. Lock, stock, and barrel." She eased into the back cushion. "How goes the packing? I wish I could help more but..." She rubbed her stomach.

"The last thing you and baby need is for you to tote around heavy boxes. You do enough as it is, freeing me up by cooking meals for all of us. Mae and Isobel help. And since the furniture goes with the house, it's mostly our personal things. The only big items are the large walnut buffet in the kitchen, Allie's trundle bed that Dad built, the cradle Søren made, our two rocking chairs, and a few trunks and the highchair in the attic. Maybe a few more things up there. Ethan and Ben will move all that Monday or Tuesday."

"All your canned goods in the root cellar go, right?"

"Absolutely. I'm not leaving those. We worked too hard on them." Grace bent her knee and pulled one leg under her.

From the back yard, summer sounds resonated. The whisper of wind in the pines, the cheerful trill of quail, the cackle of hens, Uffda's spirited woofs, Allie's gales of laughter. Every one of them comforted her.

Esther caught Grace's hand and laid it on her tummy. "Feel that?"

A smile played at the corners of Grace's mouth. She bent down, close to her sister's bulging midsection. "Hey there, little one. This is your Auntie Grace. Keep growing big and strong. We can hardly wait to meet you."

Esther's face radiated happiness. "It's a miracle, isn't it? Just think, a little over three months and I can hold him in my arms."

"Or her."

"Or her. I'm happy with either. Ben is, too." She rubbed her stomach. "Kicking spree is over. I'll call Allie for his next performance."

"Speaking of Allie, could she stay with you for the next few nights? It'd be easier for me to start packing first thing in the mornings if she wasn't underfoot—if you know what I mean."

"Of course. We'd love to have her."

"Thanks."

Later, as she brushed her hair, Grace tried to organize her thoughts. She'd been saving the attic, the kitchen, and her bedroom for last. Mae and Isobel offered to box up dishes and pots and pans. Everything would have been overwhelming without their help. She'd not heard a word about their own moving plans. She sure hoped they could all remain close.

Ethan and Ben could load boxes and take them across the street on Saturday. And, of course, the heavier things later.

Ethan. She grinned when she thought of his offer. She'd been miffed for a couple of days, but no more. His heart was in the right place. Besides, he was too good a friend to stay mad at for long. Grace just hoped things weren't awkward when he came over and that he wasn't too embarrassed about the whole deal. Goofy guy. She was more than ready for them to get back to normal.

Grace laid the brush on the bureau. After braiding her hair, she blew out the oil lamp and crawled under the covers. Tomorrow morning would be here before she knew it.

# Thirty-Three

Roses. Woodbine. Pine. Kneeling in front of the window, Grace inhaled the sweet scents wafting in on the cool morning air. The cloudless blue sky promised another scorching late July day, with rising heat rendering the main floor bearable, the upstairs roasting, the attic stifling. Until freshened by a new day.

Grace and her helpers, bless them, had worked far into the night, sorting and packing. She'd fallen into bed exhausted at midnight. Still, the three of them rose before dawn. After a quick breakfast, Isobel left for an early shift at the café while she and Mae tackled the root cellar. Now, heavy boxes of canned goods, dried herbs, and empty Mason jars awaited Ethan and Ben.

Mae had gone to her room to rest. Grace withdrew to hers.

This room. Grace turned from the window and sat on the floor, poring over every corner, every nook and cranny, stamping its image on her mind. Her bed, Double Wedding Ring quilt folded across the footboard, Allie's trundle bed, the oak bureau with mirror above, a pine washstand topped with her pink flowered bowl and pitcher, the padded rocking chair from her in-laws, two oak nightstands holding oil lamps with green globes. She touched the faded blue-and-brown rug covering the hardwood floor, then lifted her eyes to the floral wallpaper she and Esther had plastered to the walls, fits of laughter accompanying their mishaps and spills.

This room. Coming to Halstad House as a young bride, eager for what lay ahead. She and Søren crouching before their newborn's cradle, marveling at the gift God had given them. Secluding herself after the dreadful telegram from the war department, unable to put one foot in front of the other for weeks. But then, times with Allie, rocking, bedtime stories, lullabies, giggles.

This room held so much love.

Grace leaned back, the windowsill pressing into her shoulders. She closed her eyes. It was time. One more task remained. It could only be done here, surrounded by memories. Memories of joyful times, painful times, but somehow, always, memories touched by love. Yes, it was time.

The letter.

She stood and walked to the bureau. Removing the lid from the wooden box, she retrieved the envelope, holding it to her lips a moment before slitting the top with a bone-handled opener. She took the pages from within and sat on the edge of the bed. Her heart flip-flopped at the sight of Søren's distinctive handwriting. She smiled and smoothed the sheets across her lap.

May 2, 1918

Dear Grace,

    I take pen in hand to let you know I am well. The meals here can't compare to yours, and cinnamon rolls appear only in my dreams. Funny what one appreciates when hunger pangs hit, though.

    Thank you for the photographs. I kiss them both every night before I go to sleep. A couple of the men saw your picture. They tease me about how a big, dumb Norski could have won the heart of such a beautiful brown-eyed girl. I don't argue with them because I wonder the same thing myself.

    Something happened I want to tell you about, not to frighten you but to show how God can work even through me, a simple small-town boy from Emmett. Lots of guys have noticed me reading my Bible. Some ignore it, some give me a hard time, calling me Preacher or accusing me of thinking myself holier-than-thou. I don't let it bother me. Three friends kept asking me questions—Nick Karinski, Bob Taylor, and George Grimm. After spending time talking about God and the Bible, over a period of about two weeks, all three of them surrendered their lives to Him. To think, God let me be a part of this.

Four days ago, our unit was involved in a battle that took place in a dense forest. Nick, Bob, George, and I were together. I won't go into detail but Nick and I were the only ones to return. I feel the loss of Bob and George deeply, but I am comforted to know they are with Jesus and I will see them again. Nick and I both wrote to their families, letting them know of the decisions Bob and George made before they died. I hope it comforts them.

Their dying has made me consider my own mortality. Don't think me morbid—I have every intention of coming home to you. But if the unthinkable were to happen, I want to tell you this: Please don't grieve for me longer than you should.

"Did he know, Lord? Did You give him some kind of premonition?"

Let God heal your broken heart and restore joy to you. Marry again, Grace. Yes, you read that right. Find a strong, godly man who will treat you and our daughter with kindness and gentleness. You deserve the very best. You have so much love to give. Don't lock it away. I want your life to be full and happy. My desire is to stand right beside you, but if that is not to be, allow God to lead you to love and companionship.

"Oh, Søren," she murmured.

My sweet Lilya, when I think of you, there is an ache in my chest I cannot ease. I miss you more than words can say. It is necessary for me to be here and I will do my duty, but I long to be home with you. You are my life, little wife. (So now you see your Scandinavian husband can be romantic, ja?)

Grace wiped her cheek. Lilya. His pet name for her. Søren may not have spouted sentimental words very often, but when he did, he made them count.

One last thing I want to say. God has been speaking to me about my stubborn streak. I owe you an apology. He brought to my mind the times you and I sat around the table going over our bills and ledgers. I'm ashamed of my impatience. I know you tried hard to balance household accounts, and I'm afraid I made you think you were inadequate. I am sorry, sweetheart. I am proud of you and believe you are capable and smart. Will you forgive me?

"Forgive you? I already have," she whispered. "But thank you." The very thing Ethan had talked about, God had shown Søren long before. "Thank You, Lord."

While I am on the subject of finances, I meant to talk with you about something but forgot in the rush to prepare for my leavetaking. Since we do not own a strongbox and I did not want to leave important papers lying around in bureau drawers, I came up with a plan.

Grace caught her breath. She lifted one hand to her chest.

Later I realized it wasn't the best plan, but I can take care of it when I get home. Or if you'd like to do something about it beforehand, that's fine as well. Do what you think is best.

She read faster.

We have several important papers: the bill of sale from

*Roger Forester for our house, the deed to the house, and a copy of my Aunt Miriam's will. There is also a little money set aside as a nest egg. Like I said, since we do not own a strongbox, I tried to think of a place where the papers would be safe. In the steamer trunk that holds our wedding clothes, I built a false bottom.*

"Glory be!" Grace exploded off the bed and with the letter clutched in her hand, bolted from the room. With a whoop, she ran down the hall to the back landing and tore up the attic stairs. She flew past the two tiny bedrooms and into the main room. Sunlight streamed in through the windows. Flies buzzed at the screens. She fell to her knees in front of the trunk and raised the heavy lid. How many times in the last year had she been in it and never noticed anything unusual? She plucked out Søren's suit and plopped it onto the floor. She'd refold it later. Miscellaneous stockings, neckerchiefs, and who knew what all, she tossed over her shoulders, hands moving like pistons. She stared at the empty trunk. Nothing suspicious about the bottom as far as she could tell. She grabbed the letter.

*Look for a knothole and press down until it drops.*

"Søren Ivar, I see four knotholes." She reread the sentence. "Okay. Press until it drops." She bore down on the first one with her thumb. Nothing happened. The same with the second knothole. With the third, she put one thumb on top of the other and leaned into the trunk. When the knothole gave way, she almost lost her balance. "It worked! Now what?"

*A hole will be exposed. Grip it with your finger and pull. The false bottom will peel back. The papers are underneath.*

"Right." She stuck her index finger in the hole, wrapped it around the edge, and tugged. No movement. She placed her other index finger in and yanked with both, the muscles in her arms straining. "Come on..." With a screech, the corner of the false bottom let loose. Grace grabbed the corner and pulled, peeling the wood away from the edges. Just like shucking corn.

"Oh my goodness." Two leather packets lay side by side underneath. Laughing and crying at the same time, she snapped them up. In the smaller one, she found bills and coins. The nest egg. *Oh, Søren.* She shook her head and laid the packet back in the trunk. Untying the leather strap that secured the larger pouch, she slid out its contents. Papers. She pressed one hand against her chest. "I can't believe it."

Just as he'd said, the pouch contained his aunt's will, the bill of sale for Halstad House, and the deed. She placed the will on the floor beside her and scanned the second paper.

### Bill of Sale

This is to certify the purchase of the residence located at number 3 Main Street, Emmett, Washington. Included in the sale are all furnishings in said residence, the one-acre plot it sits on, all outbuildings, water rights, and mineral rights.

Both Roger Forester and Søren had signed and dated the document. At the bottom, the words *Paid in Full* after the purchase price leaped out at her. Below that, she recognized the seal of a notary public, stamped, dated, and signed.

She laid the paper on top of the will and turned to the final page. A squeal burst out of her when she examined it. Hallelujah—that blessed word *Deed*. It stated all the particulars about the residence at number 3 Main Street and it, too, bore the seal of a notary public, stamped, dated, and signed.

Grace bent forward, her forehead resting on the trunk. She couldn't contain her laughter. "Thank You, Lord. Thank You, thank You, thank You."

She glanced at the bottom of Søren's letter, to make sure she didn't miss anything about his last words to her.

*I will close now, sending you my love. Kiss Allie for me.*
Søren

"Bless you, Søren." Grace reared back and jumped to her feet. She tucked the precious papers into the packet and took off running.

The bell jingled as Grace pushed through the door. "Esther! Ben!"

Ben peered from behind the mailboxes where he sorted mail. "Hi there, Grace. Everything okay?"

She laughed and bounced from one foot to the other. "I found them."

Esther popped through the open doorway from their house. "I thought I heard your voice. Come in. Dad and Allie are napping, but we—" She frowned and glanced between her sister and her husband. "What's going on?"

Grace held the packet out in front of her, giggling and wiping tears from her eyes. "I found them. The papers." She ran to Esther and hugged her. "Can you believe it? They were there all the time."

"What?"

Esther stretched her hand toward the packet, but Grace held it out of reach. "Not yet."

"Let's see." Ben ran over.

"No. I just wanted to stop real fast." She spun around and dashed to the door. "I'm heading to Ethan's."

"Hey. Wait a minute," Ben said.

"No time."

"Grace," Esther cried out after her.

But Grace had already reached the middle of the street, sprinting in the direction of Ethan's house. "Ethan!" She knew he couldn't hear her four blocks away, but she called his name anyway. This was nothing short of a miracle. Giddy laughter burst out again.

Three blocks. Two blocks. One block. A stitch in her side threatened to undo her. *Keep running.* A half-block away she saw him. He sat on his front porch, feet on a stool, reading a book. She clasped the leather pouch to her chest with her left hand and waved with her right. "Ethan!" His name came between gasps. "Ethan!"

He raised his head, then unfolded himself from the chair and dropped the book. He hurried down the stairs. "Grace?"

Grace met him in the middle of his yard. It was a good thing he braced himself because she slammed into him at full speed.

"Oomph." Ethan grabbed her shoulders and steadied them both. "What's wrong? Are you hurt?"

She shook her head and sucked in great gulps of air.

"Allie. Is she all right?"

Grace bobbed her head. "Letter."

"What? I don't—"

She shoved the packet against his shirt. When he grabbed it, she bent over, hands on her knees, taking deep breaths. "Open... it."

Ethan untied the leather strap and pulled out the papers. "Is this what I think it is?" His eyes grew wide as he flipped through the pages. "You found them?"

"I found them." She straightened and flashed him a radiant smile.

"You found them." With a shout, he clasped her in his arms and whirled her until her feet left the ground.

All Grace could do was shriek and hang on tight.

He threw back his head and laughed.

At the sound of tires on gravel, they looked over to see Ben in his model T pulling up to the fence. He hopped out of the automobile and jogged to them, grinning. "Much as I'd like to dance a jig myself, I figure Ethan and I had better tend to some business."

Ethan deposited Grace back on terra firma. His face turned

somber. "You're right. Mr. Corelli." He raked a hand through his hair. "Even though he doesn't work on Saturdays, we'd better find him today. I heard Mr. Emmett say he was sending him to Idaho this Monday on mill business. Who knows when he'll return." He looked at Grace. "Einar and his attorney are coming Wednesday to take possession?"

"Yes."

"We don't have any time to lose then." He placed a hand on her shoulder and held up the leather pouch. "Do you trust me with these?"

"Of course, silly. I trust you with my life."

"Okay." He rubbed the back of his neck. "Ben, we need to locate Corelli. I have no idea how long it will take us or how far we'll have to go. Are you game?"

"You bet I am. But we need to drive to my place first. I've got a wife who's about ready to pitch a fit."

"Grace?" Ethan shook her shoulder gently.

Her eyes shot open and she started to sit up.

"No. It's okay." He pushed her back down. "I just wanted to let you know it's all taken care of."

"What time is it? We couldn't stay awake any longer."

"That's okay."

"Mr. Corelli?"

"Yep. We finally found him around eleven o'clock. You should've seen him. He was as excited as a schoolboy on the last day of school." Ethan lowered himself to the floor, sitting next to the sofa in Esther and Ben's front room. "We all jumped in Ben's car and drove to the judge's house. I'm afraid we got him out of bed."

"I can't imagine he was too happy about that." Grace covered a yawn with the back of her hand.

"He didn't seem to mind, but his wife was not thrilled, I can tell you. Anyway, he examined the documents and was satisfied with their authenticity. He telephoned the county sheriff. Woke *him* up, in fact. They spoke for quite a while. Evidently, the judge has been looking into Guenther's dealings and the sheriff has been looking into Einar's. When he got off the phone he asked if we would be willing to keep the Wednesday meeting with Guenther and Einar at Halstad House."

Grace wrinkled her nose. "Ick." She nestled her head deeper into the pillow.

"I know, but they're afraid if Einar or his attorney get wind that the authorities are on to them, they'll disappear." He patted her shoulder. "The sheriff and his deputies will be there. Mr. Corelli as well."

Her lashes drifted to half-mast. "You, too?"

"Yes. I'll be there."

"'Kay."

"And, hey, you can start unpacking those boxes now."

"Mm." Her eyes closed, her breathing slowed.

"You awake?" When there was no response, Ethan brushed a strand of hair away from her face. He sat a minute longer, watching her, then heaved a sigh of relief and rose to his feet.

# Thirty-Four

"I'll be glad when this is over." Grace moved the kettle to the front of the stove. She looked at Ethan. "I'm not meant for espionage."

He smirked. "I don't think the sheriff expects any cloak and dagger malarkey from us. He'll be here before Einar anyway." He scooted his chair back from the table. "We just act natural. Let him take care of everything."

"You sound awfully confident."

"It's pretty cut and dried. What could go wrong?"

Grace narrowed her eyes. "Famous last words."

"He wouldn't have set this up if he thought we'd be in any real danger." He stretched his legs out in front of him. "I promise to whisk you out the back door if it's necessary."

"Oh, I know." She flapped a hand in front of her. "It's just the jitters, I guess." She removed the teapot and a few cups from the cupboard. The cookie tin held a dozen or more oatmeal raisin cookies. She placed a half dozen on a porcelain plate, in case she needed them. Was she up for this? The prospect of seeing Einar gave her a queasy feeling.

*Greater is He that is in you than he that is in the world.*

A sudden, unexpected calm descended on her, a blanket of peace. She recognized that voice, that peace. Everything would be all right. God would guide her every step of the way. Come to think of it, she was indeed up for this. She set the tea things on the counter, turning her gaze to Ethan.

"Are you okay?" he asked.

"Mm-hmm. I'm okay. You know, it could be kind of educational, watching the officers work. Deter me from following a life of crime."

Ethan snorted. "We're all so worried about that."

At the screak of brakes and the crunch of gravel, Grace stepped to the window. "This must be the sheriff now."

"I'm surprised he didn't park out back." Ethan pushed himself off the kitchen chair.

Grace pulled the curtain aside a few inches to peek out, then gasped, whipping her head around. "It's Einar." She glanced at the clock. "He's over an hour early."

"Oh man."

She peered around the curtain again. "Mr. Guenther is a small man. I think we could take them."

"What?"

"Well, I have my skillet. You could grab a broom or something."

"Grace..." He walked toward her.

"Uh-oh. They brought someone with them. Good grief, will you look at the size of that guy. He's as big as a mountain." She turned to Ethan. "Three to two isn't good odds."

"Woman, you are making me nervous. We're not *taking* anybody." He grasped her arm, leading her away from the window. "We are going to walk back to the table. We are going to wait for the sheriff. We are going to stall for time. But if Einar starts to act even a little bit ugly, we are going to hightail it out of here. Got it?"

"Got it."

They sat side by side at the table a moment until Grace rose and moved to the counter.

"Don't you touch that skillet," Ethan said.

"Relax. I'm only getting the tea things. Would you like a cup?"

"Now?"

She pivoted, teapot in hand when Einar, Mr. Guenther, and the biggest man she'd ever laid eyes on stepped through the side door. Einar and Guenther walked to the middle of the room. The big man leaned against the wall, legs spread, arms crossed, looking fierce with his overabundance of dark hair and a dark scruffy beard.

"Gentlemen. We were just about to have a cup of tea. Will you join us?" She raised the flowered china pot toward Einar.

He shook his head, as did Mr. Guenther. The big man uncrossed his arms and took a step forward.

Einar spoke for him. "He doesn't need one either."

The man shrugged, leaned back against the wall, recrossed his arms.

"Well, maybe later." Grace set the pot on the kitchen table and stood next to Ethan's chair, wracking her brain for ways to stall until the sheriff came. She didn't feel afraid. In fact, the dread she'd felt earlier was replaced with a calm, yes, but more than that, with a sense of anticipation, as if the two of them were a part of God's plan.

Einar gave the room a once-over. He scowled at her. "I thought you'd have your things moved out by now."

"Yes, well, about that..."

"You did receive our letter, didn't you?" Mr. Guenther said.

Grace sat down, clasping her hands in her lap. She leaned toward the attorney. "Yes, I received your letter."

"It was clear?"

"It was. I found it a little harsh."

"But perfectly legal." He rocked back on his heels.

Mr. Guenther's smug smile repulsed her. "I asked my lawyer to look at it."

"Oh, you have legal representation?" Mr. Guenther shifted his feet. "What did he say?"

"I'm not sure if he found it harsh or not." She looked at Ethan. "Did he say anything to you about the letter being harsh?"

"Not that I recall."

"But he said it was legal, right?" Einar asked.

Grace nodded. "Mr. Corelli did say it was legal."

"*Anton* Corelli?" Mr. Guenther pulled a handkerchief from his pocket and wiped his upper lip.

Grace placed her thumb and two fingers on her chin as she gazed at the ceiling. "Well, I'm not sure. I never did hear his first name. Maybe Ethan knows."

Ethan's lips twitched. "I never heard either."

Einar grunted. "Who cares what his first name is? It doesn't matter."

"I suppose not," Grace said. "Unless there's another Corelli practicing law in the area." She cocked her head at Mr. Guenther.

"He's the only one I know of."

"Ah. Then his name must be Anton." She gave him a big smile. "I'm glad you cleared that up."

"Can we get back to the point? We're wasting time." Einar pinched his lips together.

"Of course... What was the point again?"

"Why aren't your things out of here?"

"Oh, right. I wanted to speak with you about that." She drew in a breath and let it out slowly. "I wondered if perhaps you may have changed your mind?"

"Pfft. Not likely. Halstad House belongs to me now. Who do you think you are? There's nothing you can do about it."

Grace had tossed around the idea of an elaborate ruse to string these men along, maybe even throwing in a few tears for fun. Kind of like being in a school play. But this was no play. It was hard, cold reality. She stared at Einar.

He glared back at her, hands clenched.

This man had evoked countless emotions in her: wariness, fear, anger, disgust. Looking at him now, she felt pity. His wickedness, his malicious schemes, all were about to catch up with him. "Einar, you plotted to steal the home of a widow and her five-year-old child."

He took a step toward her, his jaw rigid.

Ethan rose, angling himself between the two of them.

Grace twisted in her chair. "Mr. Guenther, my husband bought this house, bringing me here as a bride in 1916. I was almost eighteen at the time. A year later, God blessed us with a beautiful blue-eyed, blond-haired baby girl. She was not quite a year old when her daddy, my husband, Einar's cousin, died in a faraway battlefield in Europe. I converted our home into a boarding house, struggling and working hard from morning till long into the night to provide for my daughter and myself. We are not just names on a piece of paper."

He licked his lips and dabbed his forehead. "All perfectly legal, my dear. Perfectly legal."

"Boss?"

Everyone turned to the big man on the other side of the room.

His eyes zeroed in on Einar. "You hired me to help evict squatters from your property."

"Shut up, Wilkes."

"I didn't sign up for this."

Einar pointed a finger at him. "Shut up and do what you're told."

Wilkes switched his gaze to Grace. "Ma'am? Do you have a little girl?"

"I do."

"Did your husband buy this house for you?"

"He did."

He swallowed hard. "Was he killed in the Great War?"

"Yes, Mr. Wilkes, he was."

He closed his eyes a moment, breathing hard. "I'm sorry for your loss." The mountain of a man headed for the door.

"Get back here!" Einar stormed after him but froze when the big man turned around and leveled a steely glare his way.

Wilkes looked back at Grace and bowed his head once. "Ma'am." He walked out, closing the door with a soft click.

Einar whipped around, scorching Grace with his eyes. "This is your fault. Everything is your fault." Spittle built up in the corners of his mouth. He moved in her direction.

"Brevik!" Ethan planted his feet shoulder-width apart. "Stop right where you are."

Einar stood still, his glower burning into Ethan.

"Gentleman, gentlemen." Mr. Guenther wrung his hands.

"There is no need for this to come to fisticuffs. After all, we are civilized."

At the sound of loud thuds on the porch stairs, Einar spun to look at the door. He smacked his fist into his palm. "I knew he'd be back."

But the mountain of a man had not returned. The door opened. The county sheriff, a uniformed deputy, and Anton Corelli filed into the room.

Einar yelped, making a beeline for the parlor. His luck had run out, though. A second deputy flung the parlor door wide open, hurling himself into the kitchen. The wildly swinging door caught Einar full on the face, tossing him against the wall. Hard. Blood spurted from his nose. He covered it with one hand. When Einar tried to sidestep the deputy, his frantic eyes strayed to the back door. But he sank to the floor when a third deputy ran in from the mudroom.

Mr. Guenther watched from the middle of the room, wringing his hands while his mouth flopped open like a fish out of water.

It was over in a matter of minutes. The deputies led a cursing, wild-eyed Einar and a whining Guenther out of the house in handcuffs.

Though Grace pitied them, she didn't feel sorry for them. To the end, they'd had no qualms carrying out their detestable plans. They were in the sheriff's custody; she placed them in God's.

The sheriff walked to her and Ethan. Removing his hat, he shook their hands. "Thank you for your help. This way we didn't have to hunt all over creation for those crooks. Sorry. I expected to be here before they arrived. Hopefully they didn't give you any trouble."

Grace and Ethan exchanged glances. "We were fine," Ethan said.

"Well, thanks again." He combed his hair with his fingers and stuck his hat back on his head. "Right now, I'd better get these guys behind bars."

Mr. Corelli, who had been standing out of the way by the

woodstove, shook hands with the sheriff before moving to stand beside Grace and Ethan. He broke out in a huge grin. "Grace, this once I am going to disregard professional protocol." He wrapped her in a bear hug, squeezing her until she giggled. "There. Now we can get down to business." When he stepped back, he placed his briefcase on the table. He clicked the lock and popped open the lid. From inside, he pulled out her own leather packet. "This belongs to you. I want to assure you that everything is properly recorded. As a matter of fact, it had been before, but Guenther managed to bribe a clerk at the courthouse into replacing the true deed with his phony one. Plus, he slipped in the so-called promissory note between Einar and Søren. Believe you me, that clerk sang like a canary when threatened with prison time. He'd secreted Søren's deed away, maybe keeping it to cover himself in case this very thing were to happen. Anyway, everything is right 'n tight. Halstad House is yours, free and clear, as it should be."

Tears sprang into Grace's eyes. "Mr. Corelli, I don't know how to thank you. You've been wonderful." She wiped her cheeks. "Okay, like you said, let's get down to business. How much do I—"

"Stop right there." Mr. Corelli held up a hand. "You don't owe me a cent."

"But—"

He shook his head. "No. It is payment enough to see justice done to a man I have been suspicious of for years. It's me who should be thanking you." He pointed to the leather packet. "I suggest you put that in a safe place. Just be sure to tell someone you trust where it is." He smiled at Ethan. "Maybe this bright young man right here."

He snapped the briefcase shut and shook their hands. "You take care. If I can ever be of help, don't hesitate to call." Briefcase in hand, smile on his face, he withdrew.

Ethan let out a slow whistle and placed his hands on Grace's shoulders, swinging her around to face him. "Lillian Grace Browne Halstad, you do beat all."

"What?"

He bundled her in his arms. "There's never a dull moment around you, that's for sure." He lifted her off the ground, then set her down and pulled back, leaving his hands on her arms. His eyes danced. "Things are going to seem awfully dull around here now. What's next?"

"Dull I can handle." She wrinkled her nose, grinning up at him. "For starters, I'm going to make cinnamon rolls!"

That night, Grace gazed at Allie, blonde braid lying across the lacy border of the coverlet, one hand resting on her pillow, fingers curled, lips parted as she breathed in and out. Her daughter slept in her own trundle bed, in their own room, in their own house. Even though she knew how things stood a couple of days ago, it wasn't until Mr. Corelli had said everything was officially recorded that she dared to breathe. Grace hugged herself to contain the impulse to whoop, sing, or throw something into the air. God had worked a miracle. She had trusted Him when things looked bleak, willing to give all this up, hard as it was. But look what He had done. She clapped her hand over her mouth to suppress a giggle, then whispered, "Thank You, Lord."

She untied the red ribbon at the end of her braid, loosened the thick hair, and spread it with her fingers. In the distance, the rich, low whistle from the mill blew, its echo bouncing off the ridge to the east of town. Shift change. Isobel coughed in her room next door. The oil lamp's glow sent shadows flickering across Grace's bedroom wall. She sighed. Picking up her brush, she began counting strokes. One, two, three... Her mind wandered, and she relived the moments leading up to this day. Einar's ruthless threats, his lawyer's letter, Mr. Corelli, hours spent searching for proof of Søren's ownership, Esther and Ben's generosity, Mae and Isobel's prayers and support, Ethan's mercy marriage proposal. That guy. She smiled, remembering his offer to rescue a damsel in distress.

At least now she could marry him because she *wanted* to, not because she *had* to. Her hand stilled. Heavens to Betsy, she wanted to. She slumped to the edge of the mattress. She wanted to marry Ethan Michael Myers. And she had told him no.

She fell backward onto the bed. "I'm an idiot."

# Thirty-Five

"I'm an idiot." Ethan rubbed a hand over his face.

"You'll get no argument here." Mr. Browne repositioned his foot on the striped ottoman and shifted in his chair. "How you ever thought such a harebrained proposal would impress my daughter is beyond me."

They sat in Ben and Esther's front room. The bell's jingling and Ben's cheery hellos drifted in from the post office. A kitchen silent of its usual bustle spoke of Esther's absence. Ethan covered a cough with the back of his hand. Gratitude for having a private conversation with Grace's father vied with jittery nerves for... well, for having a private conversation with Grace's father. "I thought..."

"Hmm?"

Ethan rubbed his face again. "Man, I don't know what I thought."

Mr. Browne laced his fingers together and sank further into the chair. How could those blue eyes hold a steely glint and a twinkle at the same time?

"Do you love my Lily Grace?"

Ethan locked eyes with the man he admired so much. "I have loved her since I was twelve years old. Guess I hoped she'd figure it out by the way I acted and how I treated her."

"How did that work for you?"

"Not so well." Ethan scoffed. "I had just about worked up the courage to tell her when Søren swept her off her feet."

"That boy pursued her nonstop—no doubt about it. Now don't get me wrong. I loved him like a son."

"We were all such good friends. I stepped aside for Søren rather than fighting for her. I'm not sure if that was a mistake or not."

"Water under the bridge, my boy. There's nothing you can do about it."

"I know."

Shafts of sunlight streamed through the kitchen window. Dust motes shimmered, floating in their wake. The scent of bacon lingered in the air. Bossie lowed in the barn.

"Coming back to Emmett this year, my love for her has grown—" His voice broke. "I'd do anything for—" Emotion overtook him again.

"And?"

Ethan sighed and slumped into the chair back. "I'm afraid if I tell Grace how I feel, it would ruin everything. She says I'm her best friend. I know she's mine. Throwing in the fact that I'm in love with her could wreck the whole shebang. Maybe she'd feel sorry for me—or feel awkward around me."

Was it strange to share all this with Mr. Browne? But he needed to talk, to get this out before he burst into a thousand pieces, and his own father lived far away in California. He shook his head. If he told Grace he loved her and she couldn't handle it, he might be relocating to that sunny state himself. Or maybe Timbuktu. Except... Hadn't God charged him with watching over Grace and Allie? His stomach clenched when he remembered something else. "It was a pretty silly thing to do and I got everything backward. I apologize for not coming to you before—about asking her to marry me."

"Asking? I thought you told her about your sensible plan while you counted off the reasons to prove it was the logical thing to do."

Ouch. Heat climbed up Ethan's neck. It was bad enough to recall the incident itself. It sounded even worse coming from Mr. Browne. "Anyway, I want to do things right this time." He leaned forward, forearms on his knees. "May I have your blessing to ask your daughter to marry me?"

Mr. Browne pinched his lower lip between his thumb and finger, staring at the floor. "Hmm..."

Ethan's heart thumped.

Mr. Browne looked up. "You'll tell her you love her this time?"

"Yes, sir."

"Not just a best friend's love, but a man who's head-over-heels-in-love-with-her kind of love?"

"Yes, sir."

Mr. Browne gave a slow nod. "She deserves to hear that. You won't mention how well you two get along?"

"No, sir." Ethan's mouth wasn't just dry. He could spit cotton.

"Even if it's true, women don't want to hear it—not when you're proposing at least."

"Yes, sir."

Another nod. "You promise not to use the words logical or smart?"

"No, sir. I mean yes, sir. I promise."

"Hmm..."

Ethan ran a damp palm down his trouser leg.

The corners of Mr. Browne's mouth turned up, revealing even, white teeth. "Of course you have my blessing. There's nothing I'd like more than to see you two as man and wife."

Ethan let out a huge breath he hadn't known he'd been holding.

"And I've watched our little Allie when you're around. I can tell she loves you already. You'd be taking her on as well." Mr. Browne's face sobered, and he pointed a finger at Ethan. "Treat them right or you'll answer to me."

"I will. I love them both. I'd be honored to be Grace's husband and Allie's father. That is, if Grace will have me."

"Well said." Mr. Browne stroked his beard. "So when are you going to ask her?"

Ethan bounced one knee. He'd bungled it last time. He didn't think he could take it if it happened again. "I'll wait until the time is right."

"Son, there's no time like the present."

"I suppose. But what if—?"

"I know Grace is home." Mr. Browne leaned forward and rubbed his hands together. "What's wrong with now?"

Ethan's throat tightened. "You mean *now* now?"

"I'm glad you agree." Mr. Browne closed his eyes. "Let's pray."

Sumptuous smells filled the kitchen at Halstad House. Fresh bread cooled on the counter next to a tub of molasses cookies and two apple crumbles. Grace had been up before dawn, getting the baking out of the way so the fire in the stove could die down. July's temperatures in the nineties had given way to August afternoon highs over one hundred degrees, sending them scurrying for shade under a tree or, better yet, a trip to the Kettle River. But for now, they enjoyed working in a comfortable room.

"Those are nice stitches." Grace placed her hands over Allie's ears, bent forward, and kissed the top of her head.

The tip of Allie's tongue protruded through set lips and furrows creased her brow. "It's kinda hard to keep 'em straight."

"I know, but they don't have to be perfect. Just do the best you can. The more you practice, the better you'll get."

"Let's see." Esther set down the baby blanket she'd been working on and scooted her chair close to Allie. She peered at the quilt squares her niece held up, one a solid royal blue, the other an explosion of stars in vivid blue, green, and white. "Mmhmm. It's coming along nicely. I predict you'll be an accomplished seamstress. And quilter."

"Goody." Allie's eyes sparkled. "This is gonna be for Margaret's bed. She'll have one from *Farmor* and one from me."

Esther picked up the baby blanket again. "As you gain more experience with quilting, someday you can make a full-sized one for your hope chest. Have you heard of them?"

"Mommy told me all about that. She had lots'a stuff in her hope chest, but you had *tons* more."

Esther scoffed. "She had fewer things because sitting still was not her specialty. Your mother spent most of her time on the go."

Grace shrugged. "What can I say? It's true."

Allie rubbed her finger over a puckered spot in her stitches. "I wanna have a hope chest, too."

"I'm happy to hear it. In this day and age, people may say having a hope chest is an outdated custom, but I don't agree." Esther snipped a strand of thread and tied off the end. "When you grow up, think of all the paraphernalia you'll have."

Allie wrinkled her nose. "Huh?"

"Paraphernalia." Esther smiled and shook her head. "Basically, stuff. You can have embroidered items, knitted ones, crocheted ones, full-sized quilts—the possibilities are endless."

"Yeah, 'cept I don't know how to do all that."

"You have plenty of time to learn." Grace tweaked Allie's nose. "Right now, keep working with your Auntie Esther. I'll hang the rest of this fabric outside." Grace hoisted a washtub onto her hip and headed for the backyard.

She hummed a tune as she hung material on the clothesline—muted green for the backing of Esther's baby blanket and pale blue for Allie's doll quilt. When the last clothespin was secure, Grace straightened the edges and stood back. A gentle breeze ruffled the cloth. A robin flew from one of the apple trees to the garden fence. She wiped her hands on her apron and stepped through the gate. Squash vines ran amuck across the far end. She guessed the corn would be ripe in a couple of weeks. Corn on the cob. Yum. If the weather cooled by then, she would boil them on the stove, then slather them with butter and sprinkle them with salt. Or they could do what Allie loved—stroll down to the river, build a fire on the beach, and roast the ears in their husks right in the coals. Grace pulled up two plump carrots and picked a couple of cucumbers. Sliced into sticks, they would be just right as a complement to their lunch of bread, sliced ham, and cheese.

Grace had given the vegetables a thorough watering after the sun came up. Everything looked hale and hardy except the poor marigolds lining the perimeter. Their peaked and puny blossoms cried to her for relief. She retrieved the pail that hung on the pump and filled it with cold, clear well water. Walking along the fence line, she tipped the pail at the base of each plant. That should perk them up.

She overturned the bucket and sat. Water from the bottom of the pail and a narrow trickle from beneath the marigolds pooled, creating a small puddle. Grace eyed it. The weather had been blistering for days. She couldn't resist. Removing her shoes and stockings, she plopped one foot in, then the other, toes wiggling in its coolness. *Mmm…*

Stroking the end of her braid across her cheek, she gazed at her surroundings—a garden teeming with vegetables, fruit trees, berry bushes, a lilac hedge bordering the rise to the still untamed garden on the knoll, and, of course, Halstad House. Halstad House with its wraparound porch, clematis and wild rose vines climbing balusters and posts, a rambling house from the root cellar to the dormers in the attic. Halstad House. So much more than just a residence for Allie and her. Mae and Isobel had put down roots as well.

*Thank You for giving all this back to me, Lord.* Her heart warmed when she thought of God's provision—marred by only one thing. *Father, am I ungrateful to want something more? Someone more?* She splashed her feet in the muddy water. *I'm scared to say anything to Ethan and scared not to. What if he—*

"Grace?"

Ethan. Descending the stairs. Walking toward her. Her pulse quickened, and before she knew it, she met him halfway across the yard. Oh dear. A frown replaced his usual sunny smile.

"Hey."

"Hey yourself." His frown deepened. He took her hands, then dropped them. "We need to talk."

"Okay." If she wasn't nervous before, she sure was now. Did he come to tell her awful news? Was he mad at her for some reason? She crossed her arms only to uncross them and let them hang to her sides. "You look like you lost your best friend."

His eyes widened. "Maybe." He checked out the ground at his feet.

"Ethan?"

He rubbed the back of his neck, then raised his eyes to hers. "I need to tell you something." He straightened his shoulders and took a deep breath. "I've been afraid to, to confess—that is—to let you know how I feel about you in case—well, I didn't think you felt the same."

Butterflies fluttered in her stomach. "What do you mean? What—?"

"Please don't ask questions, okay? I'll never get this out if you interrupt." He jammed his hands into his pockets. "You told me once I was your best friend. Well, I don't love you like a best friend."

She gasped.

He whipped his hands out of his pockets. "That didn't come out right. I don't love you *just* like a best friend. What I mean is I—well I—" He raked his hand through his hair. "Doggone it, Grace. I'm in love with you. I have been for a long time."

"Ethan, I—"

"No. Let me finish."

"But—"

"Grace, please. Not a word until I'm done. Promise?"

She nodded. Heavens to Betsy. She pressed her hand against her stomach.

"I don't know if I have a chance of winning you, but I have to try. I am head-over-heels in love with you. I want to earn the right to take care of you and Allie for the rest of my life. I want to laugh with you, have adventures with you, be a shoulder to cry on when you're sad, a companion to walk through life with. I want us to hold each other up, pray together, serve the Lord together. But mostly, I want to love you." His eyes shimmered. "I don't know if you could ever..." He clamped his lips together and the frown reappeared.

She watched him a moment before giving him a slight smile. "May I speak?"

He nodded, but right away thrust out his hand. "Wait." He ran his fingers through his hair again, setting it on end. "I'm sorry about that whole mercy marriage proposal."

She watched dejection flicker across his face. "I'm not."

"You're not?"

"Nope." Grace broke into a broad grin. "Just think of the enchanting story we'll be able to tell our grandchildren."

"Our gr—" His forehead furrowed as he lowered his eyebrows. "What—I mean—"

Grace stepped closer and grabbed his lapels. "Come here, you big lug." She stood on her tiptoes, pulled him toward her, and delivered a quick peck on his lips. "I'm in love with you, too."

"You are?"

She adored the boyish grin he gave her.

He skimmed his finger along her cheek. "You are, huh?" He leaned close and delivered a good deal more than a quick peck.

Grace wondered if he'd been saving up. She had to pull away to catch her breath. She blinked and put a hand to her chest. "Willikens."

Ethan pressed his forehead against hers. "Marry me, Lils?"

"Yes."

He caught both of her hands in his, hooked them around his neck, and leaned close again.

The screen door slammed. "Hey, Auntie Esther. Mr. Ethan is kissing Mommy right on the mouth! And I think she likes it!"

"It's about time!" Esther's voice came through the open kitchen window moments before her face appeared. "Yoo-hoo." She waved her hand at them.

Grace laughed and laid her head on Ethan's shoulder.

Allie bolted down the stairs and flung herself at Ethan.

He scooped her up and set her on his hip.

Placing both hands on his cheeks, Allie turned his face to her. "Are you gonna marry us?"

"Yes."

"Will that make you my daddy?"

"It will."

Her arms shot straight up in the air. "I've been praying for that forever!"

Out of nowhere, Rascal zipped through the yard, followed by a yipping, yapping blur of a beagle.

"Whoa." Ethan pulled Grace closer before they plowed into her.

Allie wriggled down in a flash. "Uffda, wait for me! I gotta tell you 'bout our new daddy!"

Grace laid her hand on Ethan's chest. "Looks like you're acquiring a daughter and a—"

"Dog."

"And an exceedingly spoiled cat."

"And..."

"And?"

Ethan motioned with his chin. "Take a gander at the chicken coop."

Fred and his hen harem stood in single file along the fence, staring at the couple, heads bobbing right and left, keeping time with the cadence of cackles.

"Pfft...goofy chickens." Grace looked up at him. "Do you suppose they're plotting their escape?"

"Nah. Enjoying the show."

While they watched, Fred reared back, flapped his wings, and crowed.

"You know, that's just how I feel." Ethan squeezed his newly intended. "And I have another story to tell our grandchildren."

"Does it have anything to do with animals barging in on our romantic moment?"

"Nope. I'll tell them their grandma stood here in muddy bare feet while I proposed."

Grace glanced down and wiggled her toes.

Rascal, Uffda, and Allie raced past again. Allie skidded to a stop, scrunching her face against the bright sun. "Do you know how to build a swing?"

"As a matter of fact, that's one of my specialties."

"Goody." Off she took again.

Esther emerged from the mudroom. "All right, you two love-birds. Lunch in fifteen minutes." She shooed Chaucer down the stairs.

"Are you sure you're ready for this?" Grace giggled. "Things can get kind of crazy around here."

Ethan laid a hand over his heart. "Fearless is my middle name. You can't scare me off."

She looped her arms around his waist and hugged him. "That's what I'm counting on, Ethan Michael Fearless Myers."

# Esther's Buttermilk Biscuits

**Tips:**

- Don't overmix.
- Use chilled butter and buttermilk.
- Don't twist the biscuit cutter when cutting out biscuits.
- Place biscuits on the baking sheet so they touch.

**Ingredients:**

- 2 cups flour
- 4 tsp. baking powder
- ½ tsp. salt
- 1 Tbsp. sugar
- ½ cup chilled butter, cut in small pieces
- 1 cup chilled buttermilk (or ⅔ cup chilled milk)

**Directions:**

1. Preheat oven to 400°F.
2. Grease baking sheet.
3. Sift dry ingredients into a large bowl.
4. Cut butter into dry ingredients with a pastry blender until pea-sized crumbles form.
5. Make a well in the center and pour in buttermilk. Fold in gently.
6. Turn onto a lightly floured surface. Roll or pat into a 1" thick rectangle.
7. Fold in half and roll or pat again to make back into a 1" thick rectangle.
8. Do this two more times. (This gives you flaky layers.)
9. The last time, roll or pat into a 3/4" thick rectangle.
10. Using a 2" - 2½" wide biscuit cutter, press down to make biscuits. Do not twist.

11. Place biscuits on the prepared baking sheet so sides touch.
12. If desired, brush tops with melted butter or buttermilk for a more golden finish.
13. Bake at 400°F for 12-15 minutes.

Makes 8-10 biscuits.

# Grace's Cinnamon Rolls

**Dough Ingredients:**
- ¼ cup warm water
- 2¼ tsp. or 1 packet active dry yeast
- ¾ cup scalded milk, cooled
- 1 tsp. salt
- ¼ cup granulated sugar
- ¼ cup butter, melted and cooled
- 1 egg, whisked, at room temperature
- 3 to 3¼ cups flour

**Filling Ingredients:**
- ¼ cup butter, softened
- ¾ cup packed brown sugar
- 1-2 Tbsp. ground cinnamon
- ½ cup heavy cream, warm

**Directions:**
1. Stir yeast into warm water in a small bowl. Set aside and let sit 5-10 minutes until frothy.
2. Scald milk over low heat (don't boil!) until a thin layer appears on top. Cool scalded milk until it's lukewarm. Pour into a large bowl.
3. Add salt, sugar, melted butter, and egg. Stir.
4. Stir yeast mixture and add to milk mixture.
5. Add two cups of flour and stir with a spoon until it is smooth.
6. Add the rest of the flour ¼ cup at a time, kneading until it forms a moist ball. (Dough should still be moist and tacky, without sticking all over your hands. Don't add so much flour that it becomes dry or stiff.)

**First Rising:**
1. Place dough in a large, greased bowl. Cover with a damp towel and let rise in a warm place until double – about 1 hour.
2. Punch dough down. Turn onto a well-floured surface. Knead until it is smooth and doesn't stick to the surface. (Add more flour as needed if it is too sticky.)
3. Roll dough into a large, ½" thick rectangle.
4. Spread softened butter over the dough, leaving edges clear.
5. Sprinkle brown sugar and then cinnamon over the butter.
6. Roll up the dough length-wise like a log. Pinch seam closed and lay seam side down.
7. Slice into 10-12 rolls about 1½" thick.

**Second Rising:**
1. Preheat oven to 350°F.
2. Place rolls in a greased 13x9 baking pan so sides do not touch.
3. Cover with a damp towel and let rise in a warm place until double – about 30 minutes. (Rolls will touch when doubled.)
4. Warm heavy cream (not hot, just not cold).
5. Once the rolls have risen, pour the warm heavy cream over the rolls.
6. Bake in 350°F oven for 25-30 minutes or until golden brown.
7. Cool for 10 minutes and, if desired, drizzle white icing glaze over warm rolls.

**White Icing:**
(Halve icing recipe for less sweet rolls.)

- 2½ tablespoons butter, softened
- 2 cups confectioners' (powdered) sugar
- 1 teaspoon vanilla
- ¼ cup milk

1. Cream butter, 1 cup confectioners' sugar, and vanilla in a medium bowl.
2. Alternate adding the remaining confectioners' sugar and the milk. Cream until smooth.
3. Drizzle frosting over warm (but not hot) cinnamon rolls.

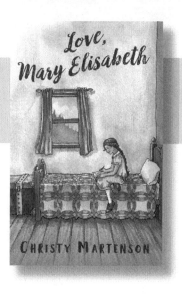

## Love, Mary Elisabeth
by CHRISTY MARTENSON
featuring illustrations by AMANDA KASTNER

Eleven-year-old Mary Elisabeth's life will never be the same.

It's 1924 and her mother has contracted tuberculosis—a deadly, terrifying disease.

Far away in Colorado, a sanatorium holds the only hope of saving her. Papa takes a grueling job at the shipyards in Bremerton to pay for her treatment. Mary Elisabeth must travel 350 miles from home to begin a new life on her uncle's farm in northeast Washington.

Her only connection to her parents is by letter.

Will that be enough to give her courage to brave the challenges that await?

> "*Love, Mary Elisabeth* is a riveting account of a young girl coming of age and learning love really does hold a family together. From its tender beginning to the heartfelt climax, the author engages her readers with wit, charm, and endurance."
>
> - CARMEN PEONE, award-winning author

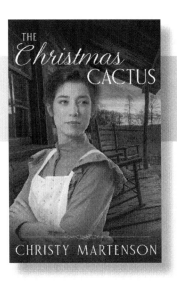

## The Christmas Cactus
### by CHRISTY MARTENSON

A broken promise. An open door.
A young woman's determination to keep her family together.

After two long years, it seems her prayers have finally been answered. Far off Washington Territory might be the back of nowhere, but it holds the dream of a home for Katie Jo O'Reilly.

With high hopes, she packs up her young siblings and heads west. But when the dream is ripped away, Katie Jo is faced with a difficult choice.

What will she risk to make a home for her family?

"I loved *The Christmas Cactus*. Wholeheartedly. Christy Martenson created a world of love and joy, introducing her readers to characters who become friends and crafting a storyline that was beautifully full of family, strength, and perseverance. In addition to all that, it passed the real test of a wonderful story: my own emotion kept leaking out in laughter and tears as I celebrated and mourned and giggled along with Katie Jo."
        - JENNI MARIE, photographer and storyteller

Made in the USA
Middletown, DE
30 April 2022